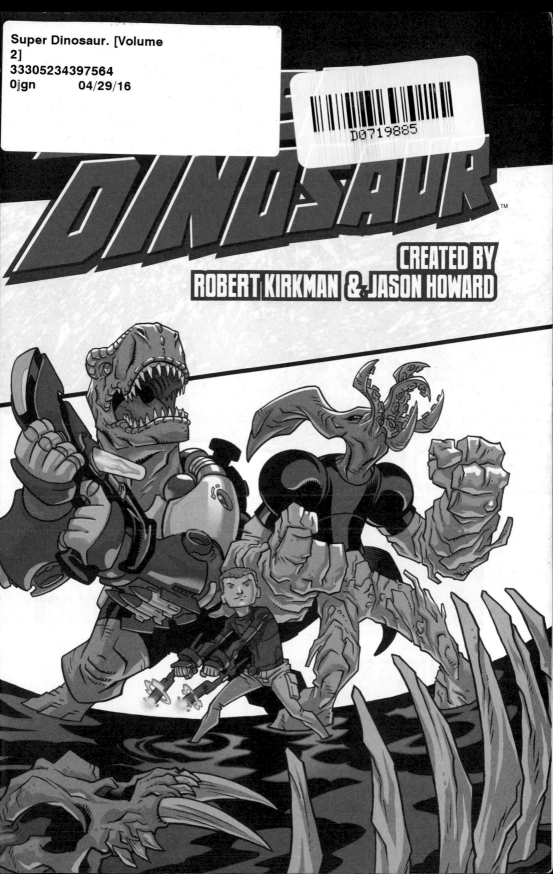

DINOSAUR ™

CREATED BY ROBERT KIRKMAN & JASON HOWARD

ROBERT [redacted]RKMAN
WRITER

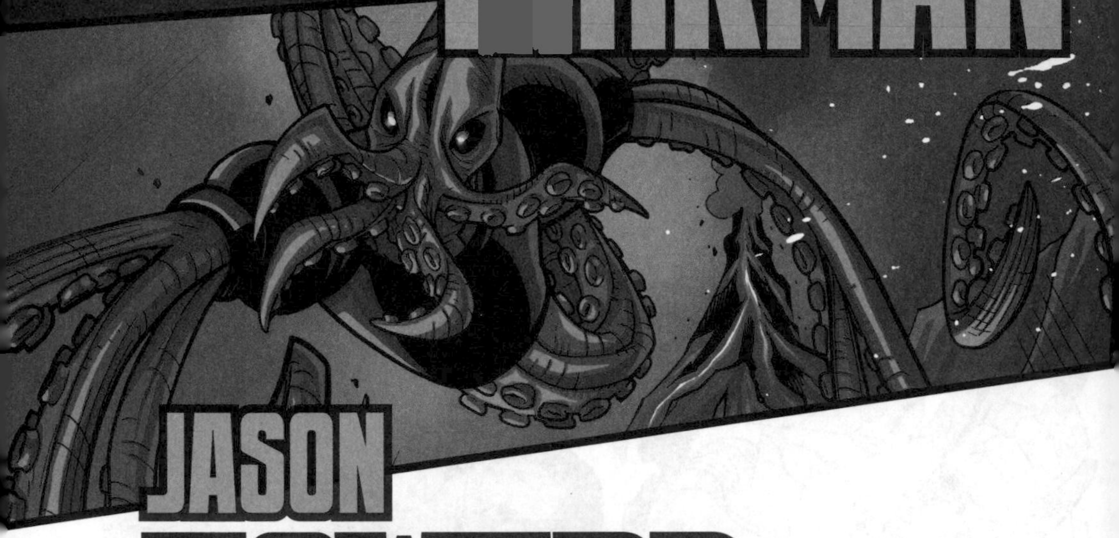

JASON HOWARD
ART & COLORS

CLIFF RATHBURN
INKER
ISSUES 9-11

RUS WOOTON
LETTERER

SINA GRACE
EDITOR

SUPER DINOSAUR, VOLUME 2
ISBN: 978-1-60706-568-5
First Printing

IMAGE COMICS, INC.
Robert Kirkman - chief operating officer
Erik Larsen - chief financial officer
Todd McFarlane - president
Marc Silvestri - chief executive officer
Jim Valentino - vice-president

Eric Stephenson - publisher
Todd Martinez - sales & licensing coordinator
Jennifer de Guzman - pr & marketing director
Branwyn Bigglestone - accounts manager
Emily Miller - administrative assistant
Jamie Parreno - marketing assistant
Sarah deLaine - events coordinator
Kevin Yuen - digital rights coordinator
Tyler Shainline - production manager
Drew Gill - art director
Jonathan Chan - design director
Monica Garcia - production artist
Vincent Kukua - production artist
Jana Cook - production artist

www.imagecomics.com

For SKYBOUND ENTERTAINMENT

Robert Kirkman - CEO
J.J. Didde - President
Sina Grace - Editorial Director
Shawn Kirkham - Director of Business Development
Tim Daniel - Digital Content Manager
Chad Manion - Assistant to Mr. Grace
Sydney Pennington - Assistant to Mr. Kirkman
Feldman Public Relations LA - Public Relations

For international rights inquiries, please contact: foreign@skybound.com

WWW.SKYBOUND.COM

PRINTED IN THE USA

LAST TIME... *AWESOME*
OUR HEROES

DEREK DYNAMO

SUPER DINOSAUR

FOUGHT THESE REALLY BAD GUYS

MAX MAXIMUS

DOOMETRODON

TRICERACHOPS

TERRORDACTYL

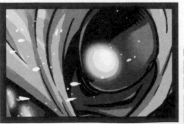

THE EXILE

DREADASAURUS

THEY WON (SORT OF)
WITH A LITTLE HELP FROM

ERIN KINGSTON

DR. DYNAMO

ERICA KINGSTON

BRUCE KINGSTON

WHEELS

SARAH KINGSTON

NOW THE ADVENTURE CONTINUES!

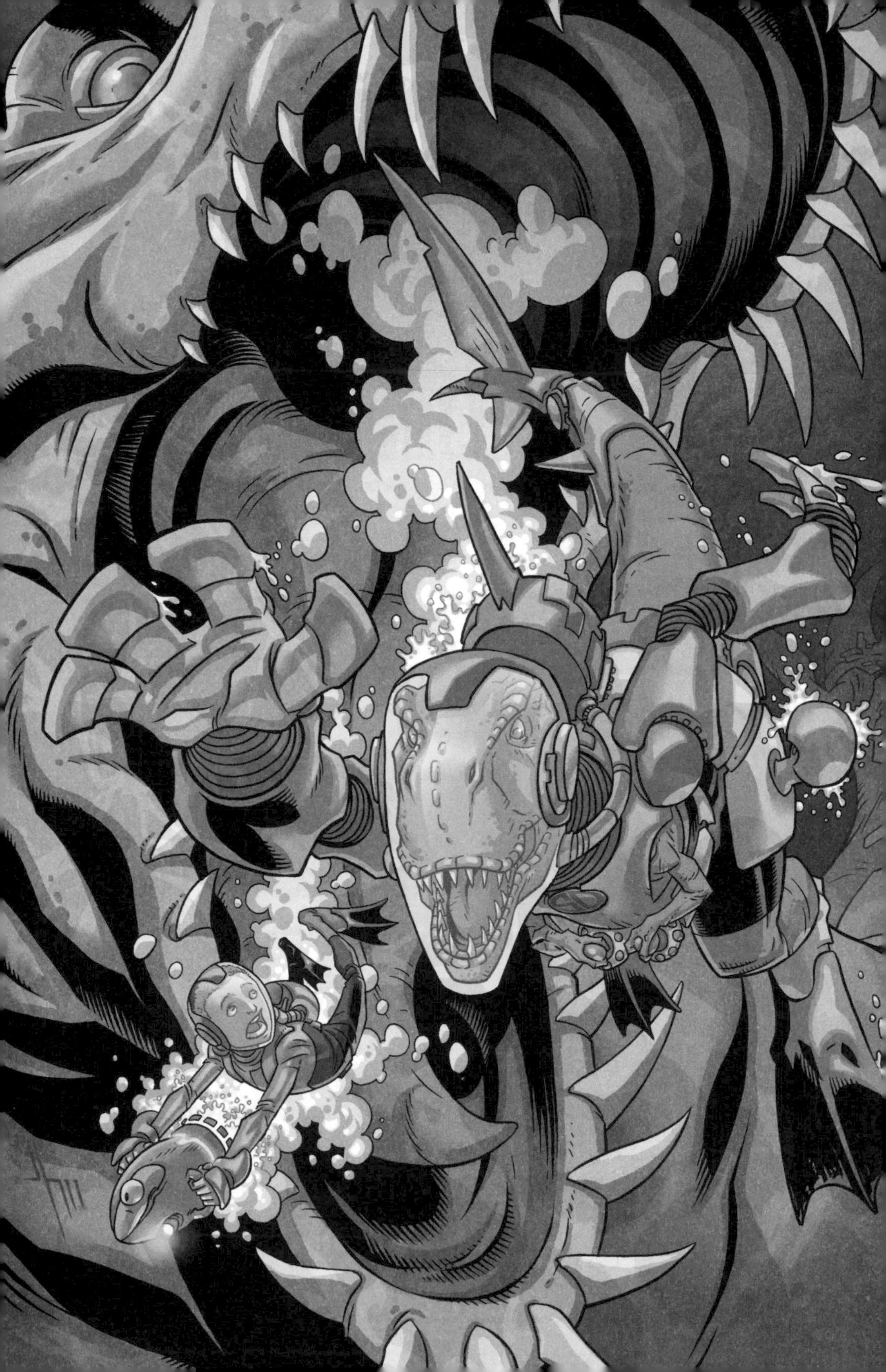

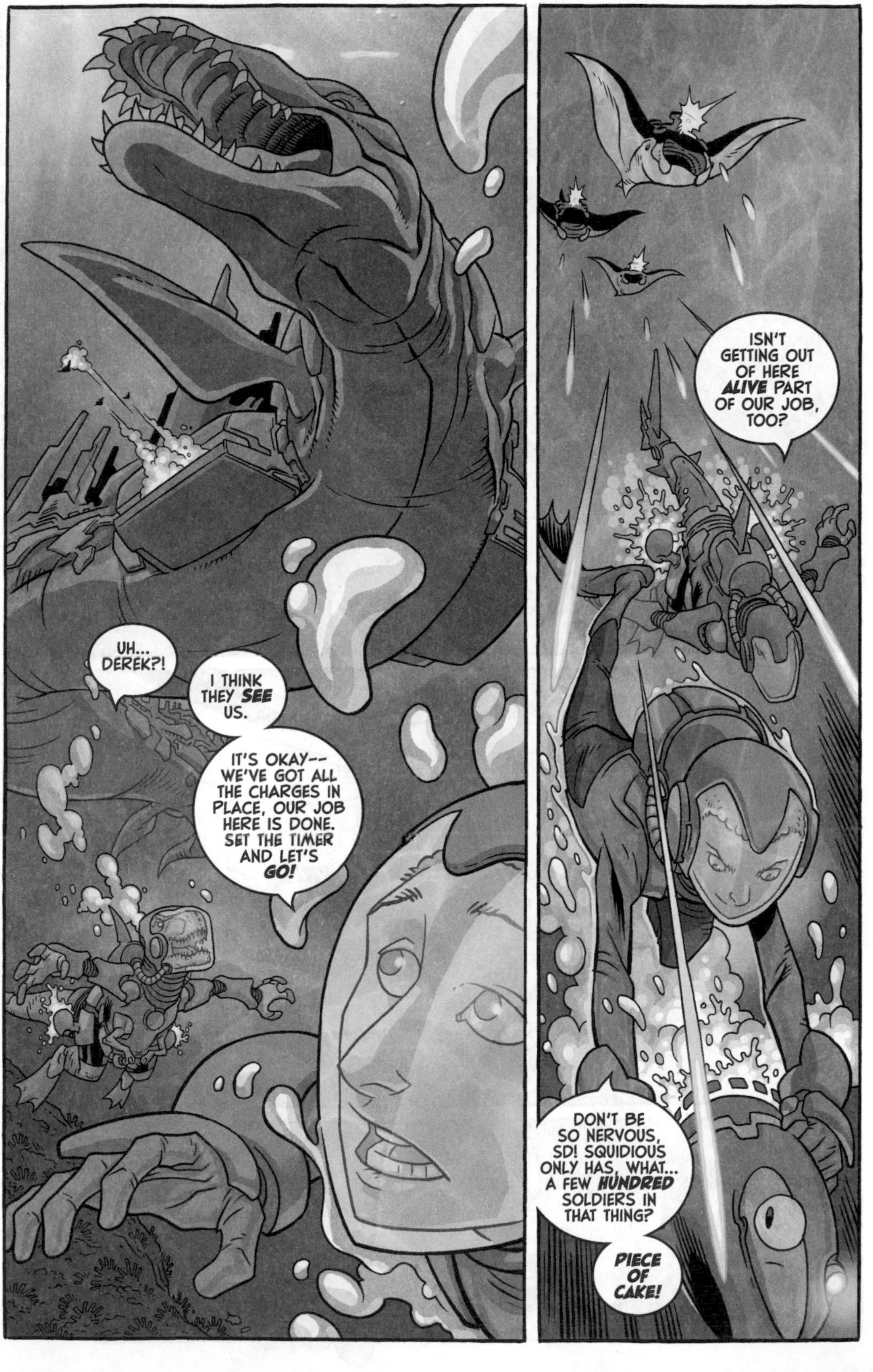
UH... DEREK?!
I THINK THEY SEE US.
IT'S OKAY-- WE'VE GOT ALL THE CHARGES IN PLACE, OUR JOB HERE IS DONE. SET THE TIMER AND LET'S GO!
ISN'T GETTING OUT OF HERE ALIVE PART OF OUR JOB, TOO?
DON'T BE SO NERVOUS, SD! SQUIDIOUS ONLY HAS, WHAT... A FEW HUNDRED SOLDIERS IN THAT THING?
PIECE OF CAKE!

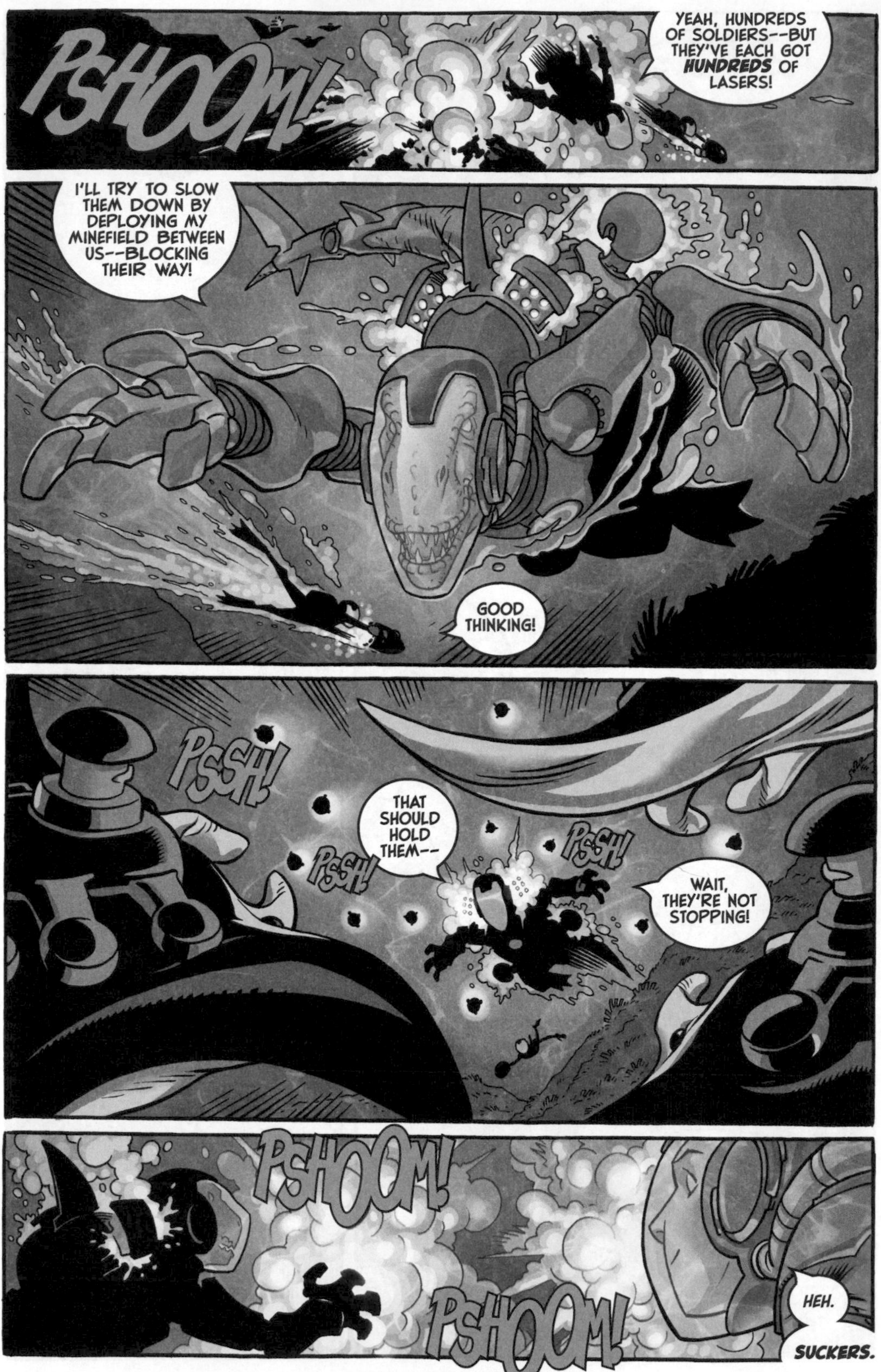
PSHOOM!
YEAH, HUNDREDS OF SOLDIERS--BUT THEY'VE EACH GOT HUNDREDS OF LASERS!
I'LL TRY TO SLOW THEM DOWN BY DEPLOYING MY MINEFIELD BETWEEN US--BLOCKING THEIR WAY!
GOOD THINKING!
PSSH!
THAT SHOULD HOLD THEM--
PSSH!
PSSH!
WAIT, THEY'RE NOT STOPPING!
PSHOOM!
PSHOOM!
HEH.
SUCKERS.

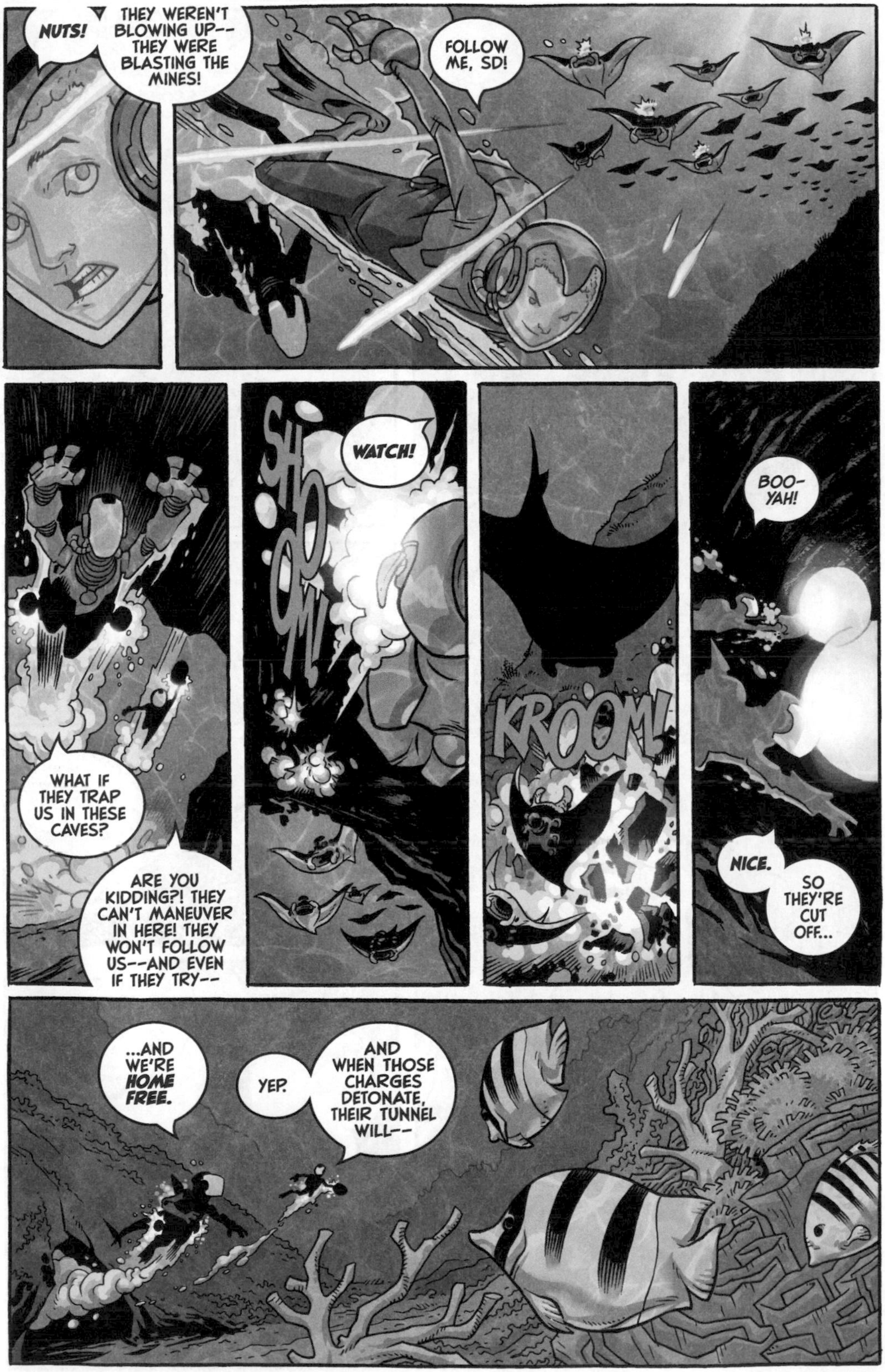
NUTS!
THEY WEREN'T BLOWING UP-- THEY WERE BLASTING THE MINES!
FOLLOW ME, SD!
WHAT IF THEY TRAP US IN THESE CAVES?
ARE YOU KIDDING?! THEY CAN'T MANEUVER IN HERE! THEY WON'T FOLLOW US--AND EVEN IF THEY TRY--
SHOOOM!
WATCH!
KROOM!
BOO-YAH!
NICE.
SO THEY'RE CUT OFF...
...AND WE'RE HOME FREE.
YEP.
AND WHEN THOSE CHARGES DETONATE, THEIR TUNNEL WILL--

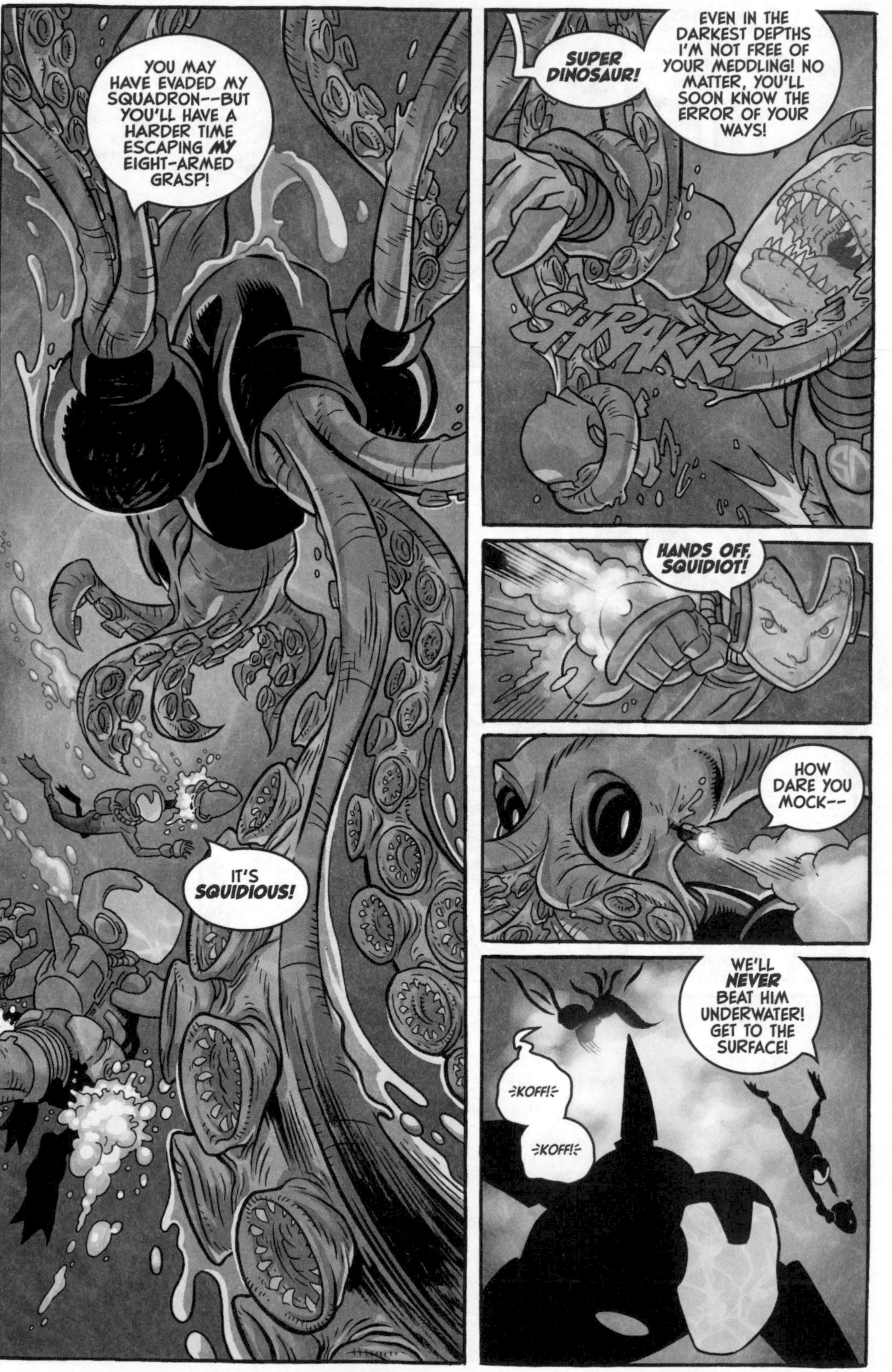
YOU MAY HAVE EVADED MY SQUADRON--BUT YOU'LL HAVE A HARDER TIME ESCAPING MY EIGHT-ARMED GRASP!
IT'S SQUIDIOUS!
SUPER DINOSAUR!
EVEN IN THE DARKEST DEPTHS I'M NOT FREE OF YOUR MEDDLING! NO MATTER, YOU'LL SOON KNOW THE ERROR OF YOUR WAYS!
SHRAKK!
HANDS OFF, SQUIDIOT!
HOW DARE YOU MOCK--
WE'LL NEVER BEAT HIM UNDERWATER! GET TO THE SURFACE!
KOFF!
KOFF!

THERE'S LAND UP AHEAD, PAST THE REEF. ***HURRY!***
HE'S CATCHING UP!
MY SUIT'S DAMAGED-- IT'S SLOWING ME DOWN!
HUFF!
HUFF!
SEE, I TOLD YOU IT WAS CLOSE.
THEY BELIEVE THEY CAN ESCAPE ME ON LAND?!
FOOLS!
THERE IS ***NOWHERE*** I CANNOT GO!

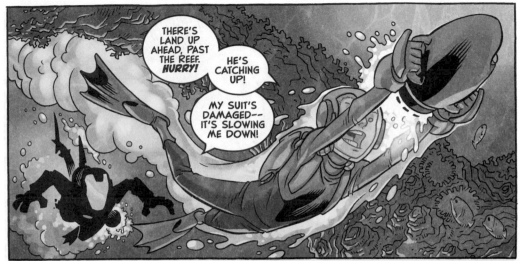

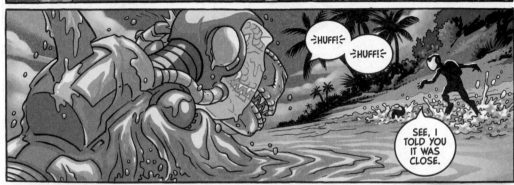

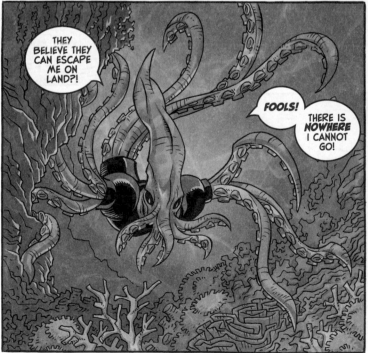

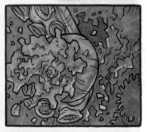

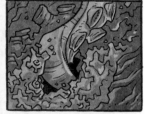

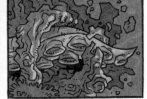

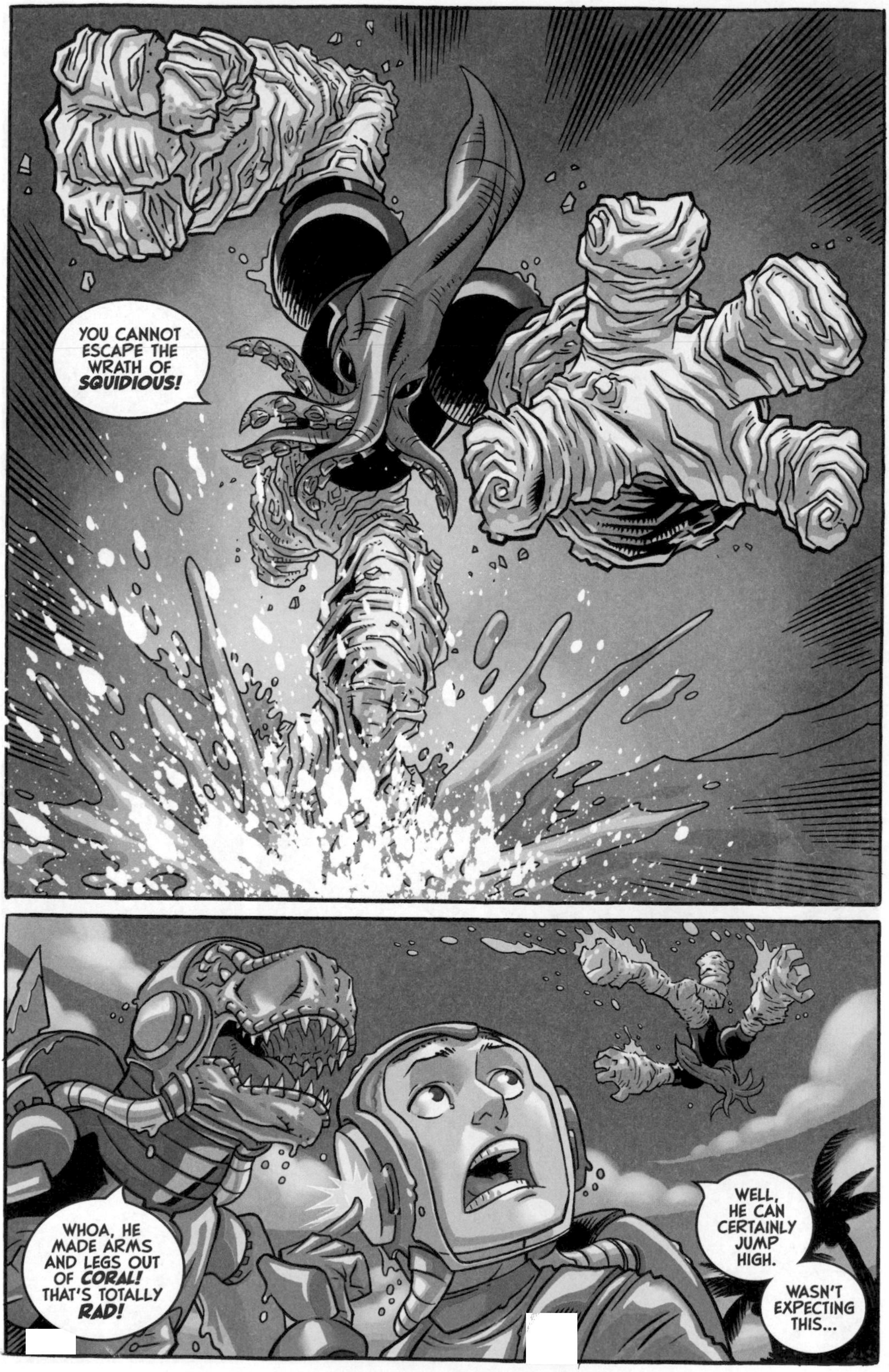
YOU CANNOT ESCAPE THE WRATH OF SQUIDIOUS!
WHOA, HE MADE ARMS AND LEGS OUT OF CORAL! THAT'S TOTALLY RAD!
WELL, HE CAN CERTAINLY JUMP HIGH.
WASN'T EXPECTING THIS...

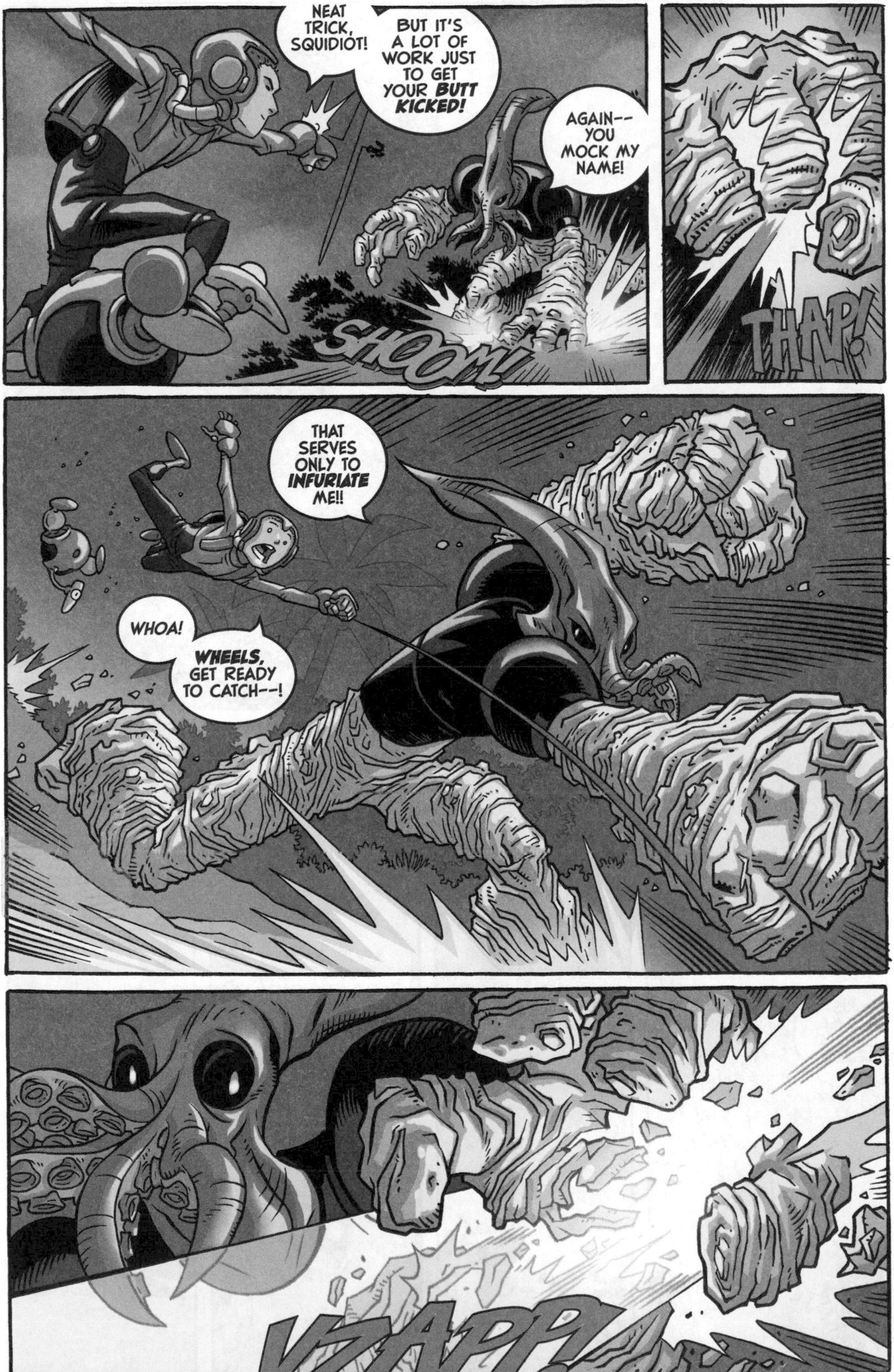
NEAT TRICK, SQUIDIOT!
BUT IT'S A LOT OF WORK JUST TO GET YOUR **BUTT KICKED!**
AGAIN-- YOU MOCK MY NAME!
SHOOOM!
THAP!
THAT SERVES ONLY TO **INFURIATE** ME!!
WHOA!
WHEELS, GET READY TO CATCH--!
VZAPP!

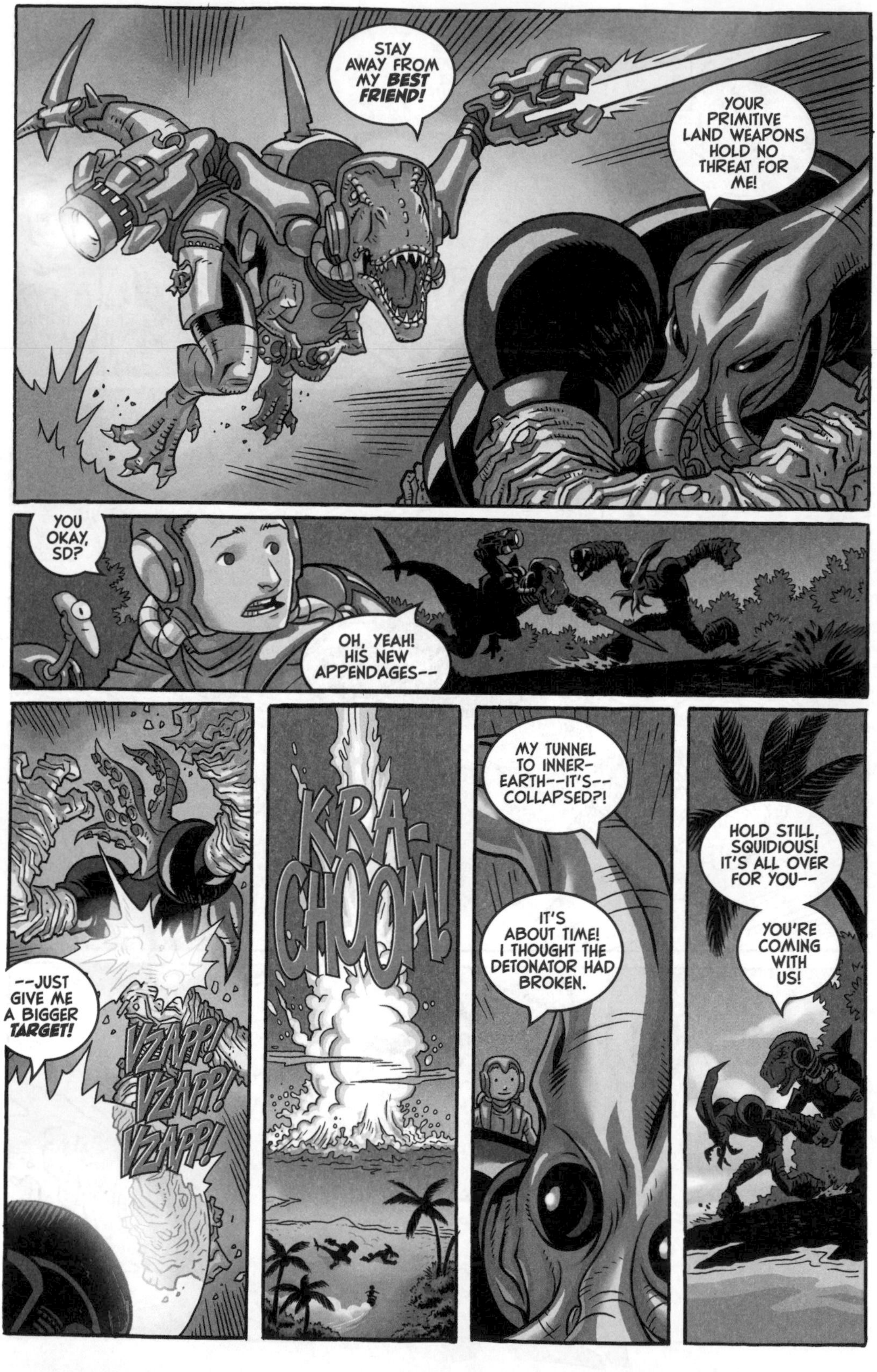
STAY AWAY FROM MY BEST FRIEND!
YOUR PRIMITIVE LAND WEAPONS HOLD NO THREAT FOR ME!
YOU OKAY, SD?
OH, YEAH! HIS NEW APPENDAGES--
--JUST GIVE ME A BIGGER TARGET!
VZAPP! VZAPP! VZAPP!
KRA-CHOOM!
MY TUNNEL TO INNER-EARTH--IT'S--COLLAPSED?!
IT'S ABOUT TIME! I THOUGHT THE DETONATOR HAD BROKEN.
HOLD STILL, SQUIDIOUS! IT'S ALL OVER FOR YOU--
YOU'RE COMING WITH US!

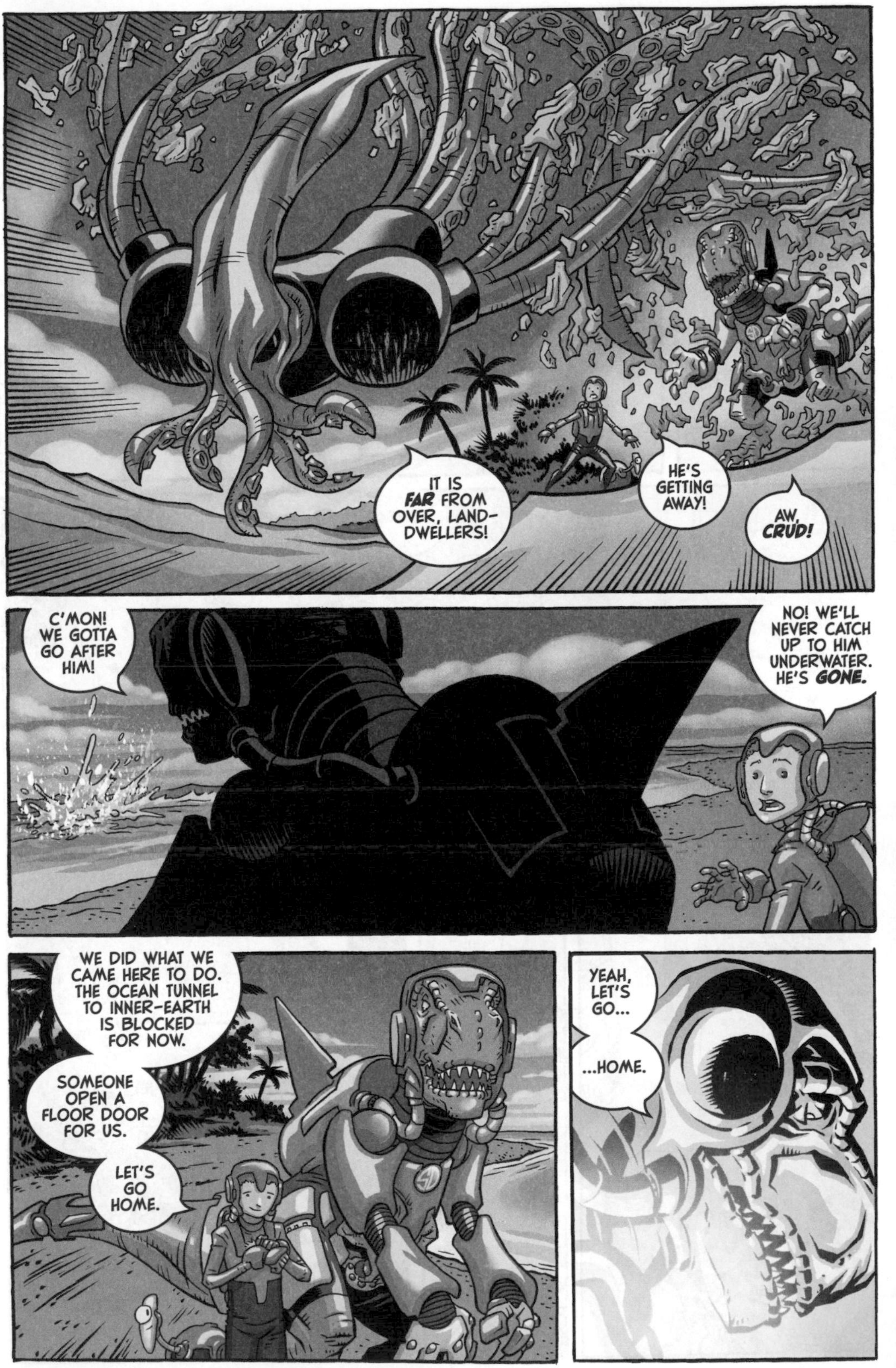
IT IS FAR FROM OVER, LAND-DWELLERS!
HE'S GETTING AWAY!
AW, CRUD!
C'MON! WE GOTTA GO AFTER HIM!
NO! WE'LL NEVER CATCH UP TO HIM UNDERWATER. HE'S GONE.
WE DID WHAT WE CAME HERE TO DO. THE OCEAN TUNNEL TO INNER-EARTH IS BLOCKED FOR NOW.
SOMEONE OPEN A FLOOR DOOR FOR US.
LET'S GO HOME.
YEAH, LET'S GO...
...HOME.

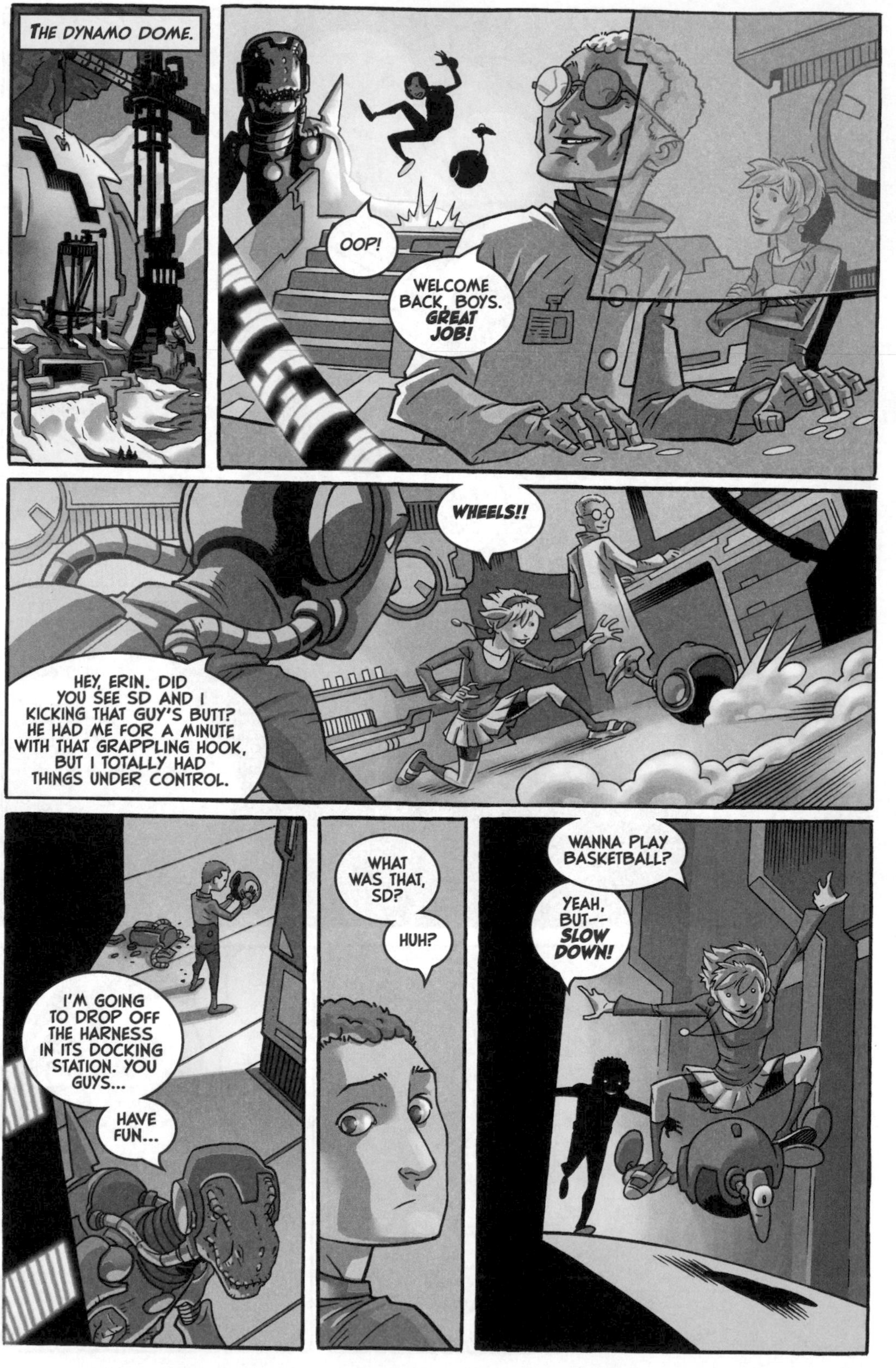
THE DYNAMO DOME.
OOP!
WELCOME BACK, BOYS. GREAT JOB!
WHEELS!!
HEY, ERIN. DID YOU SEE SD AND I KICKING THAT GUY'S BUTT? HE HAD ME FOR A MINUTE WITH THAT GRAPPLING HOOK, BUT I TOTALLY HAD THINGS UNDER CONTROL.
I'M GOING TO DROP OFF THE HARNESS IN ITS DOCKING STATION. YOU GUYS...
HAVE FUN...
WHAT WAS THAT, SD?
HUH?
WANNA PLAY BASKETBALL?
YEAH, BUT-- SLOW DOWN!

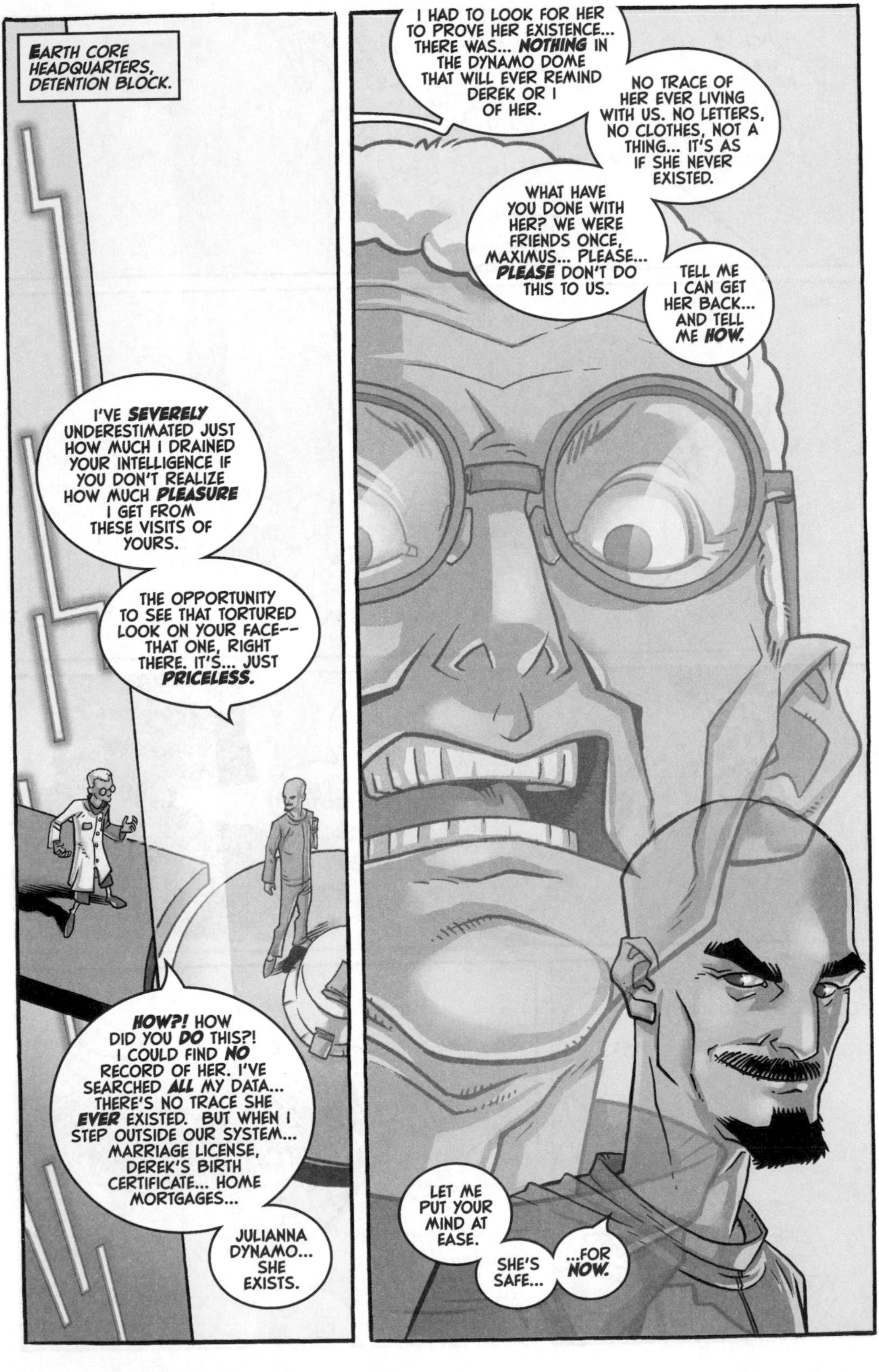
EARTH CORE HEADQUARTERS, DETENTION BLOCK.
I'VE SEVERELY UNDERESTIMATED JUST HOW MUCH I DRAINED YOUR INTELLIGENCE IF YOU DON'T REALIZE HOW MUCH PLEASURE I GET FROM THESE VISITS OF YOURS.
THE OPPORTUNITY TO SEE THAT TORTURED LOOK ON YOUR FACE-- THAT ONE, RIGHT THERE. IT'S... JUST PRICELESS.
HOW?! HOW DID YOU DO THIS?! I COULD FIND NO RECORD OF HER. I'VE SEARCHED ALL MY DATA... THERE'S NO TRACE SHE EVER EXISTED. BUT WHEN I STEP OUTSIDE OUR SYSTEM... MARRIAGE LICENSE, DEREK'S BIRTH CERTIFICATE... HOME MORTGAGES...
JULIANNA DYNAMO... SHE EXISTS.
I HAD TO LOOK FOR HER TO PROVE HER EXISTENCE... THERE WAS... NOTHING IN THE DYNAMO DOME THAT WILL EVER REMIND DEREK OR I OF HER.
NO TRACE OF HER EVER LIVING WITH US. NO LETTERS, NO CLOTHES, NOT A THING... IT'S AS IF SHE NEVER EXISTED.
WHAT HAVE YOU DONE WITH HER? WE WERE FRIENDS ONCE, MAXIMUS... PLEASE... PLEASE DON'T DO THIS TO US.
TELL ME I CAN GET HER BACK... AND TELL ME HOW.
LET ME PUT YOUR MIND AT EASE.
SHE'S SAFE...
...FOR NOW.

WHAT HAVE YOU DONE WITH MY WIFE?!

VMM!

BZZACKT!

PSSH

I'M OKAY-- IT'S FINE.

I'M LEAVING.

WHY THIS?

HOW COULD YOU DO SOMETHING SO HORRIBLE TO SOMEONE?

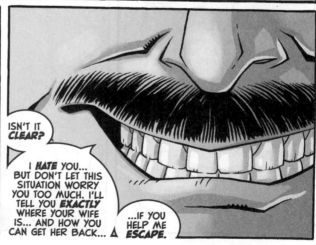

ISN'T IT CLEAR?

I HATE YOU... BUT DON'T LET THIS SITUATION WORRY YOU TOO MUCH. I'LL TELL YOU EXACTLY WHERE YOUR WIFE IS... AND HOW YOU CAN GET HER BACK...

...IF YOU HELP ME ESCAPE.

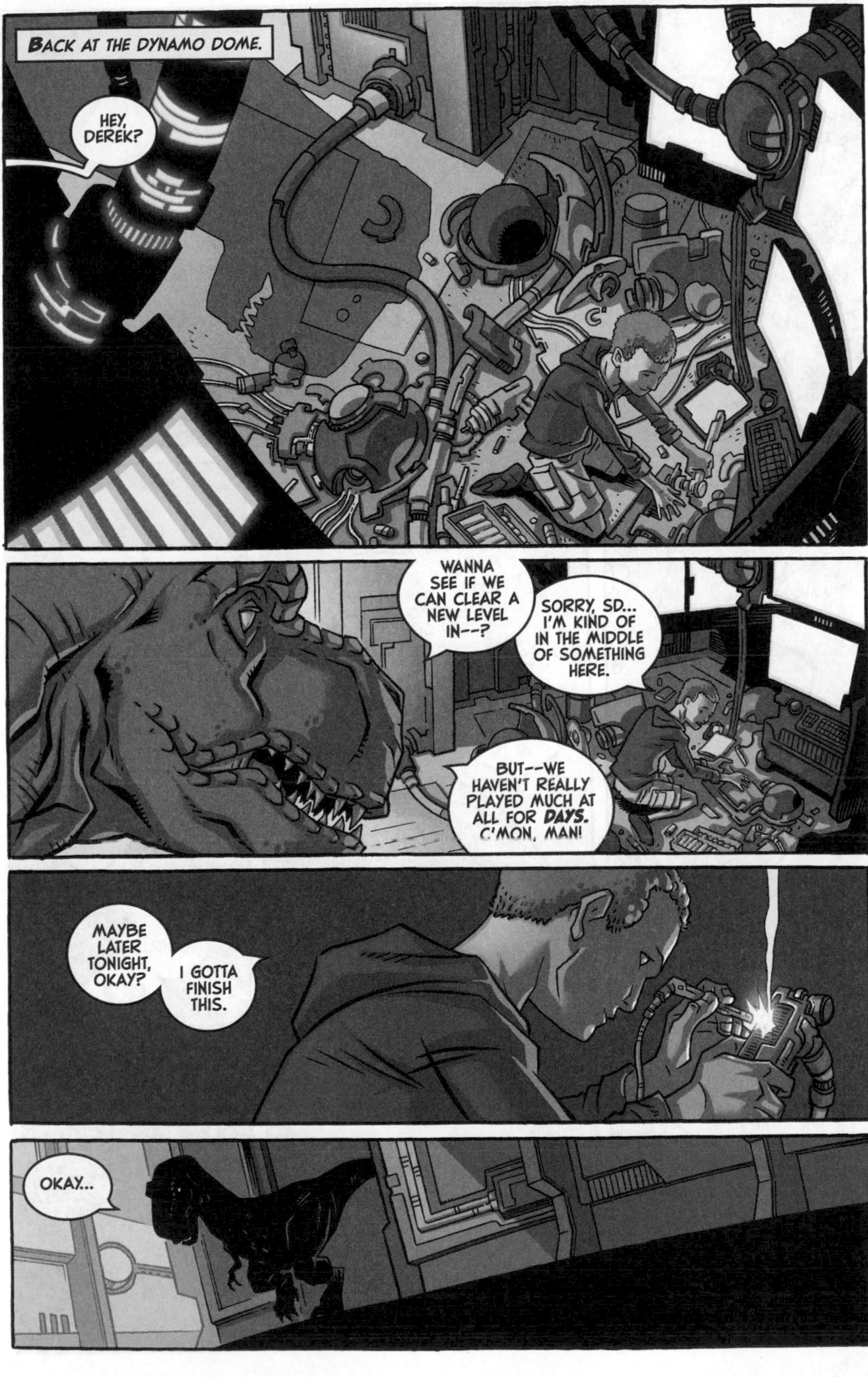
BACK AT THE DYNAMO DOME.
HEY, DEREK?
WANNA SEE IF WE CAN CLEAR A NEW LEVEL IN--?
SORRY, SD... I'M KIND OF IN THE MIDDLE OF SOMETHING HERE.
BUT--WE HAVEN'T REALLY PLAYED MUCH AT ALL FOR DAYS. C'MON, MAN!
MAYBE LATER TONIGHT, OKAY?
I GOTTA FINISH THIS.
OKAY...

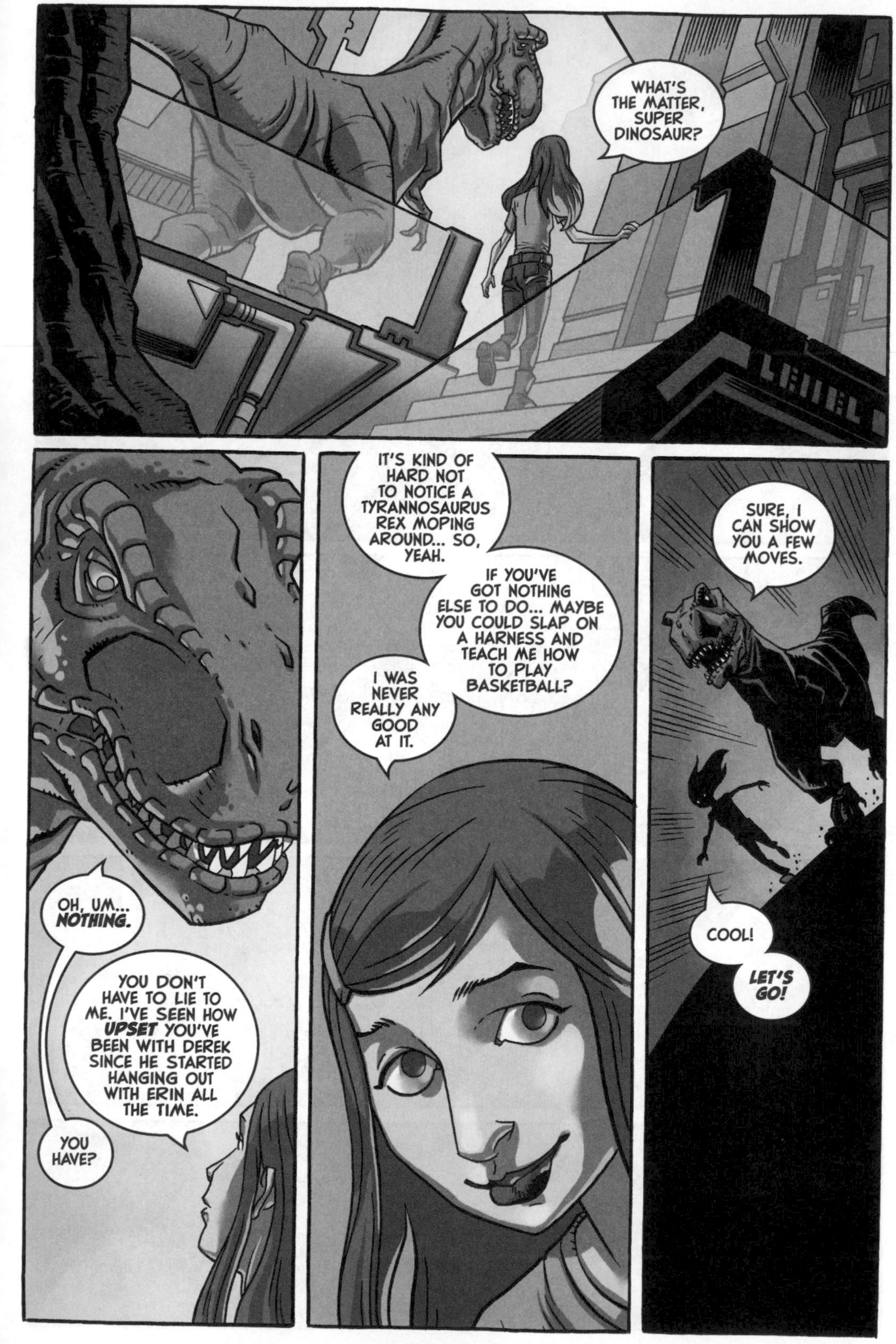
WHAT'S THE MATTER, SUPER DINOSAUR?
OH, UM... NOTHING.
YOU DON'T HAVE TO LIE TO ME. I'VE SEEN HOW UPSET YOU'VE BEEN WITH DEREK SINCE HE STARTED HANGING OUT WITH ERIN ALL THE TIME.
YOU HAVE?
IT'S KIND OF HARD NOT TO NOTICE A TYRANNOSAURUS REX MOPING AROUND... SO, YEAH.
IF YOU'VE GOT NOTHING ELSE TO DO... MAYBE YOU COULD SLAP ON A HARNESS AND TEACH ME HOW TO PLAY BASKETBALL?
I WAS NEVER REALLY ANY GOOD AT IT.
SURE, I CAN SHOW YOU A FEW MOVES.
COOL!
LET'S GO!

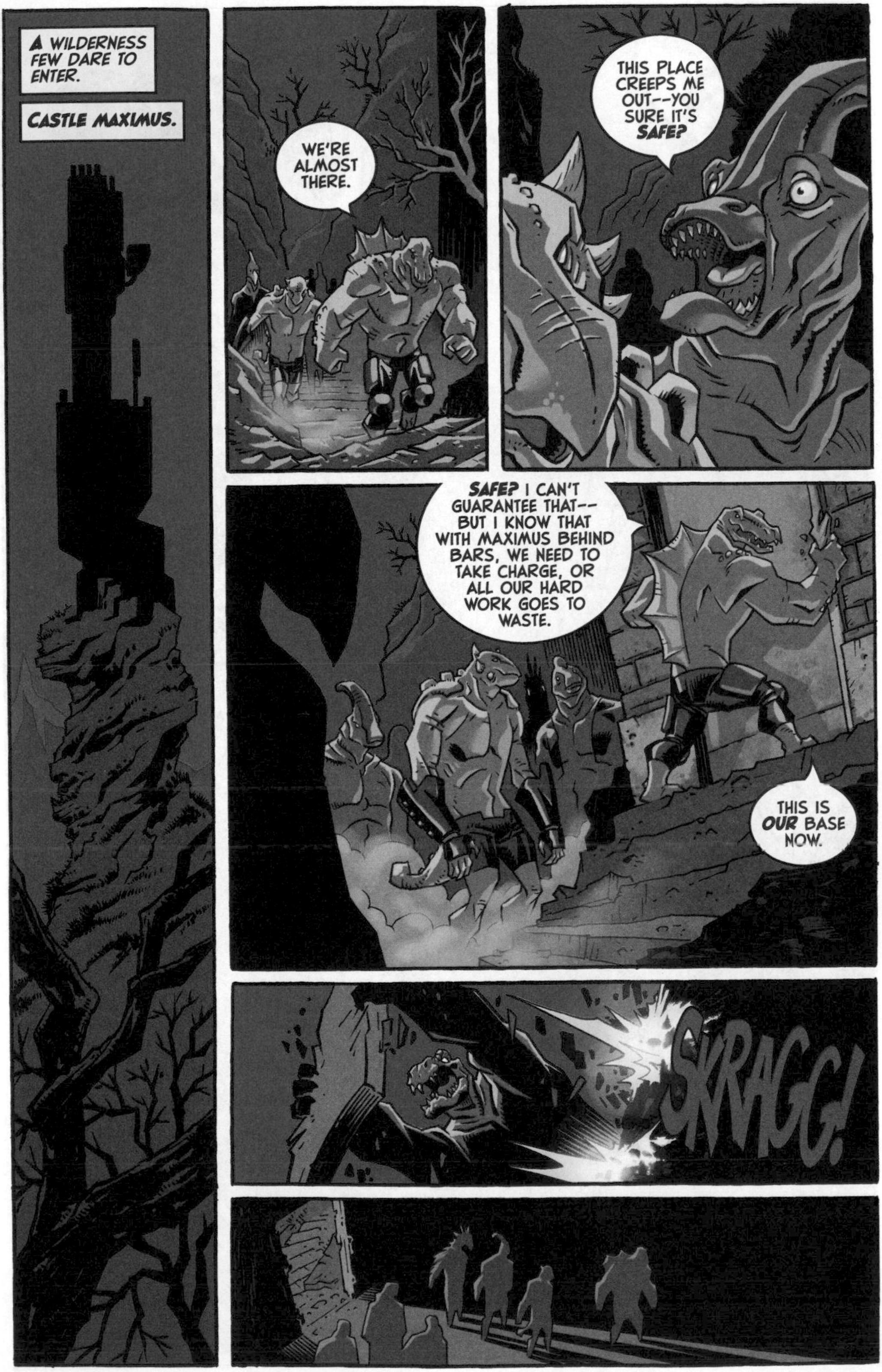
A WILDERNESS FEW DARE TO ENTER.
CASTLE MAXIMUS.
WE'RE ALMOST THERE.
THIS PLACE CREEPS ME OUT--YOU SURE IT'S SAFE?
SAFE? I CAN'T GUARANTEE THAT-- BUT I KNOW THAT WITH MAXIMUS BEHIND BARS, WE NEED TO TAKE CHARGE, OR ALL OUR HARD WORK GOES TO WASTE.
THIS IS OUR BASE NOW.
SKRAGG!

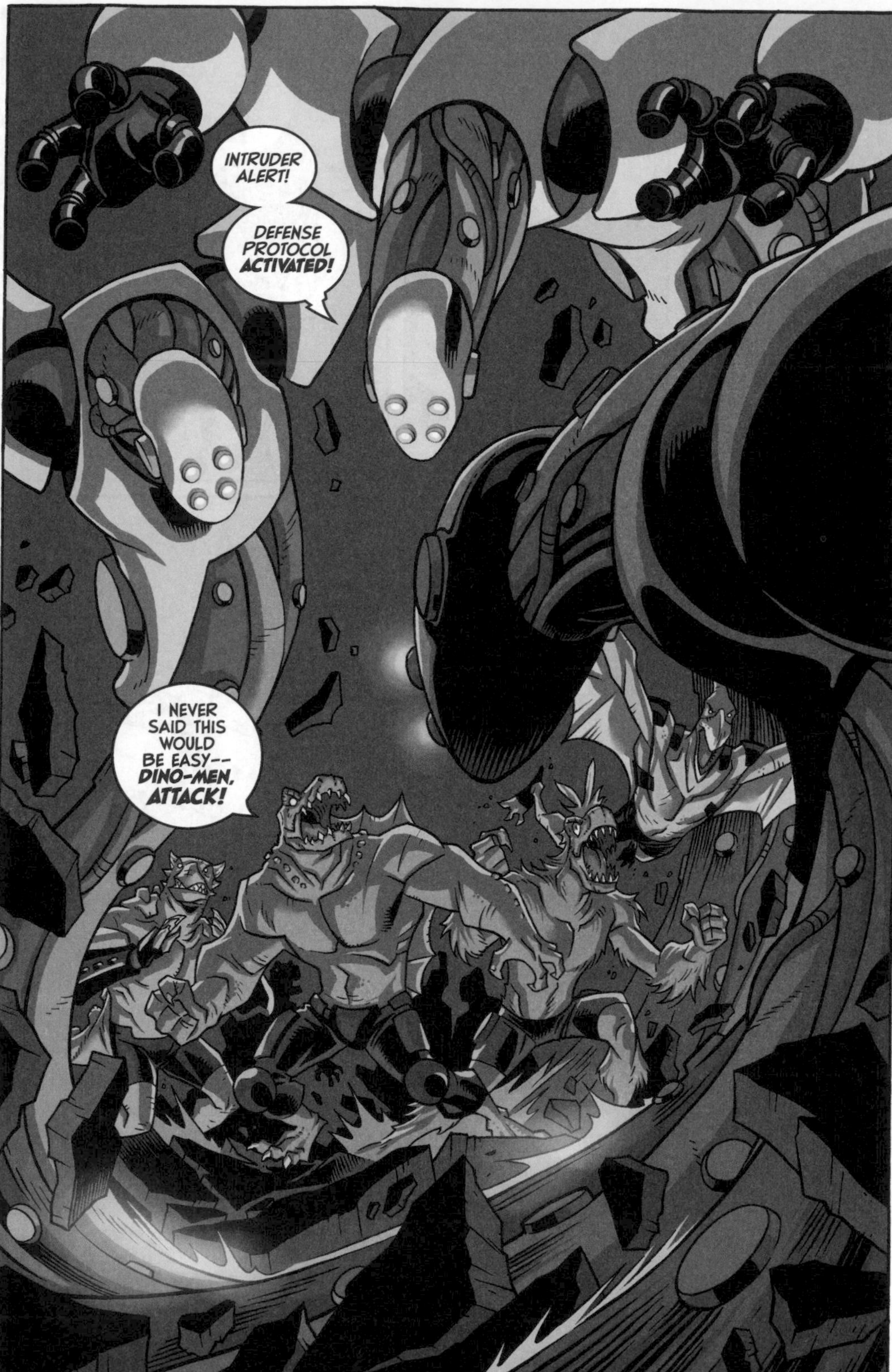
INTRUDER ALERT!
DEFENSE PROTOCOL ACTIVATED!
I NEVER SAID THIS WOULD BE EASY-- DINO-MEN, ATTACK!

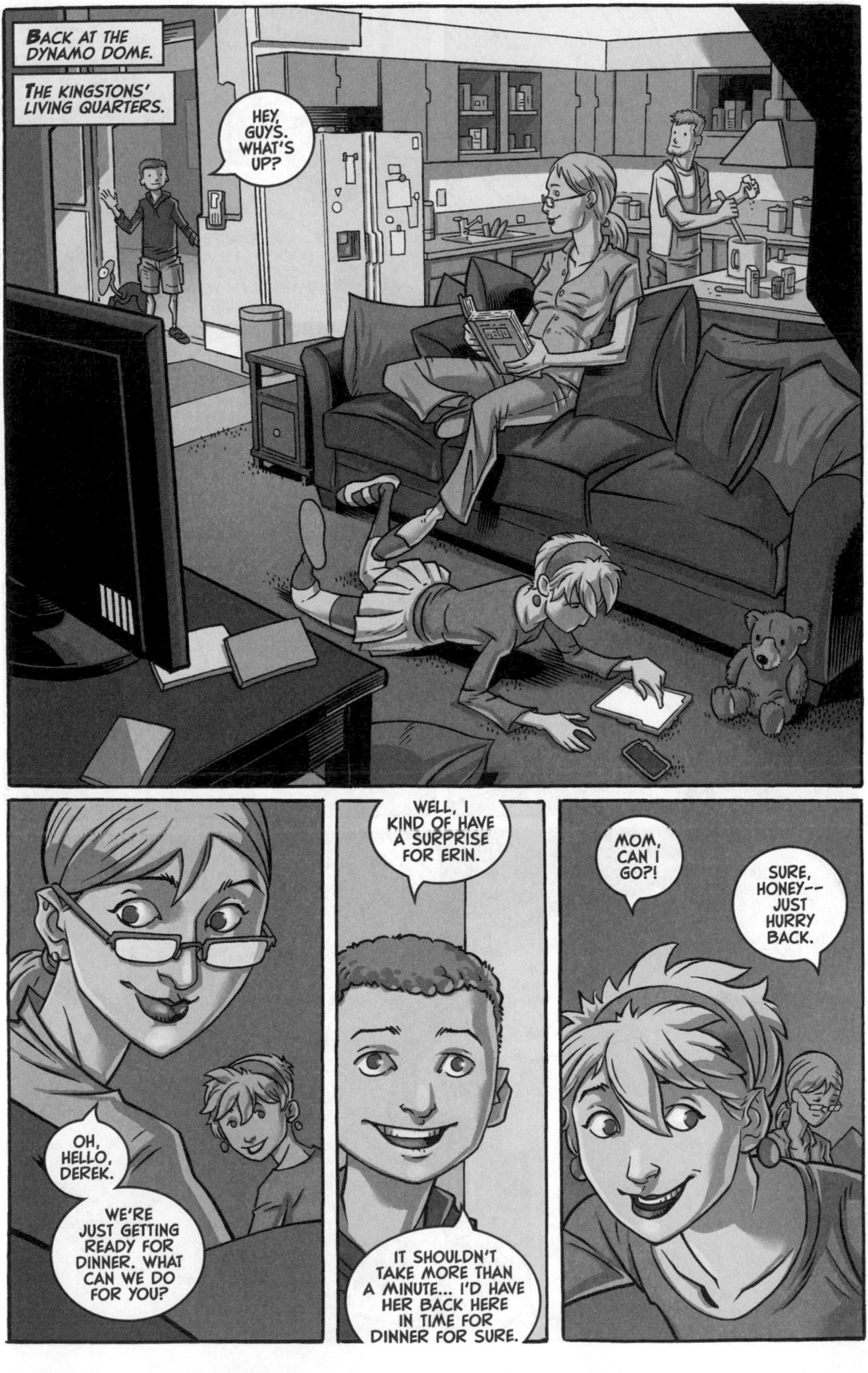
BACK AT THE DYNAMO DOME.
THE KINGSTONS' LIVING QUARTERS.
HEY, GUYS. WHAT'S UP?
OH, HELLO, DEREK.
WE'RE JUST GETTING READY FOR DINNER. WHAT CAN WE DO FOR YOU?
WELL, I KIND OF HAVE A SURPRISE FOR ERIN.
IT SHOULDN'T TAKE MORE THAN A MINUTE... I'D HAVE HER BACK HERE IN TIME FOR DINNER FOR SURE.
MOM, CAN I GO?!
SURE, HONEY-- JUST HURRY BACK.

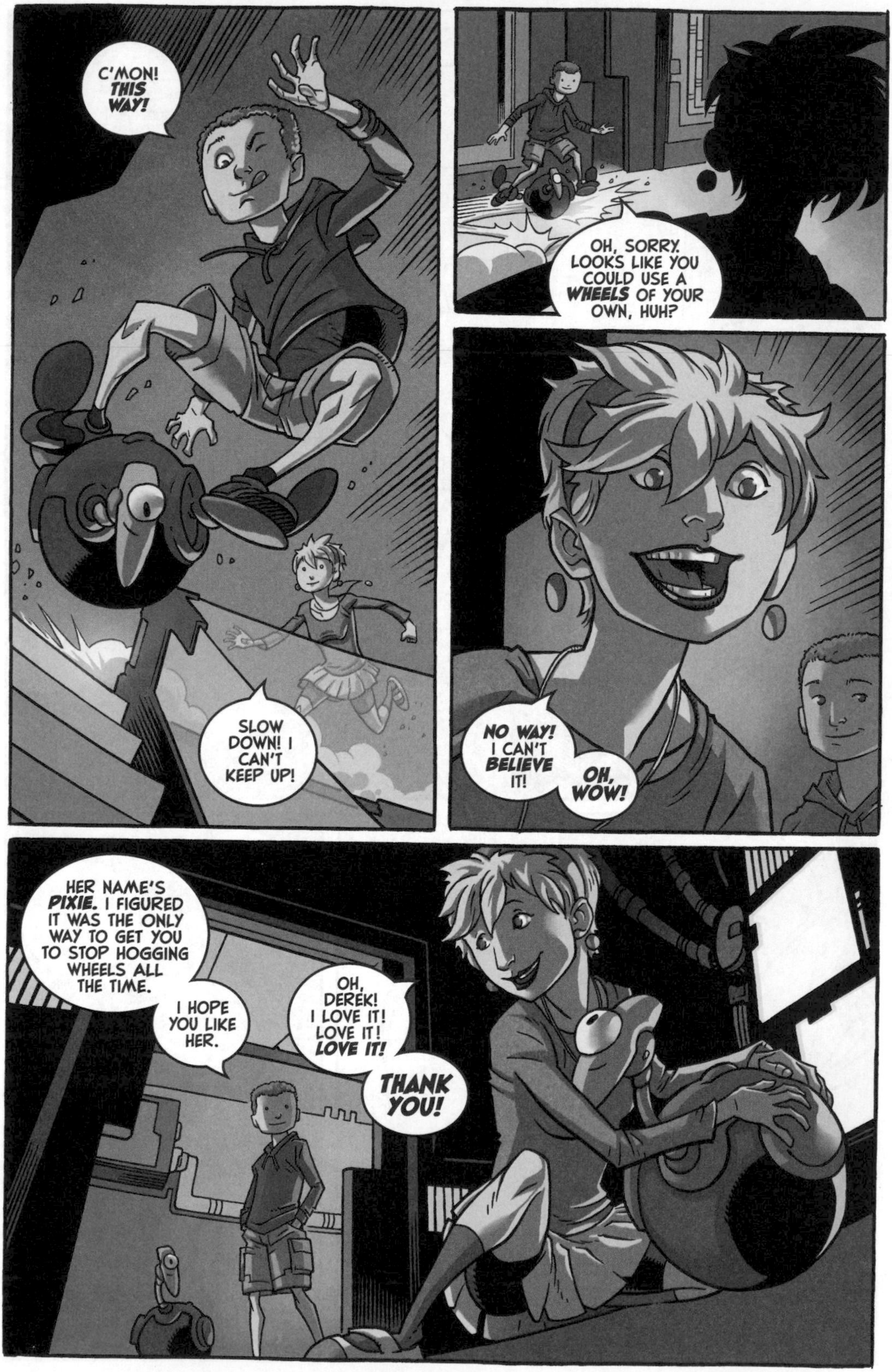
C'MON! THIS WAY!
SLOW DOWN! I CAN'T KEEP UP!
OH, SORRY. LOOKS LIKE YOU COULD USE A WHEELS OF YOUR OWN, HUH?
NO WAY! I CAN'T BELIEVE IT!
OH, WOW!
HER NAME'S PIXIE. I FIGURED IT WAS THE ONLY WAY TO GET YOU TO STOP HOGGING WHEELS ALL THE TIME.
I HOPE YOU LIKE HER.
OH, DEREK! I LOVE IT! LOVE IT! LOVE IT!
THANK YOU!

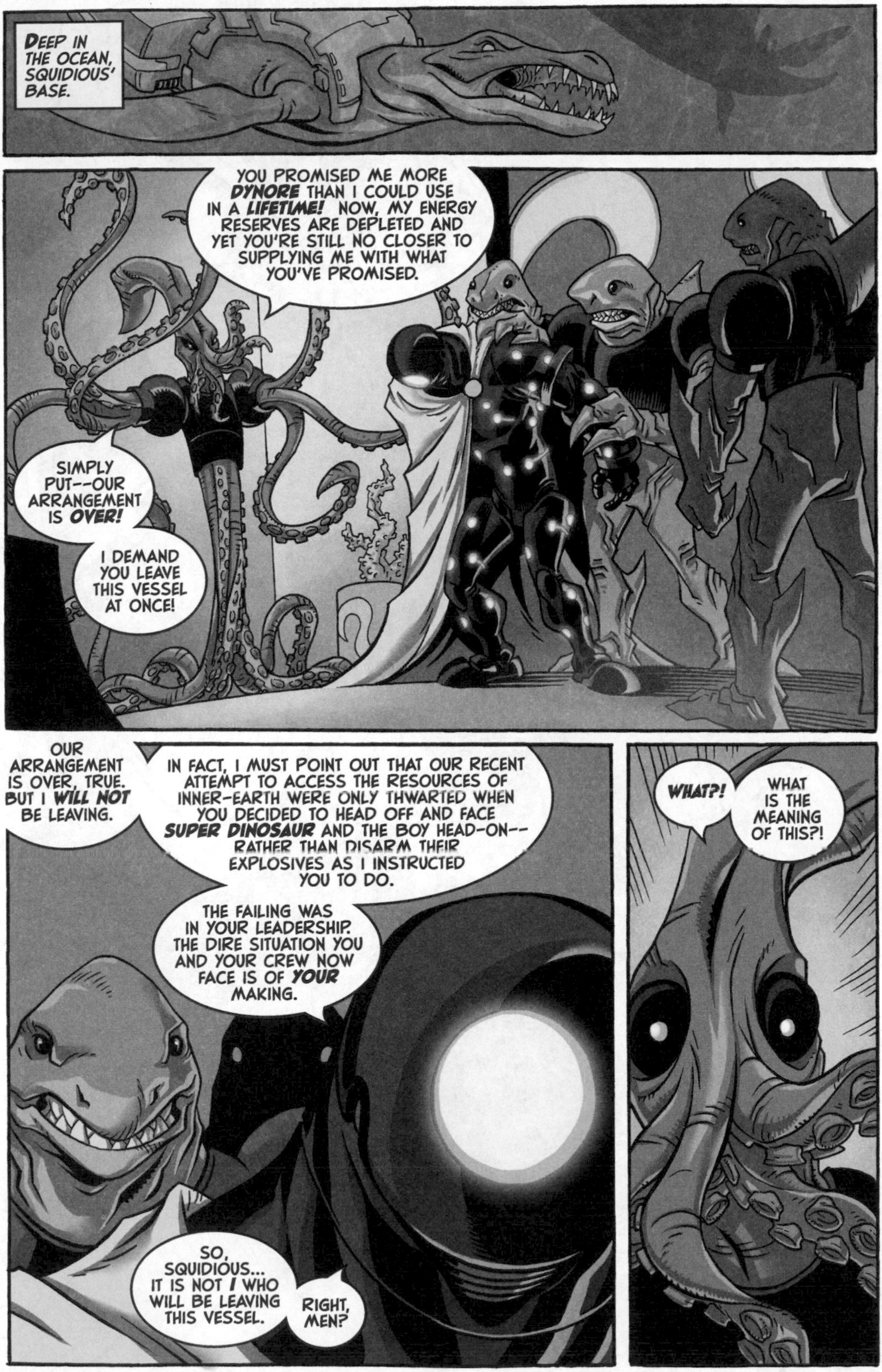
DEEP IN THE OCEAN, SQUIDIOUS' BASE.
YOU PROMISED ME MORE DYNORE THAN I COULD USE IN A LIFETIME! NOW, MY ENERGY RESERVES ARE DEPLETED AND YET YOU'RE STILL NO CLOSER TO SUPPLYING ME WITH WHAT YOU'VE PROMISED.
SIMPLY PUT--OUR ARRANGEMENT IS OVER!
I DEMAND YOU LEAVE THIS VESSEL AT ONCE!
OUR ARRANGEMENT IS OVER, TRUE. BUT I WILL NOT BE LEAVING.
IN FACT, I MUST POINT OUT THAT OUR RECENT ATTEMPT TO ACCESS THE RESOURCES OF INNER-EARTH WERE ONLY THWARTED WHEN YOU DECIDED TO HEAD OFF AND FACE SUPER DINOSAUR AND THE BOY HEAD-ON--RATHER THAN DISARM THEIR EXPLOSIVES AS I INSTRUCTED YOU TO DO.
THE FAILING WAS IN YOUR LEADERSHIP. THE DIRE SITUATION YOU AND YOUR CREW NOW FACE IS OF YOUR MAKING.
SO, SQUIDIOUS... IT IS NOT I WHO WILL BE LEAVING THIS VESSEL.
RIGHT, MEN?
WHAT?!
WHAT IS THE MEANING OF THIS?!

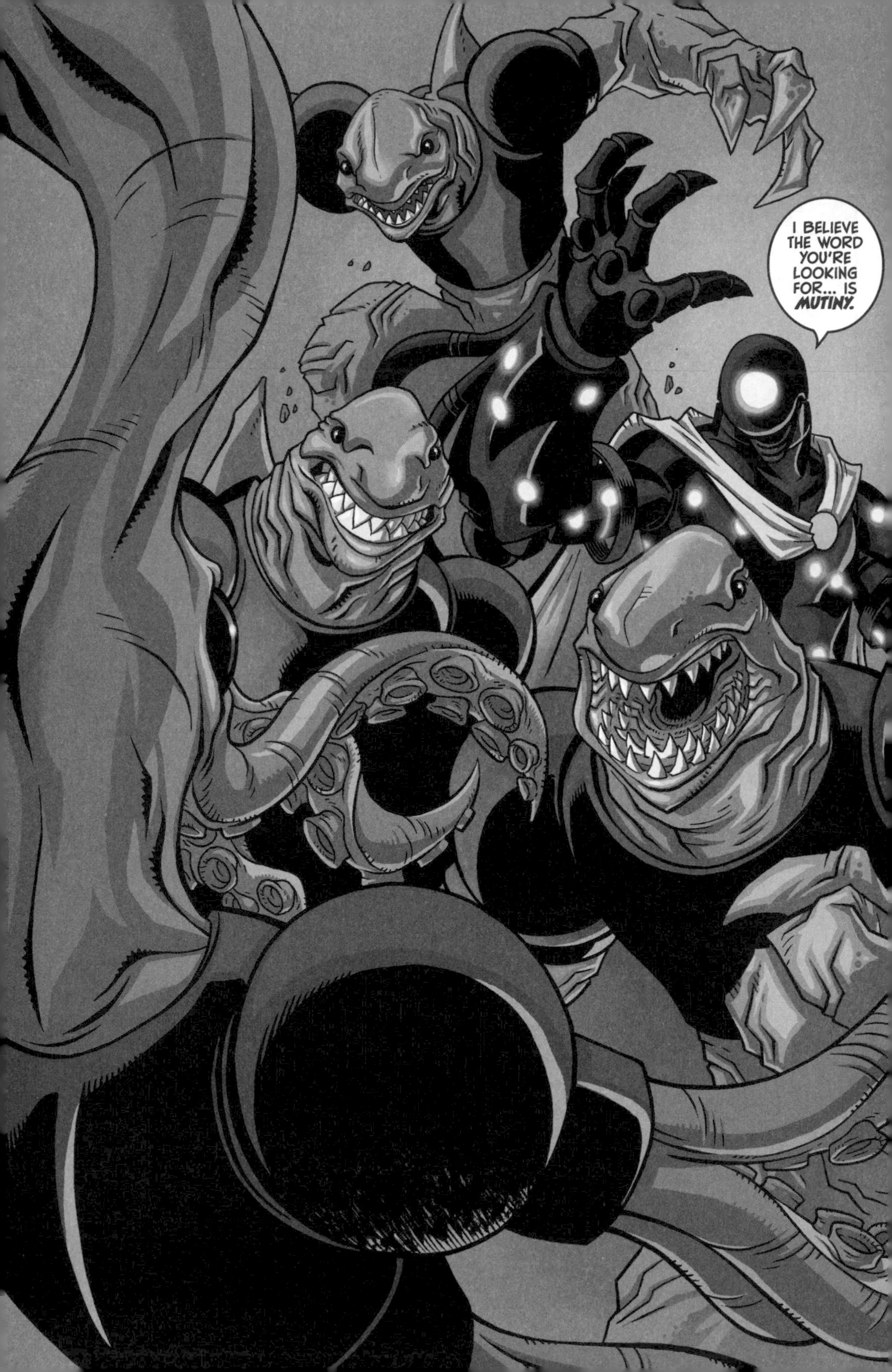
I BELIEVE THE WORD YOU'RE LOOKING FOR... IS *MUTINY.*

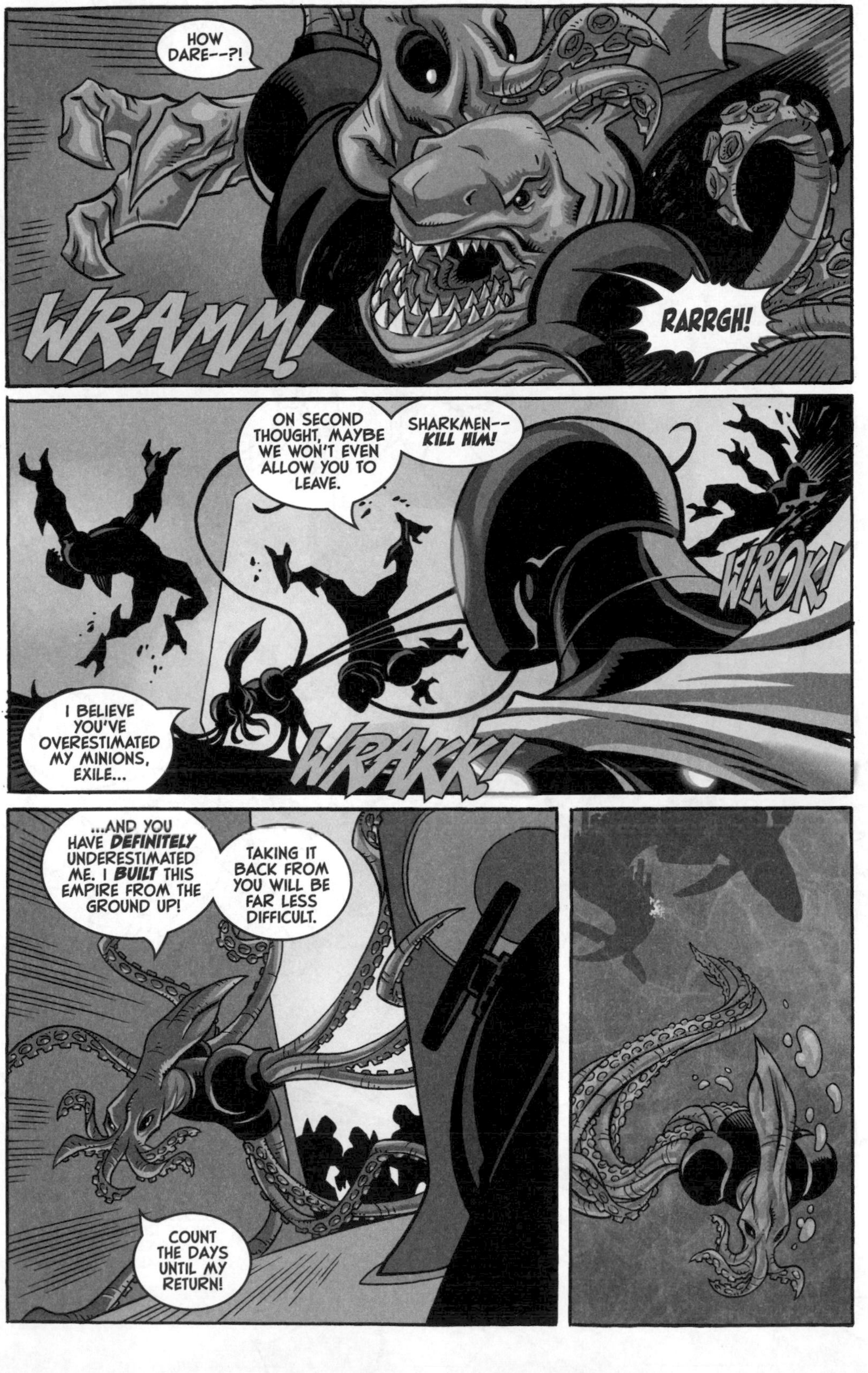
HOW DARE--?!
WRAMM!
RARRGH!
ON SECOND THOUGHT, MAYBE WE WON'T EVEN ALLOW YOU TO LEAVE.
SHARKMEN-- KILL HIM!
WROK!
I BELIEVE YOU'VE OVERESTIMATED MY MINIONS, EXILE...
WRAKK!
...AND YOU HAVE DEFINITELY UNDERESTIMATED ME. I BUILT THIS EMPIRE FROM THE GROUND UP!
TAKING IT BACK FROM YOU WILL BE FAR LESS DIFFICULT.
COUNT THE DAYS UNTIL MY RETURN!

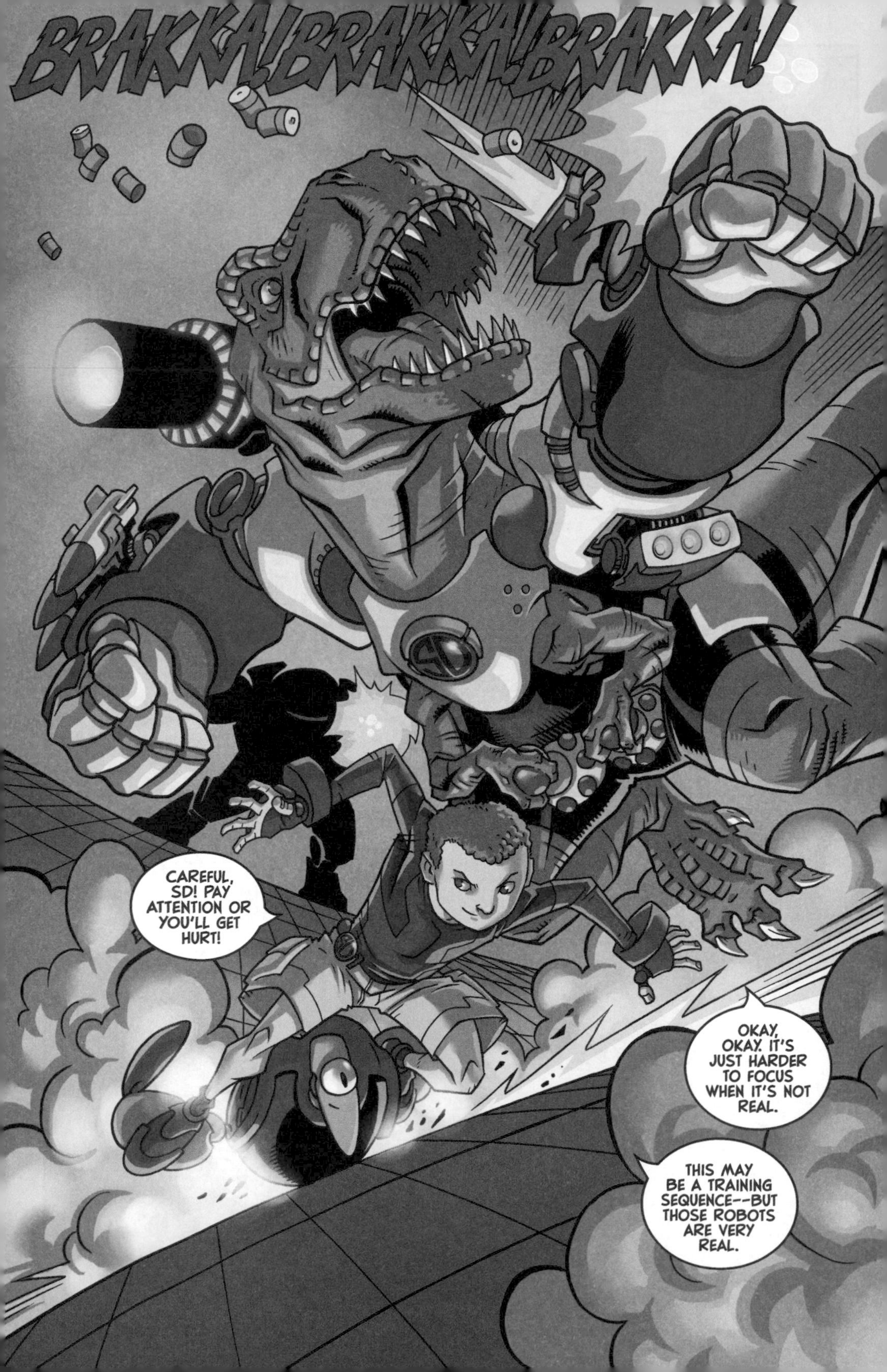
BRAKKA! BRAKKA! BRAKKA!
CAREFUL, SD! PAY ATTENTION OR YOU'LL GET HURT!
OKAY, OKAY. IT'S JUST HARDER TO FOCUS WHEN IT'S NOT REAL.
THIS MAY BE A TRAINING SEQUENCE--BUT THOSE ROBOTS ARE VERY REAL.

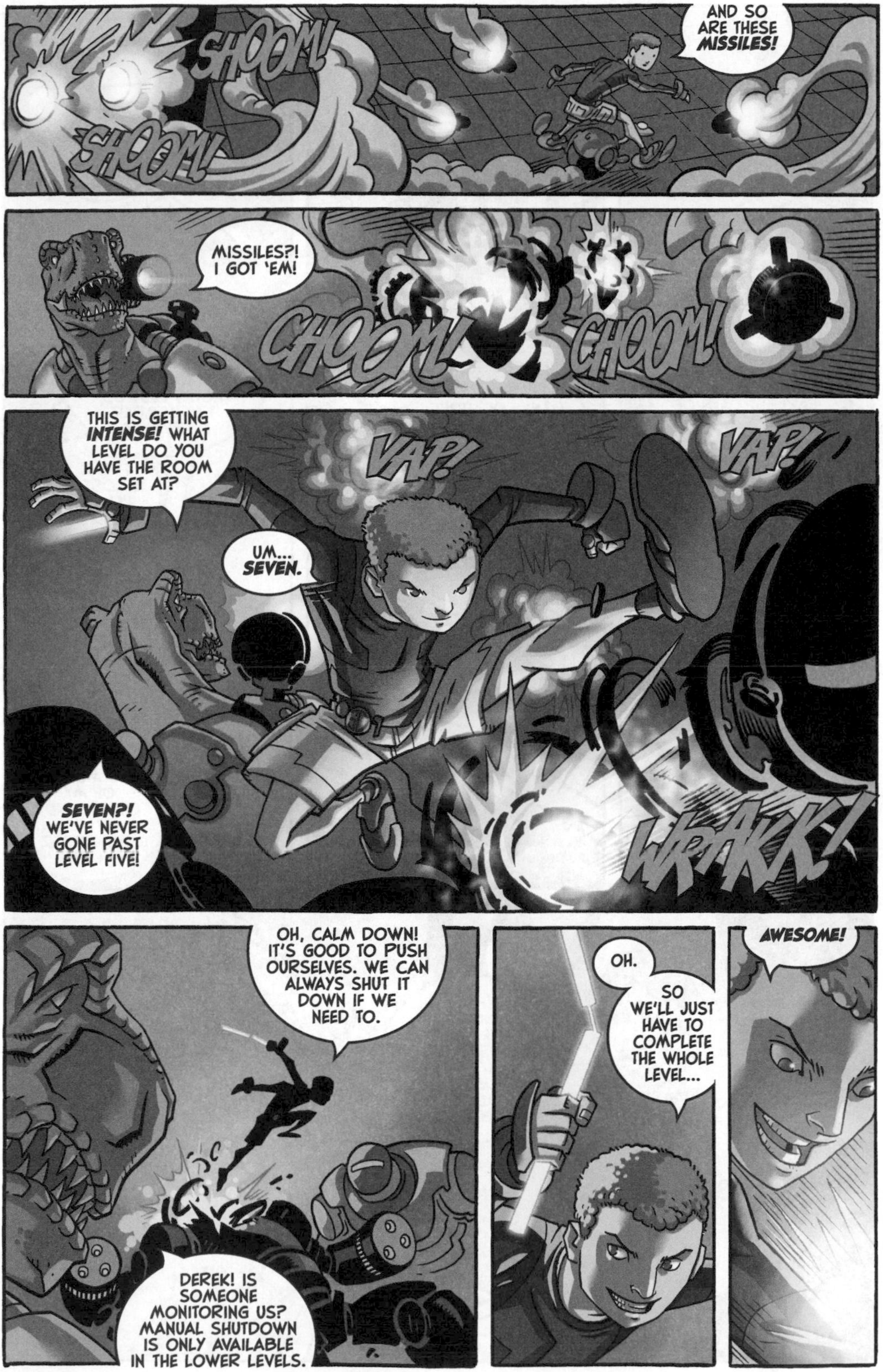
SHOOM!
SHOOM!
AND SO ARE THESE MISSILES!
MISSILES?! I GOT 'EM!
CHOOM!
CHOOM!
THIS IS GETTING INTENSE! WHAT LEVEL DO YOU HAVE THE ROOM SET AT?
VAP!
VAP!
UM... SEVEN.
SEVEN?! WE'VE NEVER GONE PAST LEVEL FIVE!
WRAKK!
OH, CALM DOWN! IT'S GOOD TO PUSH OURSELVES. WE CAN ALWAYS SHUT IT DOWN IF WE NEED TO.
DEREK! IS SOMEONE MONITORING US? MANUAL SHUTDOWN IS ONLY AVAILABLE IN THE LOWER LEVELS.
OH.
SO WE'LL JUST HAVE TO COMPLETE THE WHOLE LEVEL...
AWESOME!

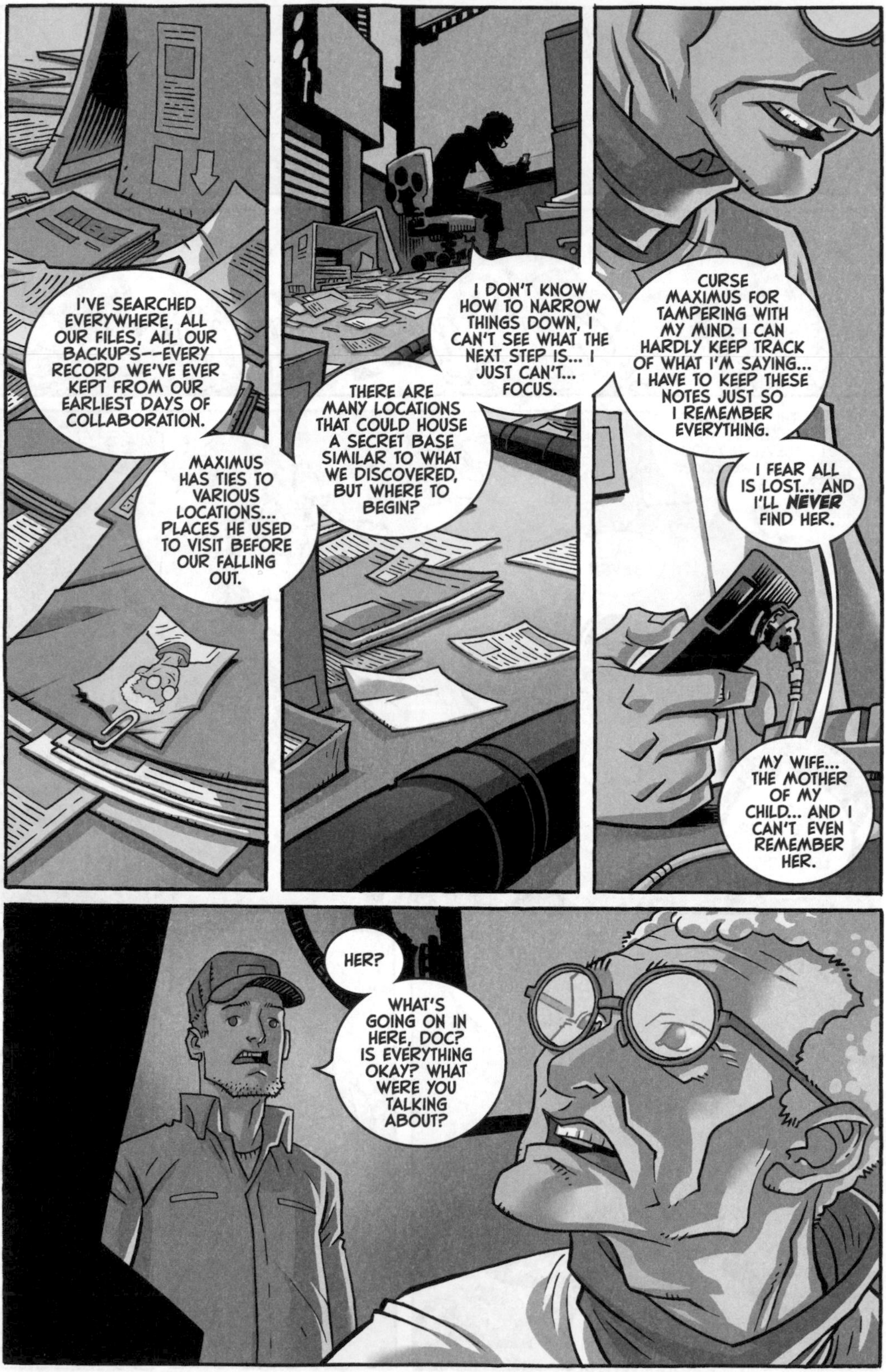
I'VE SEARCHED EVERYWHERE, ALL OUR FILES, ALL OUR BACKUPS--EVERY RECORD WE'VE EVER KEPT FROM OUR EARLIEST DAYS OF COLLABORATION.
MAXIMUS HAS TIES TO VARIOUS LOCATIONS... PLACES HE USED TO VISIT BEFORE OUR FALLING OUT.
THERE ARE MANY LOCATIONS THAT COULD HOUSE A SECRET BASE SIMILAR TO WHAT WE DISCOVERED, BUT WHERE TO BEGIN?
I DON'T KNOW HOW TO NARROW THINGS DOWN, I CAN'T SEE WHAT THE NEXT STEP IS... I JUST CAN'T... FOCUS.
CURSE MAXIMUS FOR TAMPERING WITH MY MIND. I CAN HARDLY KEEP TRACK OF WHAT I'M SAYING... I HAVE TO KEEP THESE NOTES JUST SO I REMEMBER EVERYTHING.
I FEAR ALL IS LOST... AND I'LL ***NEVER*** FIND HER.
MY WIFE... THE MOTHER OF MY CHILD... AND I CAN'T EVEN REMEMBER HER.
HER?
WHAT'S GOING ON IN HERE, DOC? IS EVERYTHING OKAY? WHAT WERE YOU TALKING ABOUT?

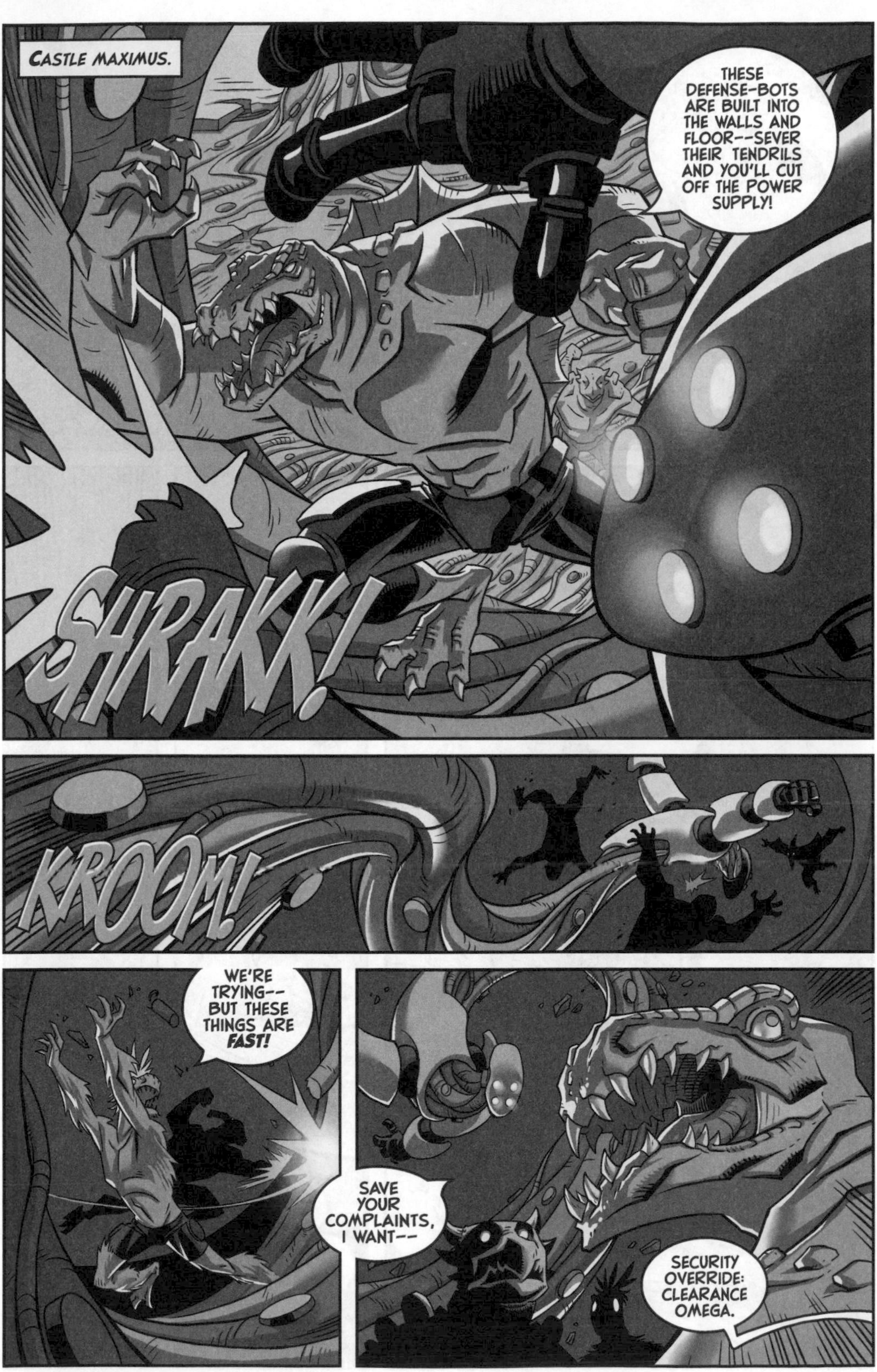
CASTLE MAXIMUS.
THESE DEFENSE-BOTS ARE BUILT INTO THE WALLS AND FLOOR--SEVER THEIR TENDRILS AND YOU'LL CUT OFF THE POWER SUPPLY!
SHRAKK!
KROOM!
WE'RE TRYING-- BUT THESE THINGS ARE FAST!
SAVE YOUR COMPLAINTS, I WANT--
SECURITY OVERRIDE: CLEARANCE OMEGA.

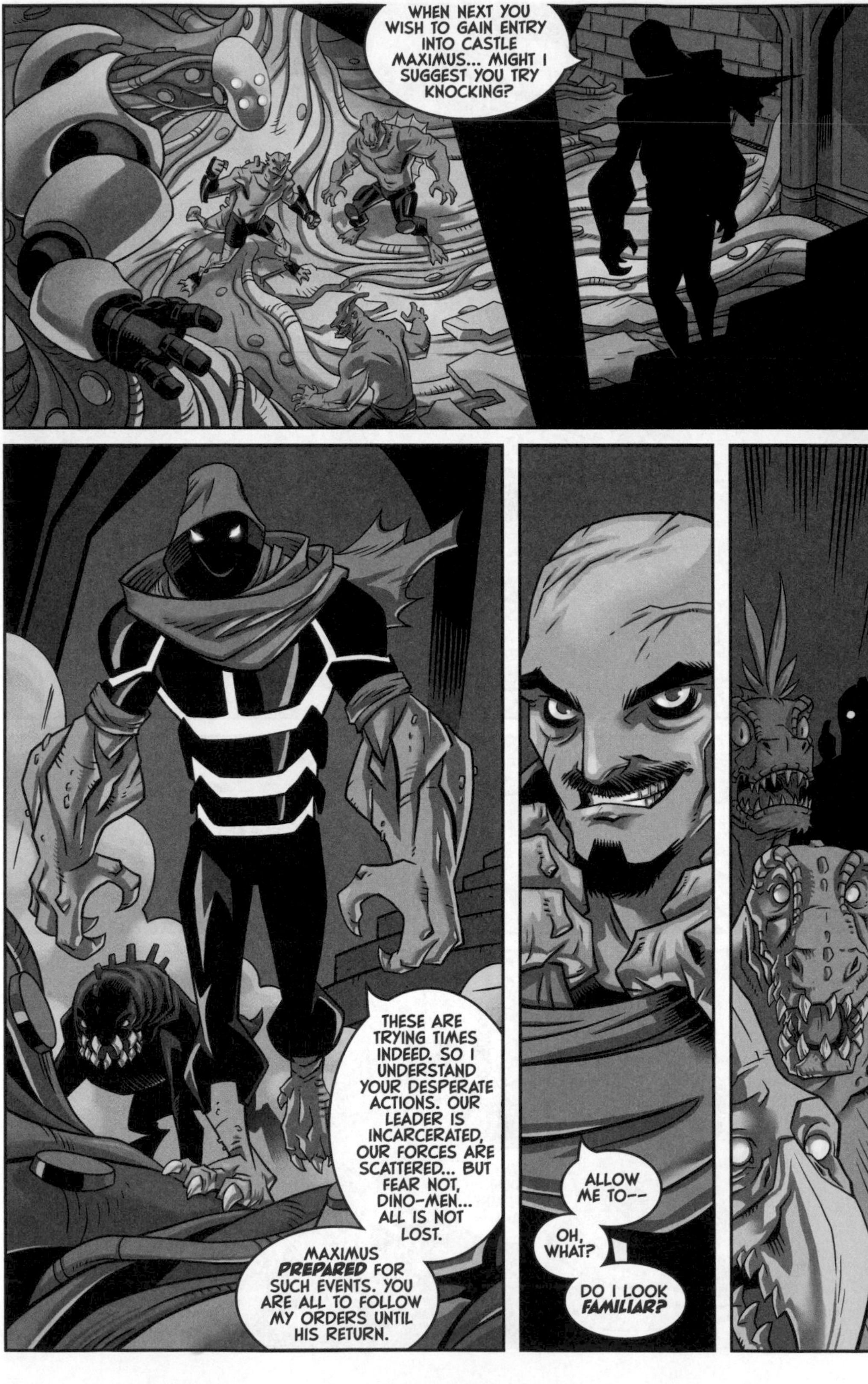
WHEN NEXT YOU WISH TO GAIN ENTRY INTO CASTLE MAXIMUS... MIGHT I SUGGEST YOU TRY KNOCKING?
THESE ARE TRYING TIMES INDEED. SO I UNDERSTAND YOUR DESPERATE ACTIONS. OUR LEADER IS INCARCERATED, OUR FORCES ARE SCATTERED... BUT FEAR NOT, DINO-MEN... ALL IS NOT LOST.
MAXIMUS **PREPARED** FOR SUCH EVENTS. YOU ARE ALL TO FOLLOW MY ORDERS UNTIL HIS RETURN.
ALLOW ME TO--
OH, WHAT?
DO I LOOK **FAMILIAR?**

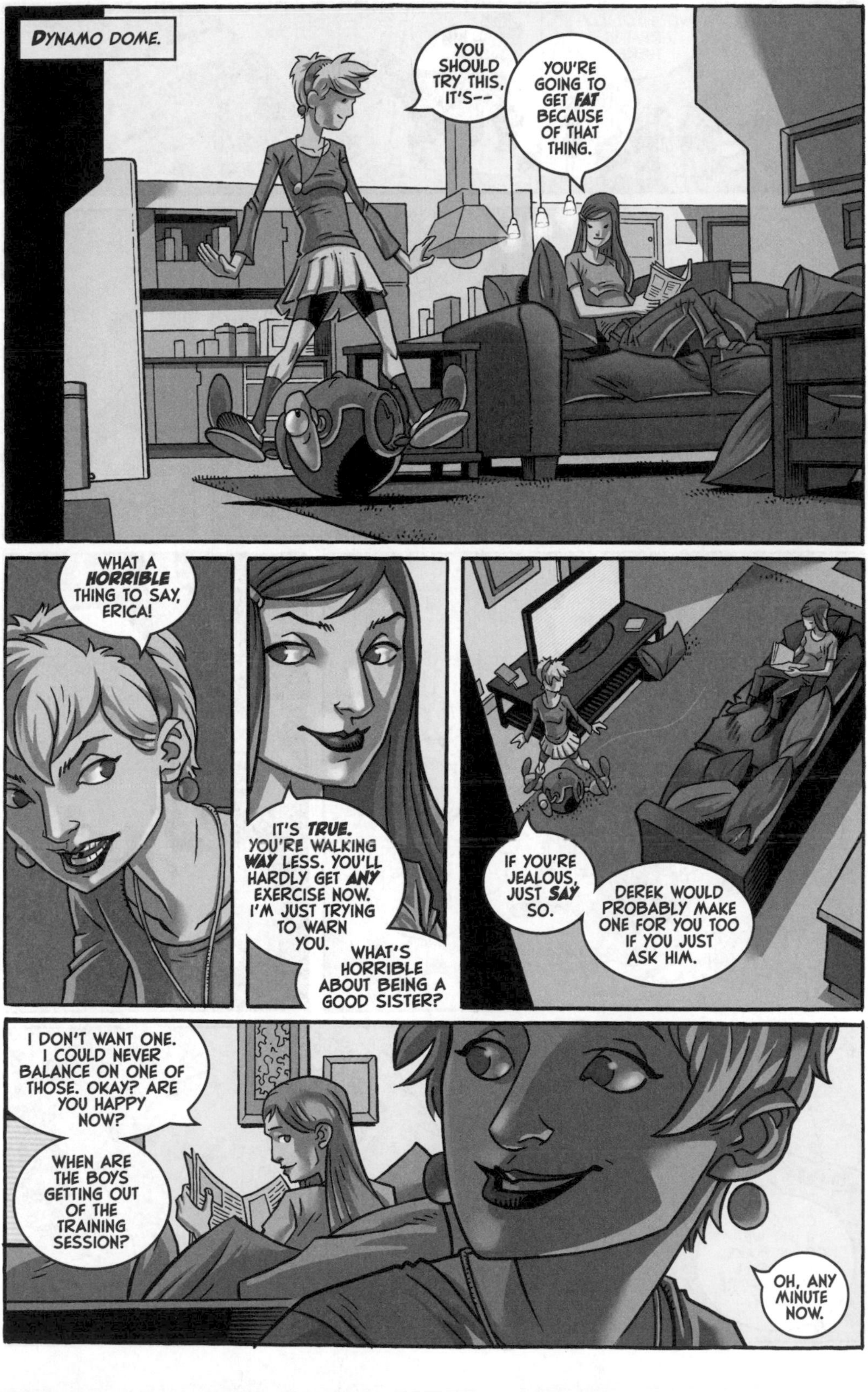
DYNAMO DOME.
YOU SHOULD TRY THIS, IT'S--
YOU'RE GOING TO GET FAT BECAUSE OF THAT THING.
WHAT A HORRIBLE THING TO SAY, ERICA!
IT'S TRUE. YOU'RE WALKING WAY LESS. YOU'LL HARDLY GET ANY EXERCISE NOW. I'M JUST TRYING TO WARN YOU.
WHAT'S HORRIBLE ABOUT BEING A GOOD SISTER?
IF YOU'RE JEALOUS, JUST SAY SO.
DEREK WOULD PROBABLY MAKE ONE FOR YOU TOO IF YOU JUST ASK HIM.
I DON'T WANT ONE. I COULD NEVER BALANCE ON ONE OF THOSE. OKAY? ARE YOU HAPPY NOW?
WHEN ARE THE BOYS GETTING OUT OF THE TRAINING SESSION?
OH, ANY MINUTE NOW.

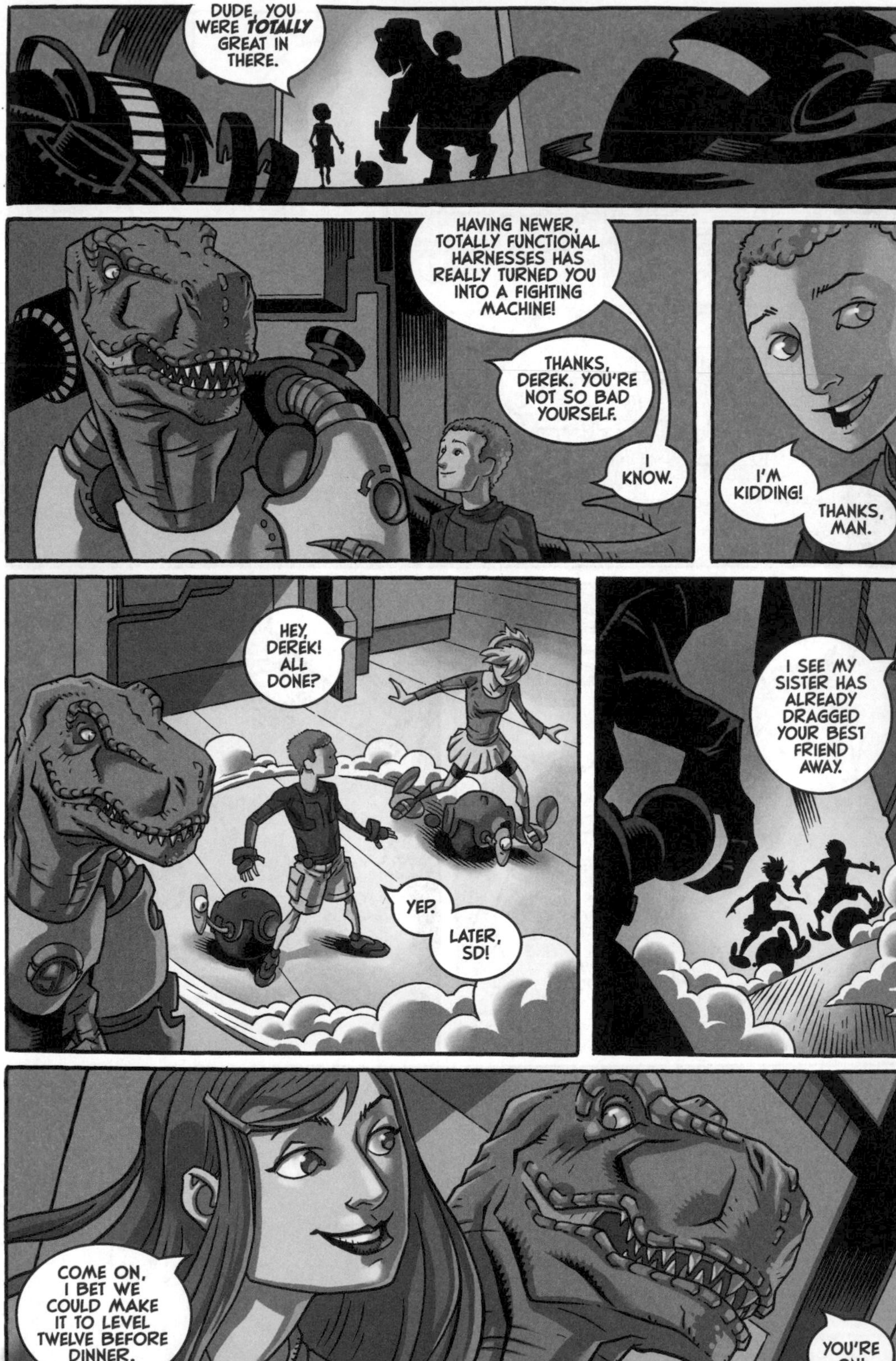
DUDE, YOU WERE TOTALLY GREAT IN THERE.
HAVING NEWER, TOTALLY FUNCTIONAL HARNESSES HAS REALLY TURNED YOU INTO A FIGHTING MACHINE!
THANKS, DEREK. YOU'RE NOT SO BAD YOURSELF.
I KNOW.
I'M KIDDING!
THANKS, MAN.
HEY, DEREK! ALL DONE?
YEP.
LATER, SD!
I SEE MY SISTER HAS ALREADY DRAGGED YOUR BEST FRIEND AWAY.
COME ON, I BET WE COULD MAKE IT TO LEVEL TWELVE BEFORE DINNER.
YOU'RE ON!

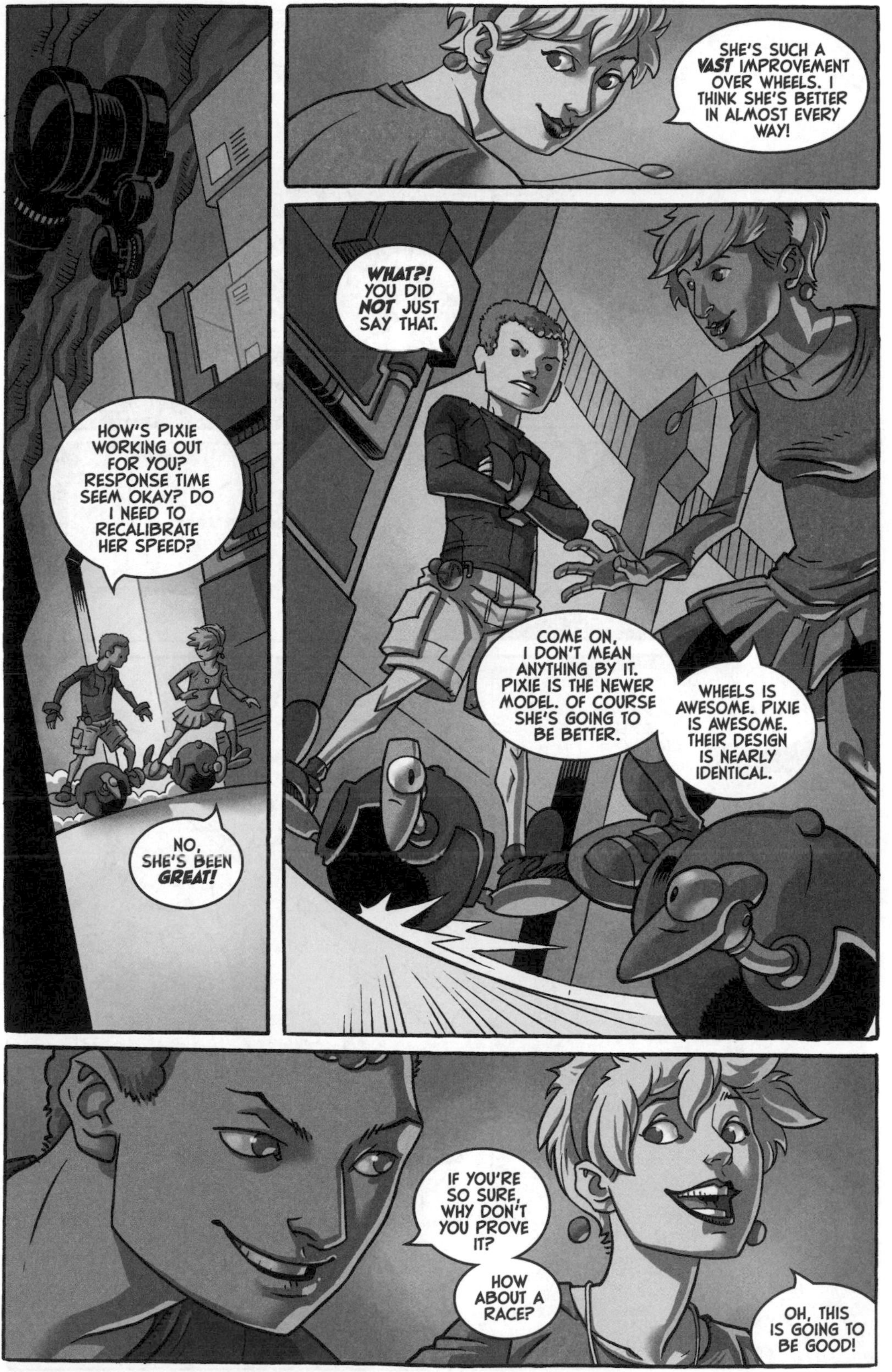
SHE'S SUCH A VAST IMPROVEMENT OVER WHEELS. I THINK SHE'S BETTER IN ALMOST EVERY WAY!
HOW'S PIXIE WORKING OUT FOR YOU? RESPONSE TIME SEEM OKAY? DO I NEED TO RECALIBRATE HER SPEED?
NO, SHE'S BEEN GREAT!
WHAT?! YOU DID NOT JUST SAY THAT.
COME ON, I DON'T MEAN ANYTHING BY IT. PIXIE IS THE NEWER MODEL. OF COURSE SHE'S GOING TO BE BETTER.
WHEELS IS AWESOME. PIXIE IS AWESOME. THEIR DESIGN IS NEARLY IDENTICAL.
IF YOU'RE SO SURE, WHY DON'T YOU PROVE IT?
HOW ABOUT A RACE?
OH, THIS IS GOING TO BE GOOD!

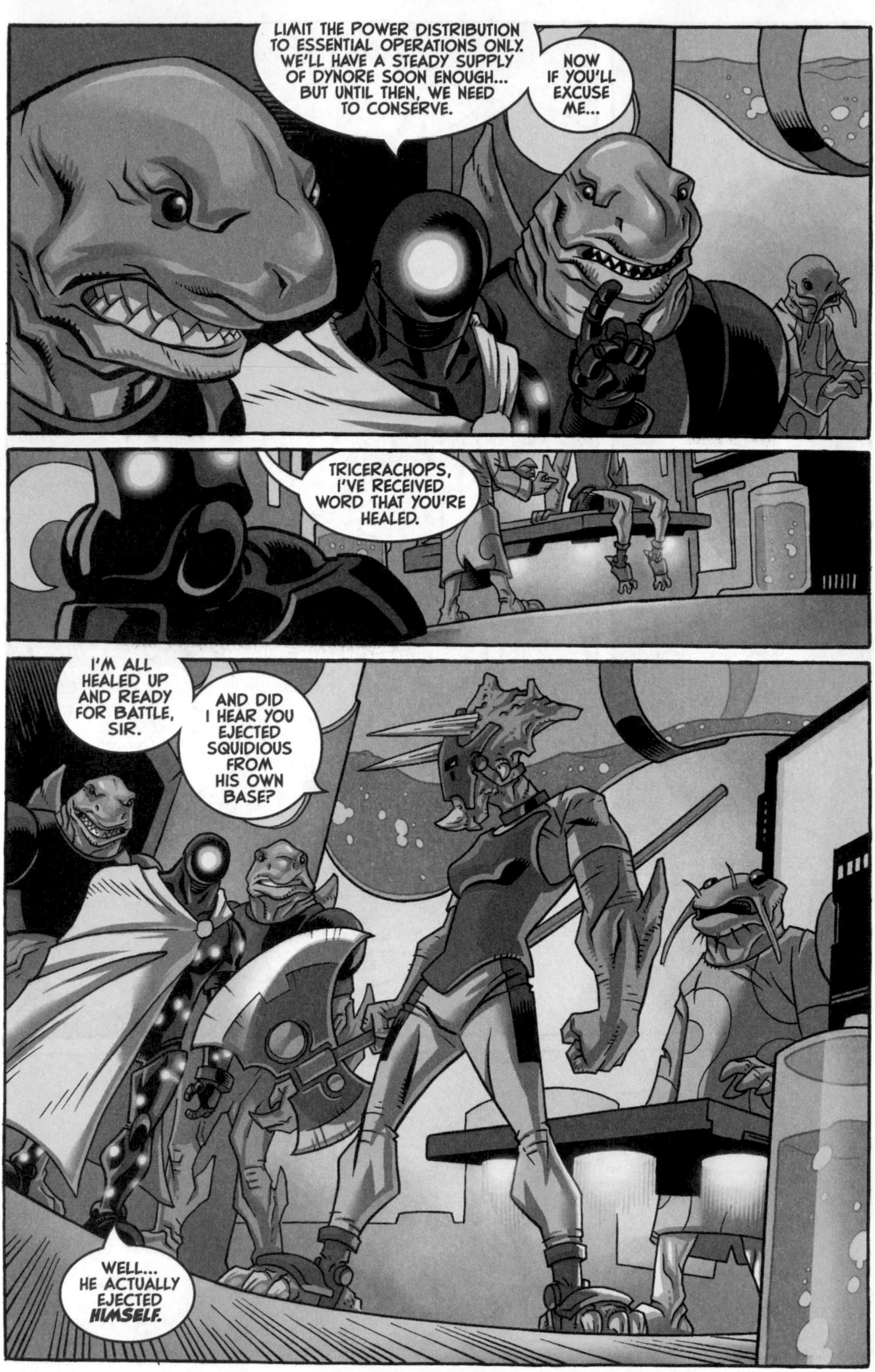
LIMIT THE POWER DISTRIBUTION TO ESSENTIAL OPERATIONS ONLY. WE'LL HAVE A STEADY SUPPLY OF DYNORE SOON ENOUGH... BUT UNTIL THEN, WE NEED TO CONSERVE.
NOW IF YOU'LL EXCUSE ME...
TRICERACHOPS, I'VE RECEIVED WORD THAT YOU'RE HEALED.
I'M ALL HEALED UP AND READY FOR BATTLE, SIR.
AND DID I HEAR YOU EJECTED SQUIDIOUS FROM HIS OWN BASE?
WELL... HE ACTUALLY EJECTED HIMSELF.

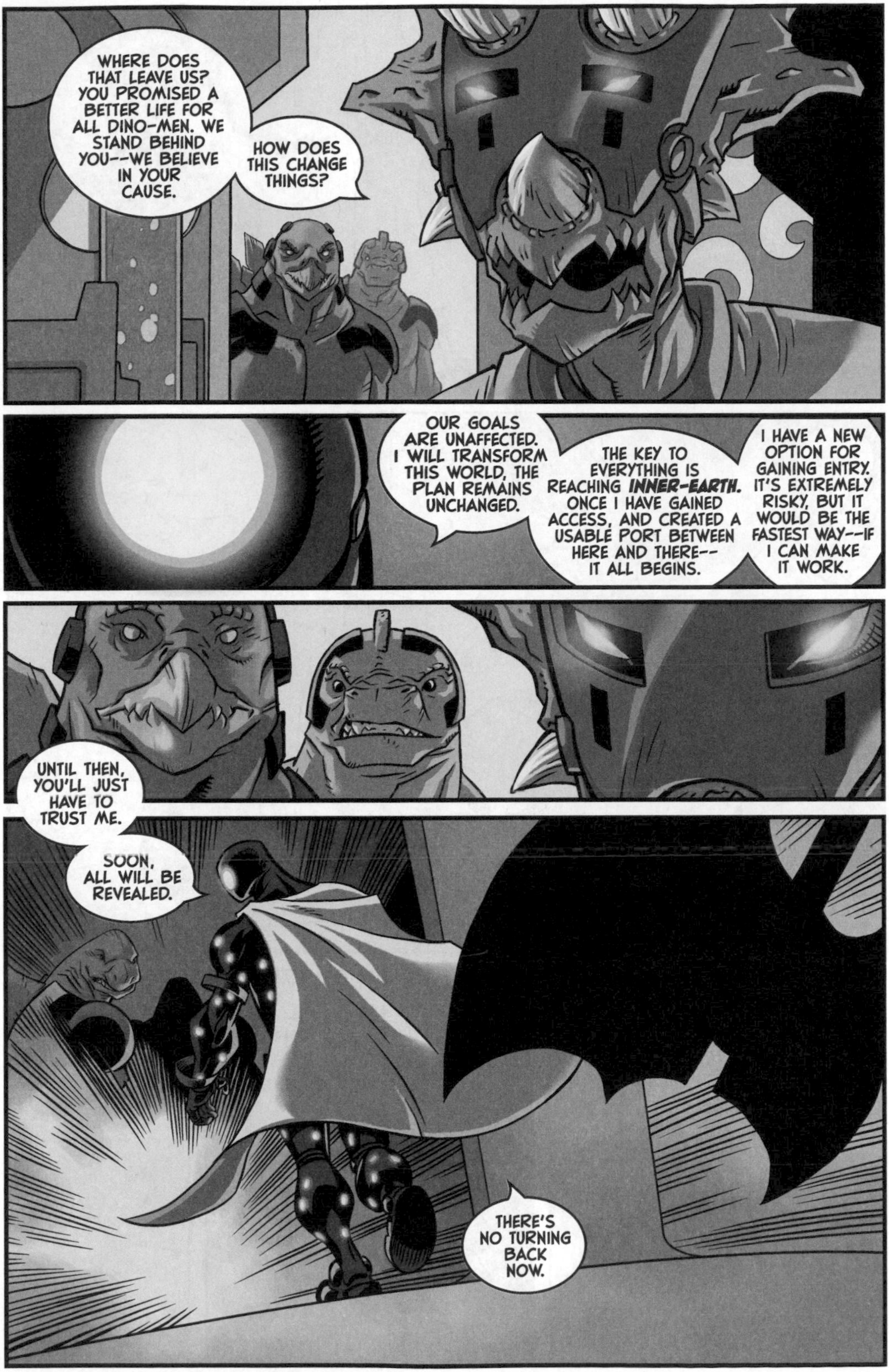
WHERE DOES THAT LEAVE US? YOU PROMISED A BETTER LIFE FOR ALL DINO-MEN. WE STAND BEHIND YOU--WE BELIEVE IN YOUR CAUSE.
HOW DOES THIS CHANGE THINGS?
OUR GOALS ARE UNAFFECTED. I WILL TRANSFORM THIS WORLD, THE PLAN REMAINS UNCHANGED.
THE KEY TO EVERYTHING IS REACHING INNER-EARTH. ONCE I HAVE GAINED ACCESS, AND CREATED A USABLE PORT BETWEEN HERE AND THERE-- IT ALL BEGINS.
I HAVE A NEW OPTION FOR GAINING ENTRY. IT'S EXTREMELY RISKY, BUT IT WOULD BE THE FASTEST WAY--IF I CAN MAKE IT WORK.
UNTIL THEN, YOU'LL JUST HAVE TO TRUST ME.
SOON, ALL WILL BE REVEALED.
THERE'S NO TURNING BACK NOW.

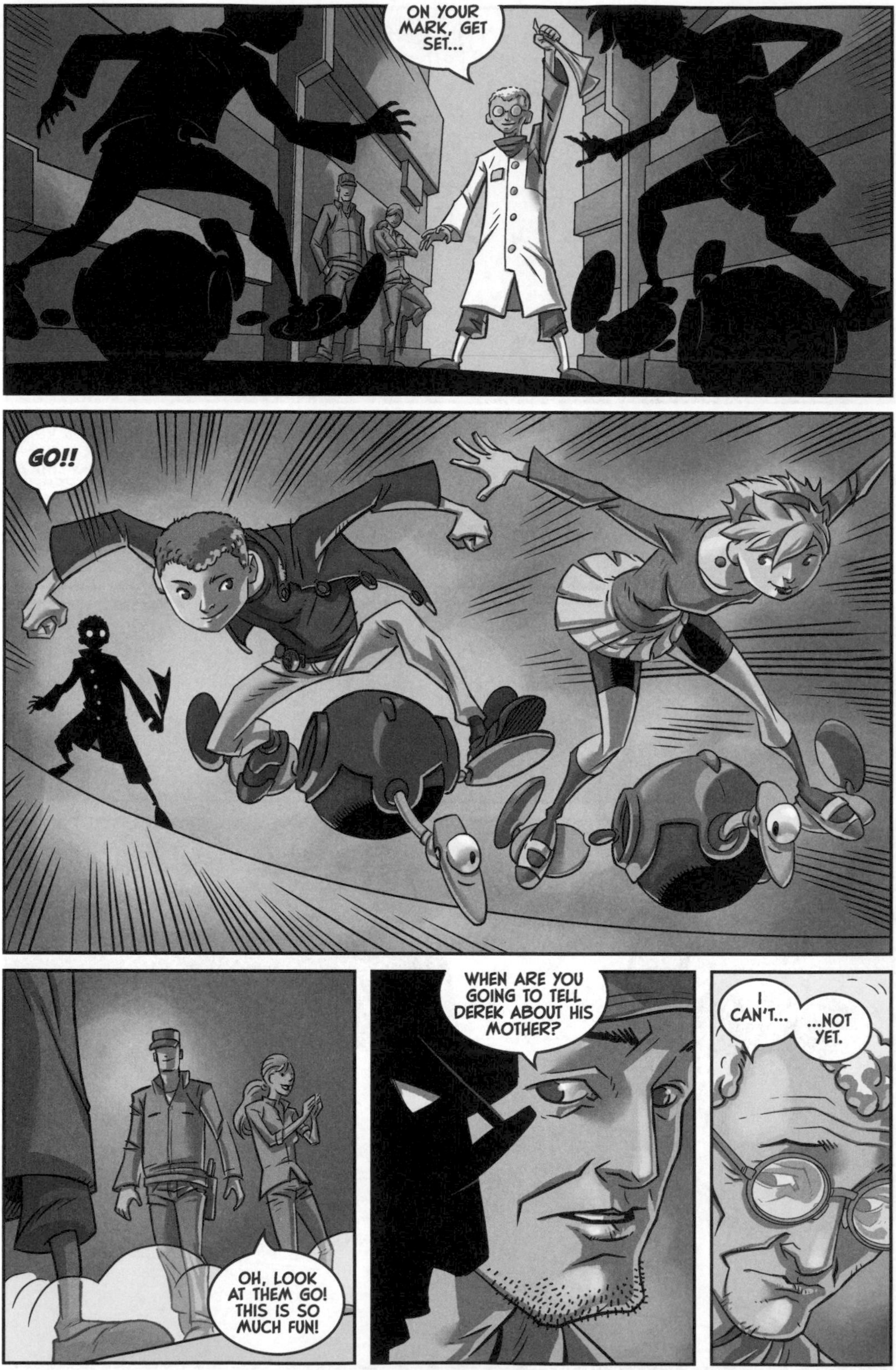
ON YOUR MARK, GET SET...
GO!!
OH, LOOK AT THEM GO! THIS IS SO MUCH FUN!
WHEN ARE YOU GOING TO TELL DEREK ABOUT HIS MOTHER?
I CAN'T...
...NOT YET.

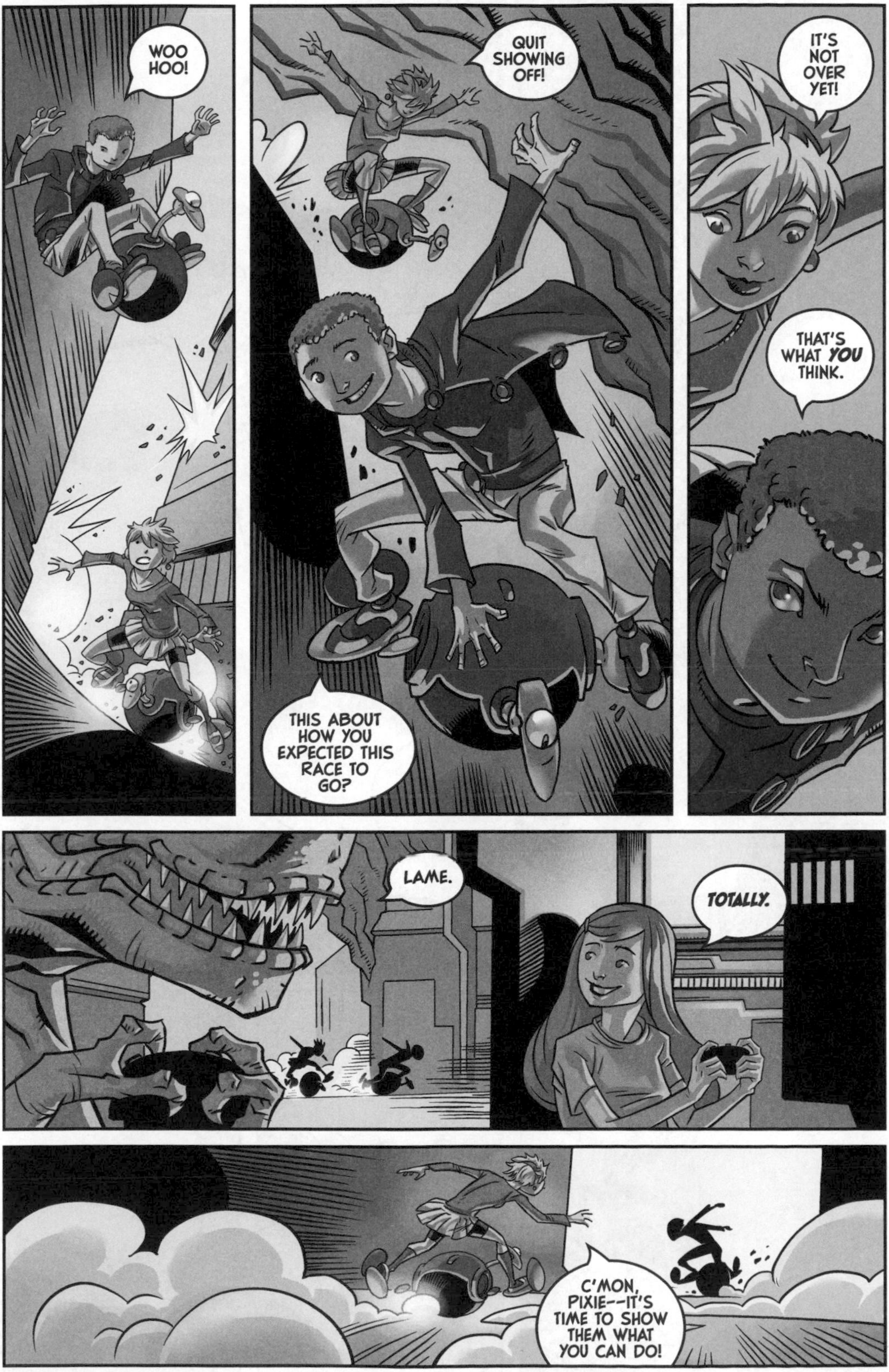
WOO HOO!
QUIT SHOWING OFF!
THIS ABOUT HOW YOU EXPECTED THIS RACE TO GO?
IT'S NOT OVER YET!
THAT'S WHAT *YOU* THINK.
LAME.
TOTALLY.
C'MON, PIXIE--IT'S TIME TO SHOW THEM WHAT YOU CAN DO!

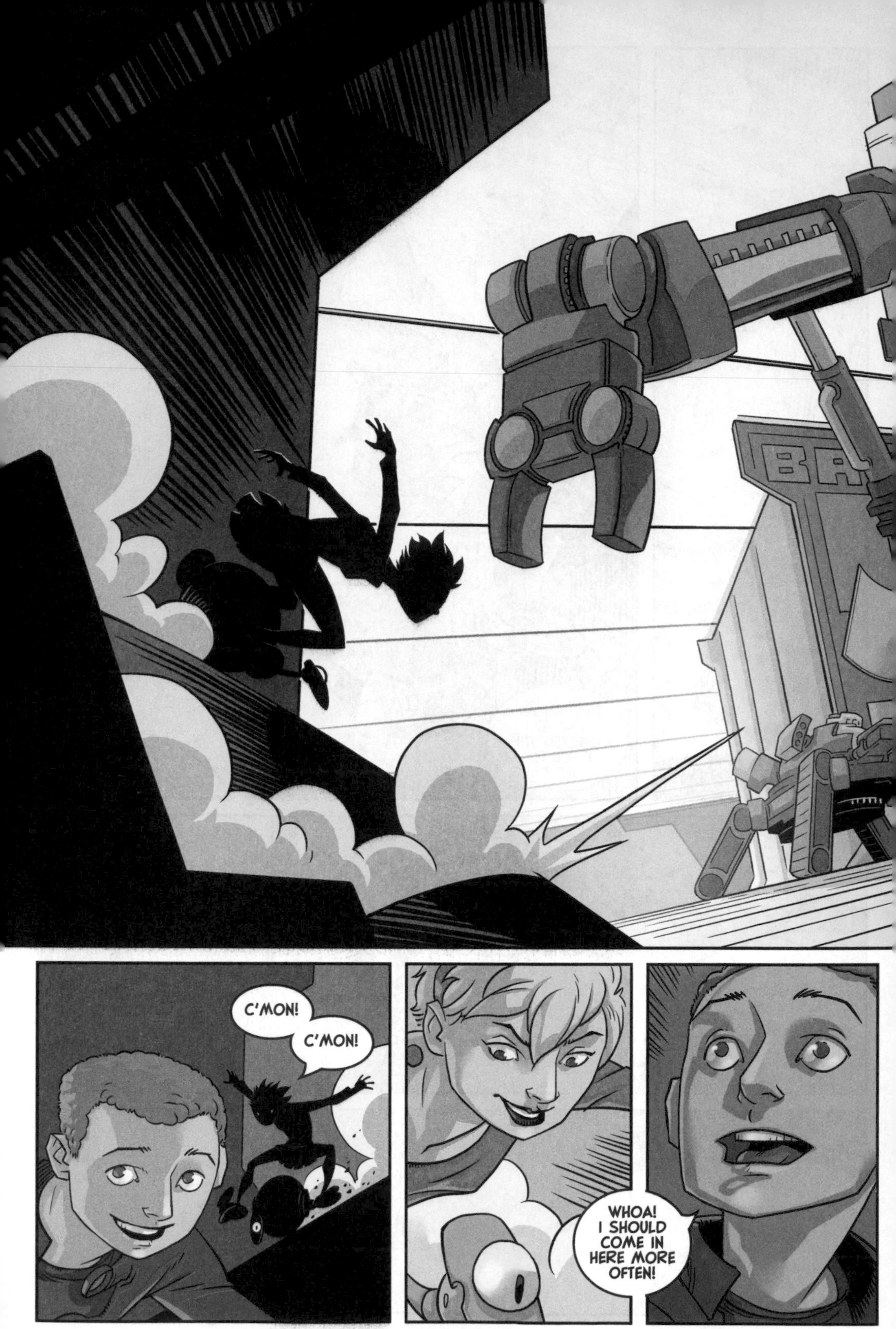
C'MON!
C'MON!
WHOA! I SHOULD COME IN HERE MORE OFTEN!

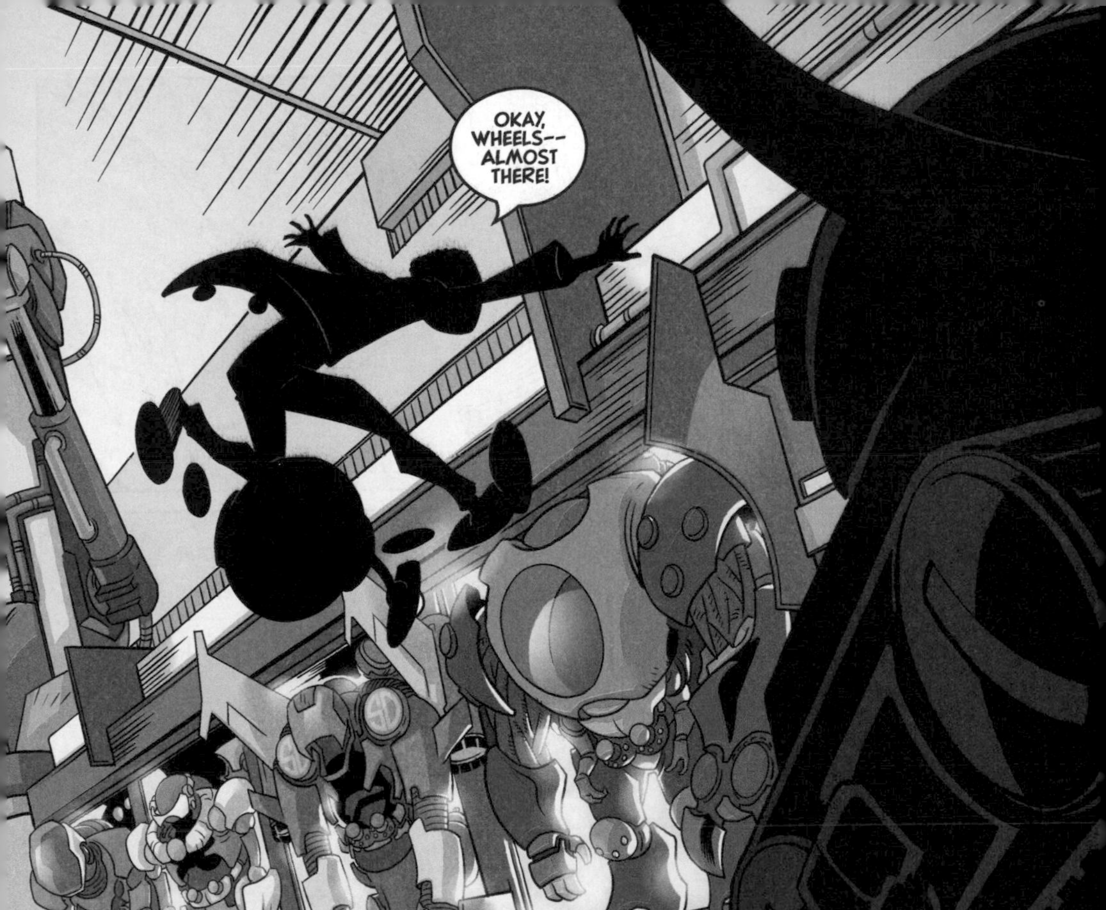
OKAY, WHEELS-- ALMOST THERE!
5
7
9

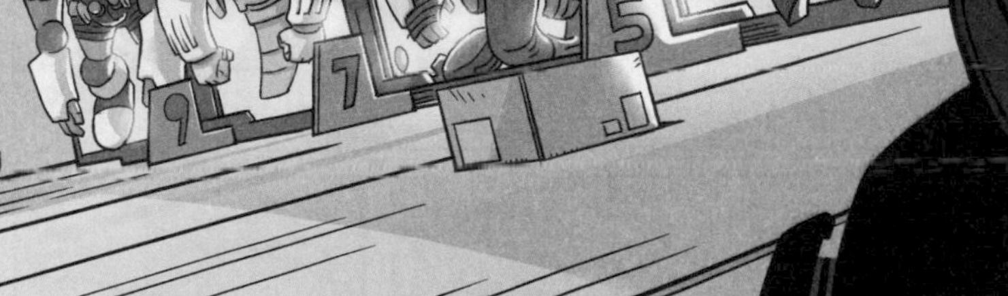
MY PARENTS MAKE SOME COOL STUFF, HUH?
I'LL COME BACK AND CHECK IT OUT **AFTER** I WIN!

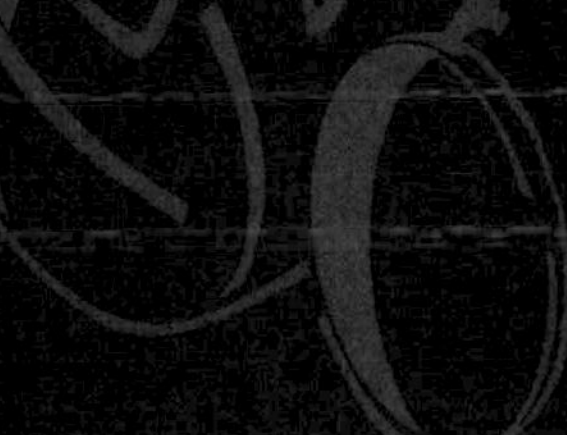
NO FAIR!

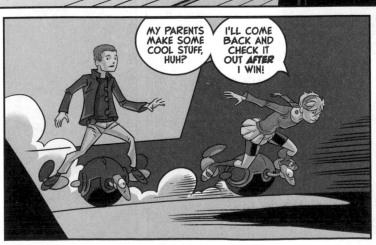

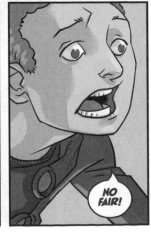

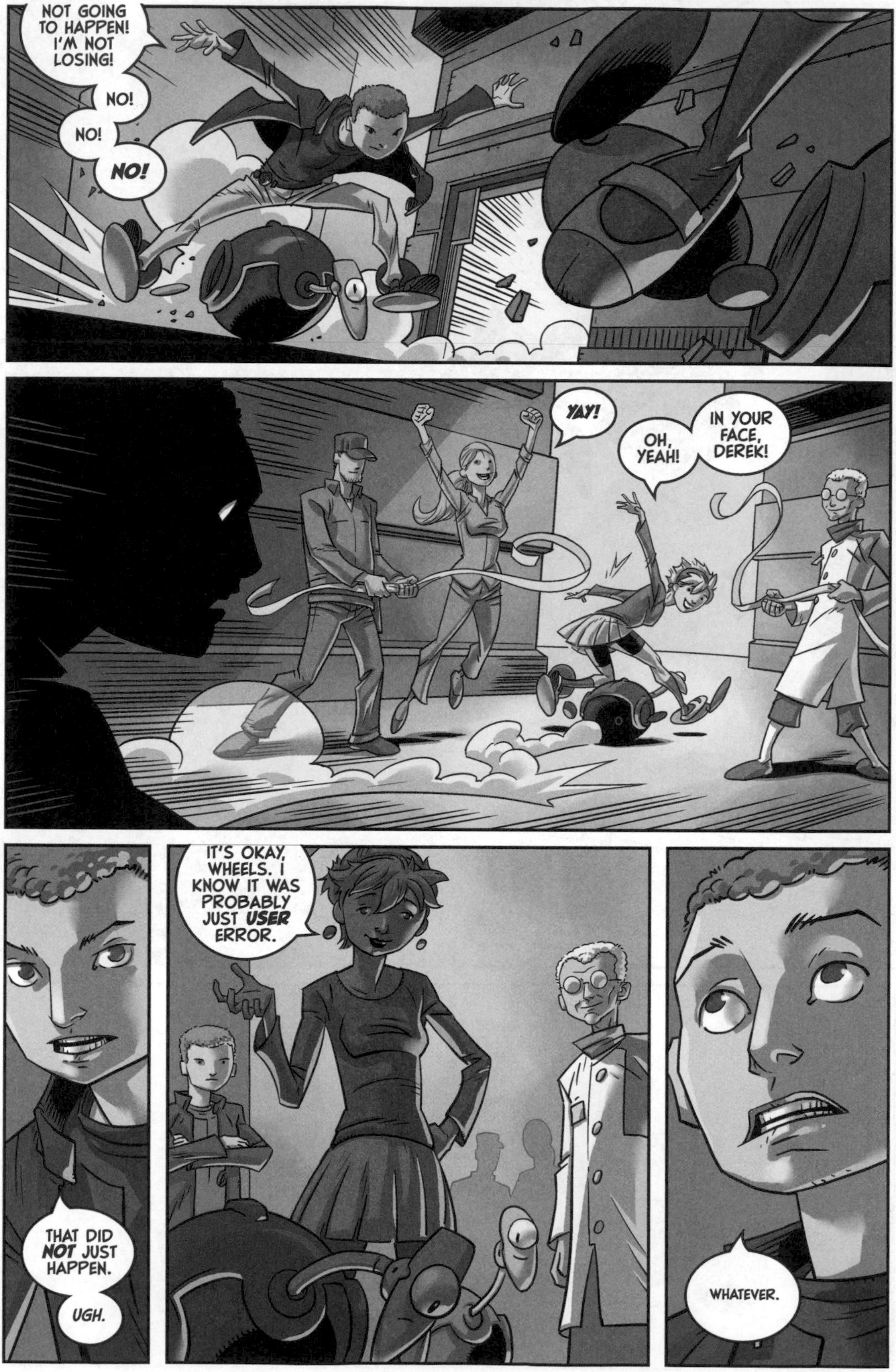
NOT GOING TO HAPPEN! I'M NOT LOSING!
NO!
NO!
NO!
YAY!
OH, YEAH!
IN YOUR FACE, DEREK!
THAT DID NOT JUST HAPPEN.
UGH.
IT'S OKAY, WHEELS. I KNOW IT WAS PROBABLY JUST USER ERROR.
WHATEVER.

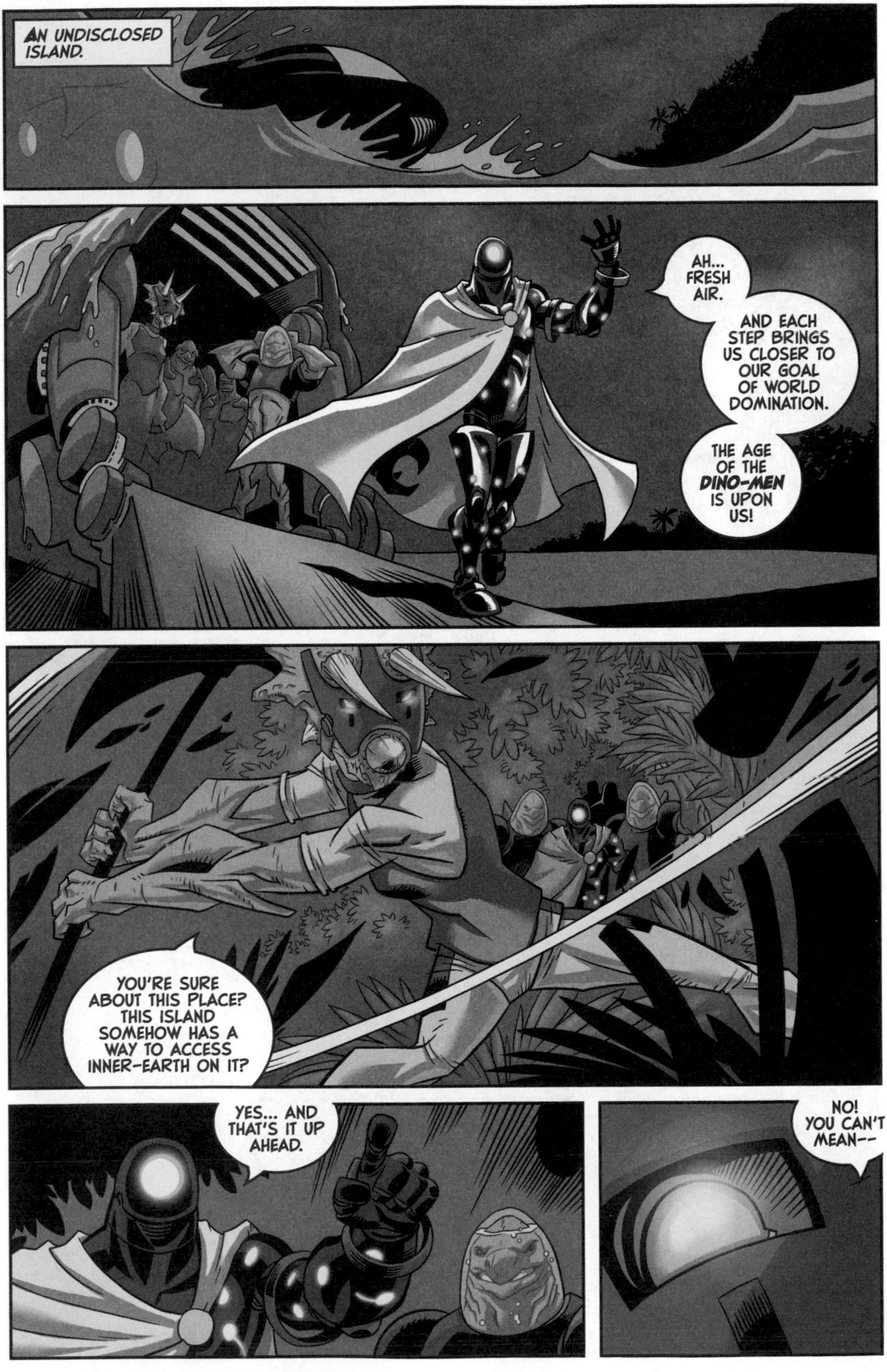
AN UNDISCLOSED ISLAND.
AH... FRESH AIR.
AND EACH STEP BRINGS US CLOSER TO OUR GOAL OF WORLD DOMINATION.
THE AGE OF THE DINO-MEN IS UPON US!
YOU'RE SURE ABOUT THIS PLACE? THIS ISLAND SOMEHOW HAS A WAY TO ACCESS INNER-EARTH ON IT?
YES... AND THAT'S IT UP AHEAD.
NO! YOU CAN'T MEAN--

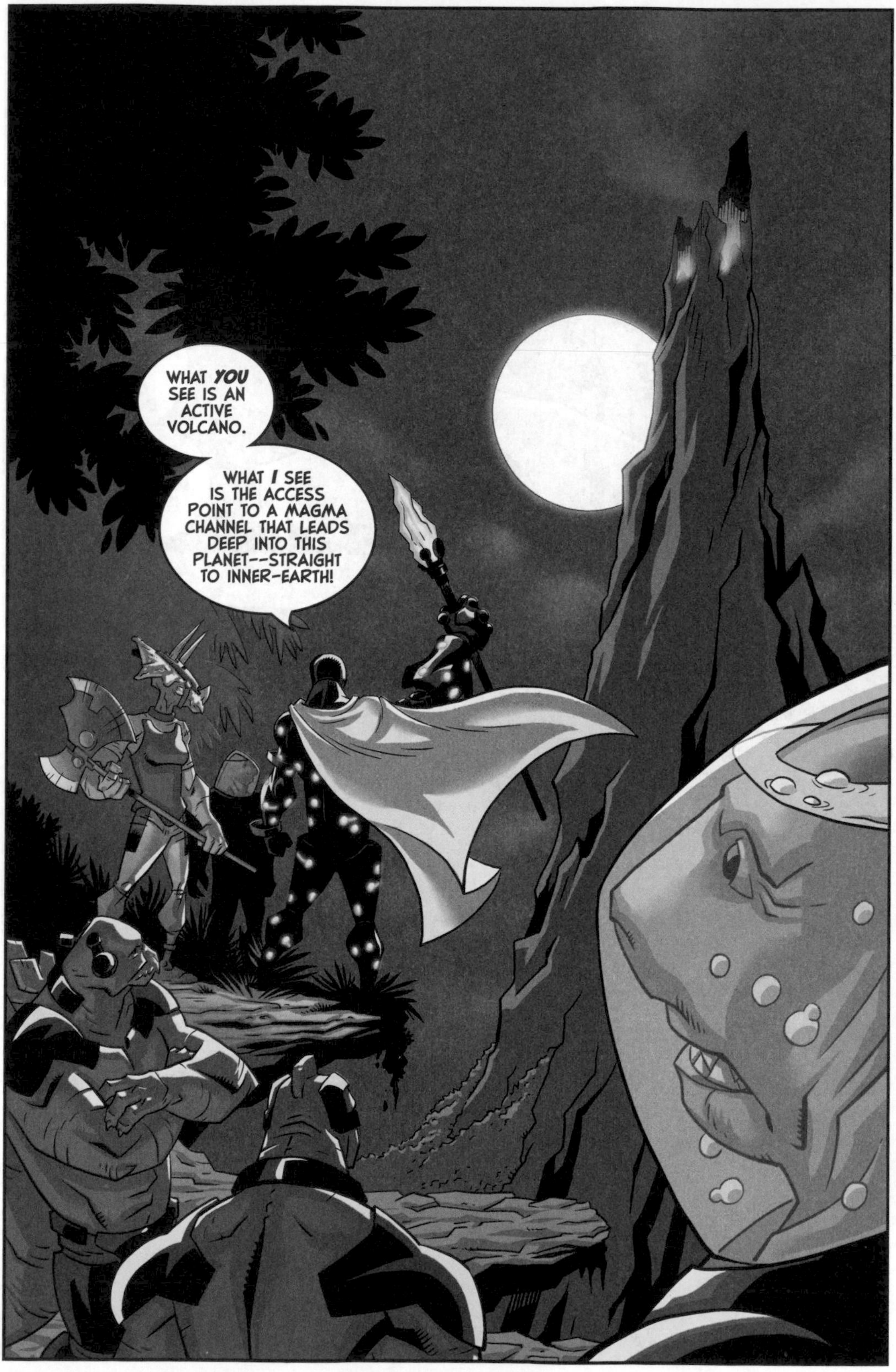
WHAT YOU SEE IS AN ACTIVE VOLCANO.
WHAT I SEE IS THE ACCESS POINT TO A MAGMA CHANNEL THAT LEADS DEEP INTO THIS PLANET--STRAIGHT TO INNER-EARTH!

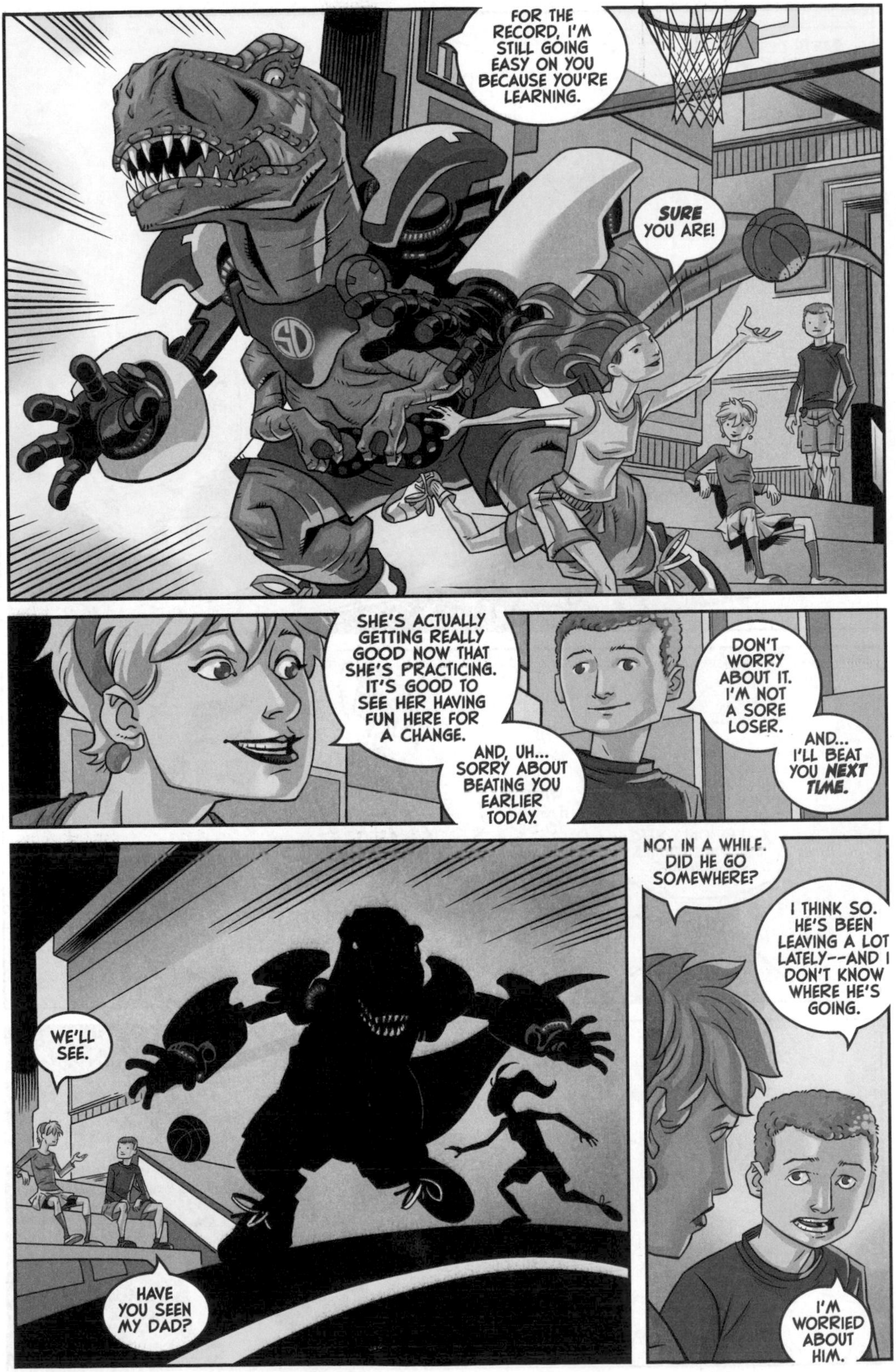
FOR THE RECORD, I'M STILL GOING EASY ON YOU BECAUSE YOU'RE LEARNING.
SURE YOU ARE!
SD
SHE'S ACTUALLY GETTING REALLY GOOD NOW THAT SHE'S PRACTICING. IT'S GOOD TO SEE HER HAVING FUN HERE FOR A CHANGE.
AND, UH... SORRY ABOUT BEATING YOU EARLIER TODAY.
DON'T WORRY ABOUT IT. I'M NOT A SORE LOSER.
AND... I'LL BEAT YOU NEXT TIME.
WE'LL SEE.
HAVE YOU SEEN MY DAD?
NOT IN A WHILE. DID HE GO SOMEWHERE?
I THINK SO. HE'S BEEN LEAVING A LOT LATELY--AND I DON'T KNOW WHERE HE'S GOING.
I'M WORRIED ABOUT HIM.

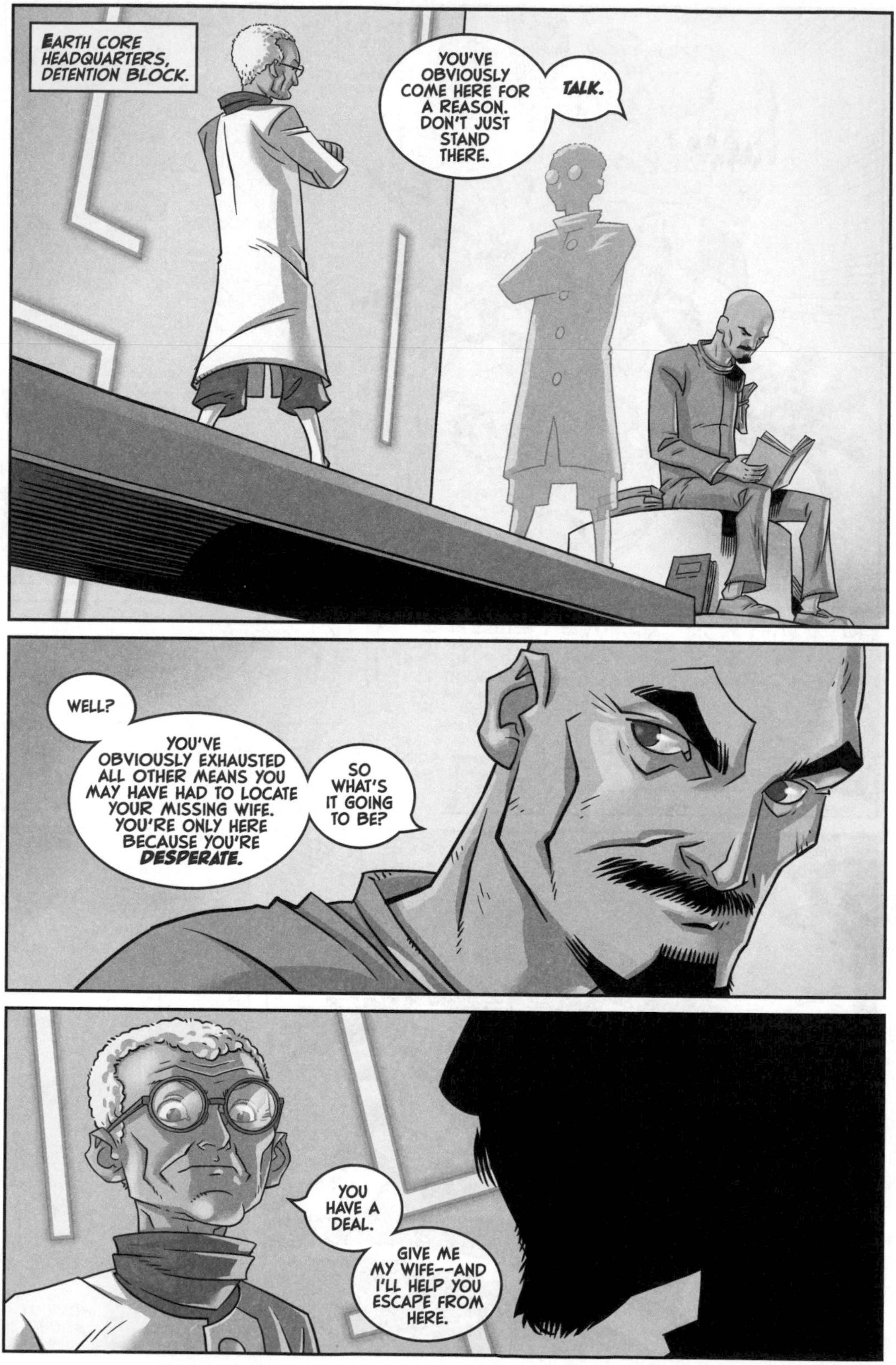
EARTH CORE HEADQUARTERS, DETENTION BLOCK.
YOU'VE OBVIOUSLY COME HERE FOR A REASON. DON'T JUST STAND THERE.
TALK.
WELL?
YOU'VE OBVIOUSLY EXHAUSTED ALL OTHER MEANS YOU MAY HAVE HAD TO LOCATE YOUR MISSING WIFE. YOU'RE ONLY HERE BECAUSE YOU'RE DESPERATE.
SO WHAT'S IT GOING TO BE?
YOU HAVE A DEAL.
GIVE ME MY WIFE--AND I'LL HELP YOU ESCAPE FROM HERE.

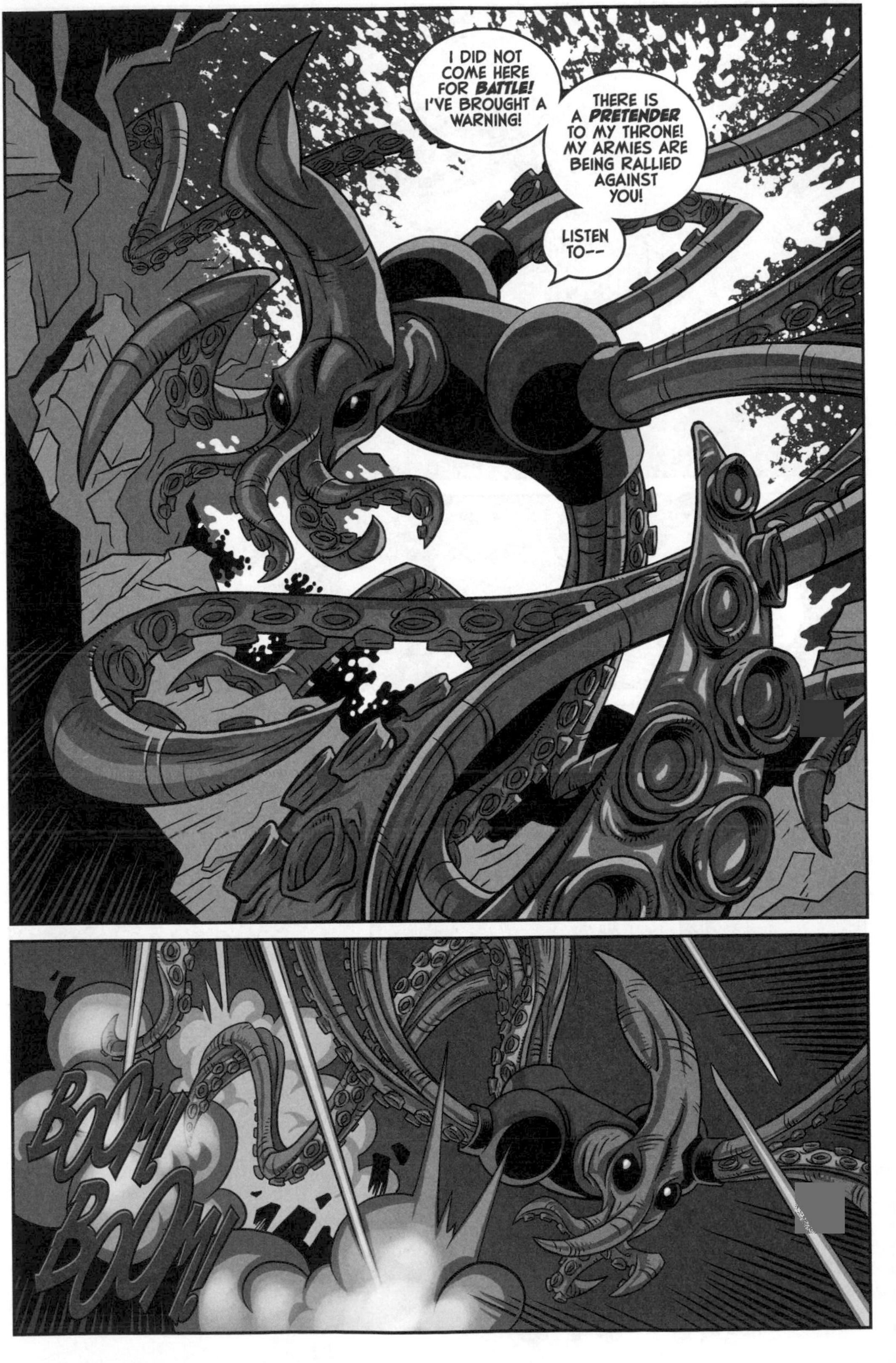
I DID NOT COME HERE FOR *BATTLE!* I'VE BROUGHT A WARNING!
THERE IS A *PRETENDER* TO MY THRONE! MY ARMIES ARE BEING RALLIED AGAINST YOU!
LISTEN TO--
BOOM!
BOOM!

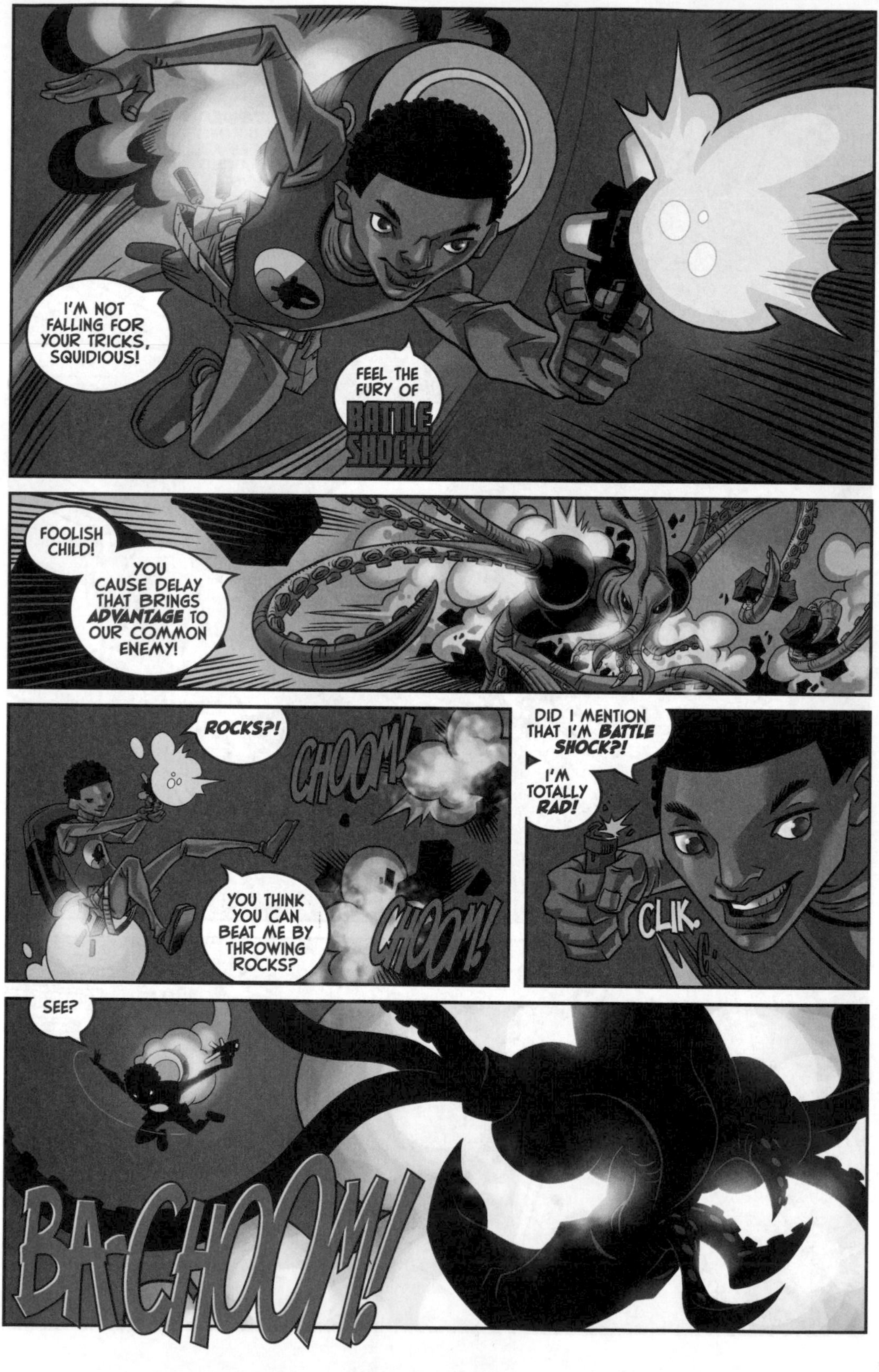
I'M NOT FALLING FOR YOUR TRICKS, SQUIDIOUS!
FEEL THE FURY OF BATTLE SHOCK!
FOOLISH CHILD!
YOU CAUSE DELAY THAT BRINGS ADVANTAGE TO OUR COMMON ENEMY!
ROCKS?!
CHOOM!
YOU THINK YOU CAN BEAT ME BY THROWING ROCKS?
CHOOM!
DID I MENTION THAT I'M BATTLE SHOCK?!
I'M TOTALLY RAD!
CLIK.
SEE?
BA-CHOOM!

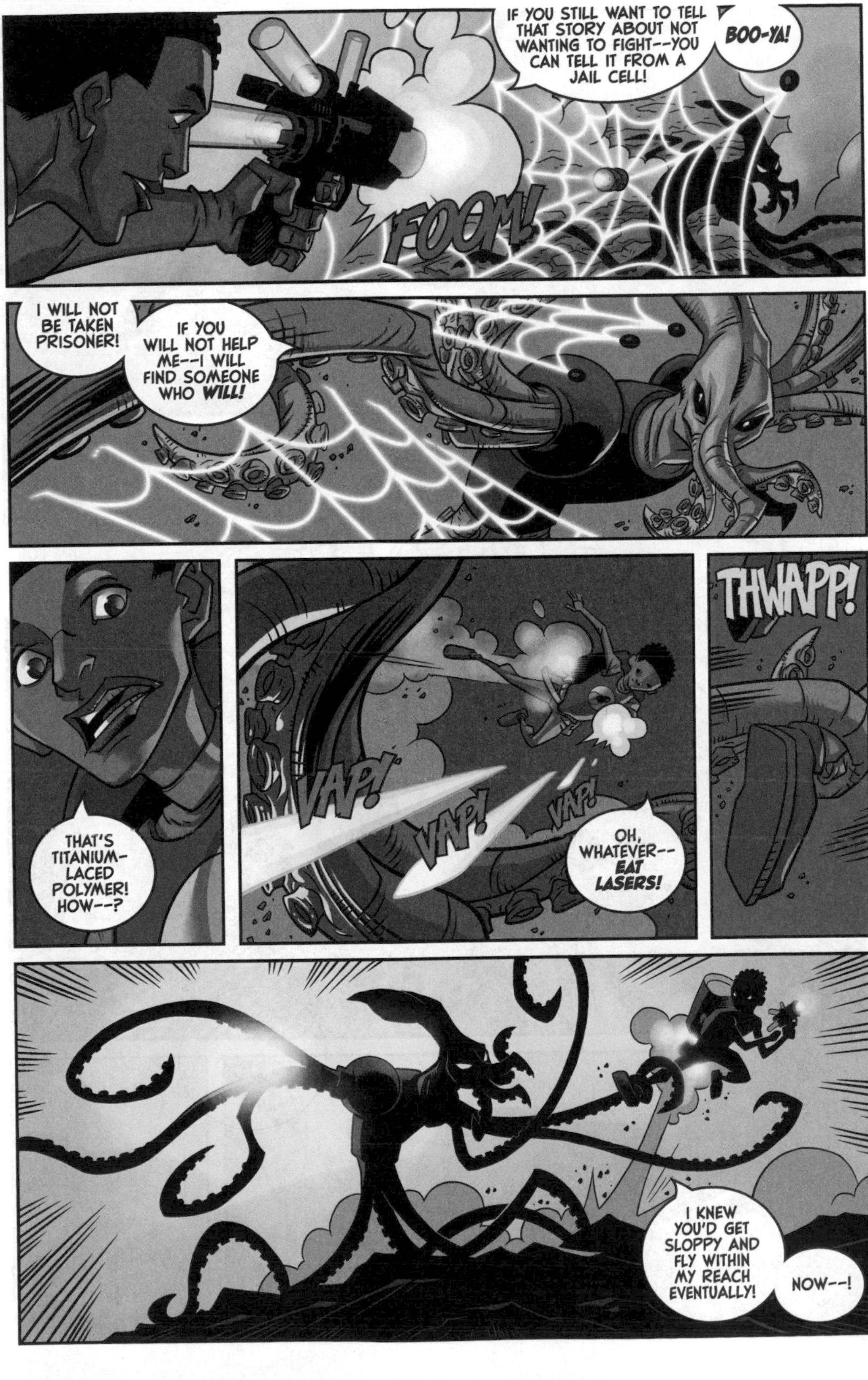
IF YOU STILL WANT TO TELL THAT STORY ABOUT NOT WANTING TO FIGHT--YOU CAN TELL IT FROM A JAIL CELL!
BOO-YA!
FOOM!
I WILL NOT BE TAKEN PRISONER!
IF YOU WILL NOT HELP ME--I WILL FIND SOMEONE WHO WILL!
THAT'S TITANIUM-LACED POLYMER! HOW--?
VAP!
VAP!
VAP!
OH, WHATEVER--EAT LASERS!
THWAPP!
I KNEW YOU'D GET SLOPPY AND FLY WITHIN MY REACH EVENTUALLY!
NOW--!

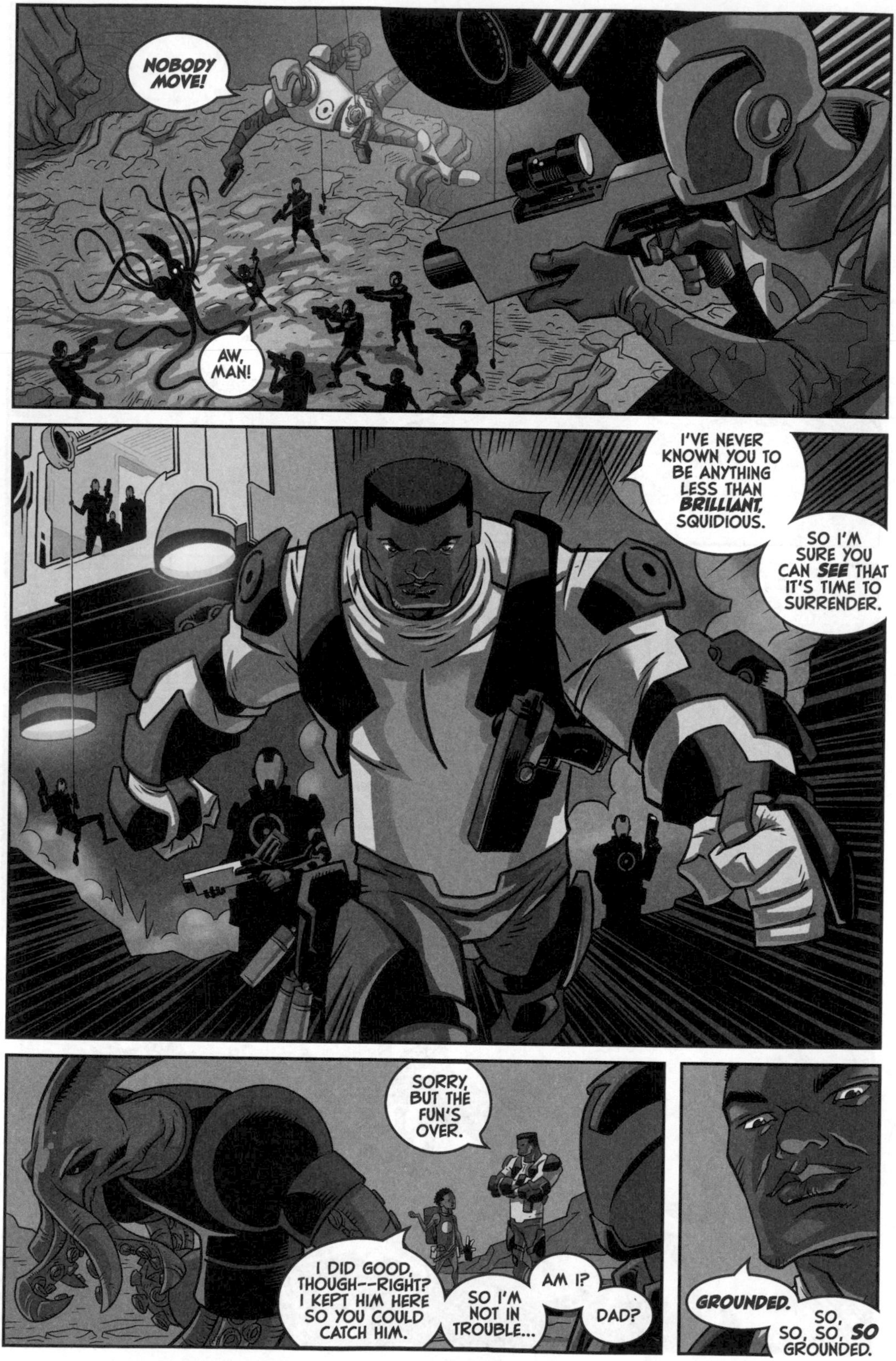
NOBODY MOVE!
AW, MAN!
I'VE NEVER KNOWN YOU TO BE ANYTHING LESS THAN BRILLIANT, SQUIDIOUS.
SO I'M SURE YOU CAN SEE THAT IT'S TIME TO SURRENDER.
SORRY, BUT THE FUN'S OVER.
I DID GOOD, THOUGH--RIGHT? I KEPT HIM HERE SO YOU COULD CATCH HIM.
SO I'M NOT IN TROUBLE...
AM I?
DAD?
GROUNDED.
SO, SO, SO, SO GROUNDED.

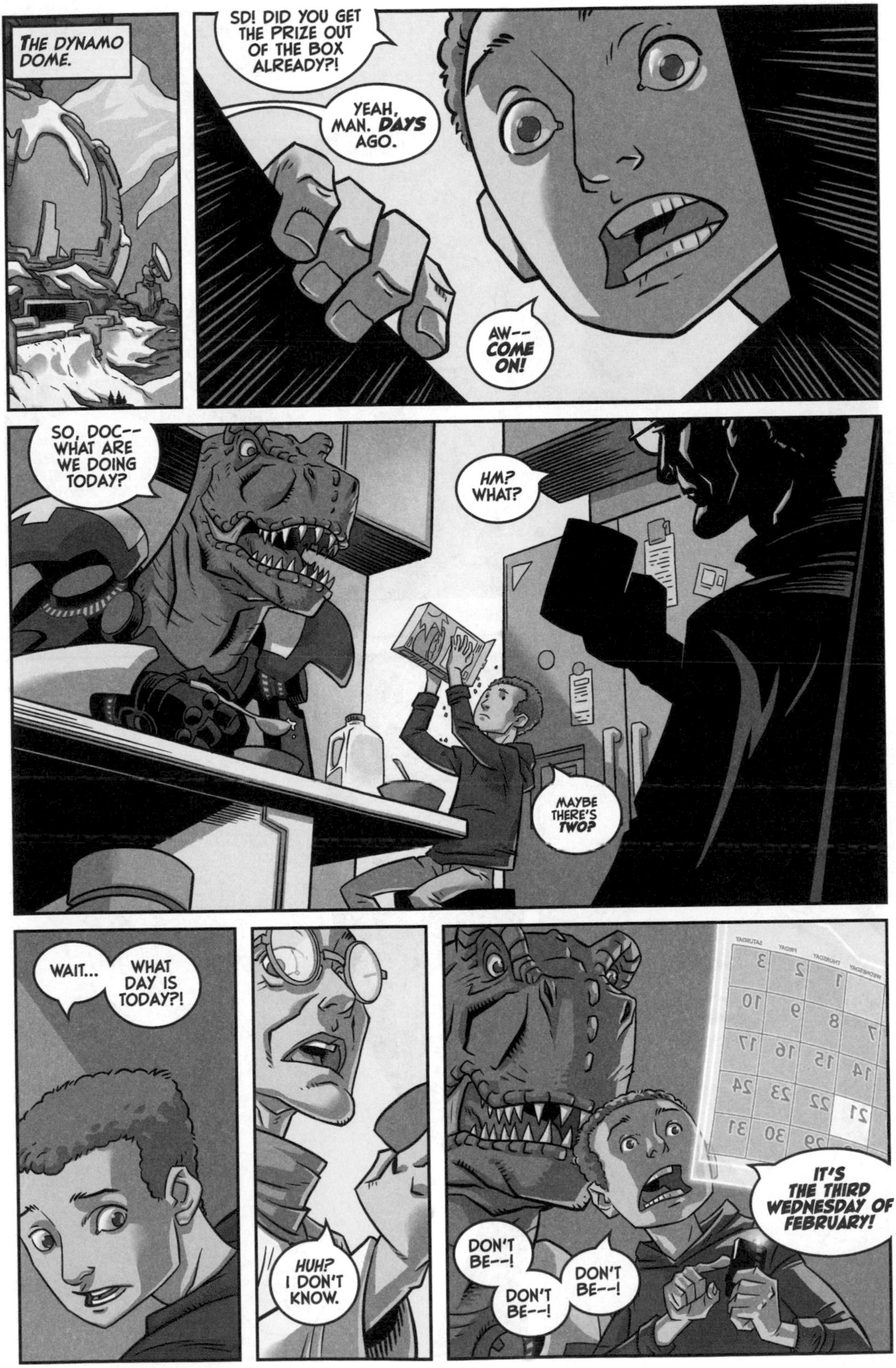
THE DYNAMO DOME.
SD! DID YOU GET THE PRIZE OUT OF THE BOX ALREADY?!
YEAH, MAN. DAYS AGO.
AW-- COME ON!
SO, DOC-- WHAT ARE WE DOING TODAY?
HM? WHAT?
MAYBE THERE'S TWO?
WAIT...
WHAT DAY IS TODAY?!
HUH? I DON'T KNOW.
IT'S THE THIRD WEDNESDAY OF FEBRUARY!
DON'T BE--!
DON'T BE--!
DON'T BE--!

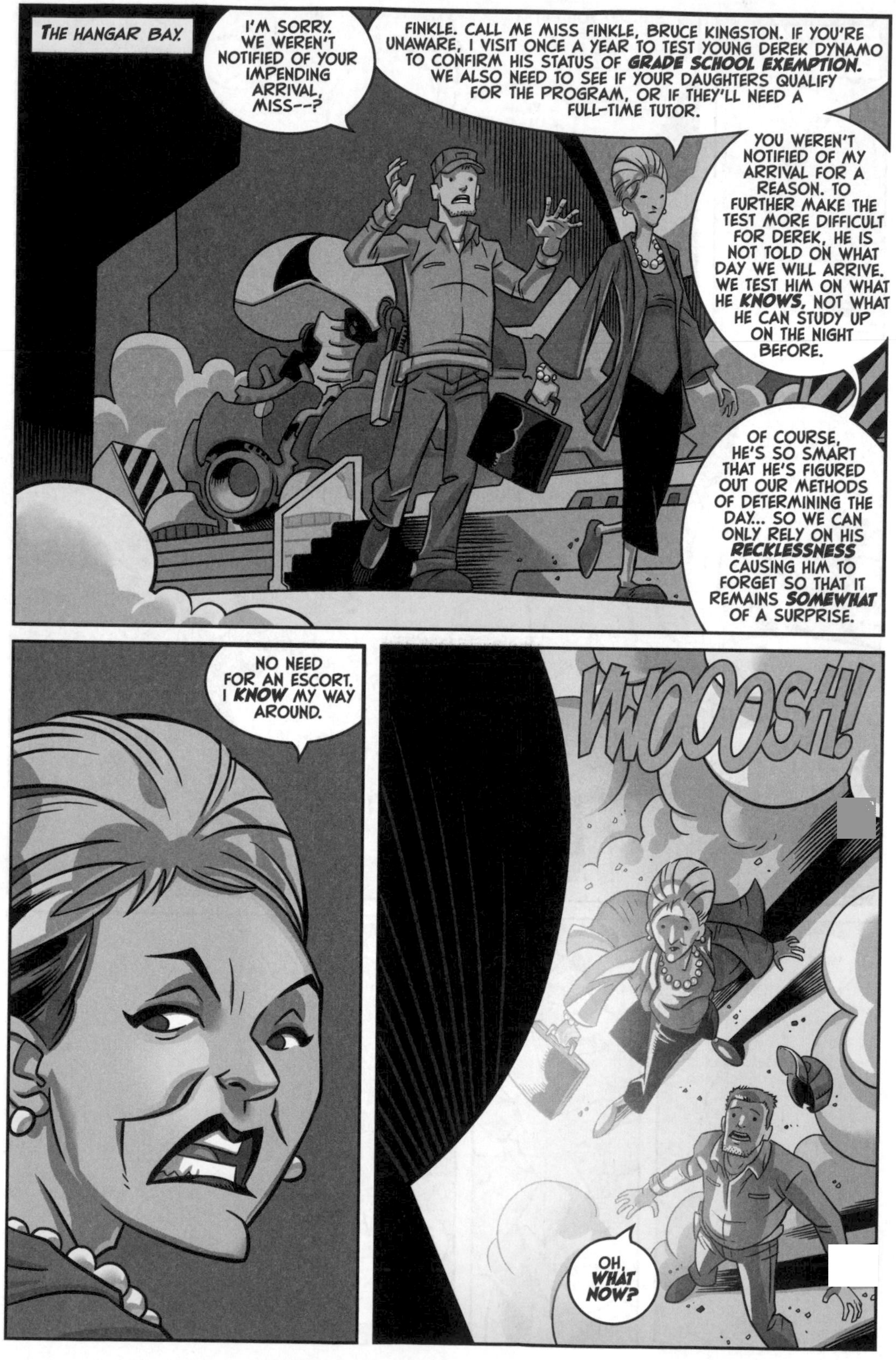
THE HANGAR BAY.
I'M SORRY. WE WEREN'T NOTIFIED OF YOUR IMPENDING ARRIVAL, MISS--?
FINKLE. CALL ME MISS FINKLE, BRUCE KINGSTON. IF YOU'RE UNAWARE, I VISIT ONCE A YEAR TO TEST YOUNG DEREK DYNAMO TO CONFIRM HIS STATUS OF GRADE SCHOOL EXEMPTION. WE ALSO NEED TO SEE IF YOUR DAUGHTERS QUALIFY FOR THE PROGRAM, OR IF THEY'LL NEED A FULL-TIME TUTOR.
YOU WEREN'T NOTIFIED OF MY ARRIVAL FOR A REASON. TO FURTHER MAKE THE TEST MORE DIFFICULT FOR DEREK, HE IS NOT TOLD ON WHAT DAY WE WILL ARRIVE. WE TEST HIM ON WHAT HE KNOWS, NOT WHAT HE CAN STUDY UP ON THE NIGHT BEFORE.
OF COURSE, HE'S SO SMART THAT HE'S FIGURED OUT OUR METHODS OF DETERMINING THE DAY... SO WE CAN ONLY RELY ON HIS RECKLESSNESS CAUSING HIM TO FORGET SO THAT IT REMAINS SOMEWHAT OF A SURPRISE.
NO NEED FOR AN ESCORT. I KNOW MY WAY AROUND.
WHOOOSH!
OH, WHAT NOW?

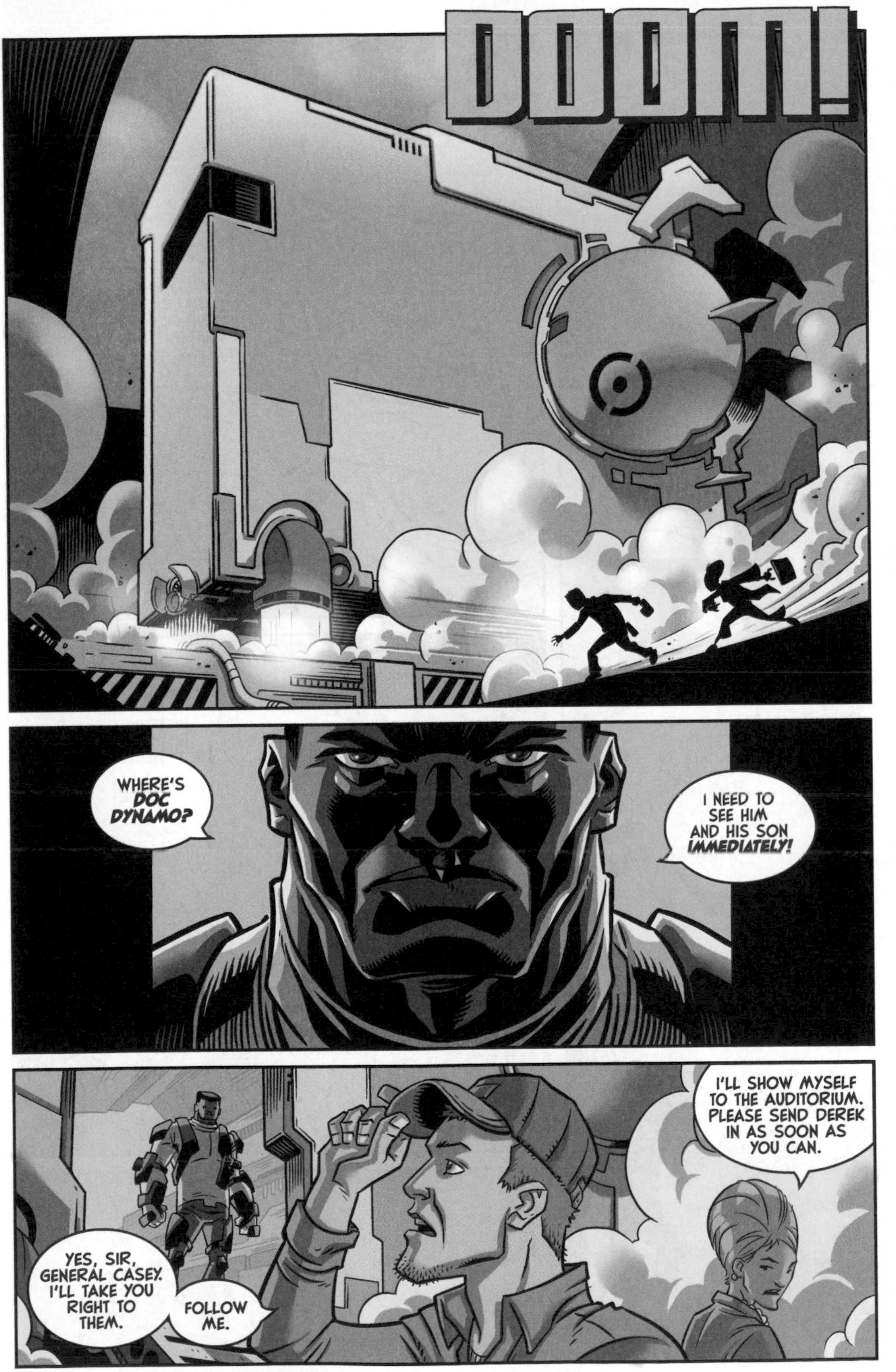
DOOM!
WHERE'S DOC DYNAMO?
I NEED TO SEE HIM AND HIS SON IMMEDIATELY!
I'LL SHOW MYSELF TO THE AUDITORIUM. PLEASE SEND DEREK IN AS SOON AS YOU CAN.
YES, SIR, GENERAL CASEY. I'LL TAKE YOU RIGHT TO THEM.
FOLLOW ME.

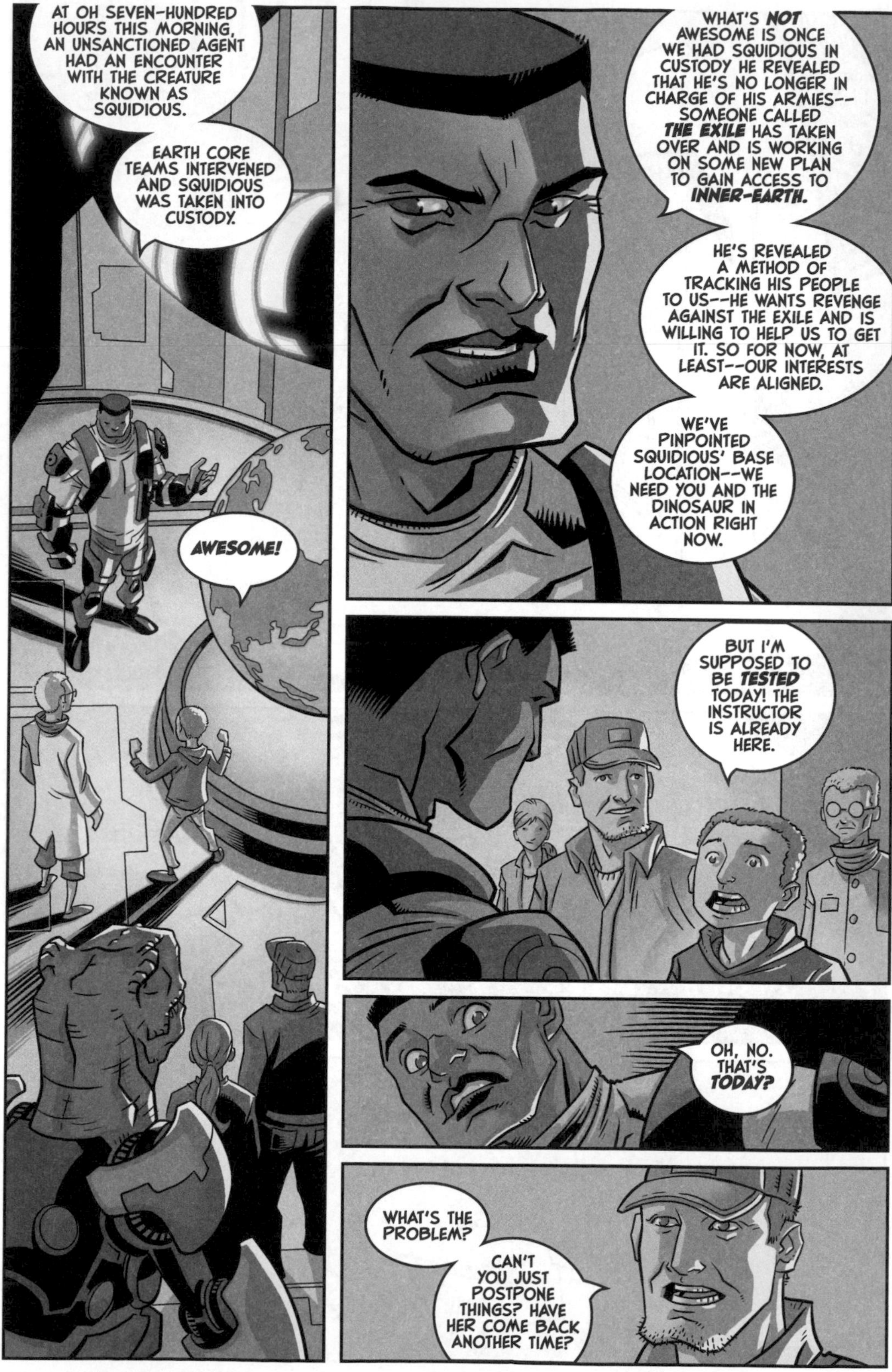
AT OH SEVEN-HUNDRED HOURS THIS MORNING, AN UNSANCTIONED AGENT HAD AN ENCOUNTER WITH THE CREATURE KNOWN AS SQUIDIOUS.
EARTH CORE TEAMS INTERVENED AND SQUIDIOUS WAS TAKEN INTO CUSTODY.
AWESOME!
WHAT'S NOT AWESOME IS ONCE WE HAD SQUIDIOUS IN CUSTODY HE REVEALED THAT HE'S NO LONGER IN CHARGE OF HIS ARMIES-- SOMEONE CALLED THE EXILE HAS TAKEN OVER AND IS WORKING ON SOME NEW PLAN TO GAIN ACCESS TO INNER-EARTH.
HE'S REVEALED A METHOD OF TRACKING HIS PEOPLE TO US--HE WANTS REVENGE AGAINST THE EXILE AND IS WILLING TO HELP US TO GET IT. SO FOR NOW, AT LEAST--OUR INTERESTS ARE ALIGNED.
WE'VE PINPOINTED SQUIDIOUS' BASE LOCATION--WE NEED YOU AND THE DINOSAUR IN ACTION RIGHT NOW.
BUT I'M SUPPOSED TO BE TESTED TODAY! THE INSTRUCTOR IS ALREADY HERE.
OH, NO. THAT'S TODAY?
WHAT'S THE PROBLEM?
CAN'T YOU JUST POSTPONE THINGS? HAVE HER COME BACK ANOTHER TIME?

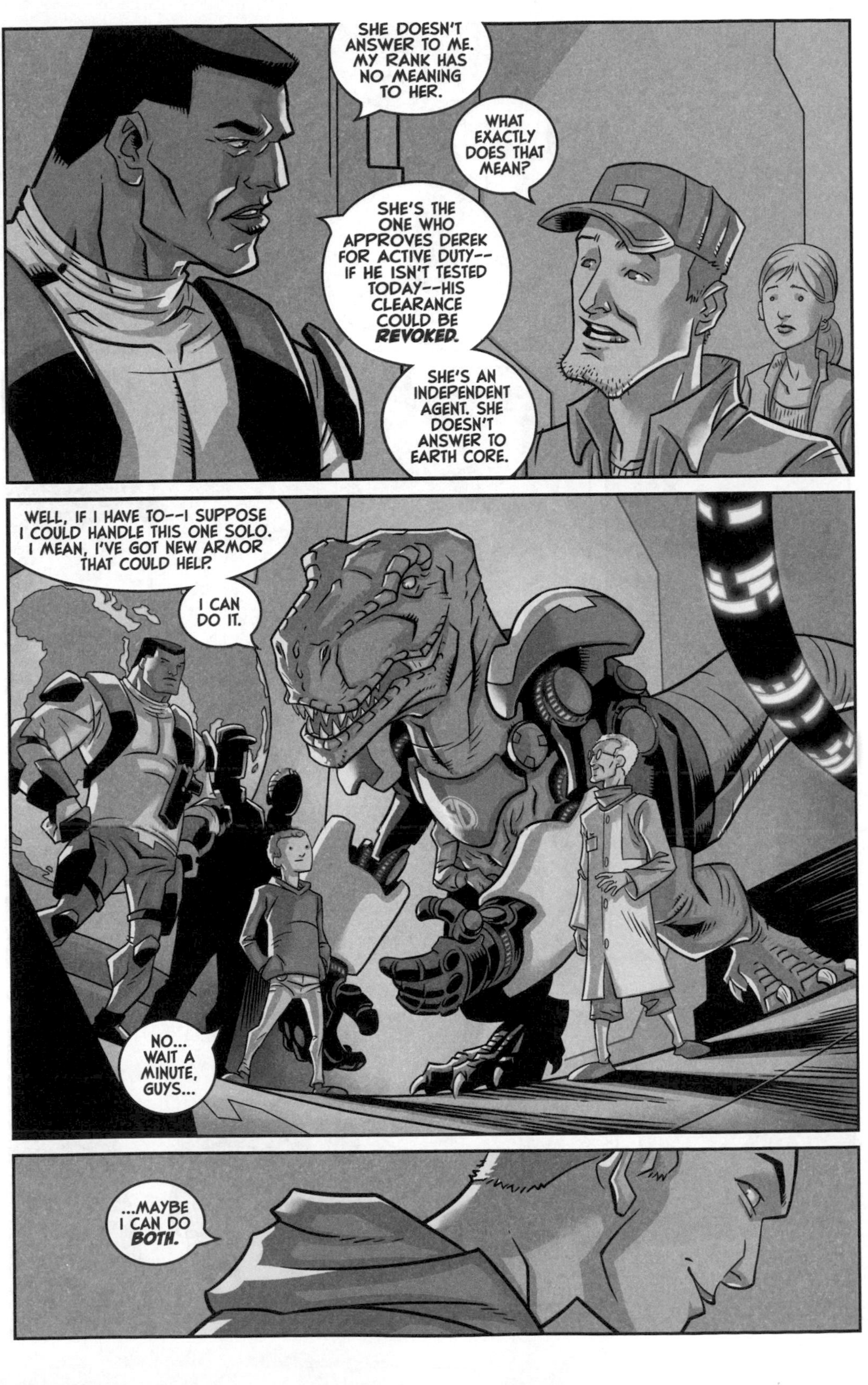
SHE DOESN'T ANSWER TO ME. MY RANK HAS NO MEANING TO HER.
WHAT EXACTLY DOES THAT MEAN?
SHE'S THE ONE WHO APPROVES DEREK FOR ACTIVE DUTY-- IF HE ISN'T TESTED TODAY--HIS CLEARANCE COULD BE **REVOKED.**
SHE'S AN INDEPENDENT AGENT. SHE DOESN'T ANSWER TO EARTH CORE.
WELL, IF I HAVE TO--I SUPPOSE I COULD HANDLE THIS ONE SOLO. I MEAN, I'VE GOT NEW ARMOR THAT COULD HELP.
I CAN DO IT.
NO... WAIT A MINUTE, GUYS...
...MAYBE I CAN DO **BOTH.**

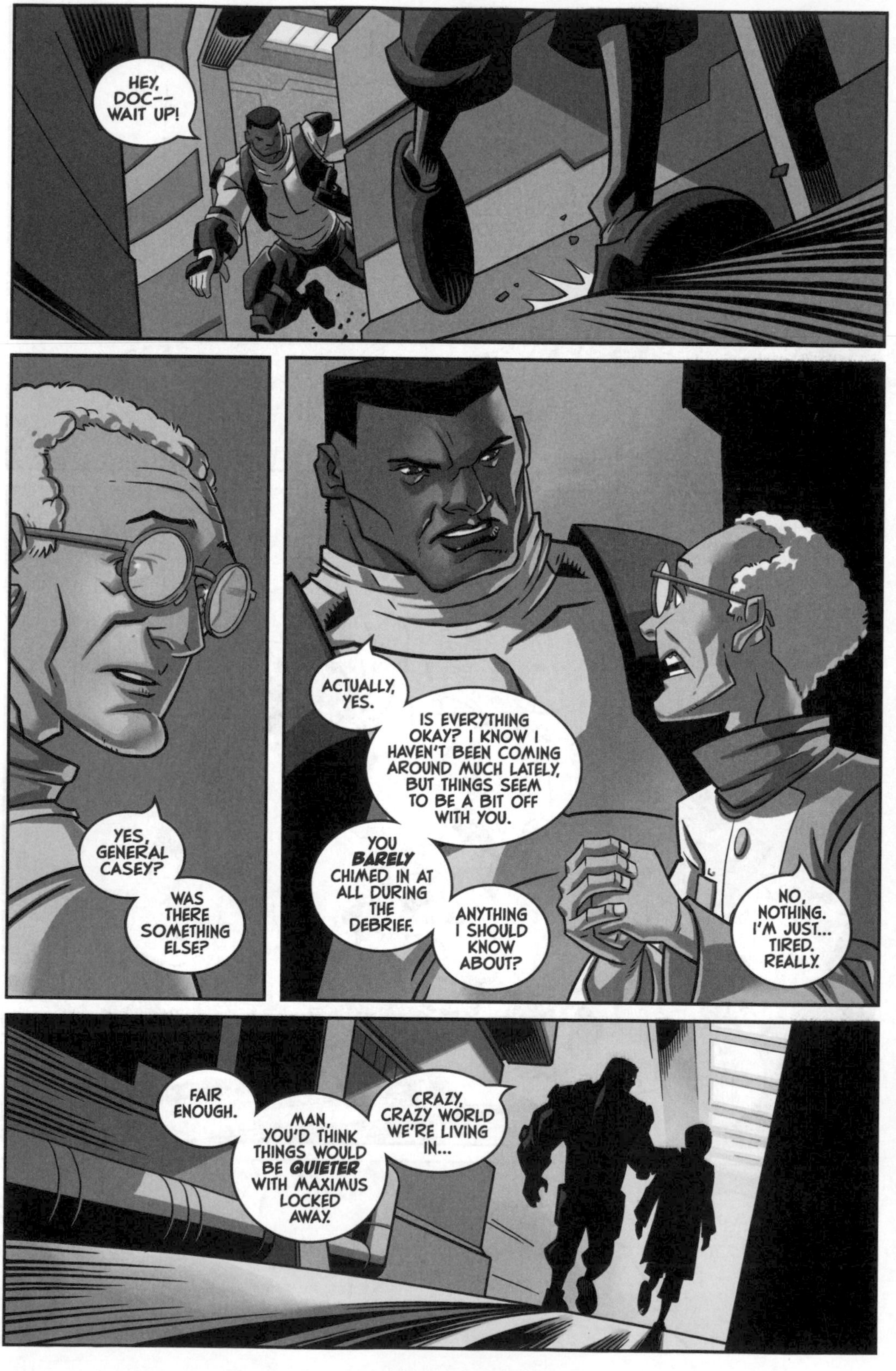
HEY, DOC-- WAIT UP!
YES, GENERAL CASEY?
WAS THERE SOMETHING ELSE?
ACTUALLY, YES.
IS EVERYTHING OKAY? I KNOW I HAVEN'T BEEN COMING AROUND MUCH LATELY, BUT THINGS SEEM TO BE A BIT OFF WITH YOU.
YOU BARELY CHIMED IN AT ALL DURING THE DEBRIEF.
ANYTHING I SHOULD KNOW ABOUT?
NO, NOTHING. I'M JUST... TIRED. REALLY.
FAIR ENOUGH.
MAN, YOU'D THINK THINGS WOULD BE QUIETER WITH MAXIMUS LOCKED AWAY.
CRAZY, CRAZY WORLD WE'RE LIVING IN...

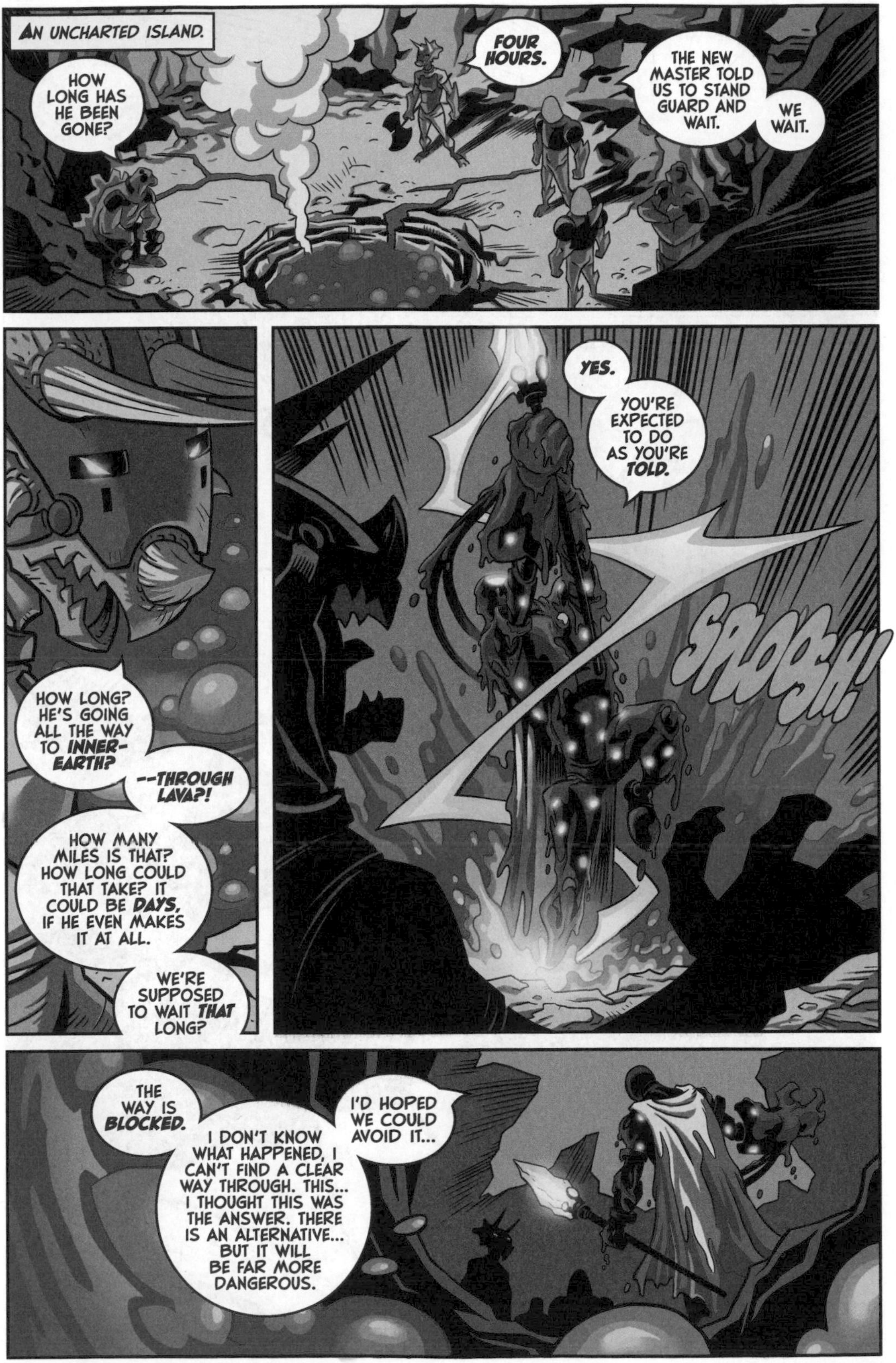
AN UNCHARTED ISLAND.
HOW LONG HAS HE BEEN GONE?
FOUR HOURS.
THE NEW MASTER TOLD US TO STAND GUARD AND WAIT.
WE WAIT.
HOW LONG? HE'S GOING ALL THE WAY TO INNER-EARTH?
--THROUGH LAVA?!
HOW MANY MILES IS THAT? HOW LONG COULD THAT TAKE? IT COULD BE DAYS, IF HE EVEN MAKES IT AT ALL.
WE'RE SUPPOSED TO WAIT THAT LONG?
YES.
YOU'RE EXPECTED TO DO AS YOU'RE TOLD.
SPLOOSH!
THE WAY IS BLOCKED.
I DON'T KNOW WHAT HAPPENED, I CAN'T FIND A CLEAR WAY THROUGH. THIS... I THOUGHT THIS WAS THE ANSWER. THERE IS AN ALTERNATIVE... BUT IT WILL BE FAR MORE DANGEROUS.
I'D HOPED WE COULD AVOID IT...

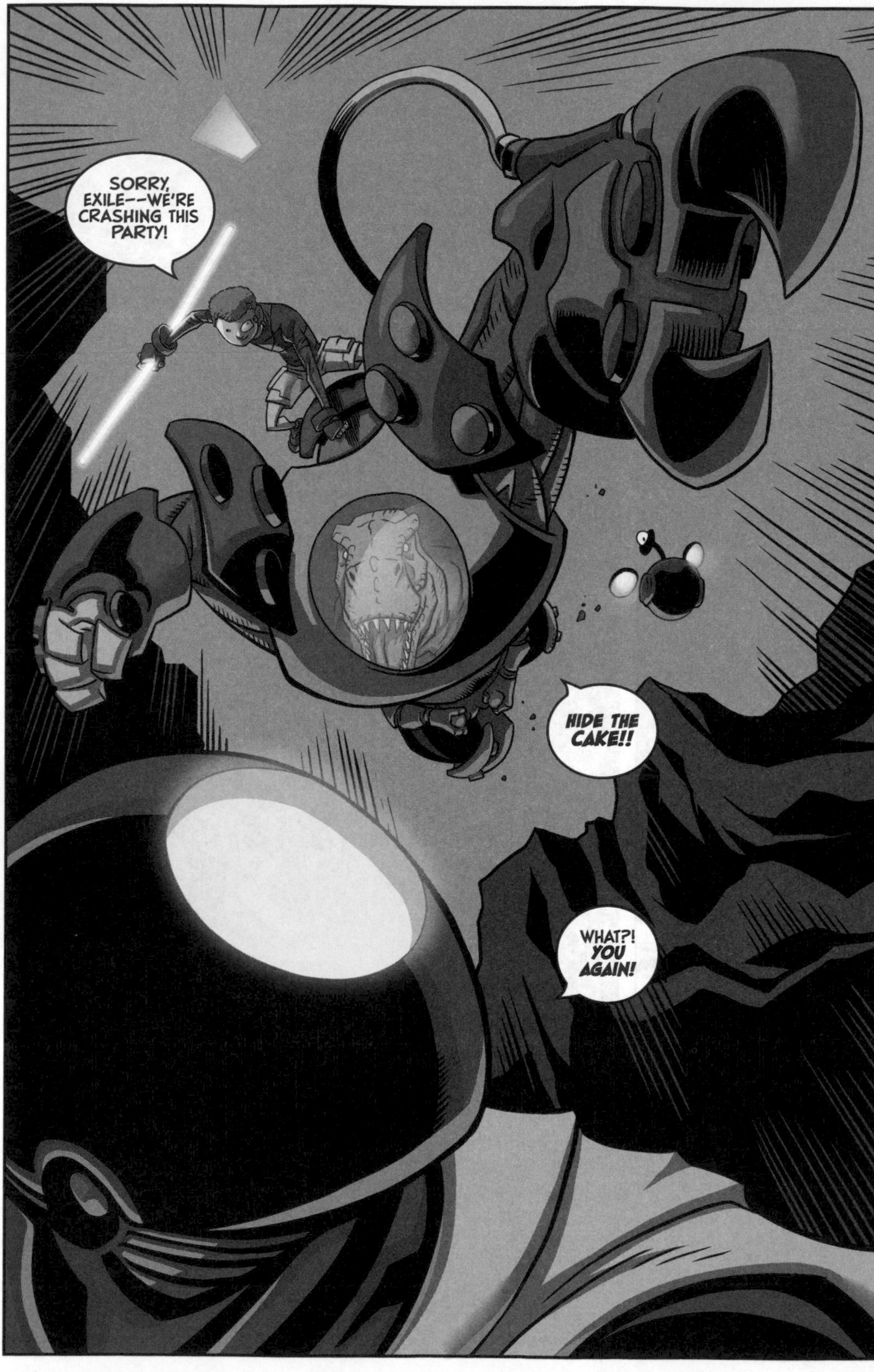
SORRY, EXILE--WE'RE CRASHING THIS PARTY!
HIDE THE CAKE!!
WHAT?! YOU AGAIN!

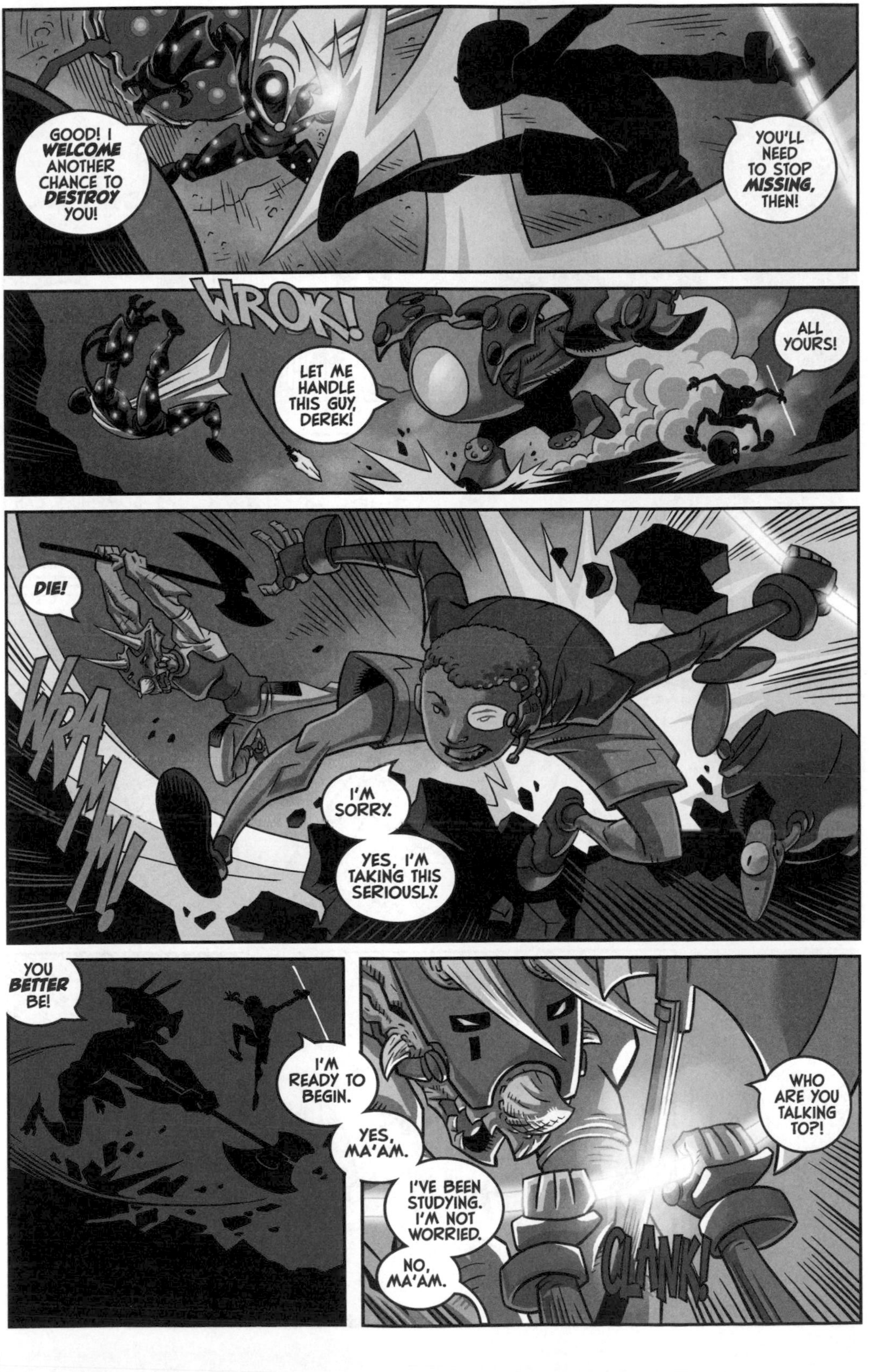
GOOD! I **WELCOME** ANOTHER CHANCE TO **DESTROY** YOU!
YOU'LL NEED TO STOP **MISSING,** THEN!
WROK!
LET ME HANDLE THIS GUY, DEREK!
ALL YOURS!
DIE!
WRAMM!
I'M SORRY.
YES, I'M TAKING THIS SERIOUSLY.
YOU **BETTER** BE!
I'M READY TO BEGIN.
YES, MA'AM.
I'VE BEEN STUDYING. I'M NOT WORRIED.
NO, MA'AM.
WHO ARE YOU TALKING TO?!
CLANK!

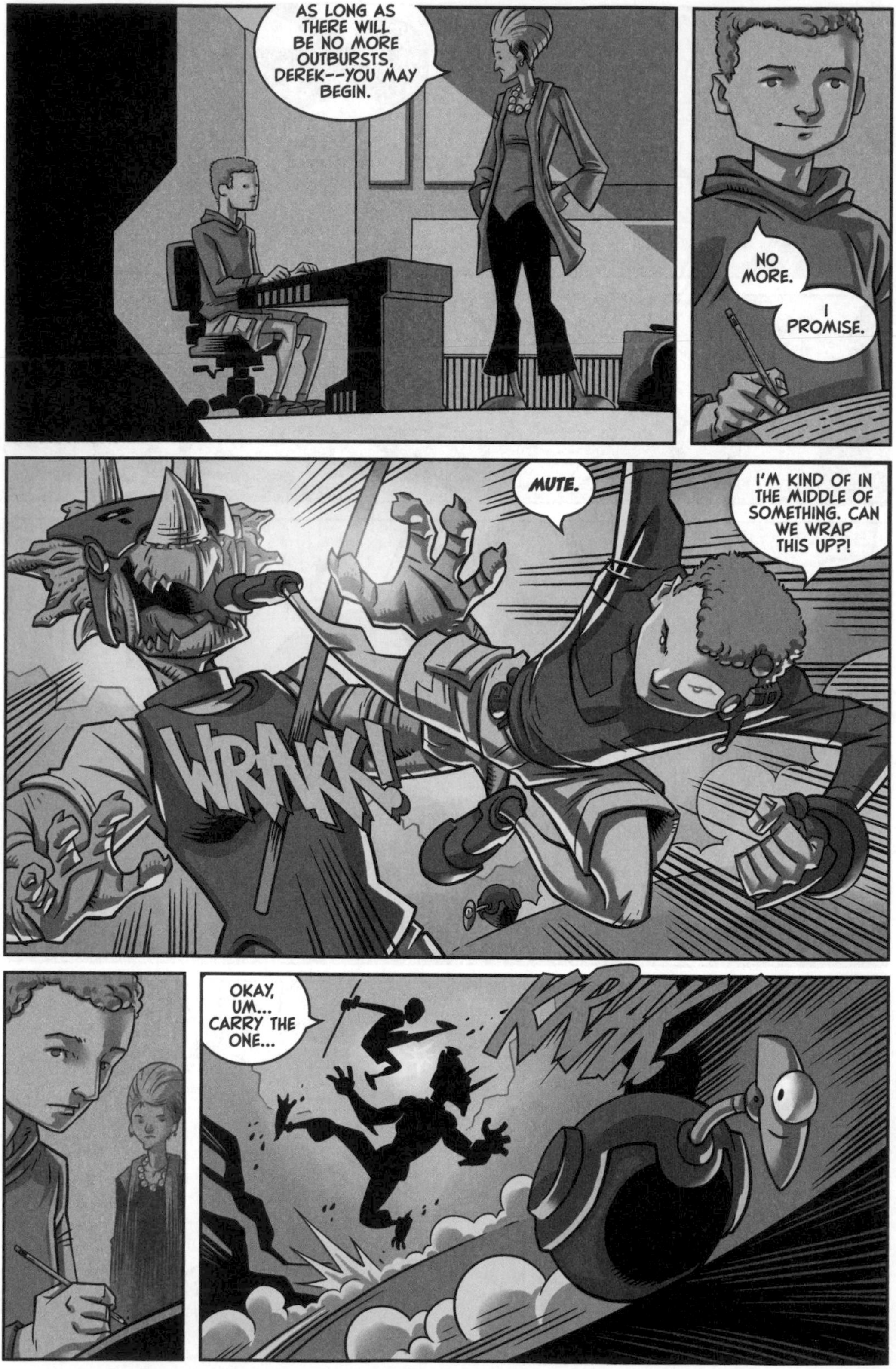
AS LONG AS THERE WILL BE NO MORE OUTBURSTS, DEREK--YOU MAY BEGIN.
NO MORE.
I PROMISE.
MUTE.
I'M KIND OF IN THE MIDDLE OF SOMETHING. CAN WE WRAP THIS UP?!
WRAKK!
OKAY, UM... CARRY THE ONE...
KRAK

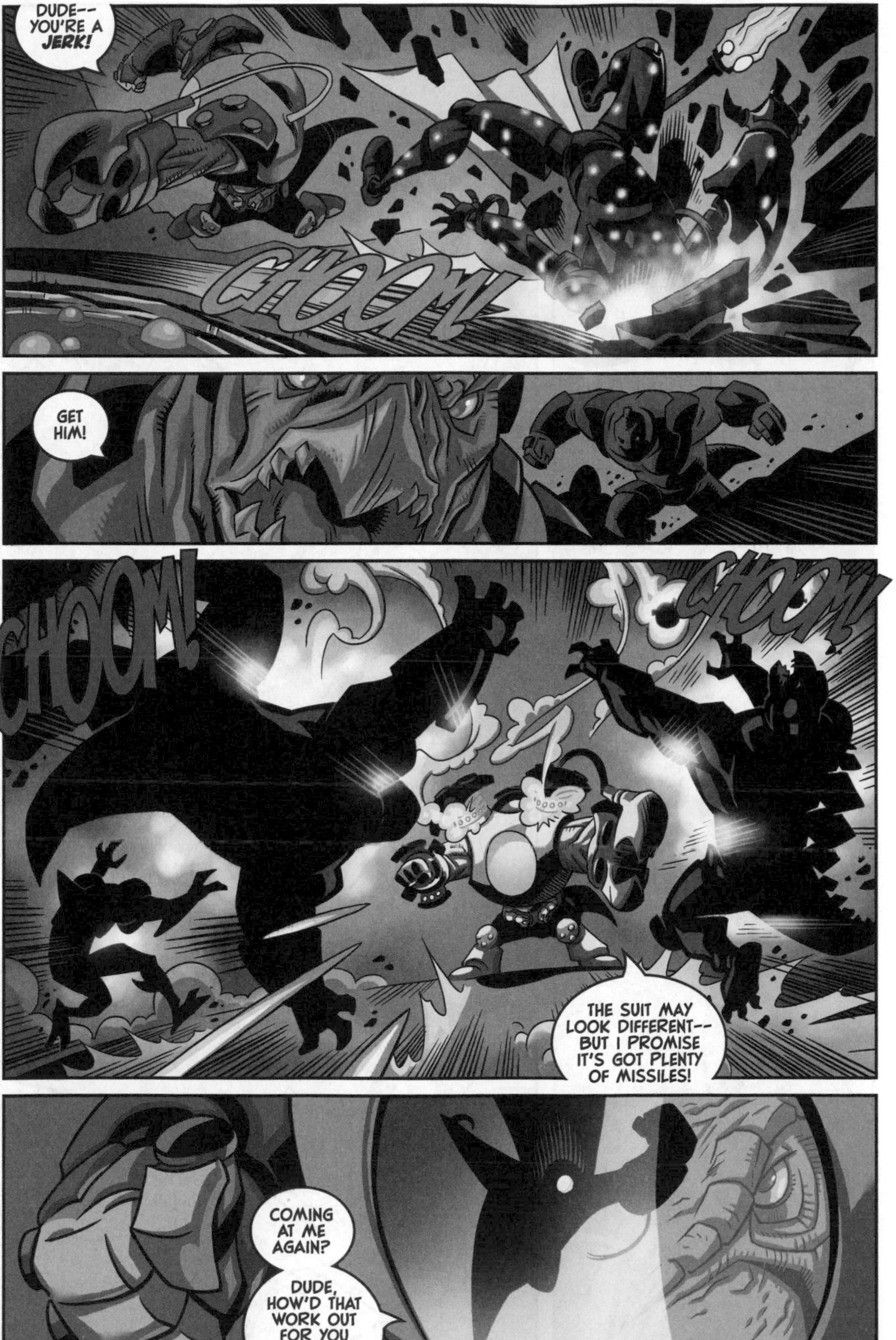
DUDE-- YOU'RE A JERK!
CHOOM!
GET HIM!
CHOOM!
CHOOM!
THE SUIT MAY LOOK DIFFERENT-- BUT I PROMISE IT'S GOT PLENTY OF MISSILES!
COMING AT ME AGAIN?
DUDE, HOW'D THAT WORK OUT FOR YOU LAST TIME?!

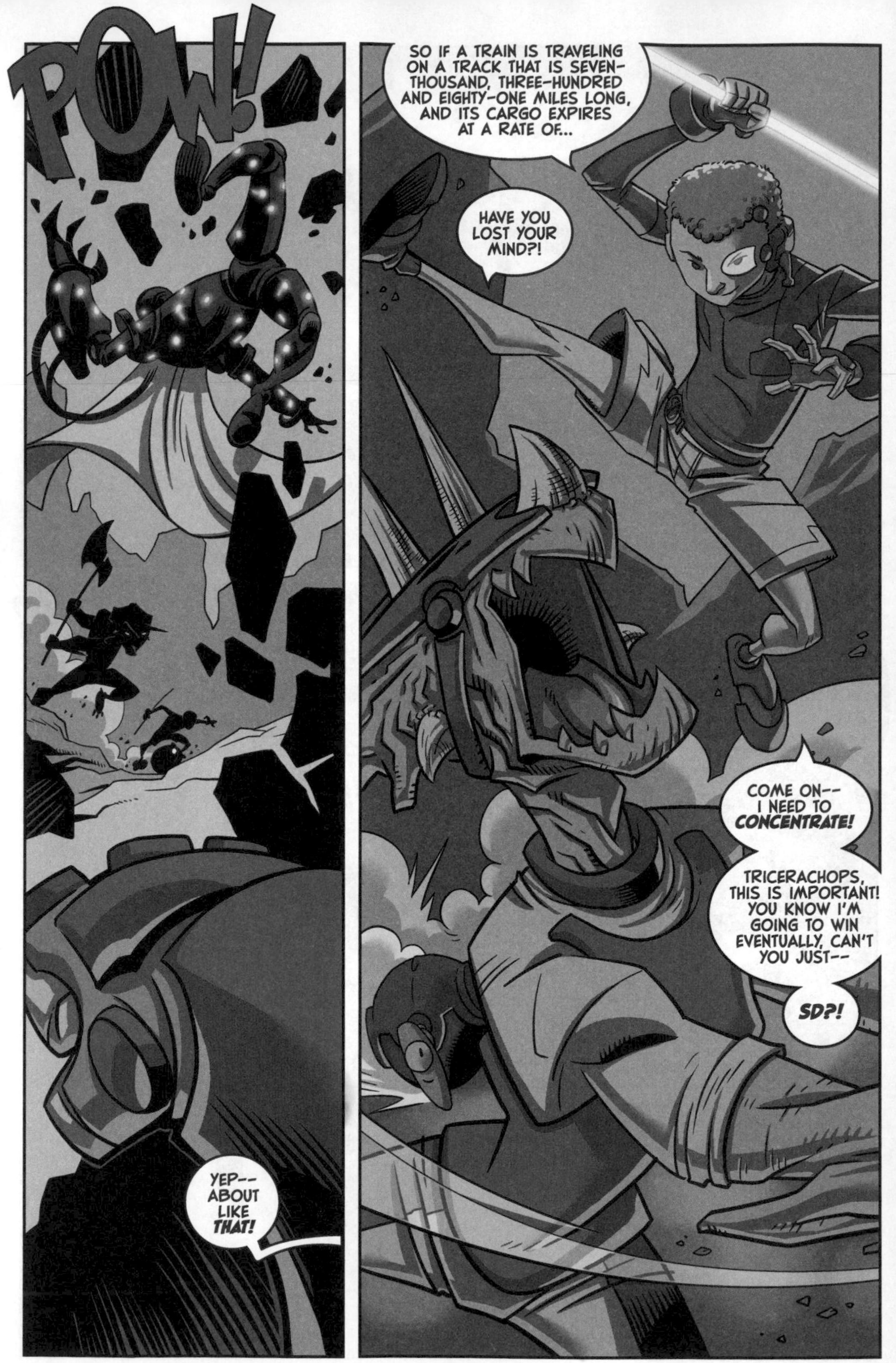
POW!!
YEP--ABOUT LIKE THAT!
SO IF A TRAIN IS TRAVELING ON A TRACK THAT IS SEVEN-THOUSAND, THREE-HUNDRED AND EIGHTY-ONE MILES LONG, AND ITS CARGO EXPIRES AT A RATE OF...
HAVE YOU LOST YOUR MIND?!
COME ON-- I NEED TO CONCENTRATE!
TRICERACHOPS, THIS IS IMPORTANT! YOU KNOW I'M GOING TO WIN EVENTUALLY, CAN'T YOU JUST--
SD?!

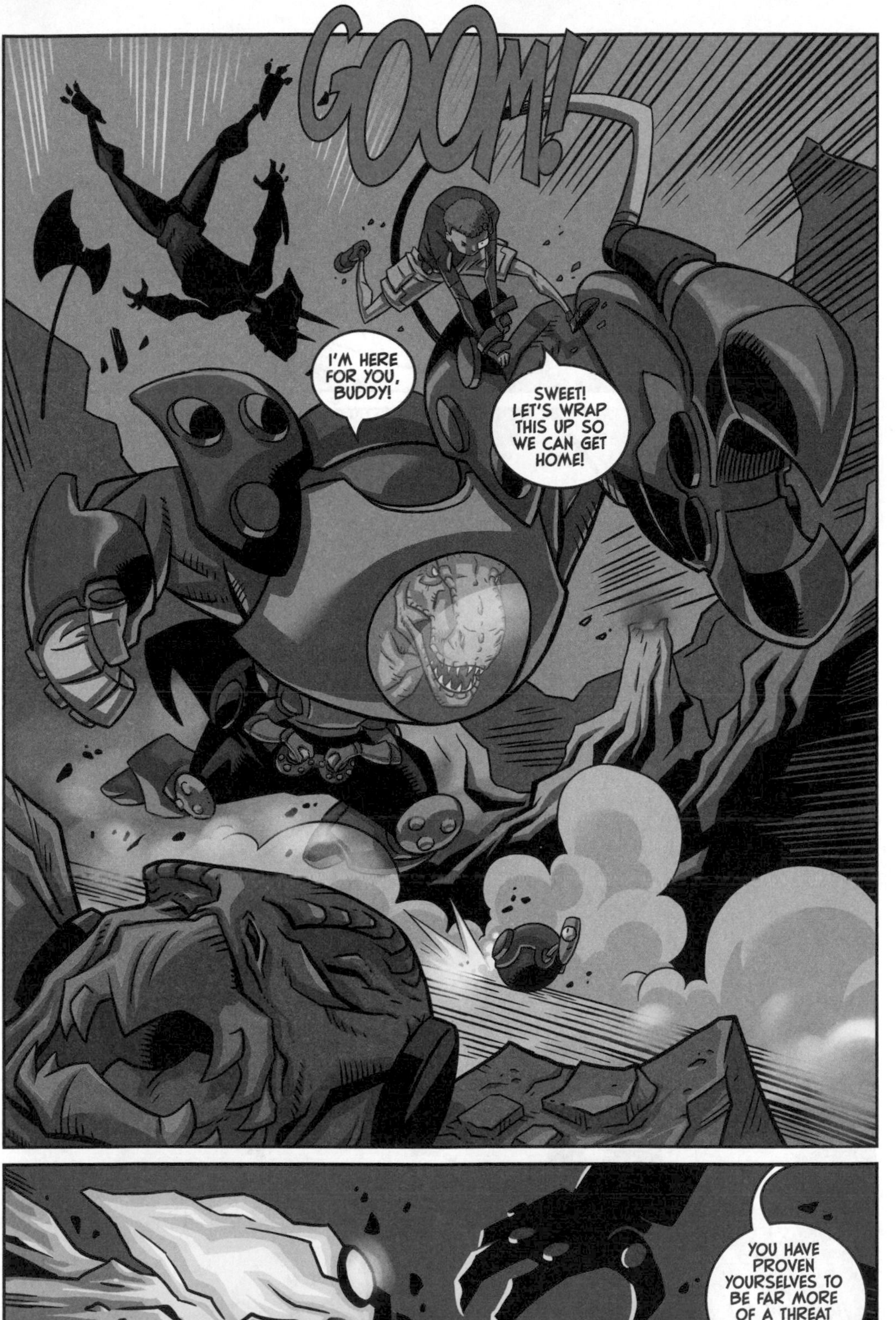
GOOM!
I'M HERE FOR YOU, BUDDY!
SWEET! LET'S WRAP THIS UP SO WE CAN GET HOME!

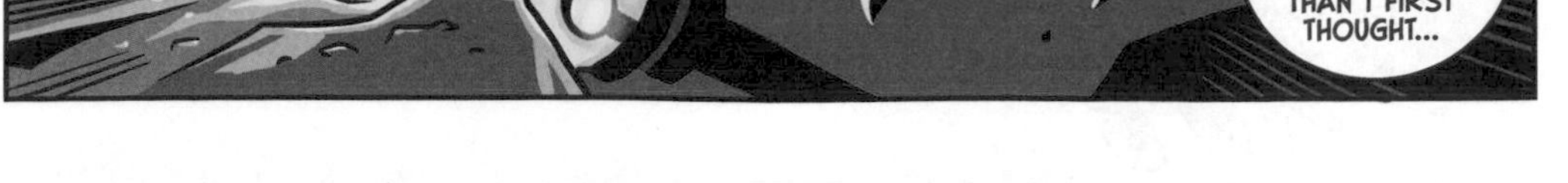
YOU HAVE PROVEN YOURSELVES TO BE FAR MORE OF A THREAT THAN I FIRST THOUGHT...

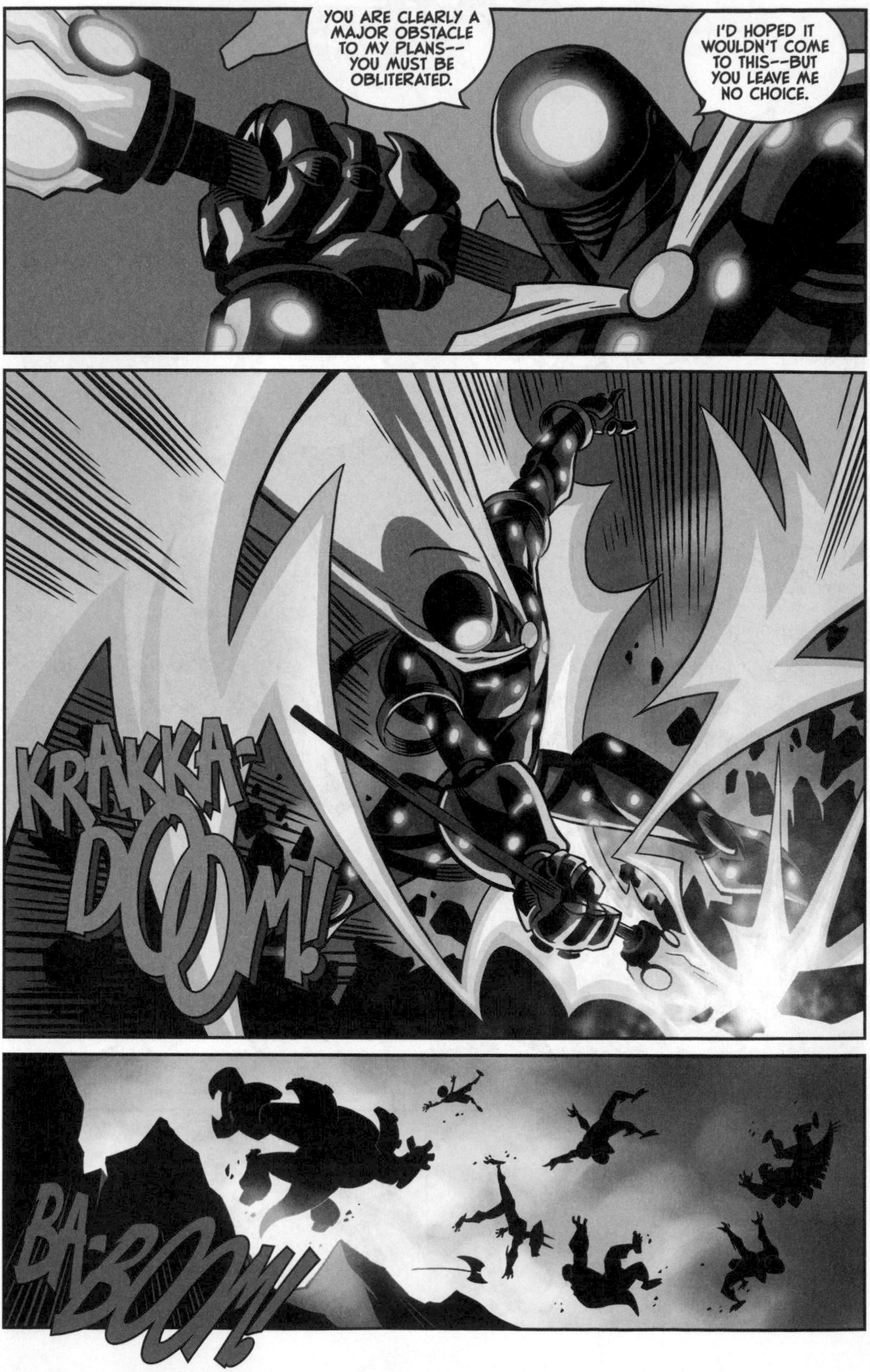
YOU ARE CLEARLY A MAJOR OBSTACLE TO MY PLANS-- YOU MUST BE OBLITERATED.
I'D HOPED IT WOULDN'T COME TO THIS--BUT YOU LEAVE ME NO CHOICE.
KRAKKA-DOOM!
BA-BOOM!

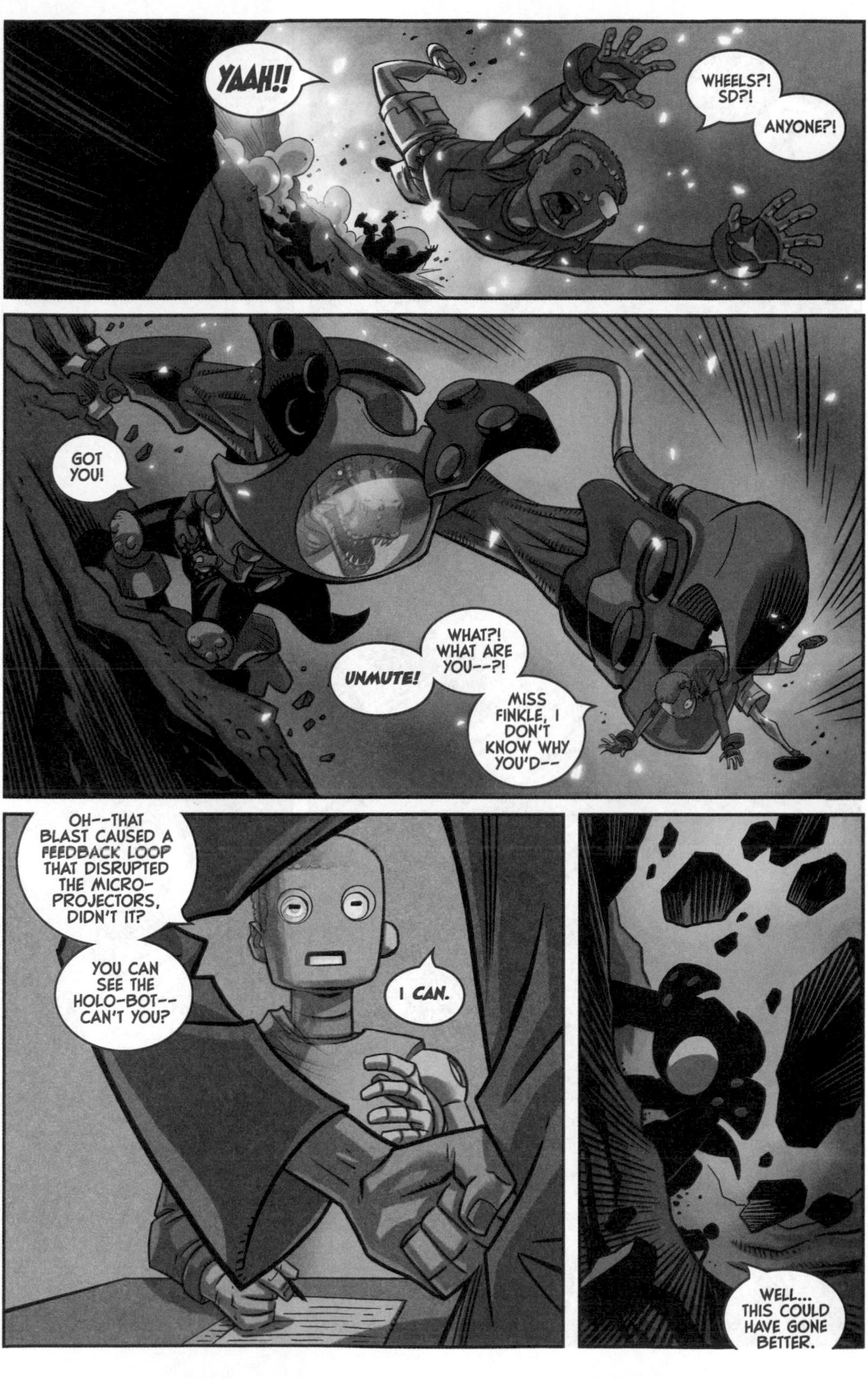
YAAH!!
WHEELS?! SD?!
ANYONE?!
GOT YOU!
UNMUTE!
WHAT?! WHAT ARE YOU--?!
MISS FINKLE, I DON'T KNOW WHY YOU'D--
OH--THAT BLAST CAUSED A FEEDBACK LOOP THAT DISRUPTED THE MICRO-PROJECTORS, DIDN'T IT?
YOU CAN SEE THE HOLO-BOT--CAN'T YOU?
I CAN.
WELL... THIS COULD HAVE GONE BETTER.

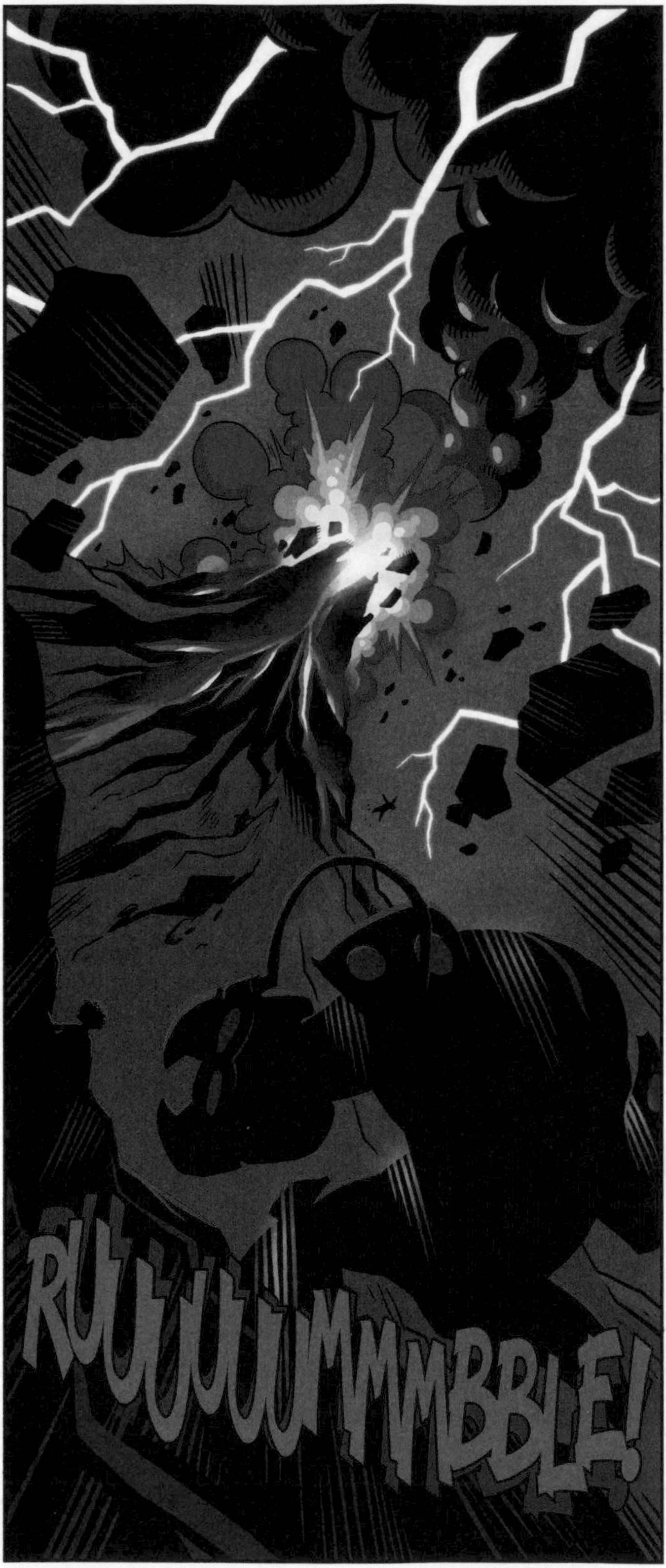
RUUUUUMMMBBLE!

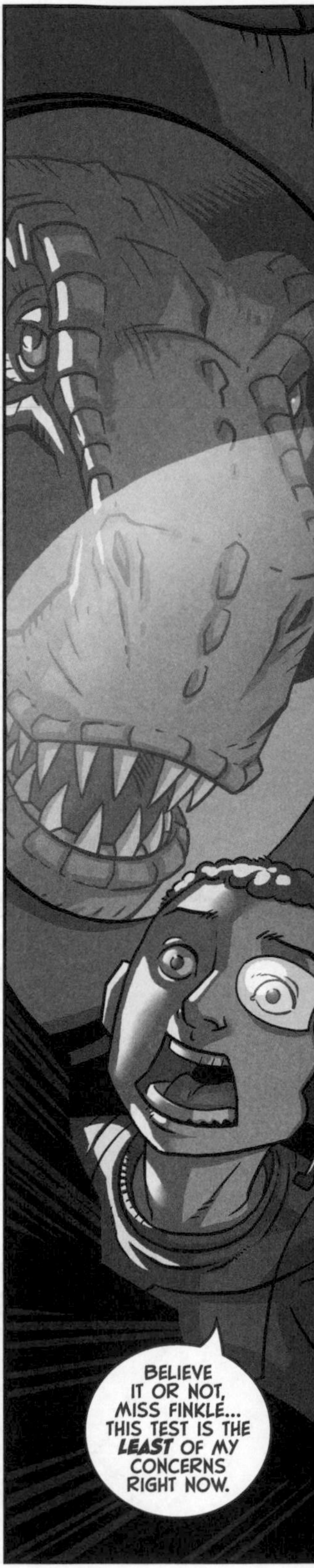
BELIEVE IT OR NOT, MISS FINKLE... THIS TEST IS THE *LEAST* OF MY CONCERNS RIGHT NOW.

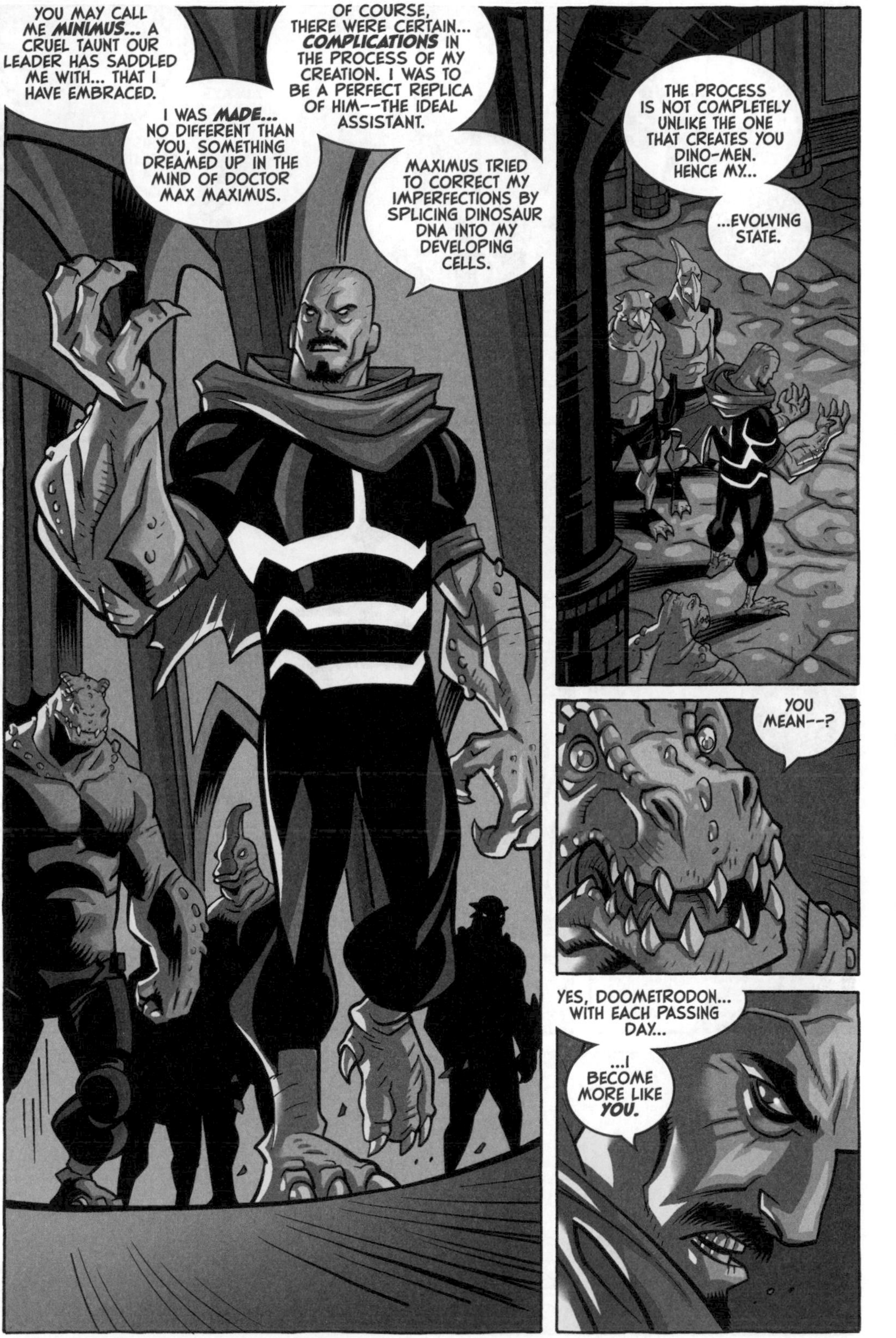

YOU MAY CALL ME MINIMUS... A CRUEL TAUNT OUR LEADER HAS SADDLED ME WITH... THAT I HAVE EMBRACED.
I WAS MADE... NO DIFFERENT THAN YOU, SOMETHING DREAMED UP IN THE MIND OF DOCTOR MAX MAXIMUS.
OF COURSE, THERE WERE CERTAIN... COMPLICATIONS IN THE PROCESS OF MY CREATION. I WAS TO BE A PERFECT REPLICA OF HIM--THE IDEAL ASSISTANT.
MAXIMUS TRIED TO CORRECT MY IMPERFECTIONS BY SPLICING DINOSAUR DNA INTO MY DEVELOPING CELLS.
THE PROCESS IS NOT COMPLETELY UNLIKE THE ONE THAT CREATES YOU DINO-MEN. HENCE MY...
...EVOLVING STATE.
YOU MEAN--?
YES, DOOMETRODON... WITH EACH PASSING DAY...
...I BECOME MORE LIKE YOU.

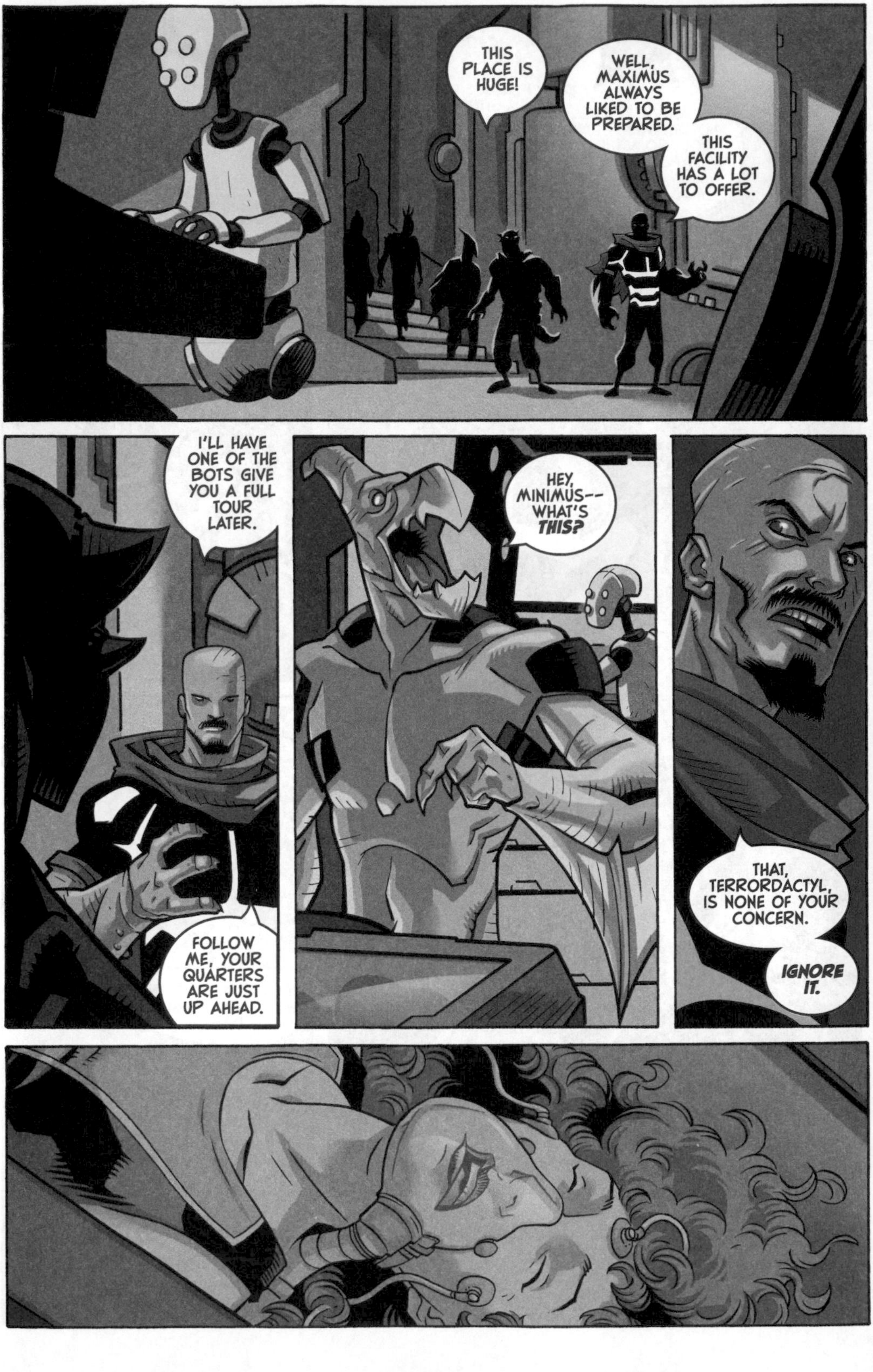
THIS PLACE IS HUGE!
WELL, MAXIMUS ALWAYS LIKED TO BE PREPARED.
THIS FACILITY HAS A LOT TO OFFER.
I'LL HAVE ONE OF THE BOTS GIVE YOU A FULL TOUR LATER.
FOLLOW ME, YOUR QUARTERS ARE JUST UP AHEAD.
HEY, MINIMUS-- WHAT'S THIS?
THAT, TERRORDACTYL, IS NONE OF YOUR CONCERN.
IGNORE IT.

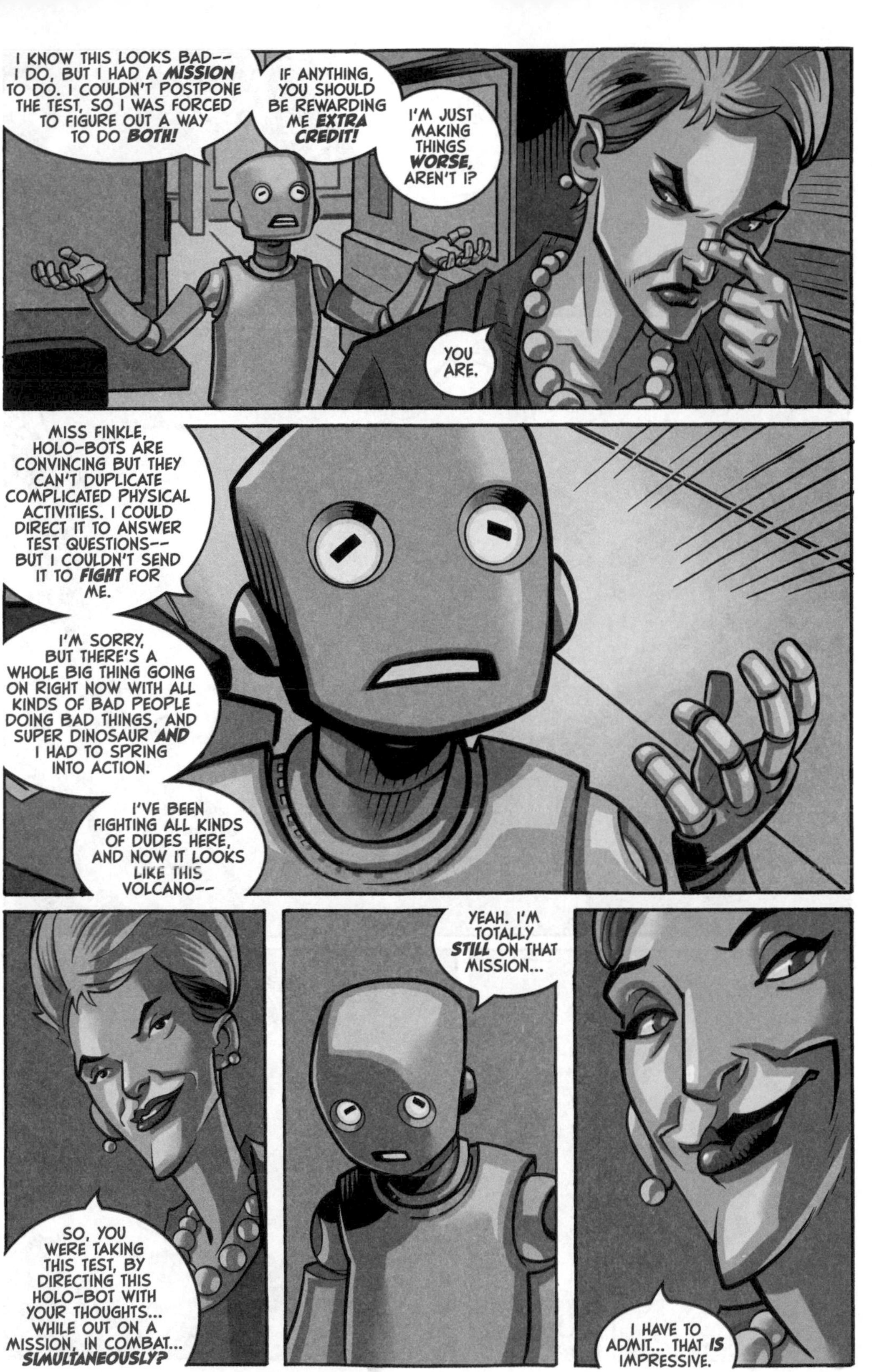
I KNOW THIS LOOKS BAD-- I DO, BUT I HAD A MISSION TO DO. I COULDN'T POSTPONE THE TEST, SO I WAS FORCED TO FIGURE OUT A WAY TO DO BOTH!
IF ANYTHING, YOU SHOULD BE REWARDING ME EXTRA CREDIT!
I'M JUST MAKING THINGS WORSE, AREN'T I?
YOU ARE.
MISS FINKLE, HOLO-BOTS ARE CONVINCING BUT THEY CAN'T DUPLICATE COMPLICATED PHYSICAL ACTIVITIES. I COULD DIRECT IT TO ANSWER TEST QUESTIONS-- BUT I COULDN'T SEND IT TO FIGHT FOR ME.
I'M SORRY, BUT THERE'S A WHOLE BIG THING GOING ON RIGHT NOW WITH ALL KINDS OF BAD PEOPLE DOING BAD THINGS, AND SUPER DINOSAUR AND I HAD TO SPRING INTO ACTION.
I'VE BEEN FIGHTING ALL KINDS OF DUDES HERE, AND NOW IT LOOKS LIKE THIS VOLCANO--
SO, YOU WERE TAKING THIS TEST, BY DIRECTING THIS HOLO-BOT WITH YOUR THOUGHTS... WHILE OUT ON A MISSION, IN COMBAT... SIMULTANEOUSLY?
YEAH. I'M TOTALLY STILL ON THAT MISSION...
I HAVE TO ADMIT... THAT IS IMPRESSIVE.

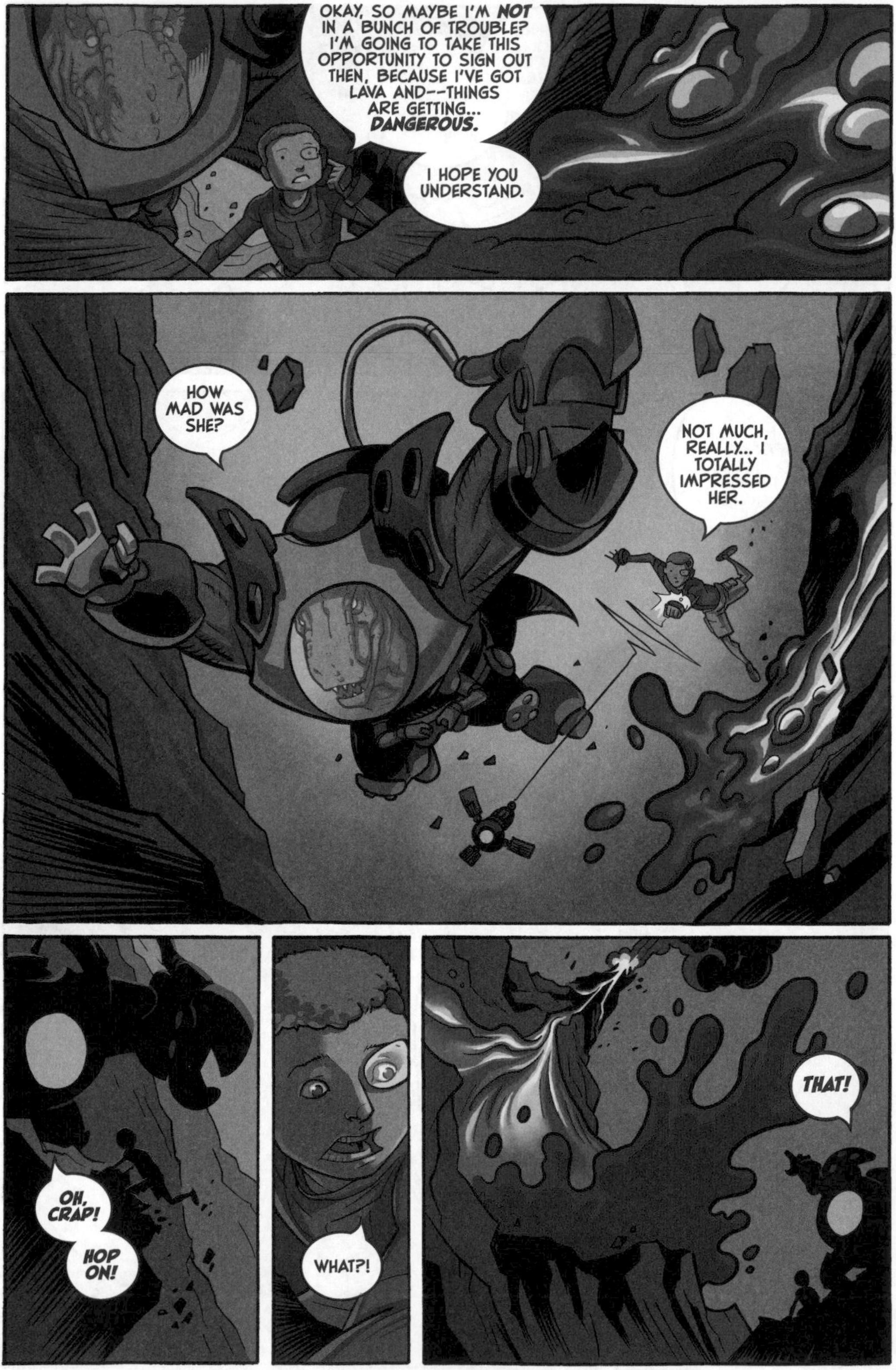
OKAY, SO MAYBE I'M **NOT** IN A BUNCH OF TROUBLE? I'M GOING TO TAKE THIS OPPORTUNITY TO SIGN OUT THEN, BECAUSE I'VE GOT LAVA AND--THINGS ARE GETTING... ***DANGEROUS.***
I HOPE YOU UNDERSTAND.
HOW MAD WAS SHE?
NOT MUCH, REALLY... I TOTALLY IMPRESSED HER.
OH, CRAP!
HOP ON!
WHAT?!
THAT!

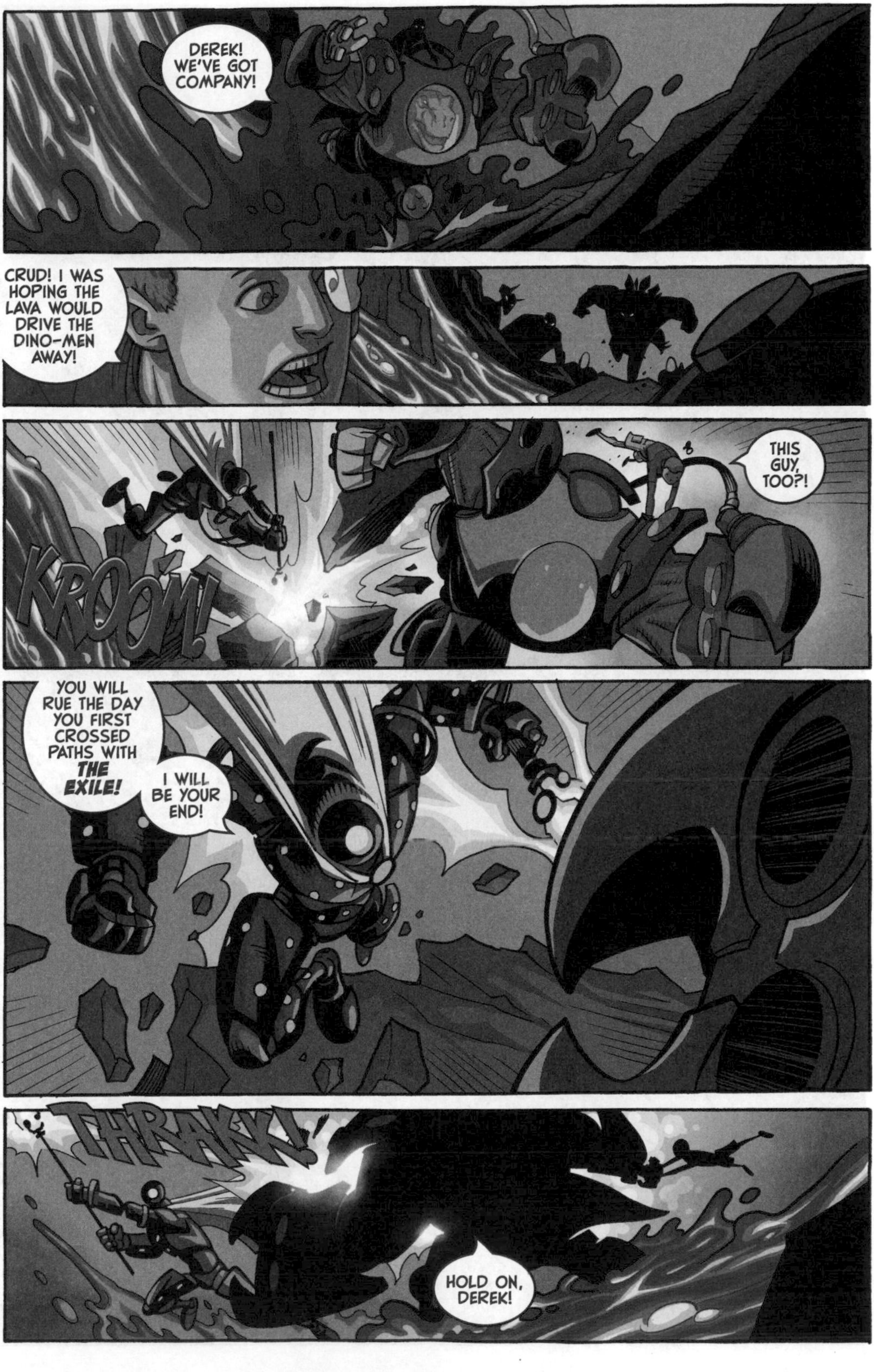
DEREK! WE'VE GOT COMPANY!
CRUD! I WAS HOPING THE LAVA WOULD DRIVE THE DINO-MEN AWAY!
KROOM!
THIS GUY, TOO?!
YOU WILL RUE THE DAY YOU FIRST CROSSED PATHS WITH THE EXILE!
I WILL BE YOUR END!
THRAKK!
HOLD ON, DEREK!

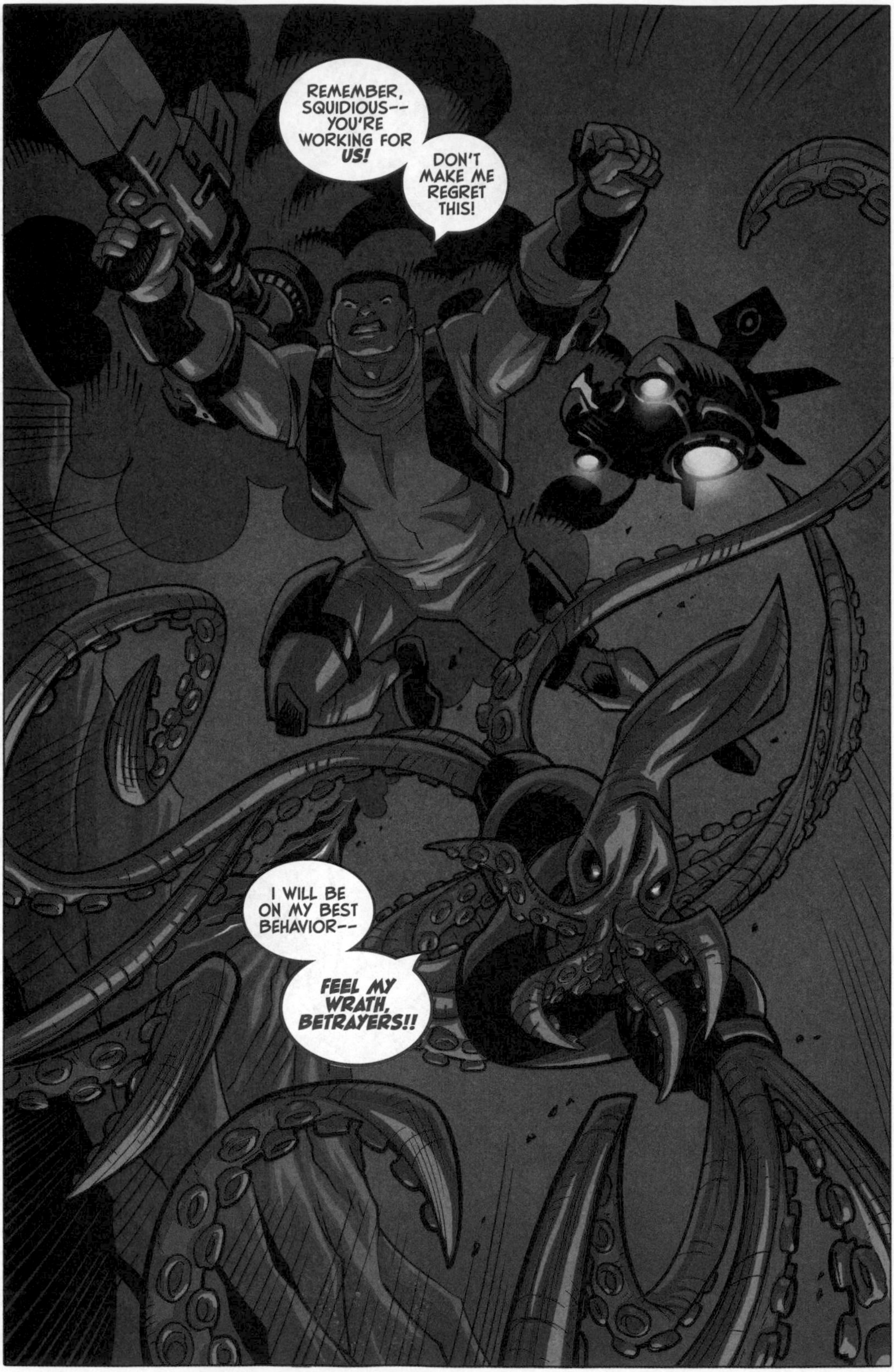

REMEMBER, SQUIDIOUS-- YOU'RE WORKING FOR *US!*
DON'T MAKE ME REGRET THIS!
I WILL BE ON MY BEST BEHAVIOR--
FEEL MY WRATH, BETRAYERS!!

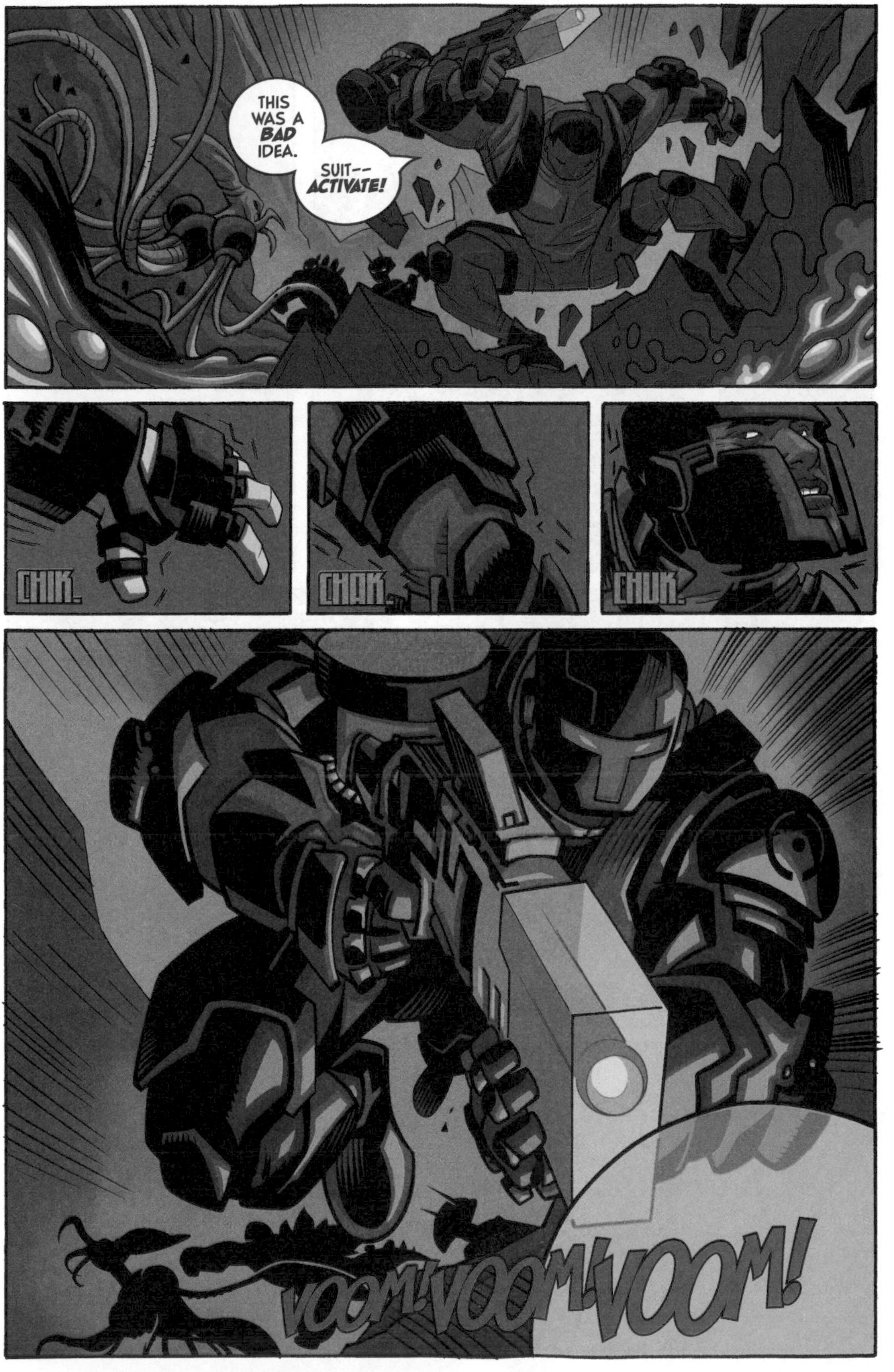
THIS WAS A BAD IDEA.
SUIT-- ACTIVATE!
CHIK.
CHAK.
CHUK.
VOOM! VOOM! VOOM!

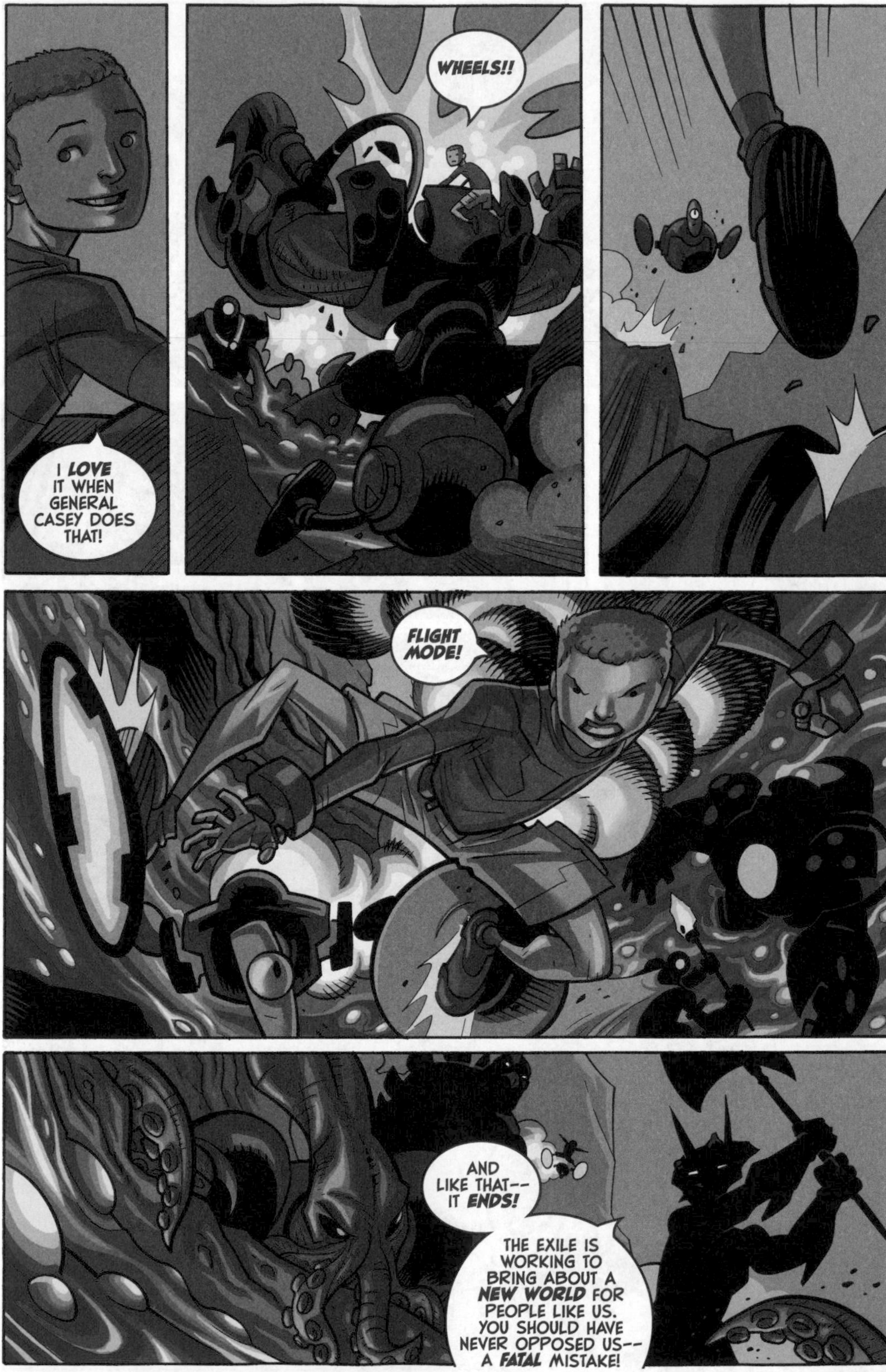
I LOVE IT WHEN GENERAL CASEY DOES THAT!
WHEELS!!
FLIGHT MODE!
AND LIKE THAT-- IT ENDS!
THE EXILE IS WORKING TO BRING ABOUT A NEW WORLD FOR PEOPLE LIKE US. YOU SHOULD HAVE NEVER OPPOSED US-- A FATAL MISTAKE!

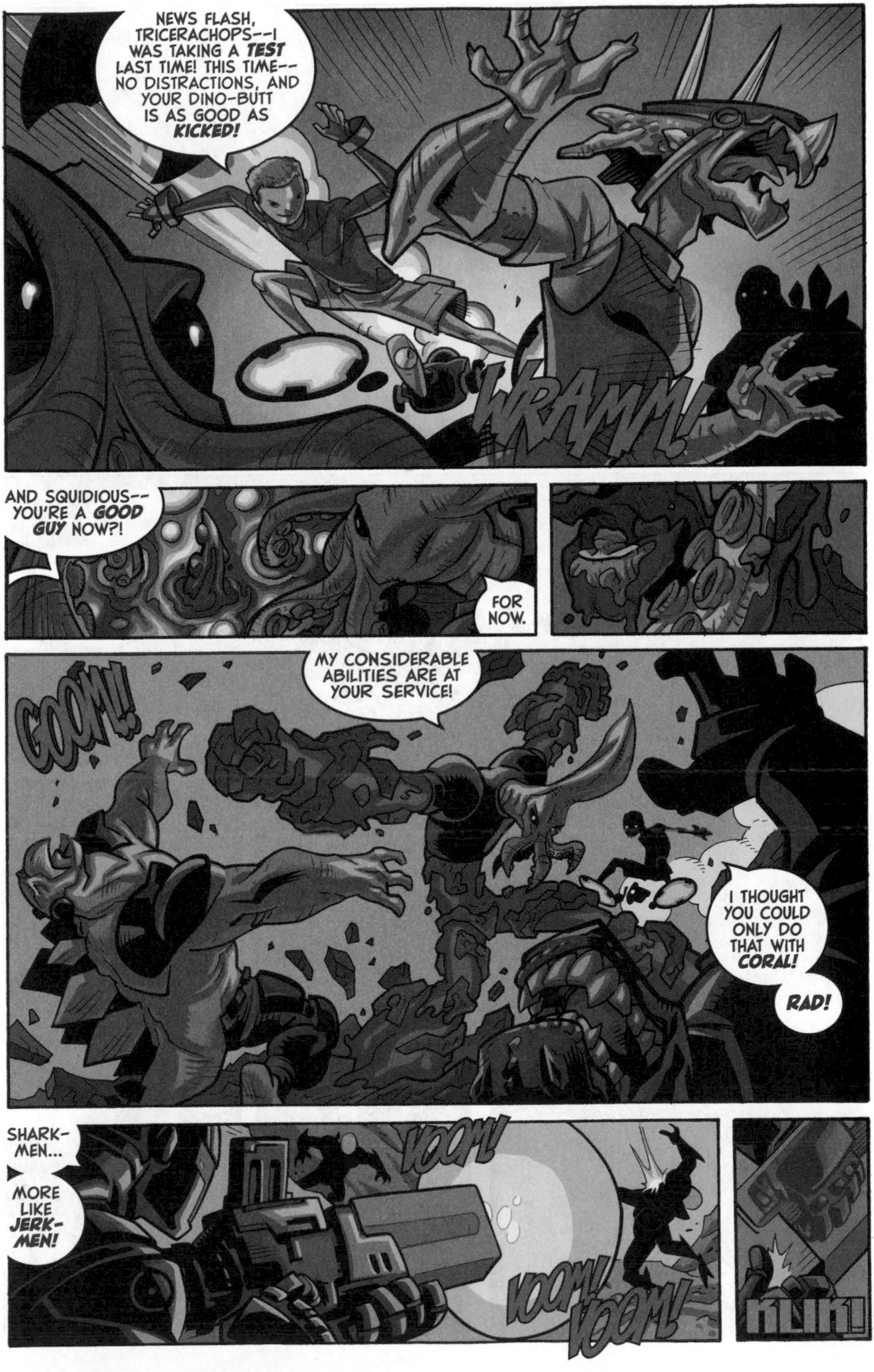
NEWS FLASH, TRICERACHOPS--I WAS TAKING A TEST LAST TIME! THIS TIME--NO DISTRACTIONS, AND YOUR DINO-BUTT IS AS GOOD AS KICKED!
WRAMM!
AND SQUIDIOUS--YOU'RE A GOOD GUY NOW?!
FOR NOW.
GOOM!!
MY CONSIDERABLE ABILITIES ARE AT YOUR SERVICE!
I THOUGHT YOU COULD ONLY DO THAT WITH CORAL!
RAD!
SHARK-MEN...
MORE LIKE JERK-MEN!
VOOM!
VOOM! VOOM!
KLIK!

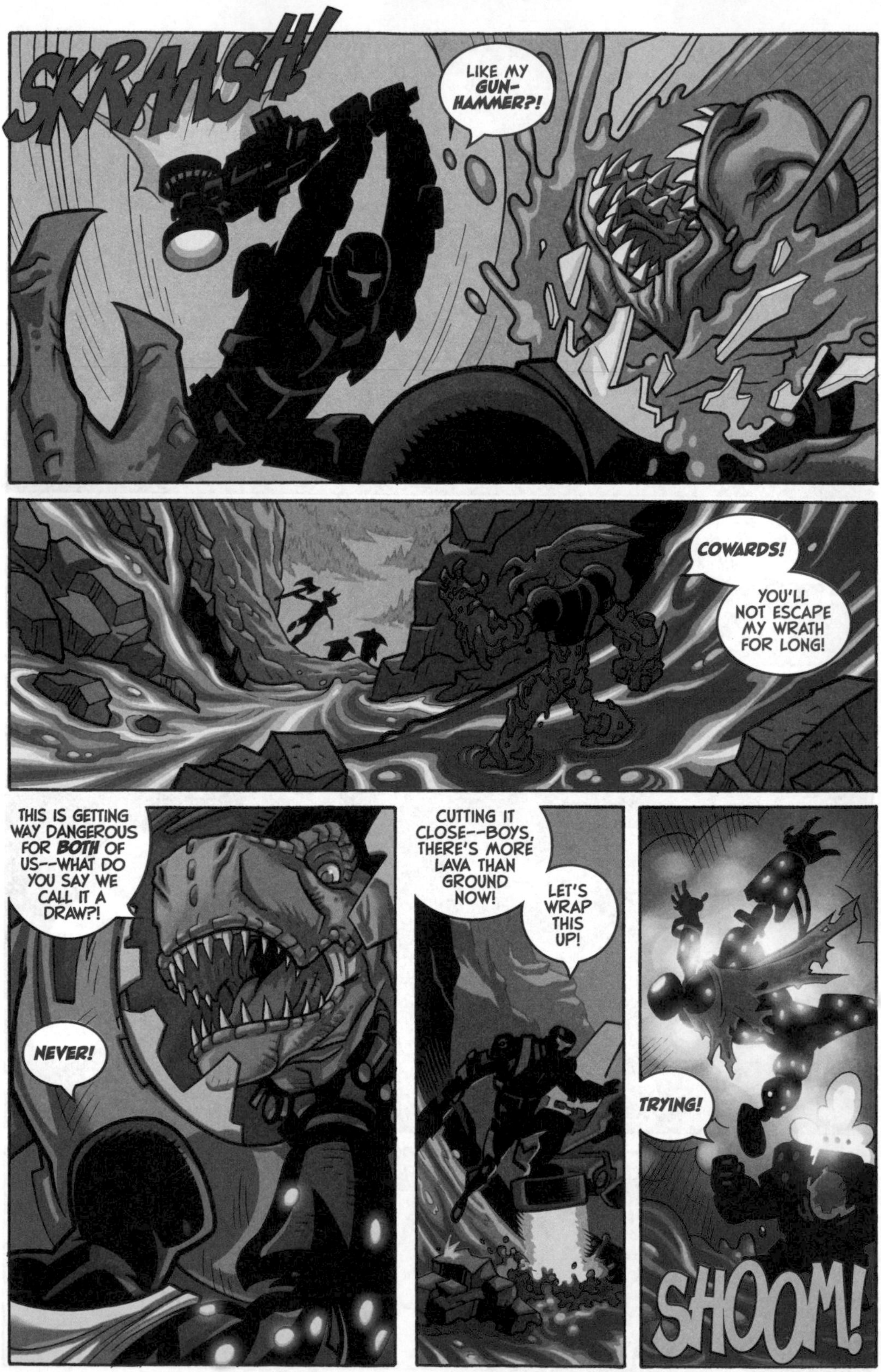
SKRAASH!
LIKE MY GUN-HAMMER?!
COWARDS!
YOU'LL NOT ESCAPE MY WRATH FOR LONG!
THIS IS GETTING WAY DANGEROUS FOR BOTH OF US--WHAT DO YOU SAY WE CALL IT A DRAW?!
NEVER!
CUTTING IT CLOSE--BOYS, THERE'S MORE LAVA THAN GROUND NOW!
LET'S WRAP THIS UP!
TRYING!
...
SHOOM!

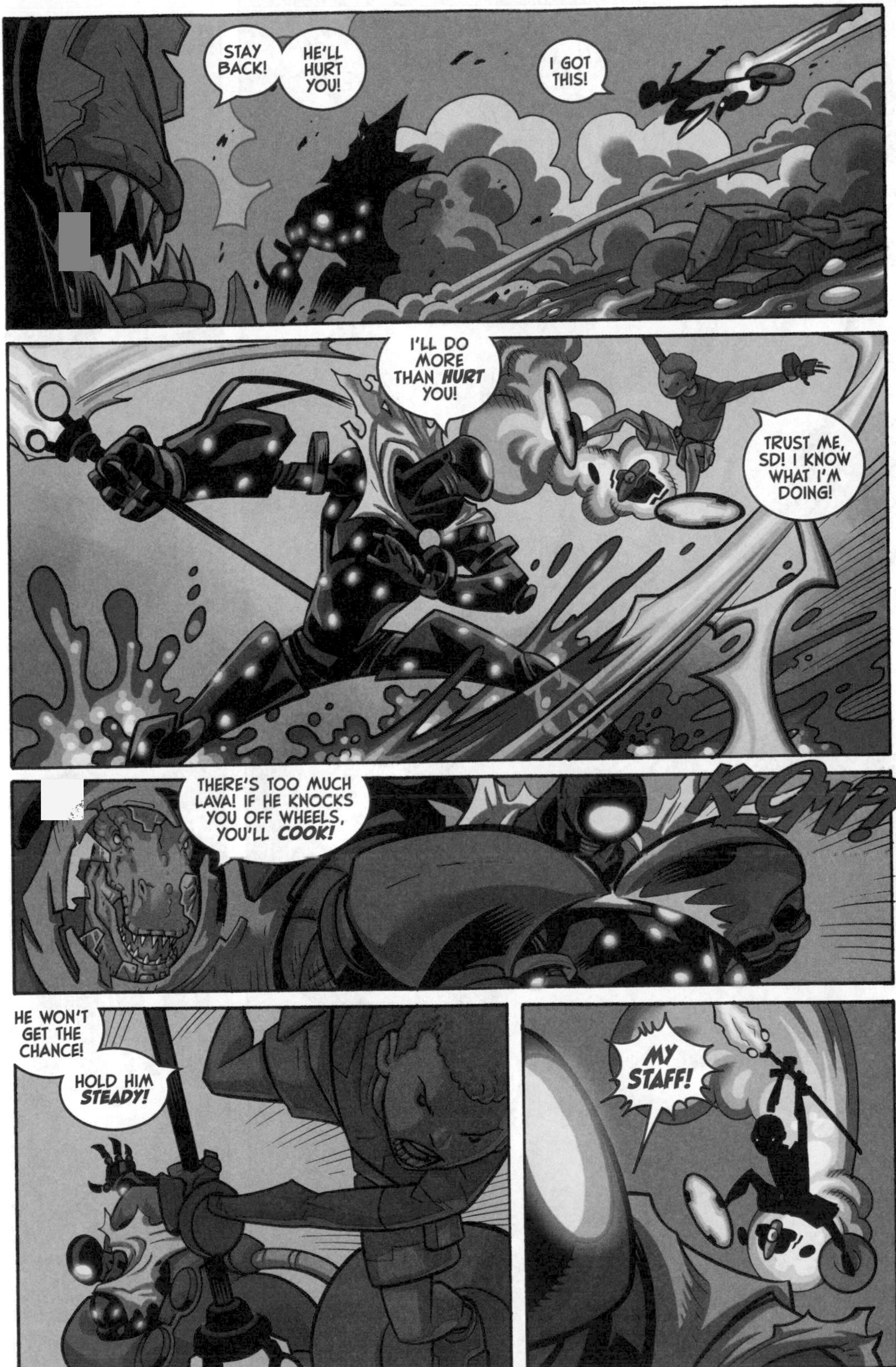
STAY BACK!
HE'LL HURT YOU!
I GOT THIS!
I'LL DO MORE THAN HURT YOU!
TRUST ME, SD! I KNOW WHAT I'M DOING!
THERE'S TOO MUCH LAVA! IF HE KNOCKS YOU OFF WHEELS, YOU'LL COOK!
KLONK!
HE WON'T GET THE CHANCE!
HOLD HIM STEADY!
MY STAFF!

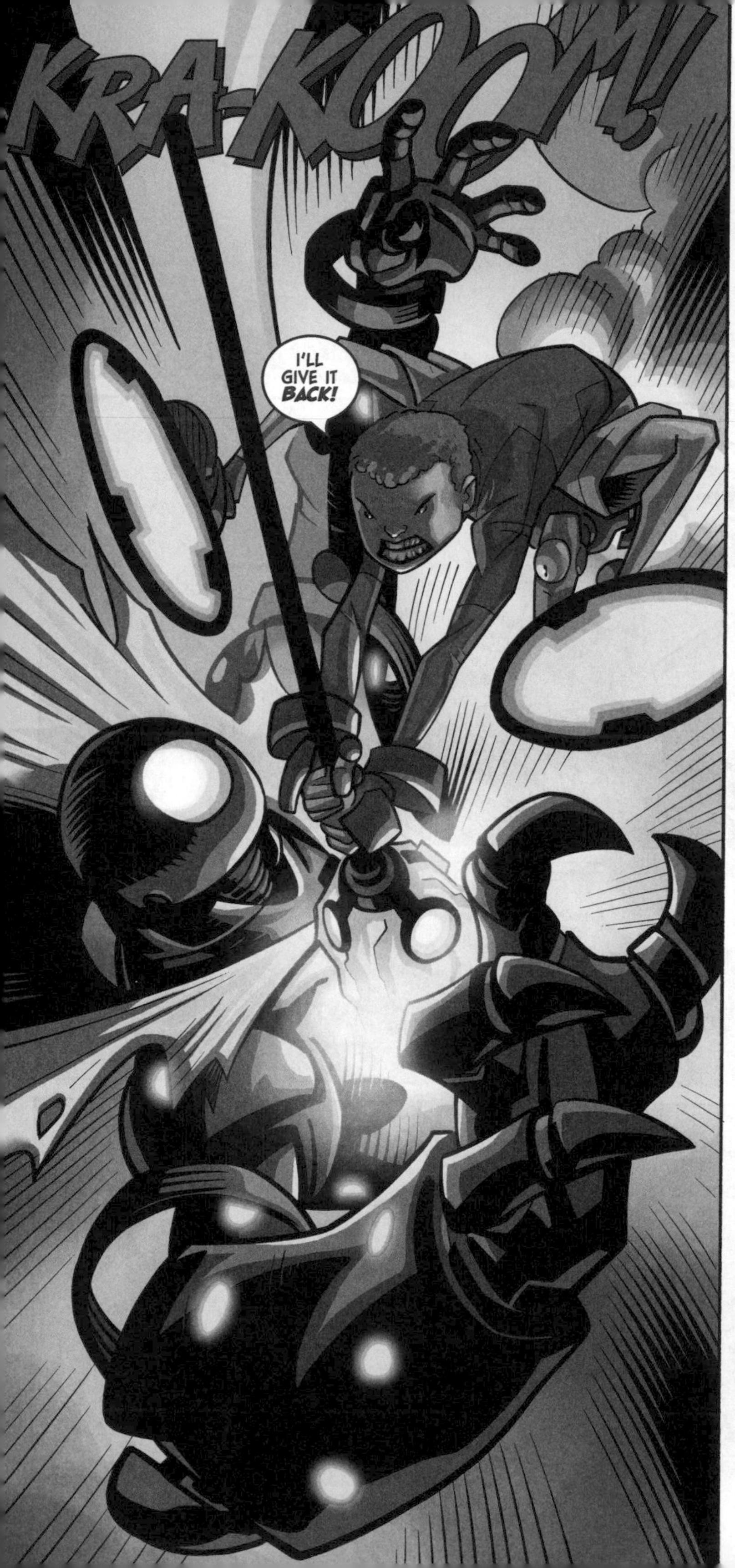
KRA-KOOOM!
I'LL GIVE IT BACK!

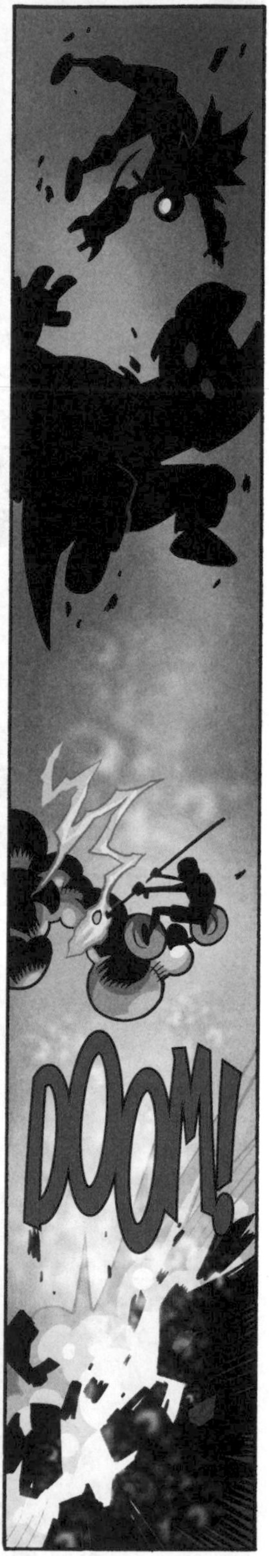
DOOM!

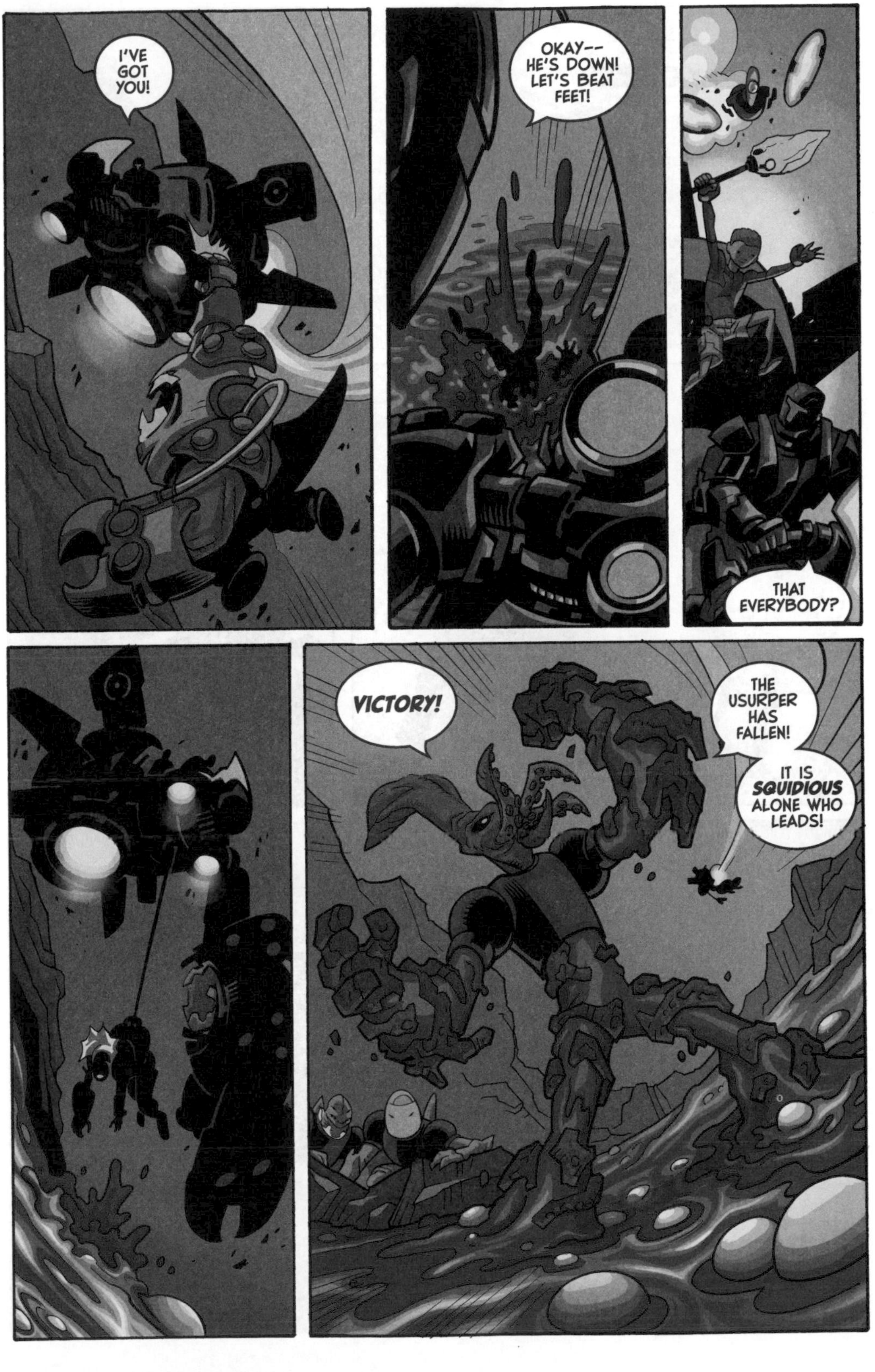
I'VE GOT YOU!
OKAY-- HE'S DOWN! LET'S BEAT FEET!
THAT EVERYBODY?
VICTORY!
THE USURPER HAS FALLEN!
IT IS SQUIDIOUS ALONE WHO LEADS!

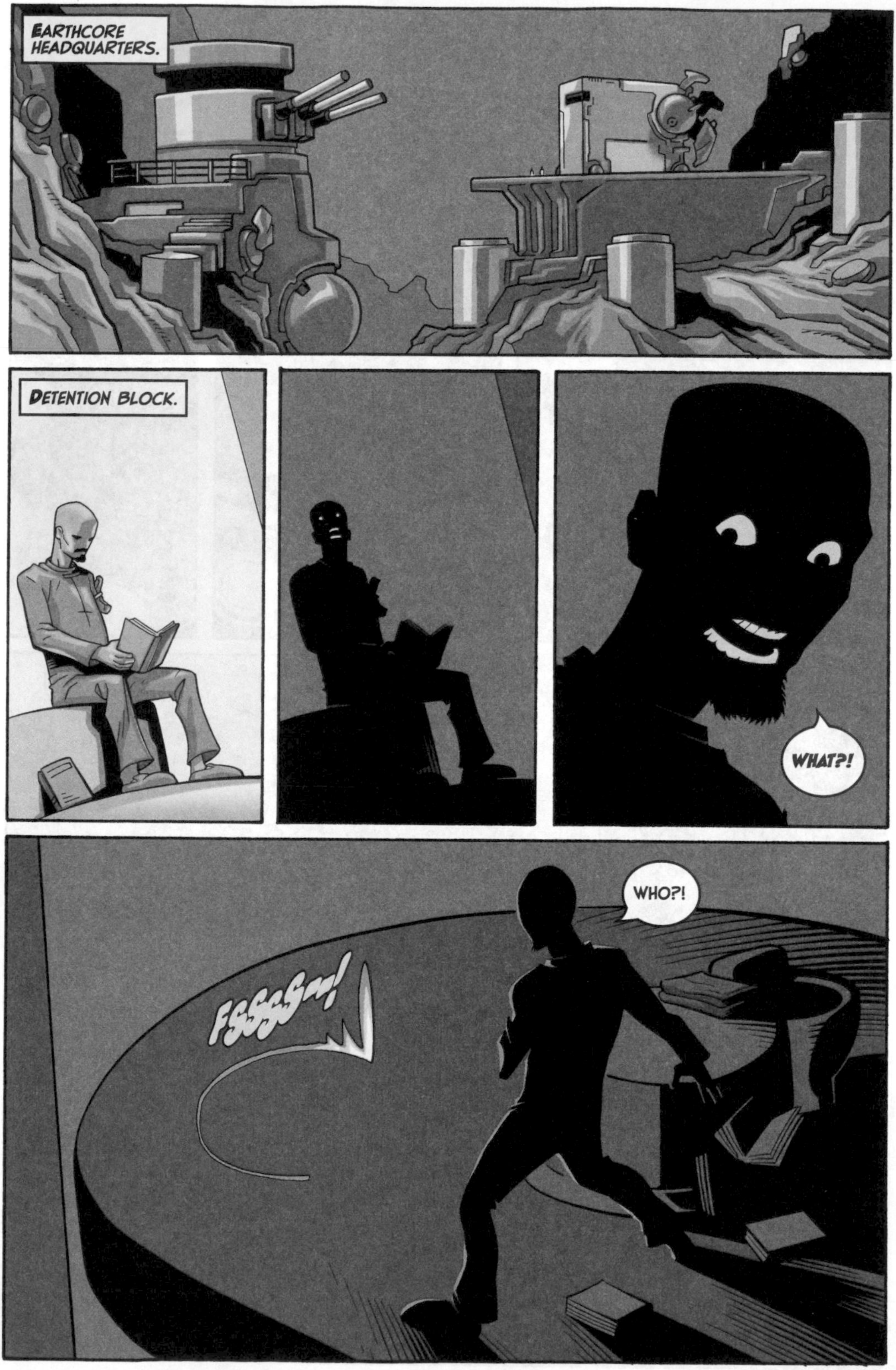
EARTHCORE HEADQUARTERS.
DETENTION BLOCK.
WHAT?!
WHO?!
FSSSSSH!

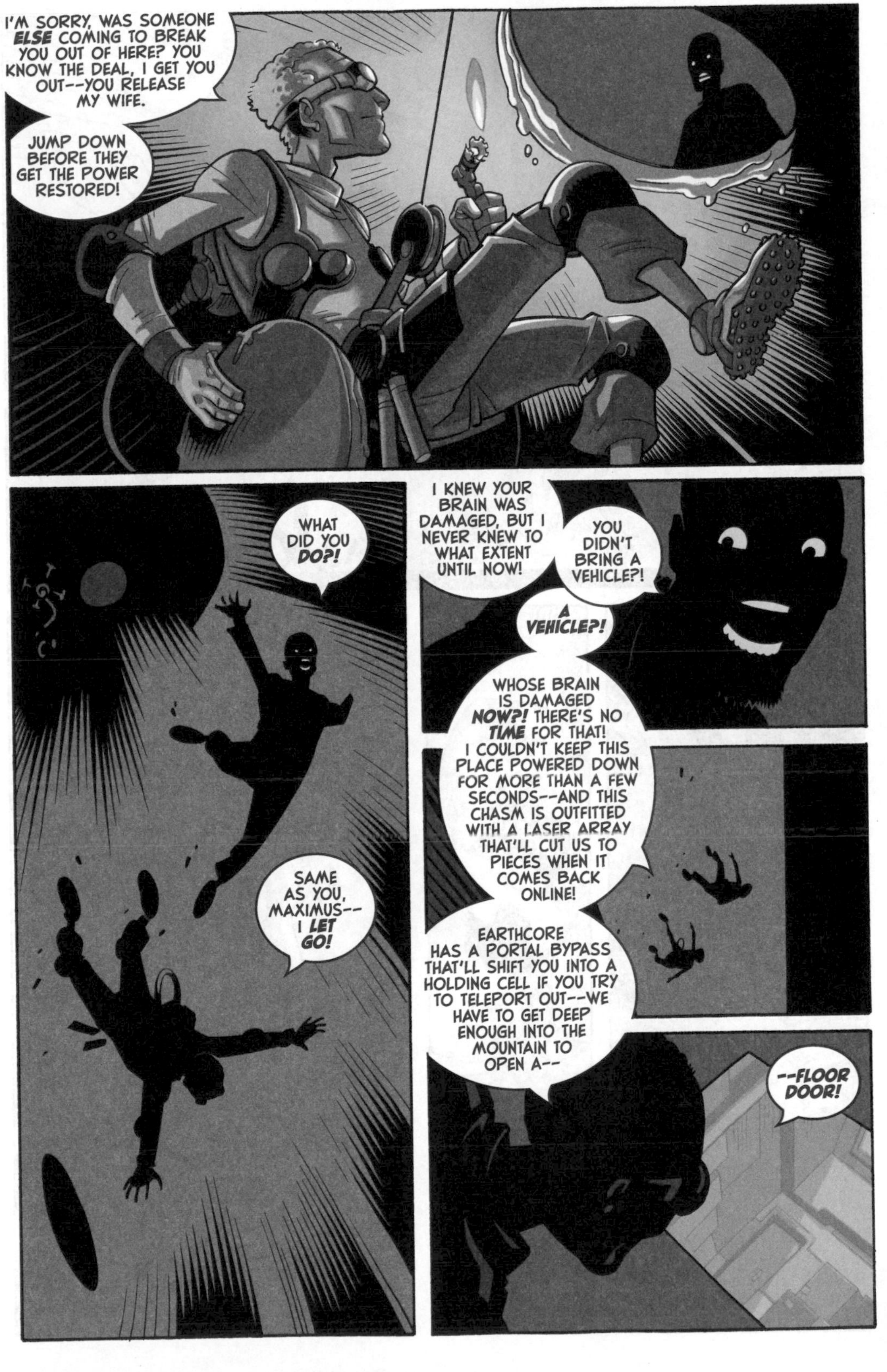
I'M SORRY, WAS SOMEONE ELSE COMING TO BREAK YOU OUT OF HERE? YOU KNOW THE DEAL, I GET YOU OUT--YOU RELEASE MY WIFE.
JUMP DOWN BEFORE THEY GET THE POWER RESTORED!
WHAT DID YOU DO?!
SAME AS YOU, MAXIMUS--I LET GO!
I KNEW YOUR BRAIN WAS DAMAGED, BUT I NEVER KNEW TO WHAT EXTENT UNTIL NOW!
YOU DIDN'T BRING A VEHICLE?!
A VEHICLE?!
WHOSE BRAIN IS DAMAGED NOW?! THERE'S NO TIME FOR THAT! I COULDN'T KEEP THIS PLACE POWERED DOWN FOR MORE THAN A FEW SECONDS--AND THIS CHASM IS OUTFITTED WITH A LASER ARRAY THAT'LL CUT US TO PIECES WHEN IT COMES BACK ONLINE!
EARTHCORE HAS A PORTAL BYPASS THAT'LL SHIFT YOU INTO A HOLDING CELL IF YOU TRY TO TELEPORT OUT--WE HAVE TO GET DEEP ENOUGH INTO THE MOUNTAIN TO OPEN A--
--FLOOR DOOR!

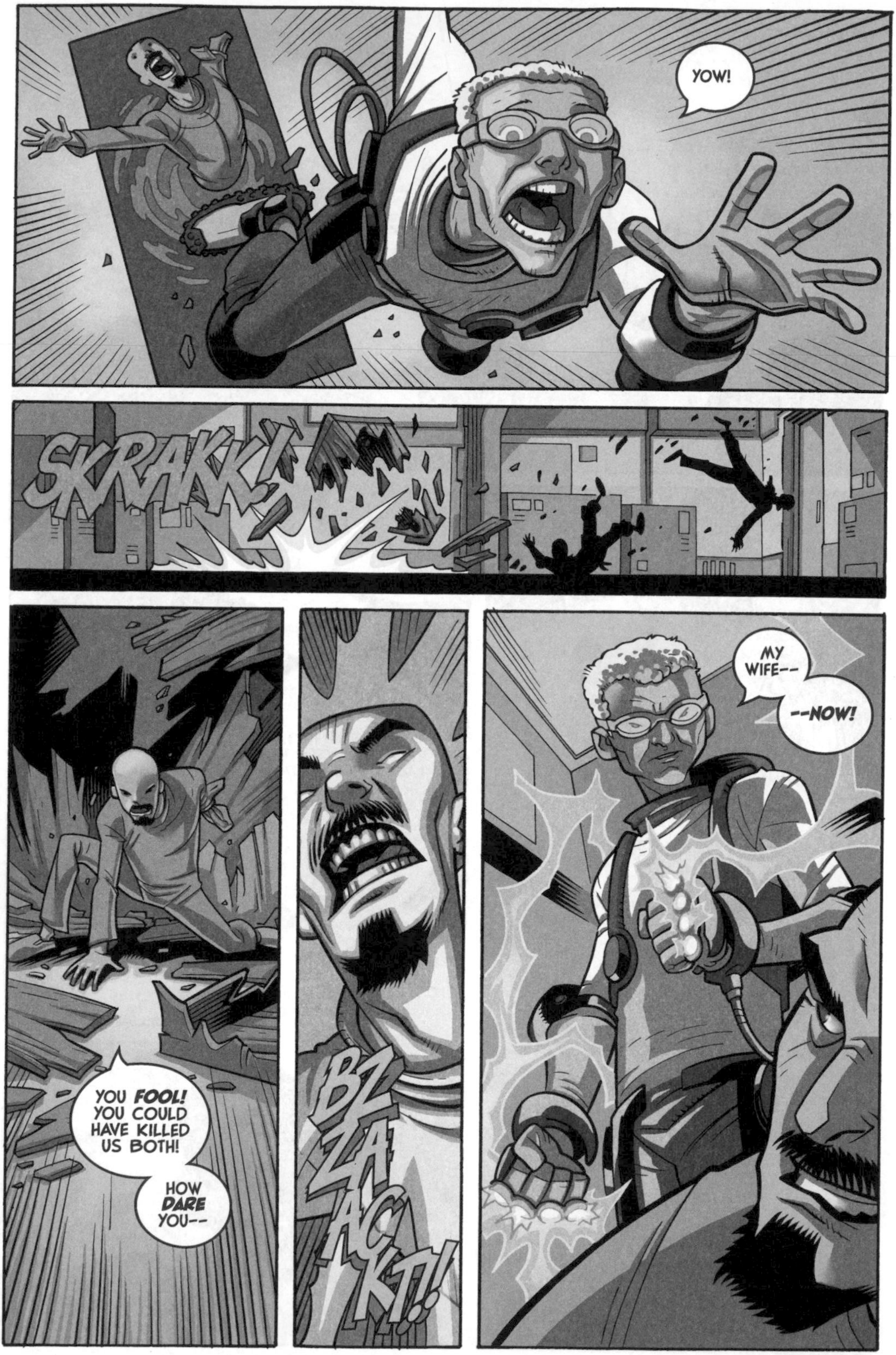
YOW!
SKRAKK!
YOU FOOL! YOU COULD HAVE KILLED US BOTH!
HOW DARE YOU--
BZZACKT!!
MY WIFE--
--NOW!

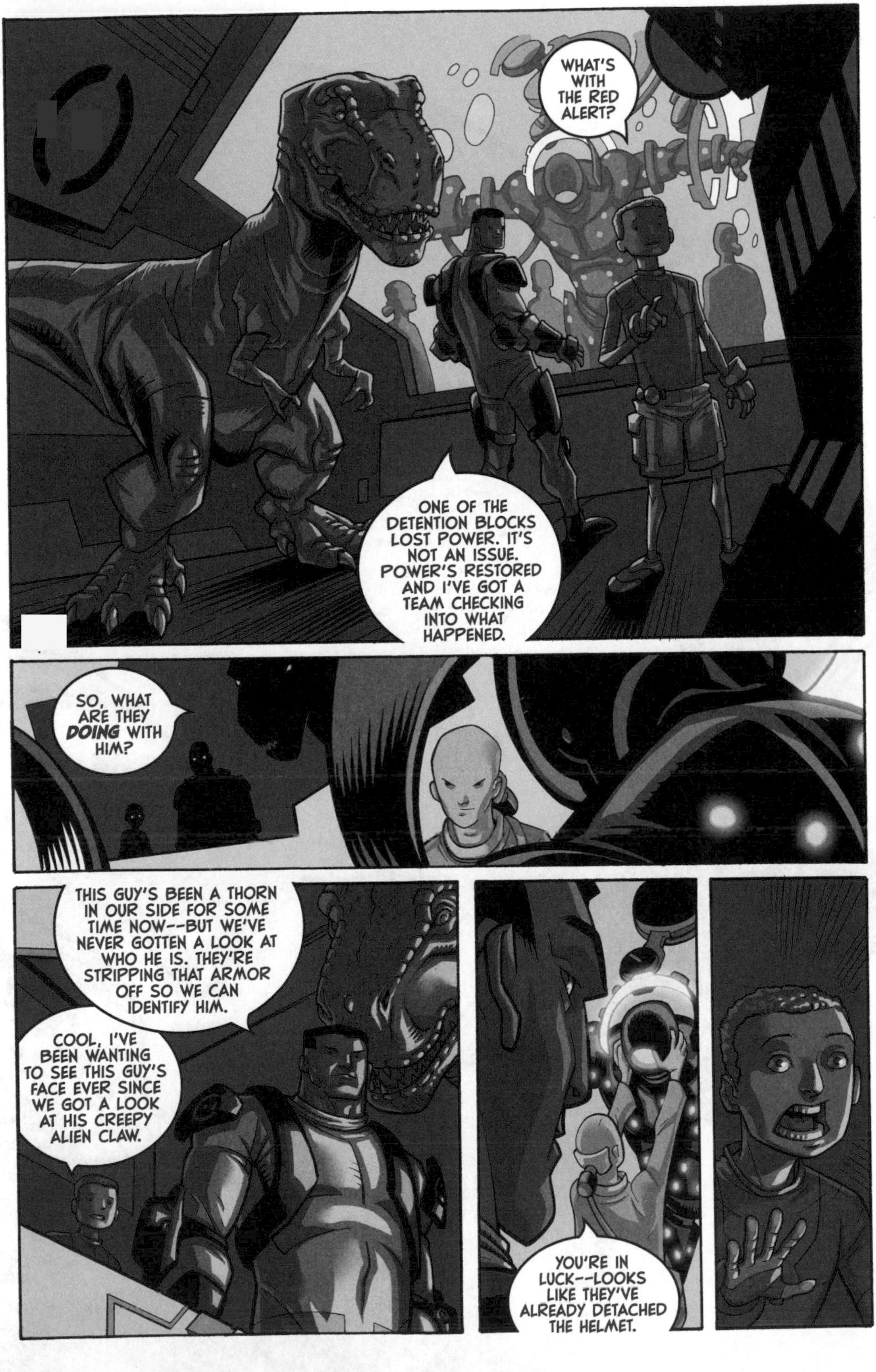
WHAT'S WITH THE RED ALERT?
ONE OF THE DETENTION BLOCKS LOST POWER. IT'S NOT AN ISSUE. POWER'S RESTORED AND I'VE GOT A TEAM CHECKING INTO WHAT HAPPENED.
SO, WHAT ARE THEY *DOING* WITH HIM?
THIS GUY'S BEEN A THORN IN OUR SIDE FOR SOME TIME NOW--BUT WE'VE NEVER GOTTEN A LOOK AT WHO HE IS. THEY'RE STRIPPING THAT ARMOR OFF SO WE CAN IDENTIFY HIM.
COOL, I'VE BEEN WANTING TO SEE THIS GUY'S FACE EVER SINCE WE GOT A LOOK AT HIS CREEPY ALIEN CLAW.
YOU'RE IN LUCK--LOOKS LIKE THEY'VE ALREADY DETACHED THE HELMET.

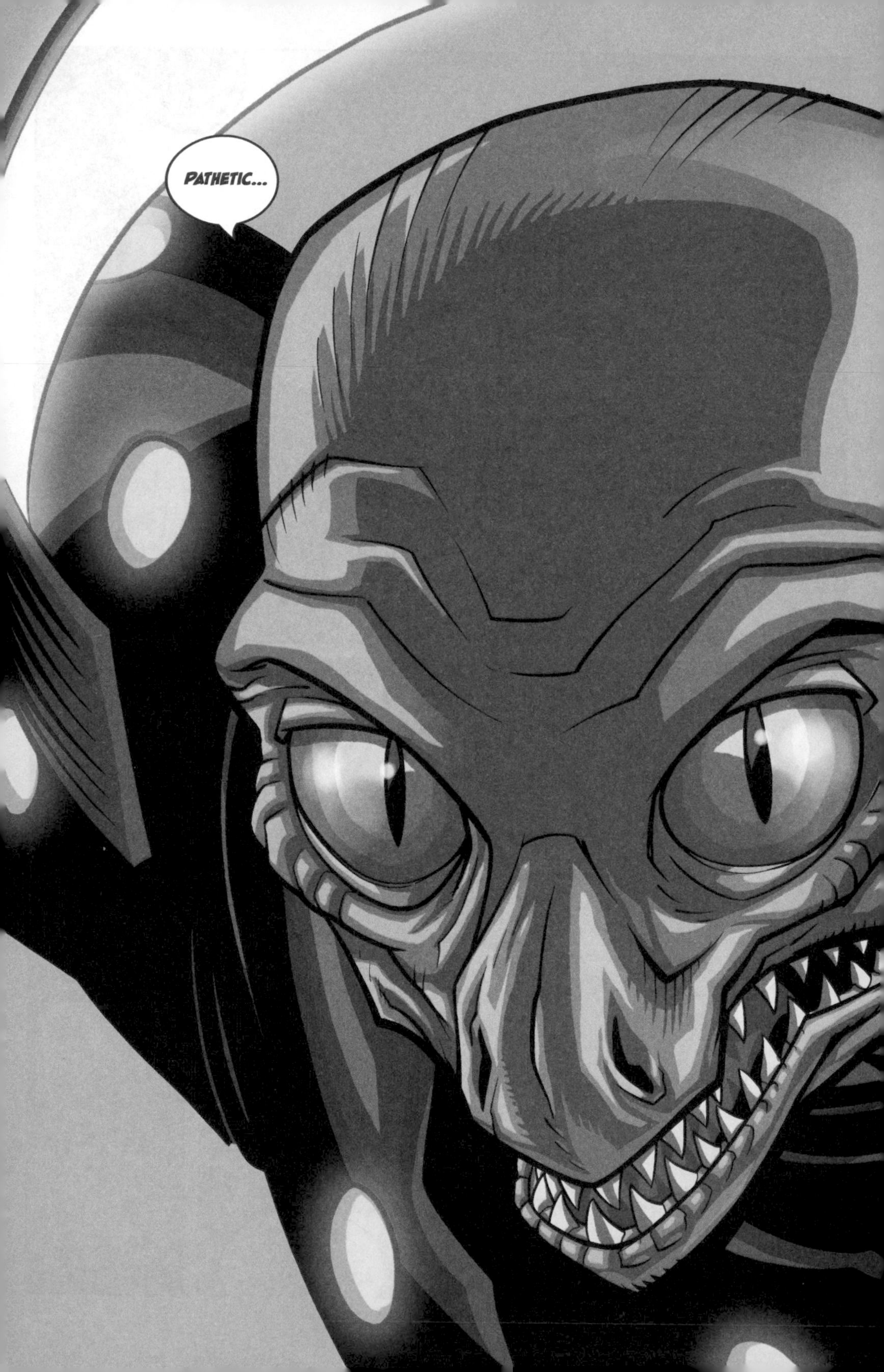
PATHETIC...

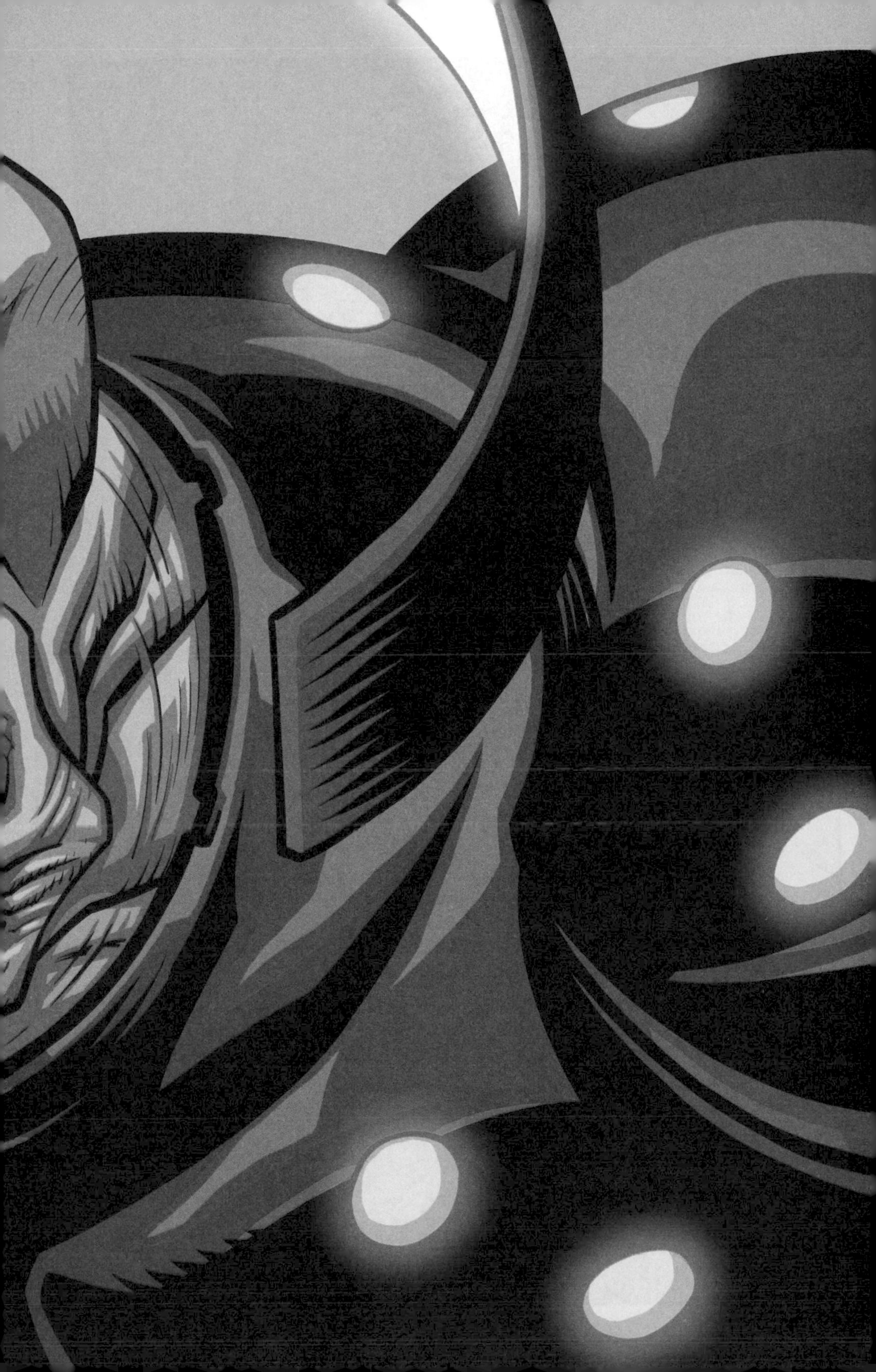

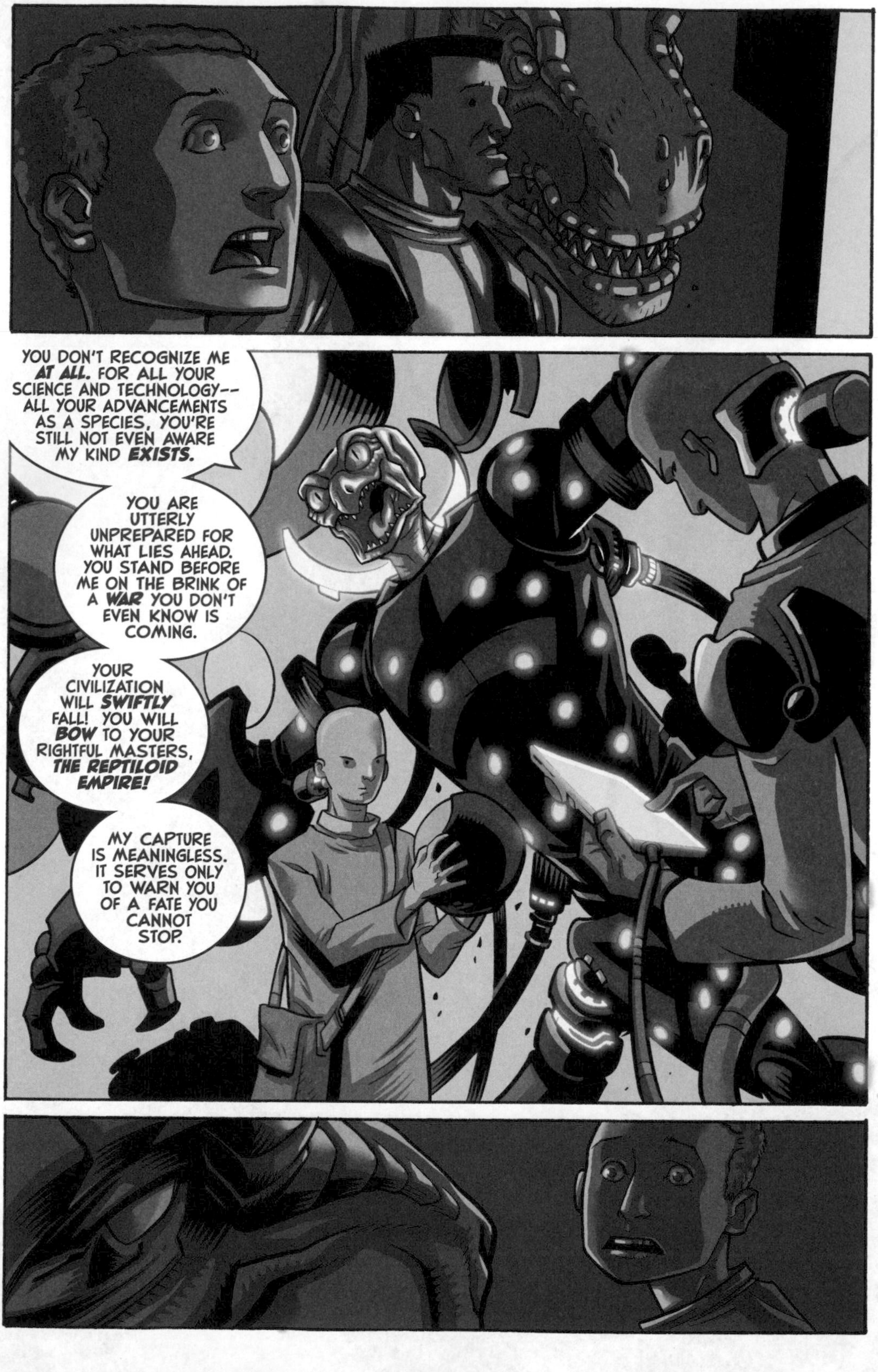
YOU DON'T RECOGNIZE ME AT ALL. FOR ALL YOUR SCIENCE AND TECHNOLOGY-- ALL YOUR ADVANCEMENTS AS A SPECIES, YOU'RE STILL NOT EVEN AWARE MY KIND EXISTS.
YOU ARE UTTERLY UNPREPARED FOR WHAT LIES AHEAD. YOU STAND BEFORE ME ON THE BRINK OF A WAR YOU DON'T EVEN KNOW IS COMING.
YOUR CIVILIZATION WILL SWIFTLY FALL! YOU WILL BOW TO YOUR RIGHTFUL MASTERS, THE REPTILOID EMPIRE!
MY CAPTURE IS MEANINGLESS. IT SERVES ONLY TO WARN YOU OF A FATE YOU CANNOT STOP.

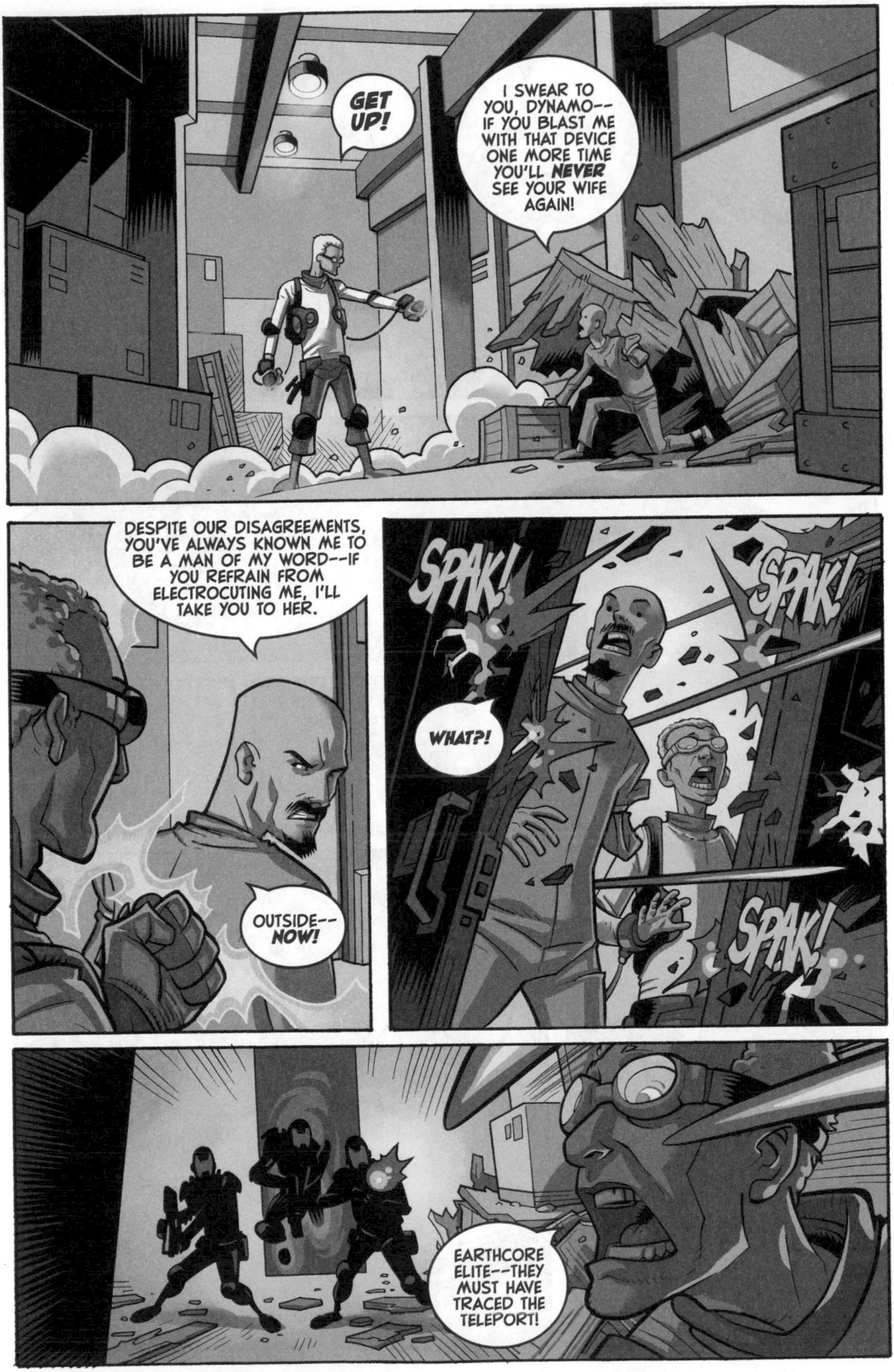
GET UP!
I SWEAR TO YOU, DYNAMO-- IF YOU BLAST ME WITH THAT DEVICE ONE MORE TIME YOU'LL NEVER SEE YOUR WIFE AGAIN!
DESPITE OUR DISAGREEMENTS, YOU'VE ALWAYS KNOWN ME TO BE A MAN OF MY WORD--IF YOU REFRAIN FROM ELECTROCUTING ME, I'LL TAKE YOU TO HER.
OUTSIDE-- NOW!
SPAK!
SPAK!
WHAT?!
SPAK!
EARTHCORE ELITE--THEY MUST HAVE TRACED THE TELEPORT!

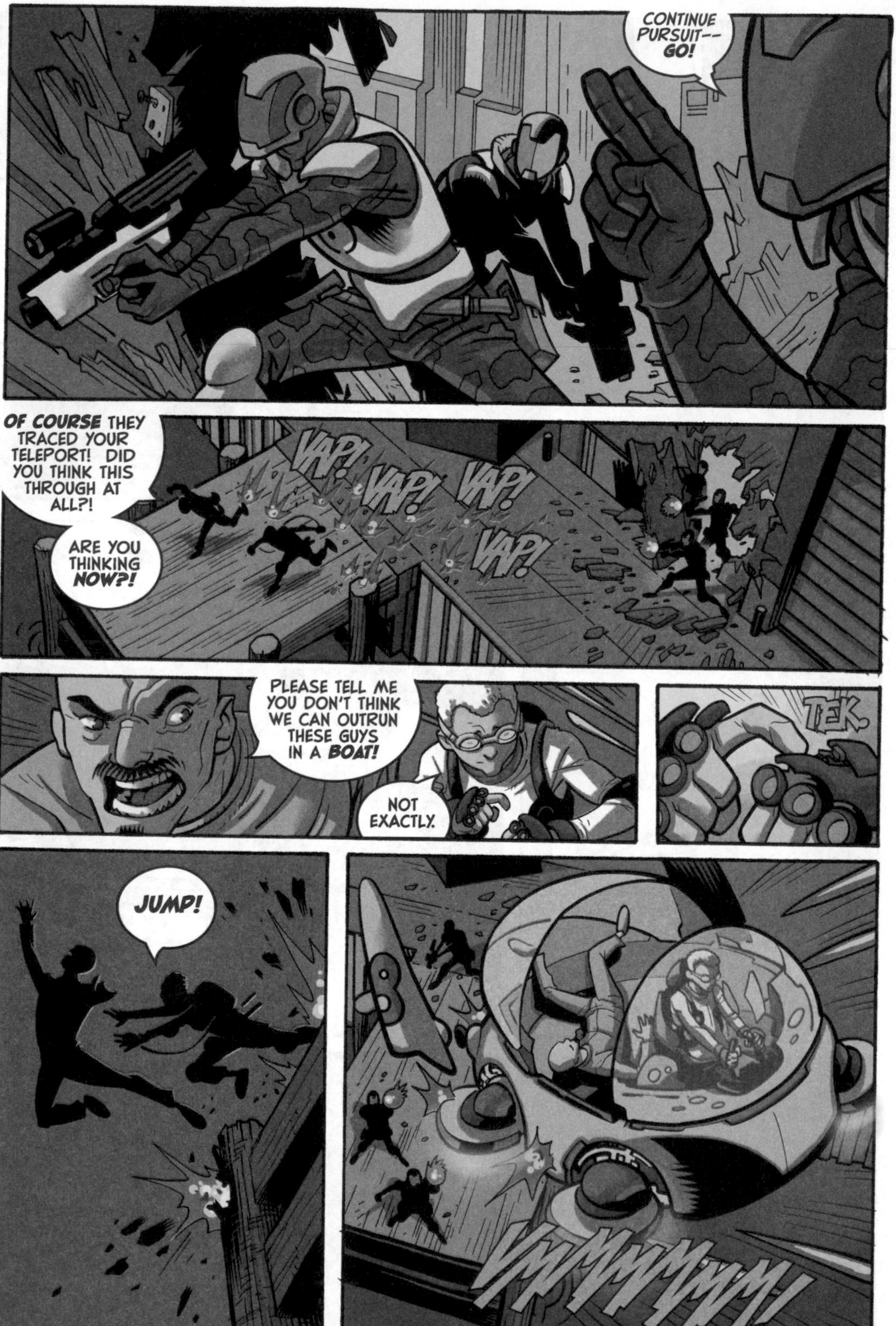
CONTINUE PURSUIT-- GO!
OF COURSE THEY TRACED YOUR TELEPORT! DID YOU THINK THIS THROUGH AT ALL?!
ARE YOU THINKING NOW?!
VAP! VAP! VAP! VAP!
PLEASE TELL ME YOU DON'T THINK WE CAN OUTRUN THESE GUYS IN A BOAT!
NOT EXACTLY.
TEK.
JUMP!
VMMMMMMM!

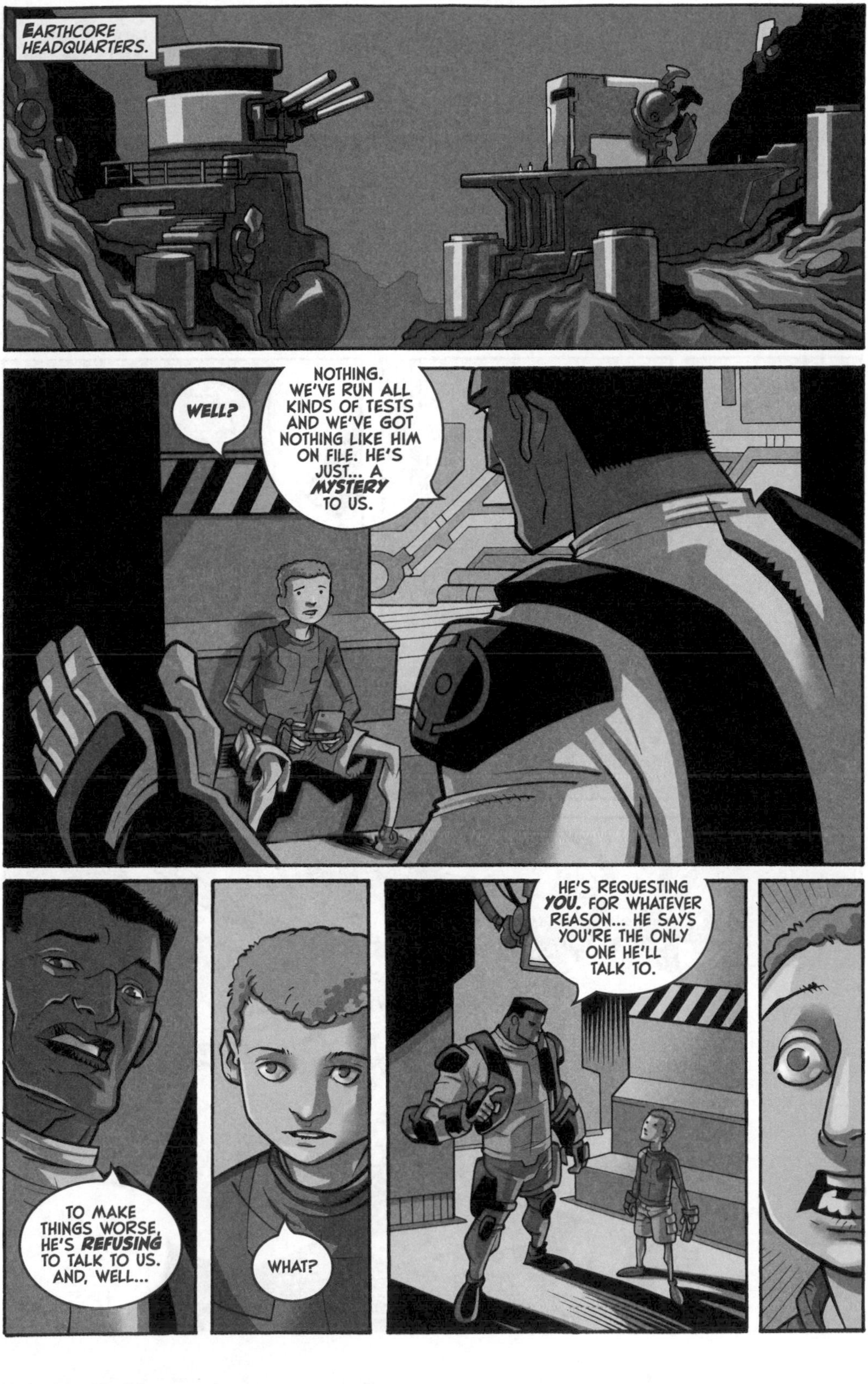
EARTHCORE HEADQUARTERS.
WELL?
NOTHING. WE'VE RUN ALL KINDS OF TESTS AND WE'VE GOT NOTHING LIKE HIM ON FILE. HE'S JUST... A MYSTERY TO US.
TO MAKE THINGS WORSE, HE'S REFUSING TO TALK TO US. AND, WELL...
WHAT?
HE'S REQUESTING YOU. FOR WHATEVER REASON... HE SAYS YOU'RE THE ONLY ONE HE'LL TALK TO.

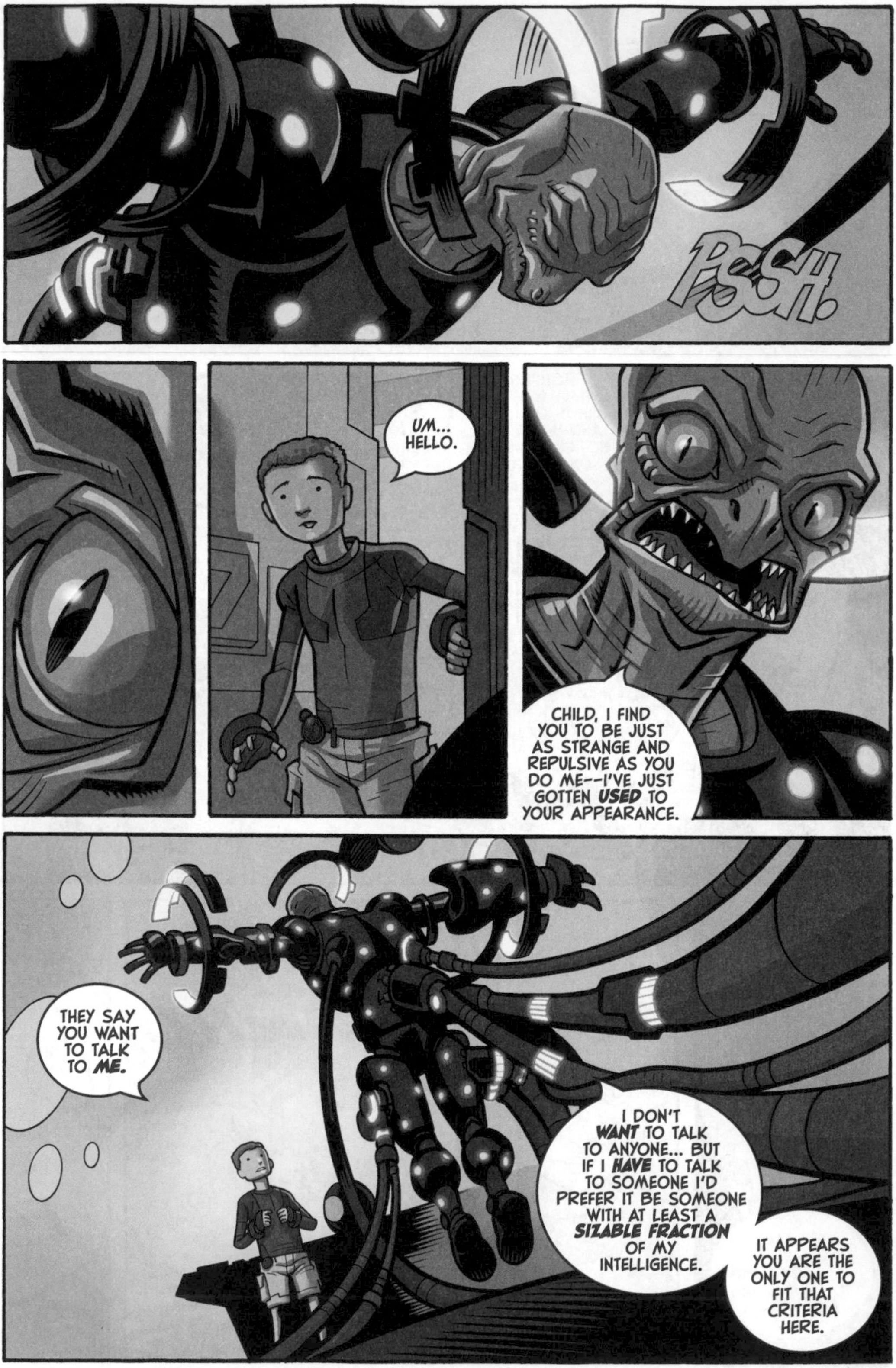
PSSH.
UM... HELLO.
CHILD, I FIND YOU TO BE JUST AS STRANGE AND REPULSIVE AS YOU DO ME--I'VE JUST GOTTEN USED TO YOUR APPEARANCE.
THEY SAY YOU WANT TO TALK TO ME.
I DON'T WANT TO TALK TO ANYONE... BUT IF I HAVE TO TALK TO SOMEONE I'D PREFER IT BE SOMEONE WITH AT LEAST A SIZABLE FRACTION OF MY INTELLIGENCE.
IT APPEARS YOU ARE THE ONLY ONE TO FIT THAT CRITERIA HERE.

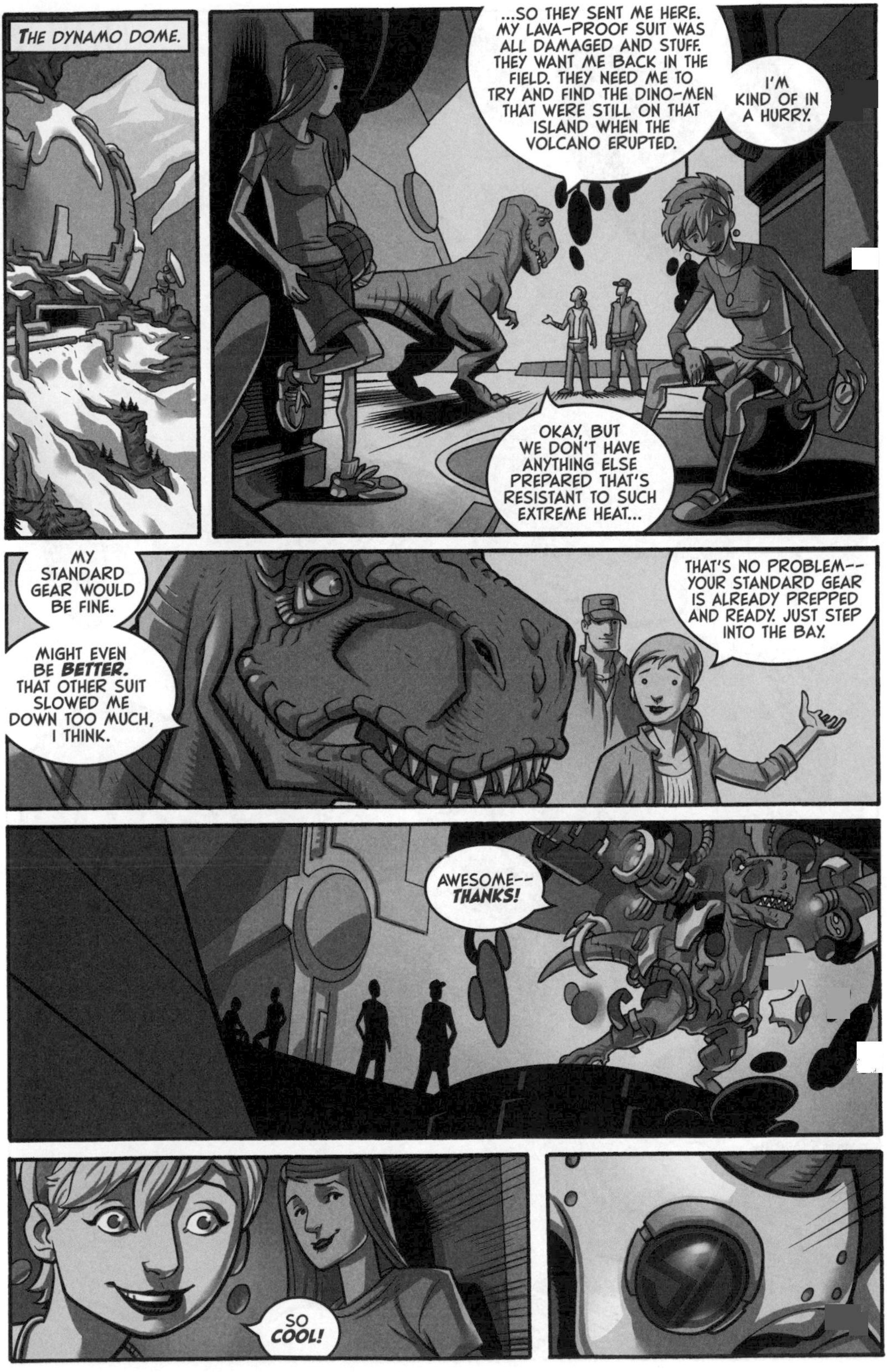
THE DYNAMO DOME.
...SO THEY SENT ME HERE. MY LAVA-PROOF SUIT WAS ALL DAMAGED AND STUFF. THEY WANT ME BACK IN THE FIELD. THEY NEED ME TO TRY AND FIND THE DINO-MEN THAT WERE STILL ON THAT ISLAND WHEN THE VOLCANO ERUPTED.
I'M KIND OF IN A HURRY.
OKAY, BUT WE DON'T HAVE ANYTHING ELSE PREPARED THAT'S RESISTANT TO SUCH EXTREME HEAT...
MY STANDARD GEAR WOULD BE FINE.
MIGHT EVEN BE BETTER. THAT OTHER SUIT SLOWED ME DOWN TOO MUCH, I THINK.
THAT'S NO PROBLEM-- YOUR STANDARD GEAR IS ALREADY PREPPED AND READY. JUST STEP INTO THE BAY.
AWESOME-- THANKS!
SO COOL!

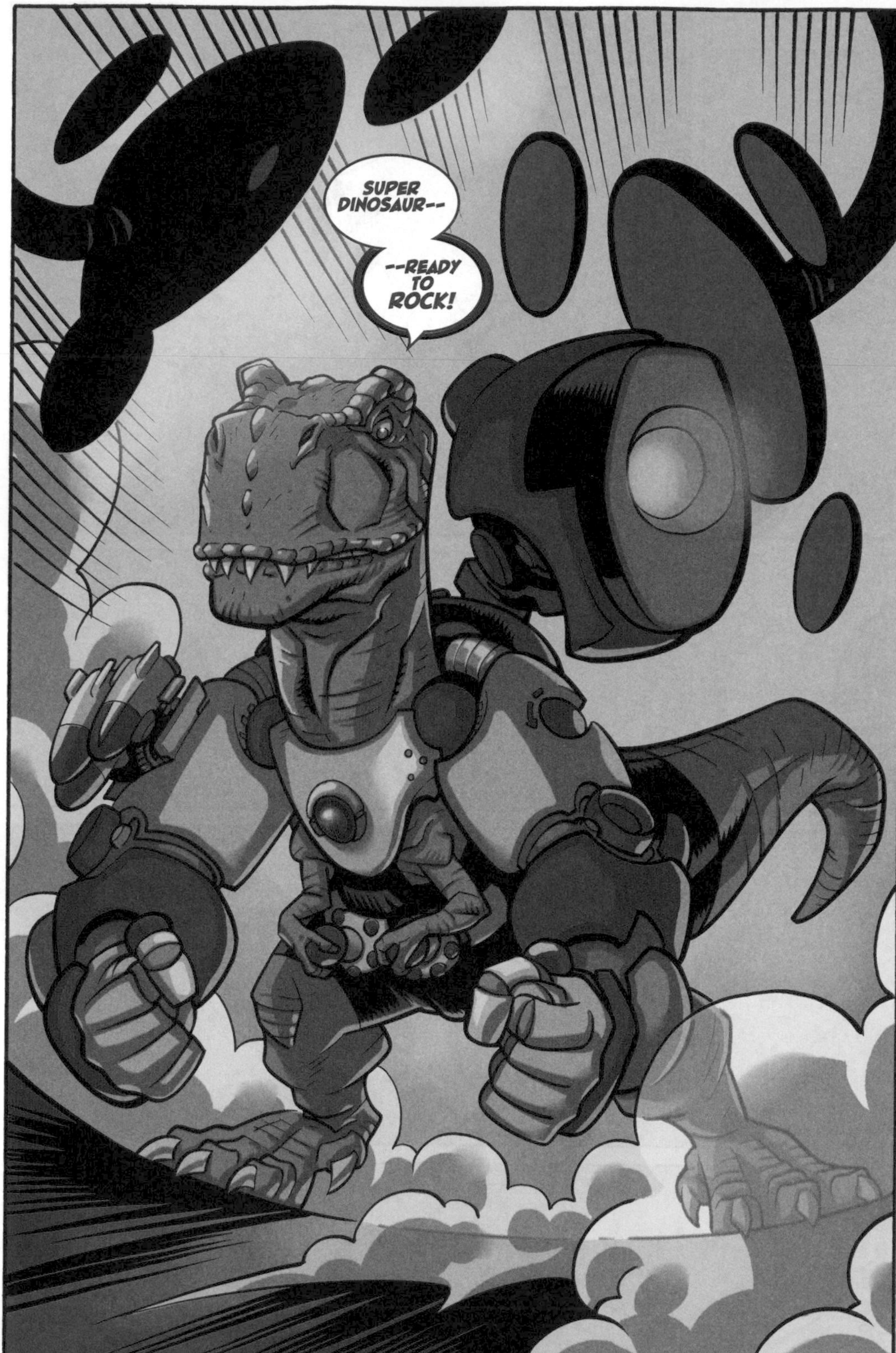
SUPER DINOSAUR--
--READY TO ROCK!

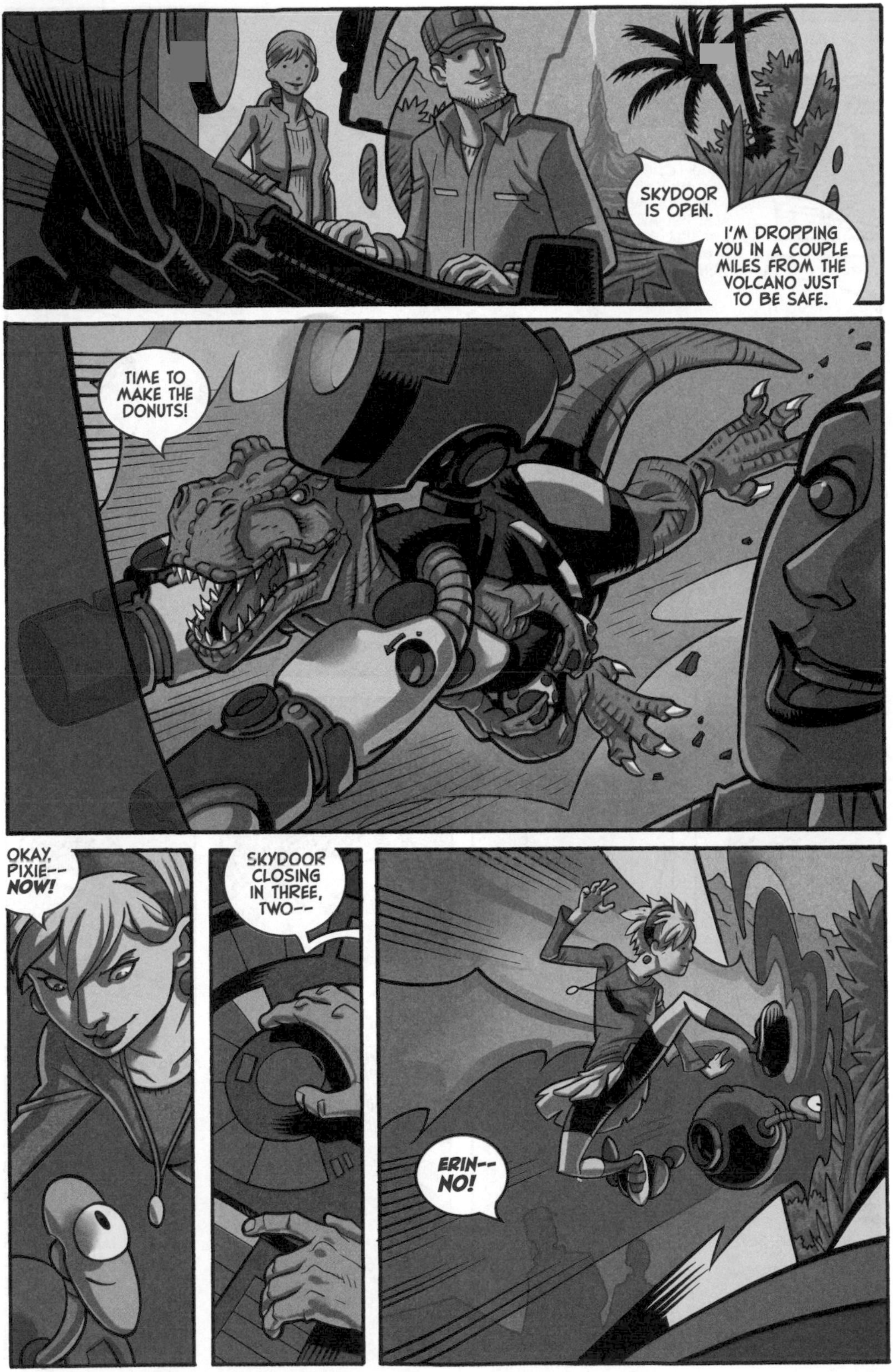
SKYDOOR IS OPEN.
I'M DROPPING YOU IN A COUPLE MILES FROM THE VOLCANO JUST TO BE SAFE.
TIME TO MAKE THE DONUTS!
OKAY, PIXIE-- NOW!
SKYDOOR CLOSING IN THREE, TWO--
ERIN-- NO!

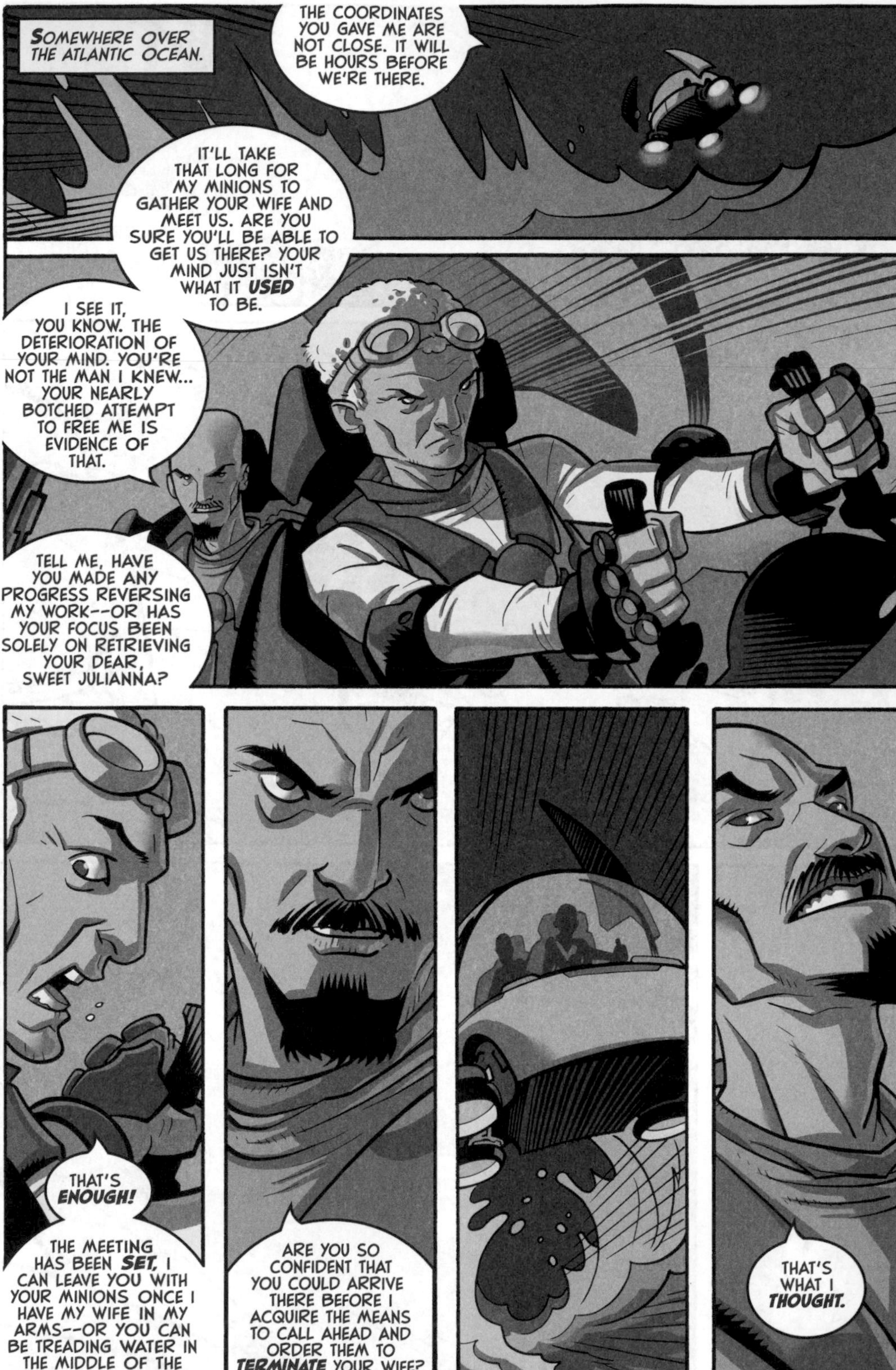
SOMEWHERE OVER THE ATLANTIC OCEAN.
THE COORDINATES YOU GAVE ME ARE NOT CLOSE. IT WILL BE HOURS BEFORE WE'RE THERE.
IT'LL TAKE THAT LONG FOR MY MINIONS TO GATHER YOUR WIFE AND MEET US. ARE YOU SURE YOU'LL BE ABLE TO GET US THERE? YOUR MIND JUST ISN'T WHAT IT USED TO BE.
I SEE IT, YOU KNOW. THE DETERIORATION OF YOUR MIND. YOU'RE NOT THE MAN I KNEW... YOUR NEARLY BOTCHED ATTEMPT TO FREE ME IS EVIDENCE OF THAT.
TELL ME, HAVE YOU MADE ANY PROGRESS REVERSING MY WORK--OR HAS YOUR FOCUS BEEN SOLELY ON RETRIEVING YOUR DEAR, SWEET JULIANNA?
THAT'S ENOUGH!
THE MEETING HAS BEEN SET, I CAN LEAVE YOU WITH YOUR MINIONS ONCE I HAVE MY WIFE IN MY ARMS--OR YOU CAN BE TREADING WATER IN THE MIDDLE OF THE OCEAN WHEN I ARRIVE.
ARE YOU SO CONFIDENT THAT YOU COULD ARRIVE THERE BEFORE I ACQUIRE THE MEANS TO CALL AHEAD AND ORDER THEM TO TERMINATE YOUR WIFE?
THAT'S WHAT I THOUGHT.

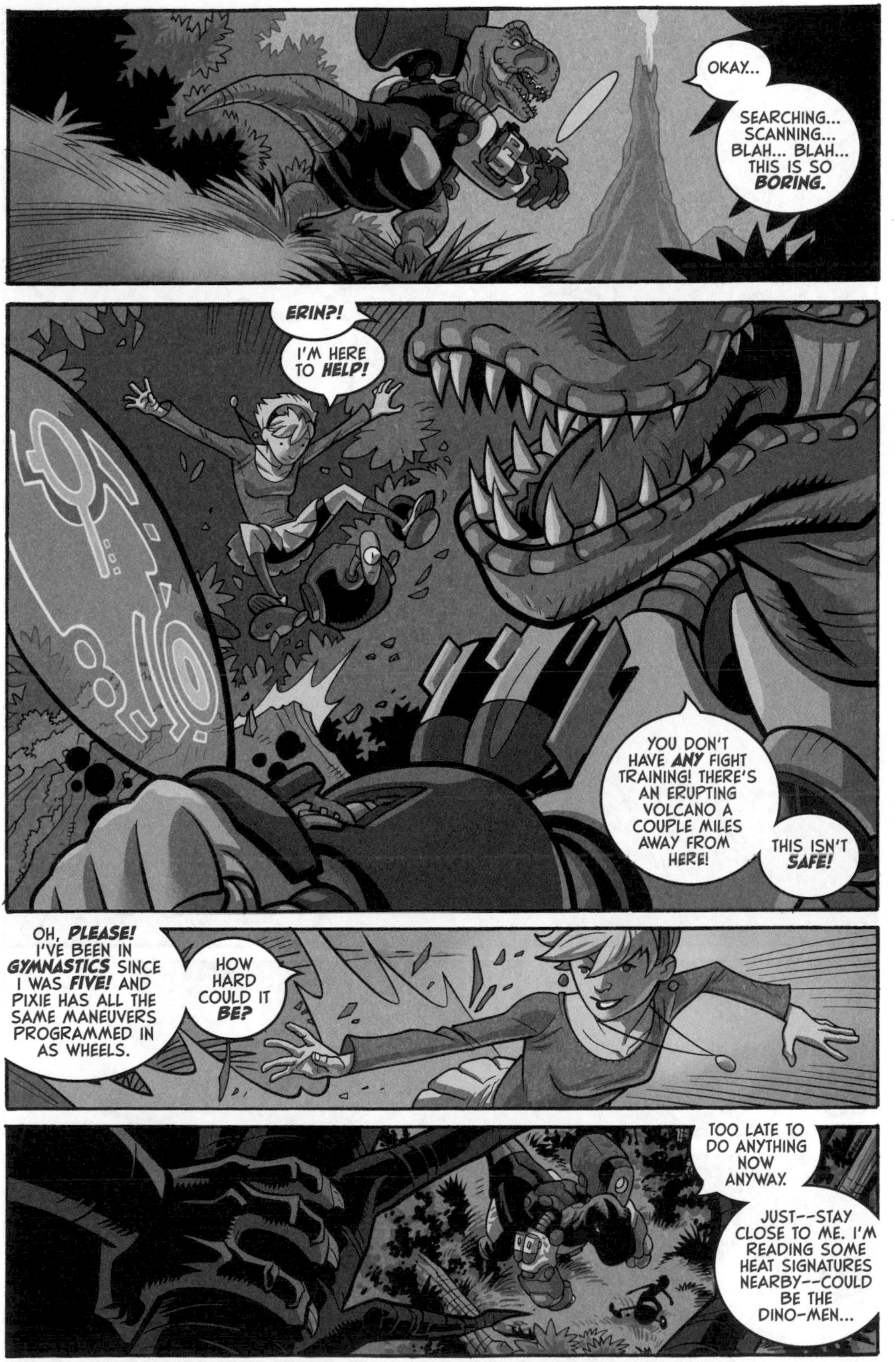
OKAY...
SEARCHING... SCANNING... BLAH... BLAH... THIS IS SO BORING.
ERIN?!
I'M HERE TO HELP!
YOU DON'T HAVE ANY FIGHT TRAINING! THERE'S AN ERUPTING VOLCANO A COUPLE MILES AWAY FROM HERE!
THIS ISN'T SAFE!
OH, PLEASE! I'VE BEEN IN GYMNASTICS SINCE I WAS FIVE! AND PIXIE HAS ALL THE SAME MANEUVERS PROGRAMMED IN AS WHEELS.
HOW HARD COULD IT BE?
TOO LATE TO DO ANYTHING NOW ANYWAY.
JUST--STAY CLOSE TO ME. I'M READING SOME HEAT SIGNATURES NEARBY--COULD BE THE DINO-MEN...

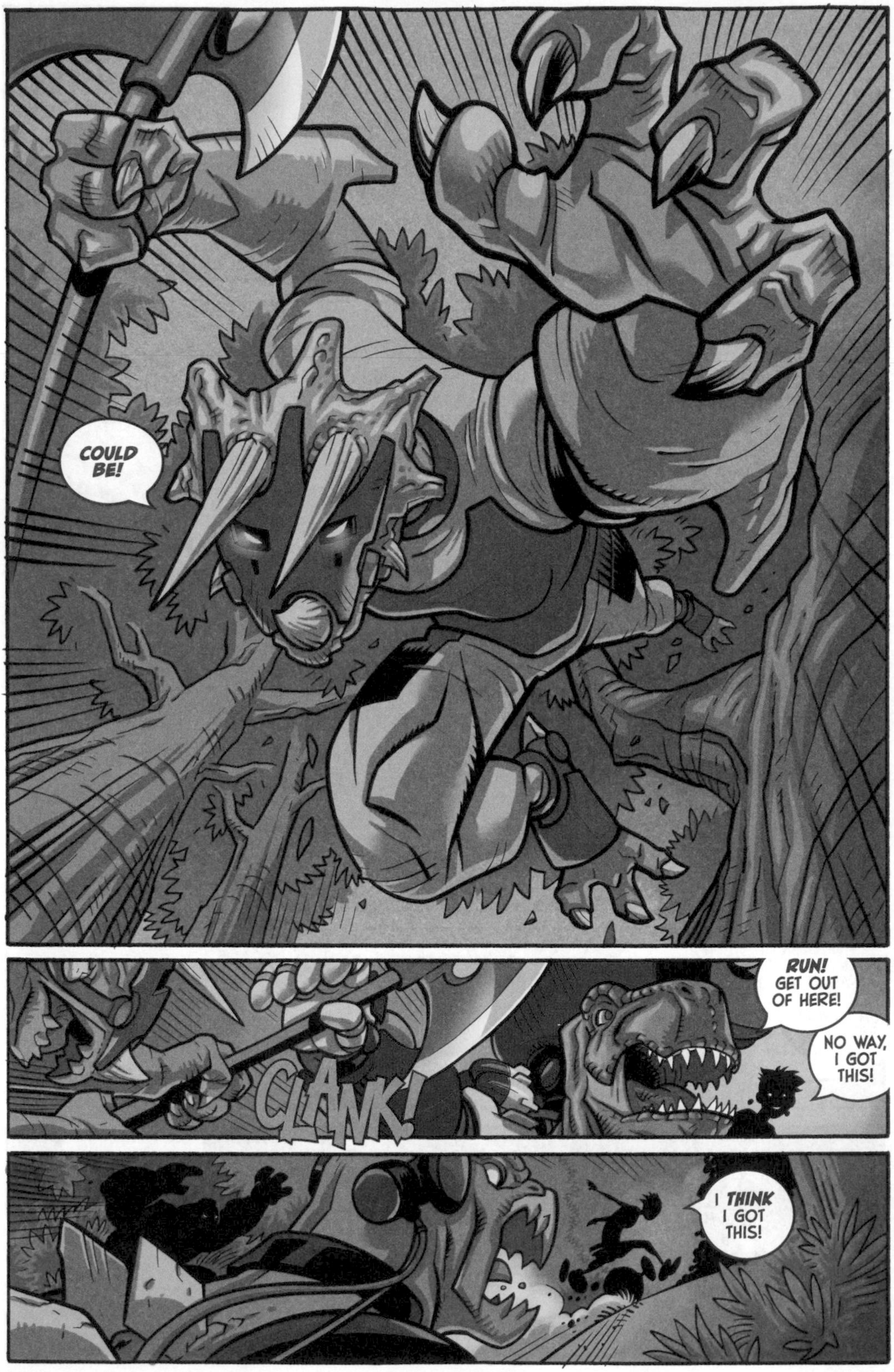
COULD BE!
CLANK!
RUN! GET OUT OF HERE!
NO WAY, I GOT THIS!
I THINK I GOT THIS!

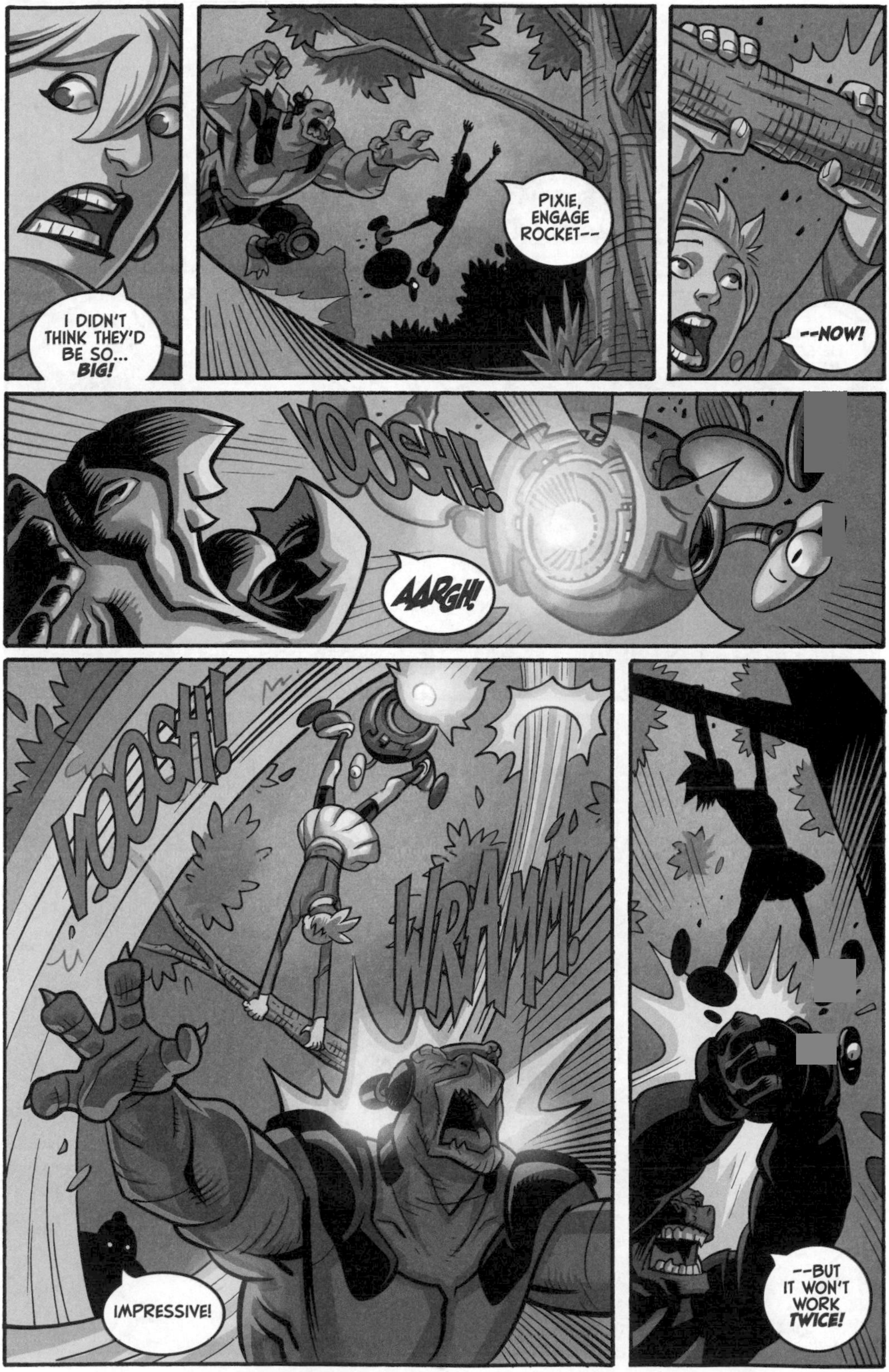
I DIDN'T THINK THEY'D BE SO... *BIG!*
PIXIE, ENGAGE ROCKET--
--NOW!
VOOSH!!
AARGH!
VOOSH!
WRAMM!
IMPRESSIVE!
--BUT IT WON'T WORK *TWICE!*

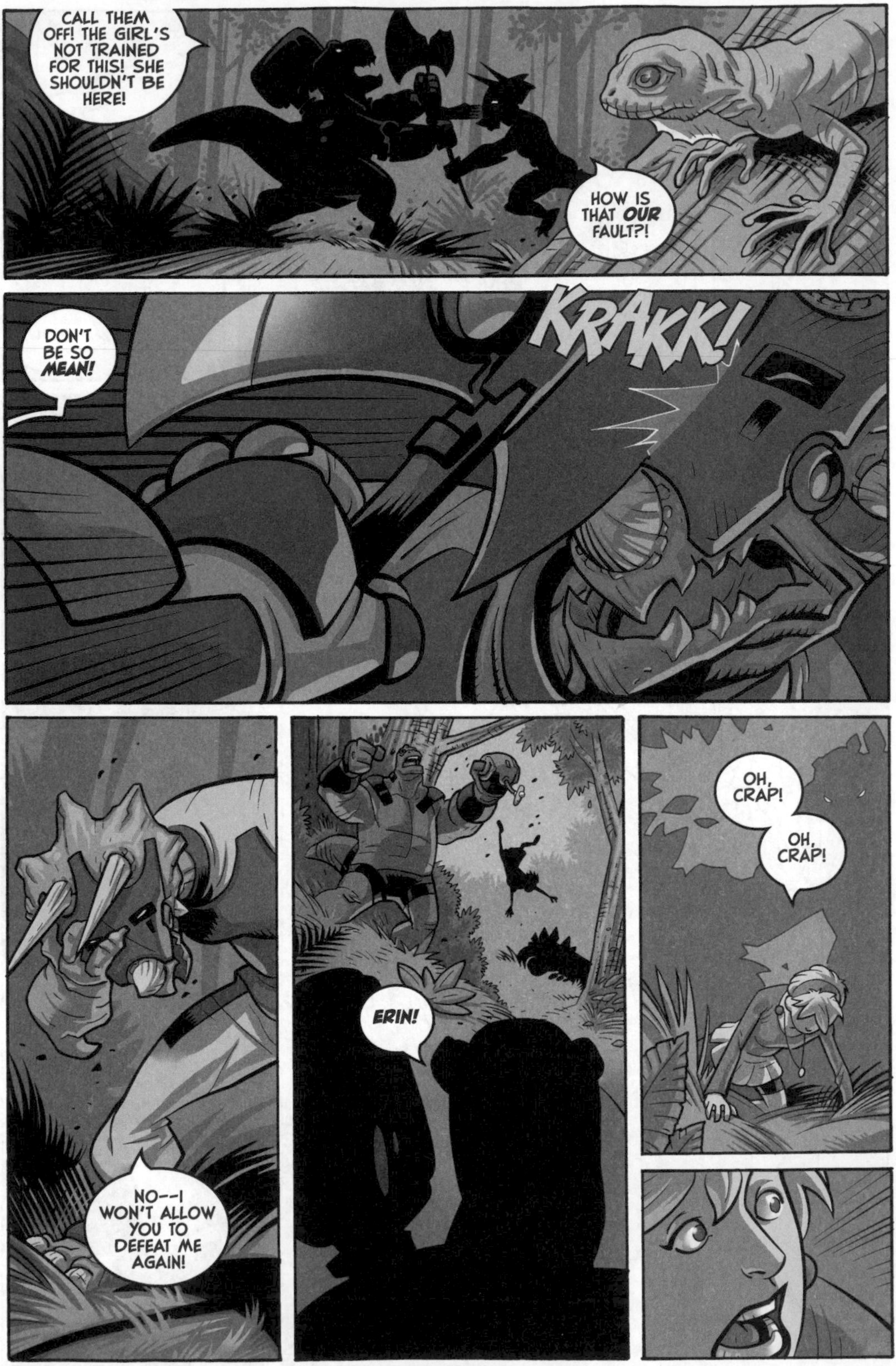
CALL THEM OFF! THE GIRL'S NOT TRAINED FOR THIS! SHE SHOULDN'T BE HERE!
HOW IS THAT *OUR* FAULT?!
DON'T BE SO *MEAN!*
KRAKK!
NO--I WON'T ALLOW YOU TO DEFEAT ME AGAIN!
ERIN!
OH, CRAP!
OH, CRAP!

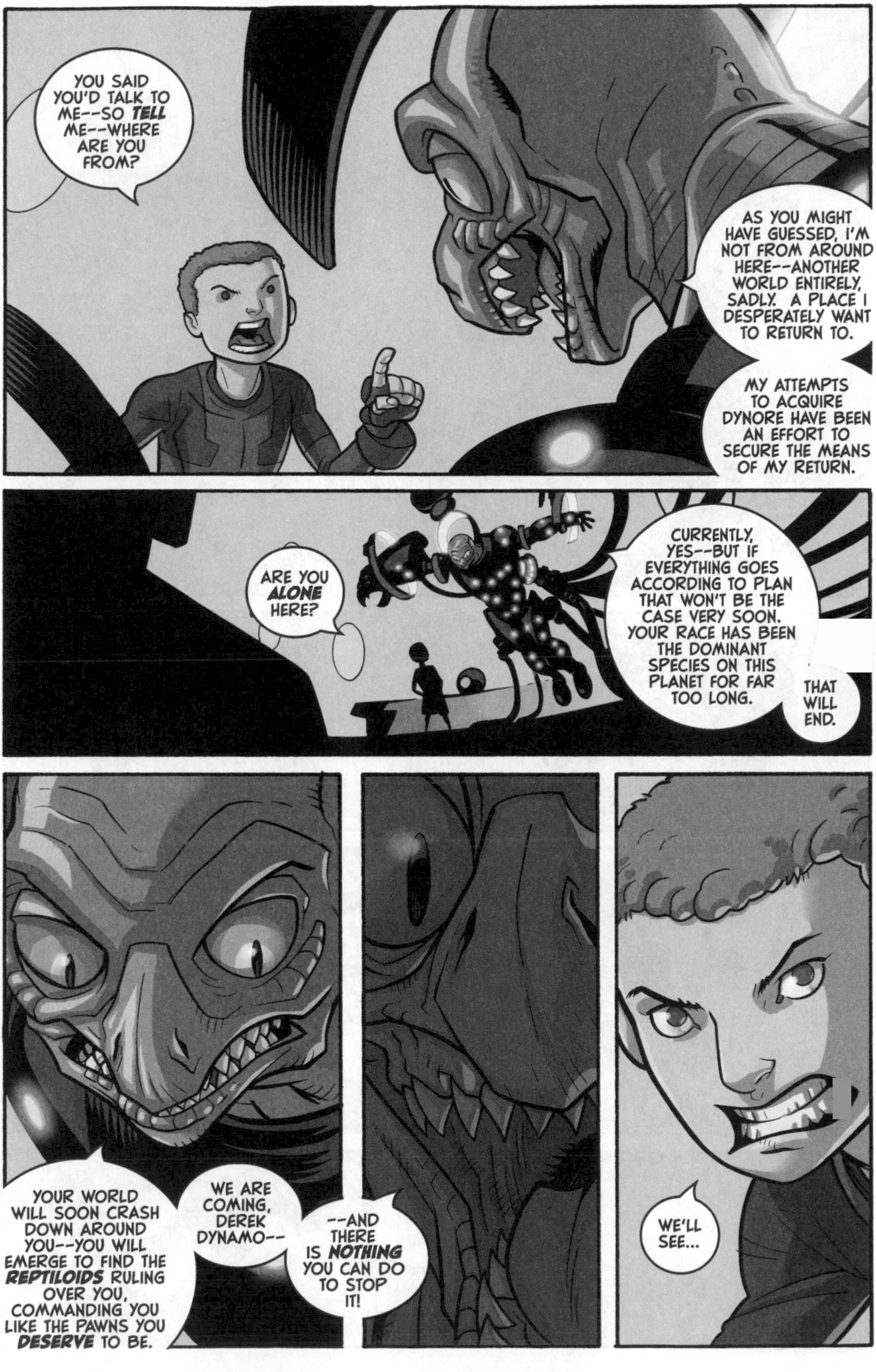
YOU SAID YOU'D TALK TO ME--SO TELL ME--WHERE ARE YOU FROM?
AS YOU MIGHT HAVE GUESSED, I'M NOT FROM AROUND HERE--ANOTHER WORLD ENTIRELY, SADLY. A PLACE I DESPERATELY WANT TO RETURN TO.
MY ATTEMPTS TO ACQUIRE DYNORE HAVE BEEN AN EFFORT TO SECURE THE MEANS OF MY RETURN.
ARE YOU ALONE HERE?
CURRENTLY, YES--BUT IF EVERYTHING GOES ACCORDING TO PLAN THAT WON'T BE THE CASE VERY SOON. YOUR RACE HAS BEEN THE DOMINANT SPECIES ON THIS PLANET FOR FAR TOO LONG.
THAT WILL END.
YOUR WORLD WILL SOON CRASH DOWN AROUND YOU--YOU WILL EMERGE TO FIND THE REPTILOIDS RULING OVER YOU, COMMANDING YOU LIKE THE PAWNS YOU DESERVE TO BE.
WE ARE COMING, DEREK DYNAMO--
--AND THERE IS NOTHING YOU CAN DO TO STOP IT!
WE'LL SEE...

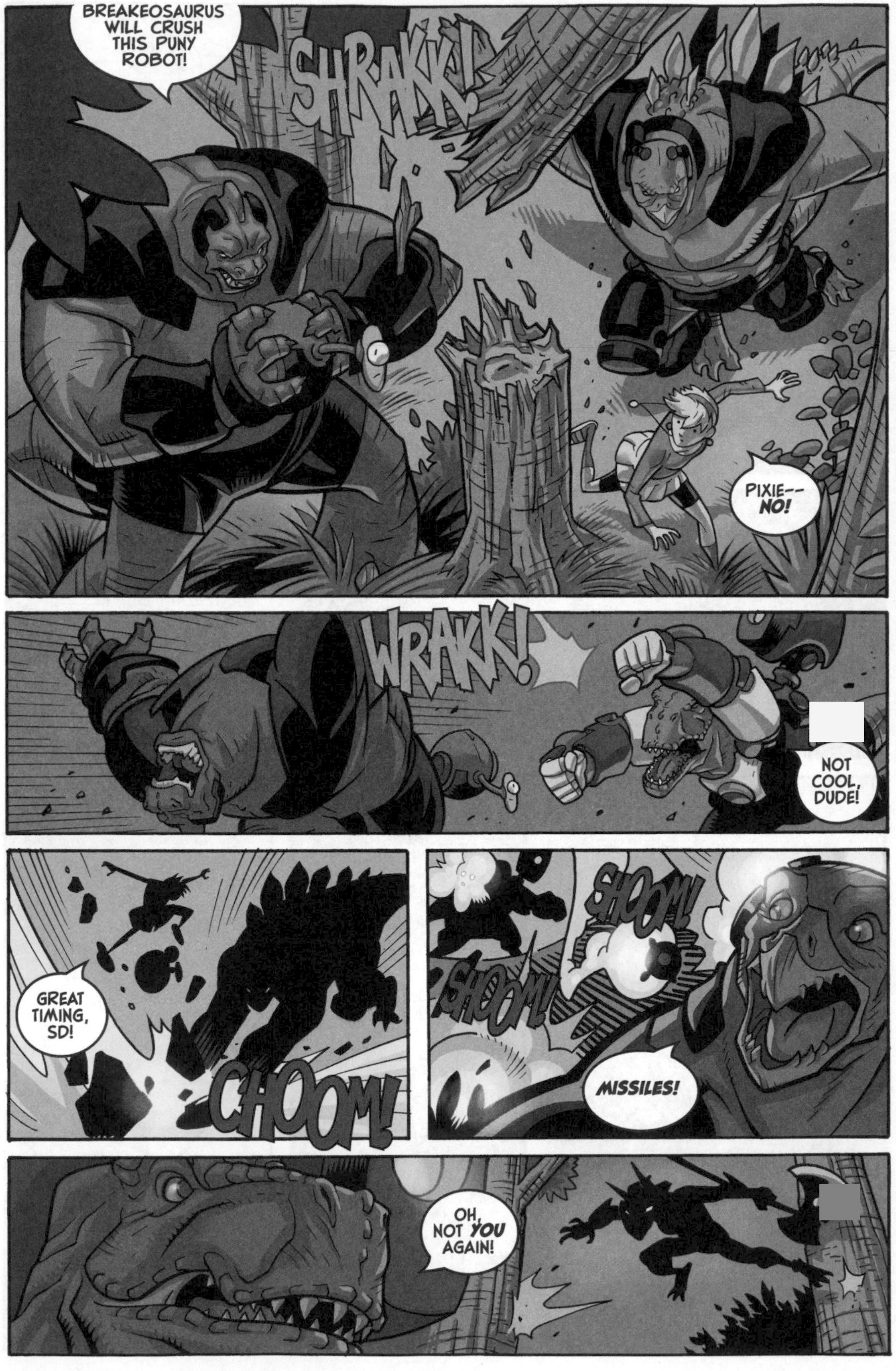
BREAKEOSAURUS WILL CRUSH THIS PUNY ROBOT!
SHRAKK!
PIXIE-- NO!
WRAKK!
NOT COOL, DUDE!
GREAT TIMING, SD!
CHOOM!
SHOOM!
SHOOM!
MISSILES!
OH, NOT YOU AGAIN!

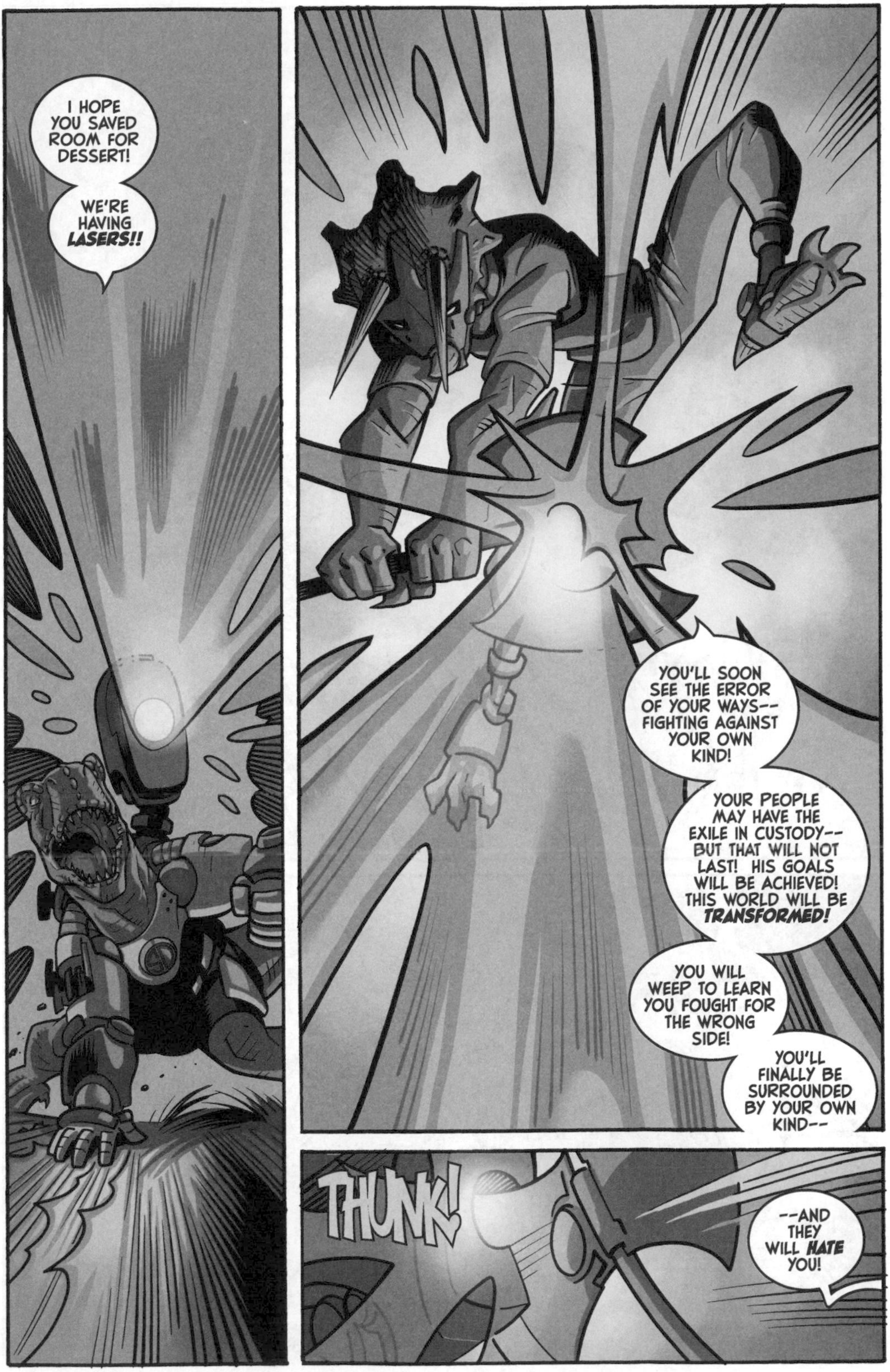
I HOPE YOU SAVED ROOM FOR DESSERT!
WE'RE HAVING LASERS!!
YOU'LL SOON SEE THE ERROR OF YOUR WAYS-- FIGHTING AGAINST YOUR OWN KIND!
YOUR PEOPLE MAY HAVE THE EXILE IN CUSTODY-- BUT THAT WILL NOT LAST! HIS GOALS WILL BE ACHIEVED! THIS WORLD WILL BE TRANSFORMED!
YOU WILL WEEP TO LEARN YOU FOUGHT FOR THE WRONG SIDE!
YOU'LL FINALLY BE SURROUNDED BY YOUR OWN KIND--
THUNK!
--AND THEY WILL HATE YOU!

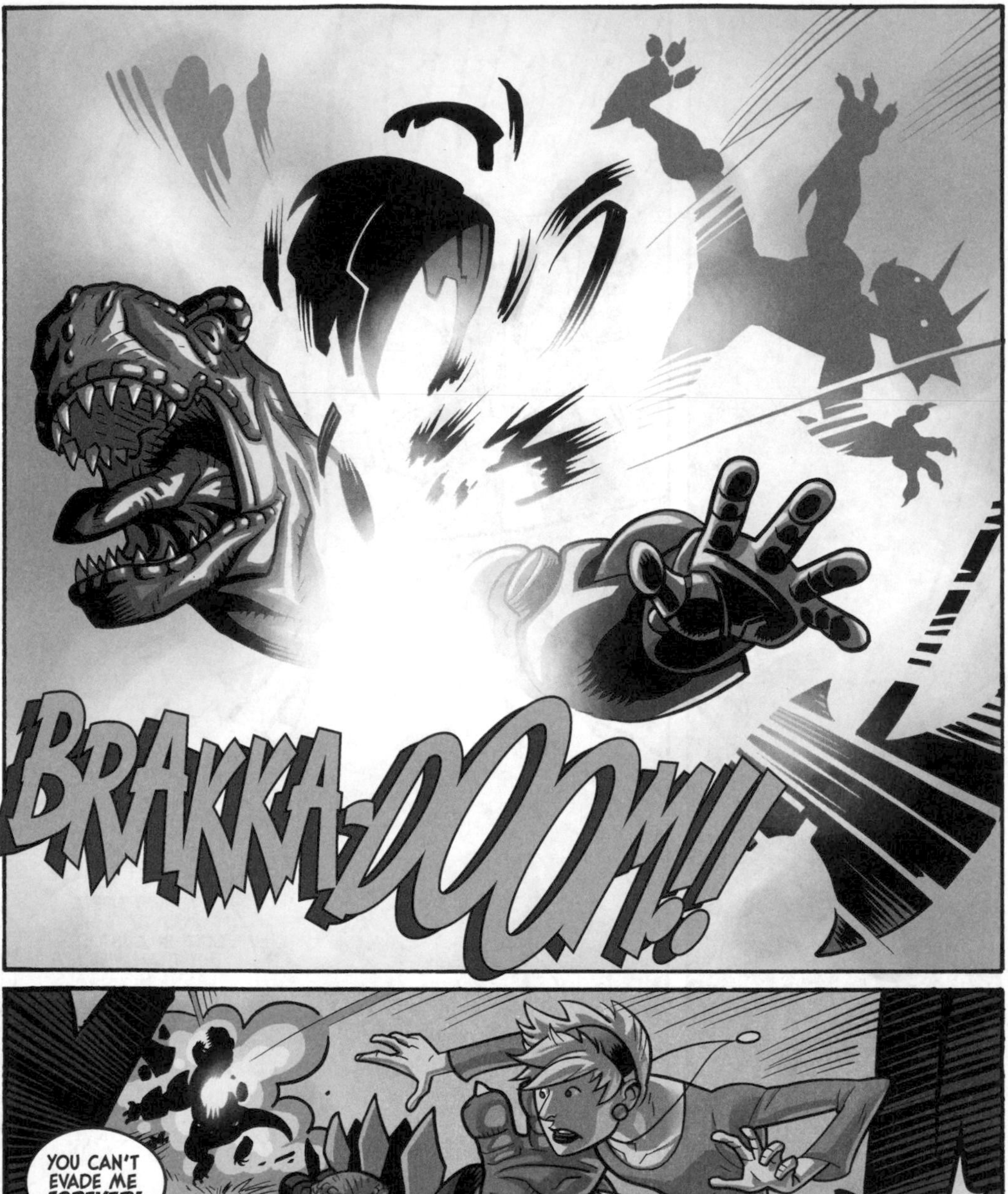
BRAKKA-DOOOM!!

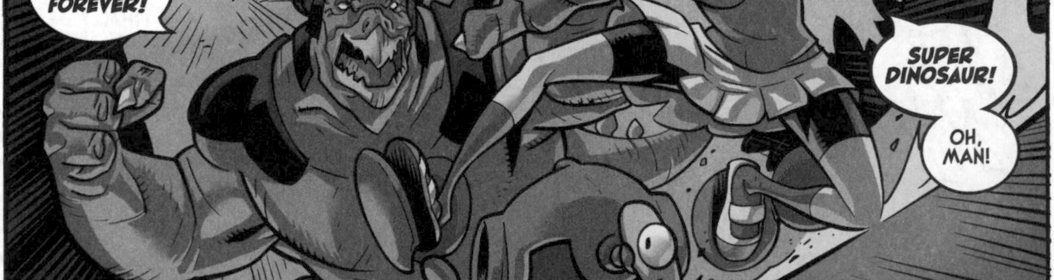
YOU CAN'T EVADE ME **FOREVER!**
SUPER DINOSAUR!
OH, MAN!

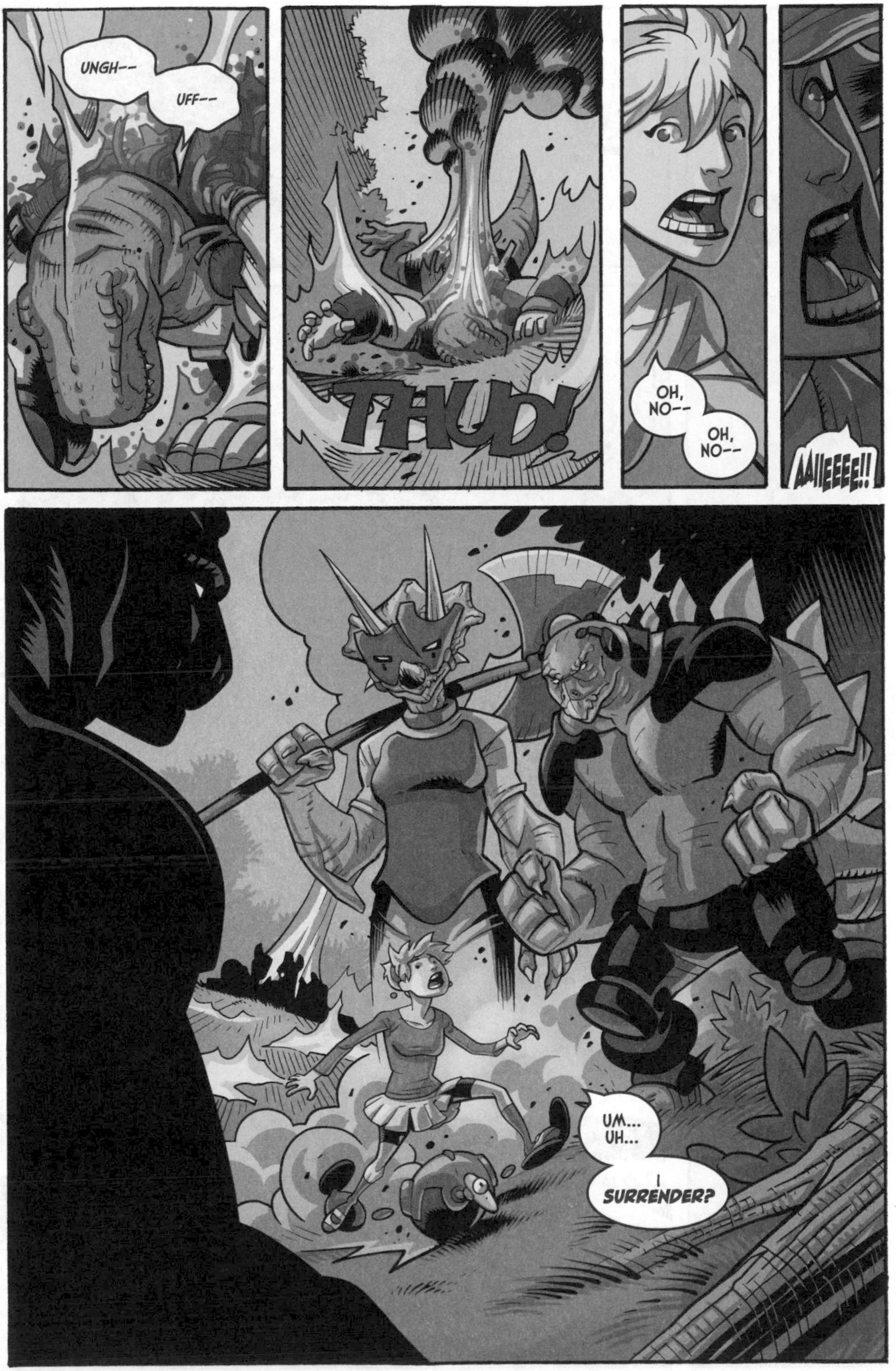
UNGH--
UFF--
THUD!
OH, NO--
OH, NO--
AAIIEEEE!!
UM... UH...
I SURRENDER?

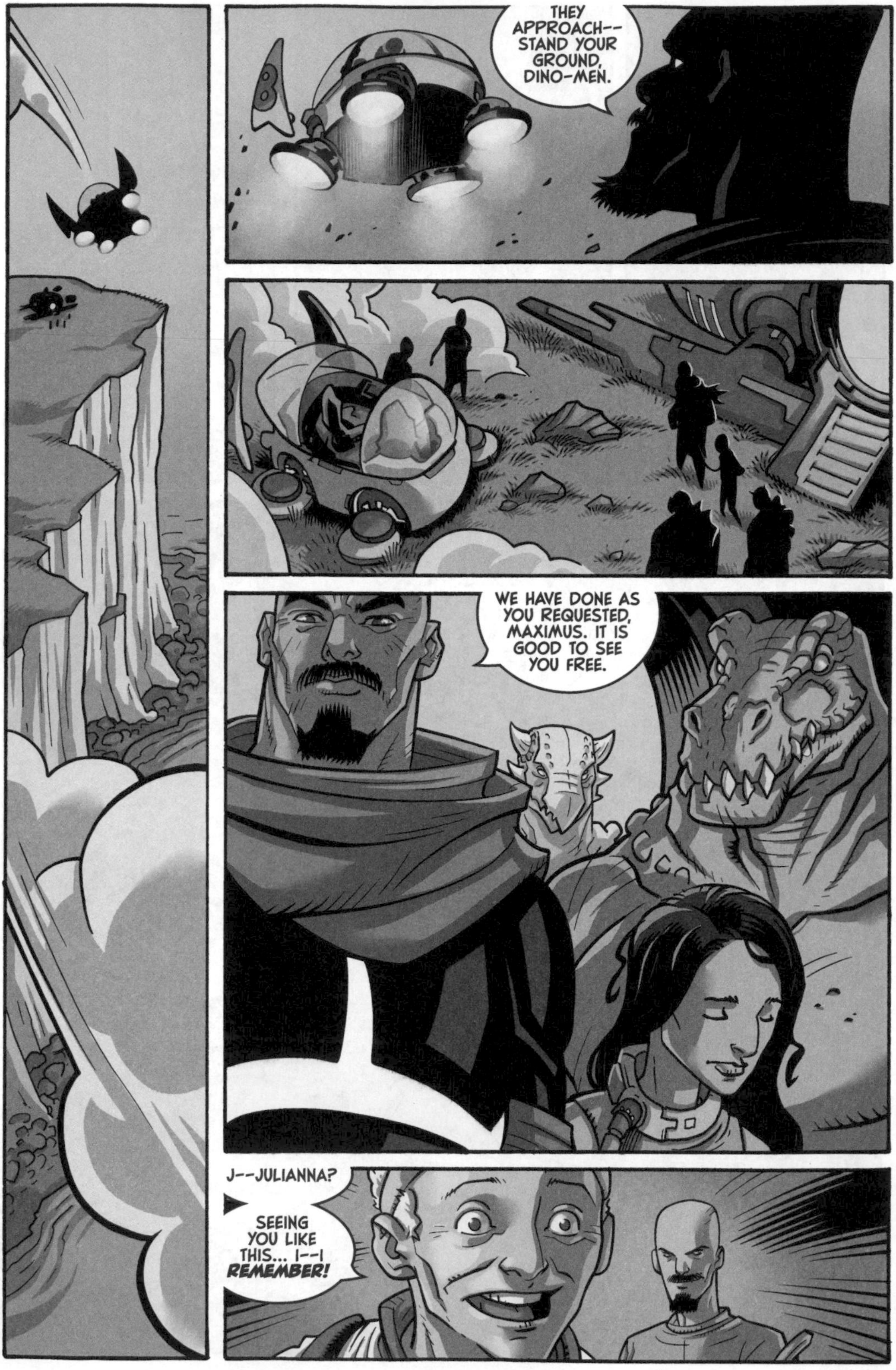
THEY APPROACH-- STAND YOUR GROUND, DINO-MEN.
WE HAVE DONE AS YOU REQUESTED, MAXIMUS. IT IS GOOD TO SEE YOU FREE.
J--JULIANNA?
SEEING YOU LIKE THIS... I--I *REMEMBER!*

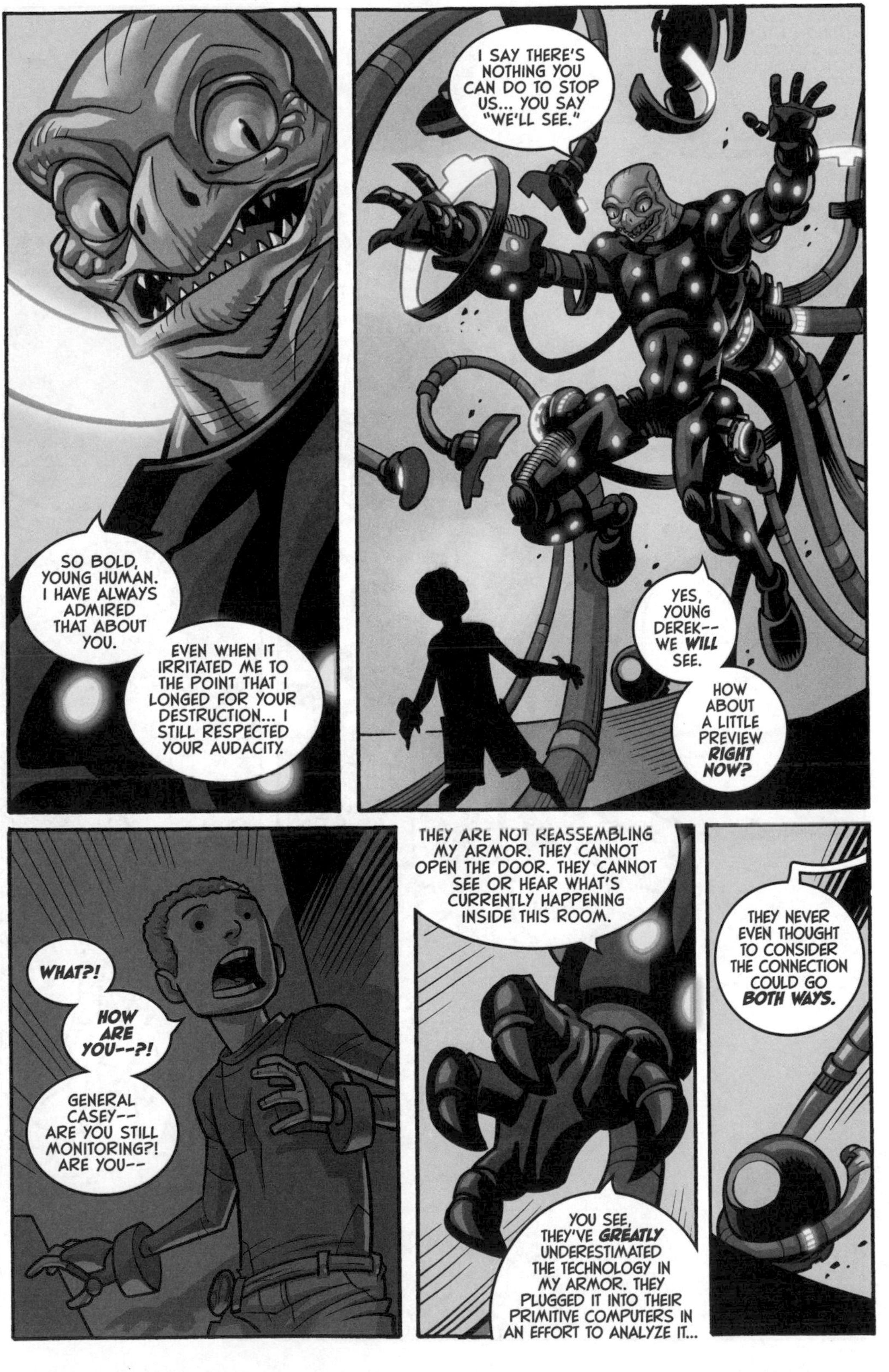
SO BOLD, YOUNG HUMAN. I HAVE ALWAYS ADMIRED THAT ABOUT YOU.
EVEN WHEN IT IRRITATED ME TO THE POINT THAT I LONGED FOR YOUR DESTRUCTION... I STILL RESPECTED YOUR AUDACITY.
I SAY THERE'S NOTHING YOU CAN DO TO STOP US... YOU SAY "WE'LL SEE."
YES, YOUNG DEREK-- WE *WILL* SEE.
HOW ABOUT A LITTLE PREVIEW ***RIGHT NOW?***
WHAT?!
HOW ARE YOU--?!
GENERAL CASEY-- ARE YOU STILL MONITORING?! ARE YOU--
THEY ARE NOT REASSEMBLING MY ARMOR. THEY CANNOT OPEN THE DOOR. THEY CANNOT SEE OR HEAR WHAT'S CURRENTLY HAPPENING INSIDE THIS ROOM.
YOU SEE, THEY'VE ***GREATLY*** UNDERESTIMATED THE TECHNOLOGY IN MY ARMOR. THEY PLUGGED IT INTO THEIR PRIMITIVE COMPUTERS IN AN EFFORT TO ANALYZE IT...
THEY NEVER EVEN THOUGHT TO CONSIDER THE CONNECTION COULD GO ***BOTH WAYS.***

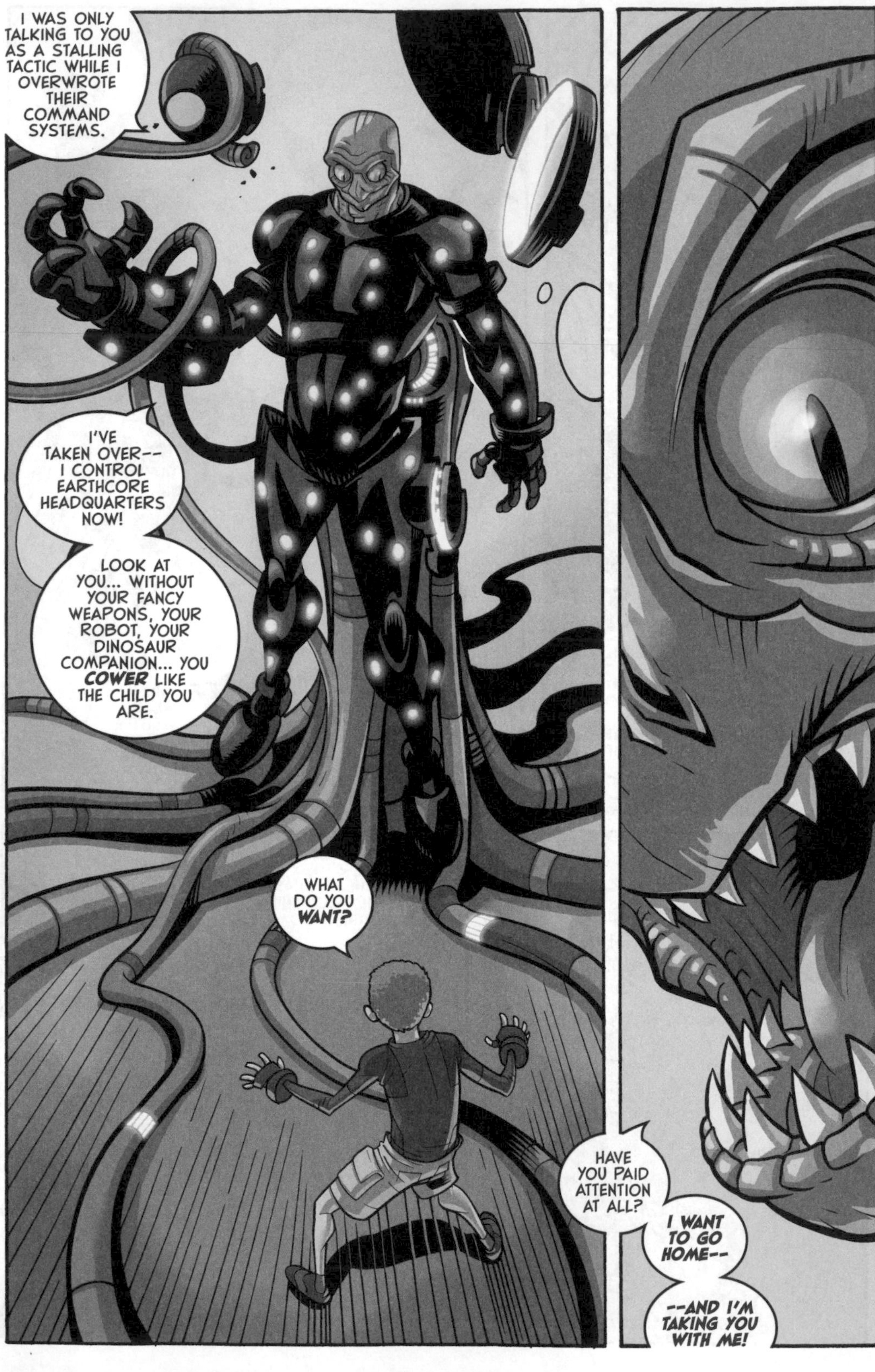
I WAS ONLY TALKING TO YOU AS A STALLING TACTIC WHILE I OVERWROTE THEIR COMMAND SYSTEMS.
I'VE TAKEN OVER-- I CONTROL EARTHCORE HEADQUARTERS NOW!
LOOK AT YOU... WITHOUT YOUR FANCY WEAPONS, YOUR ROBOT, YOUR DINOSAUR COMPANION... YOU COWER LIKE THE CHILD YOU ARE.
WHAT DO YOU WANT?
HAVE YOU PAID ATTENTION AT ALL?
I WANT TO GO HOME--
--AND I'M TAKING YOU WITH ME!

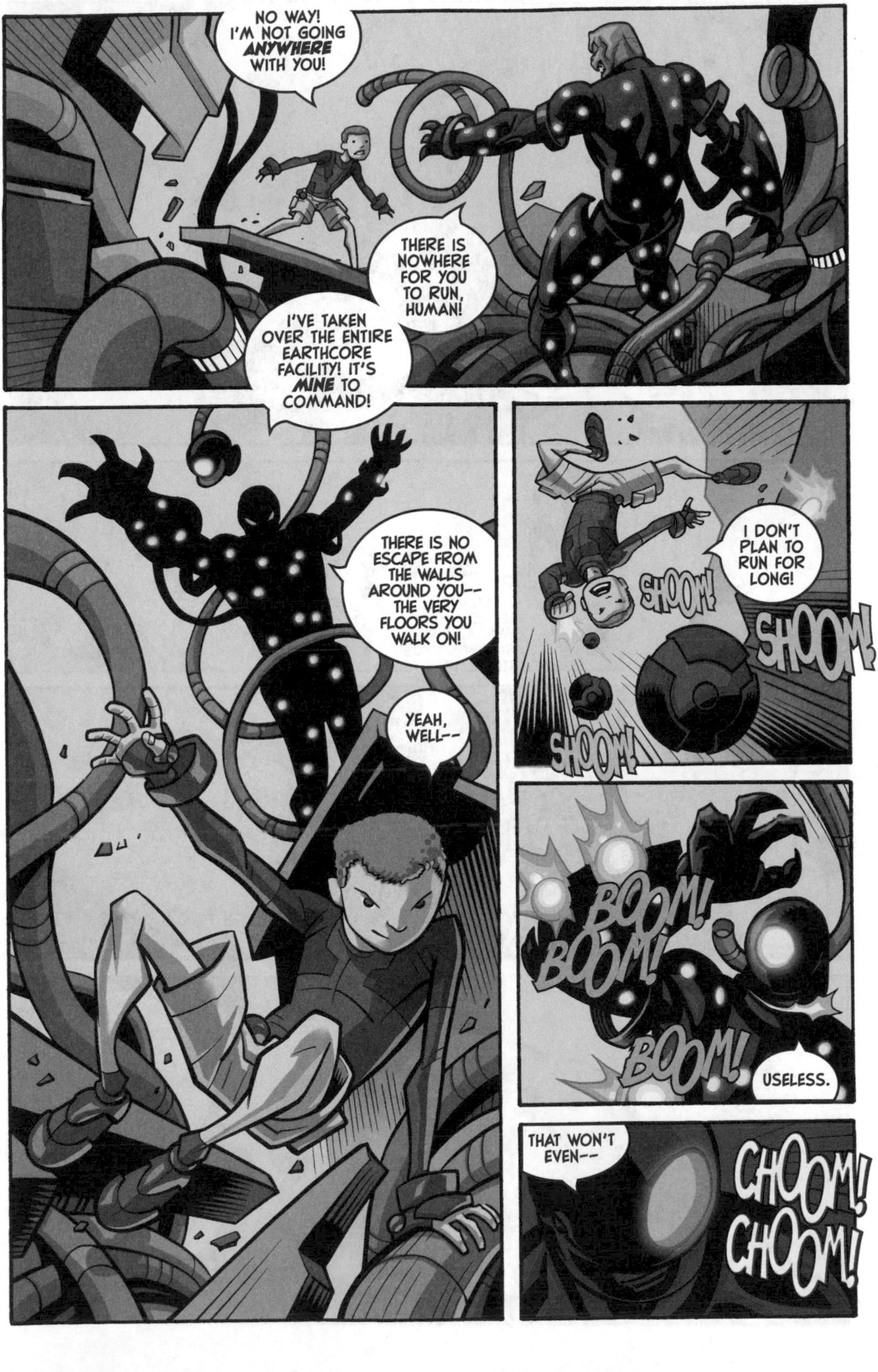
NO WAY! I'M NOT GOING ANYWHERE WITH YOU!
THERE IS NOWHERE FOR YOU TO RUN, HUMAN!
I'VE TAKEN OVER THE ENTIRE EARTHCORE FACILITY! IT'S MINE TO COMMAND!
THERE IS NO ESCAPE FROM THE WALLS AROUND YOU-- THE VERY FLOORS YOU WALK ON!
YEAH, WELL--
I DON'T PLAN TO RUN FOR LONG!
SHOOM!
SHOOM!
SHOOM!
BOOM!
BOOM!
BOOM!
USELESS.
THAT WON'T EVEN--
CHOOM!
CHOOM!

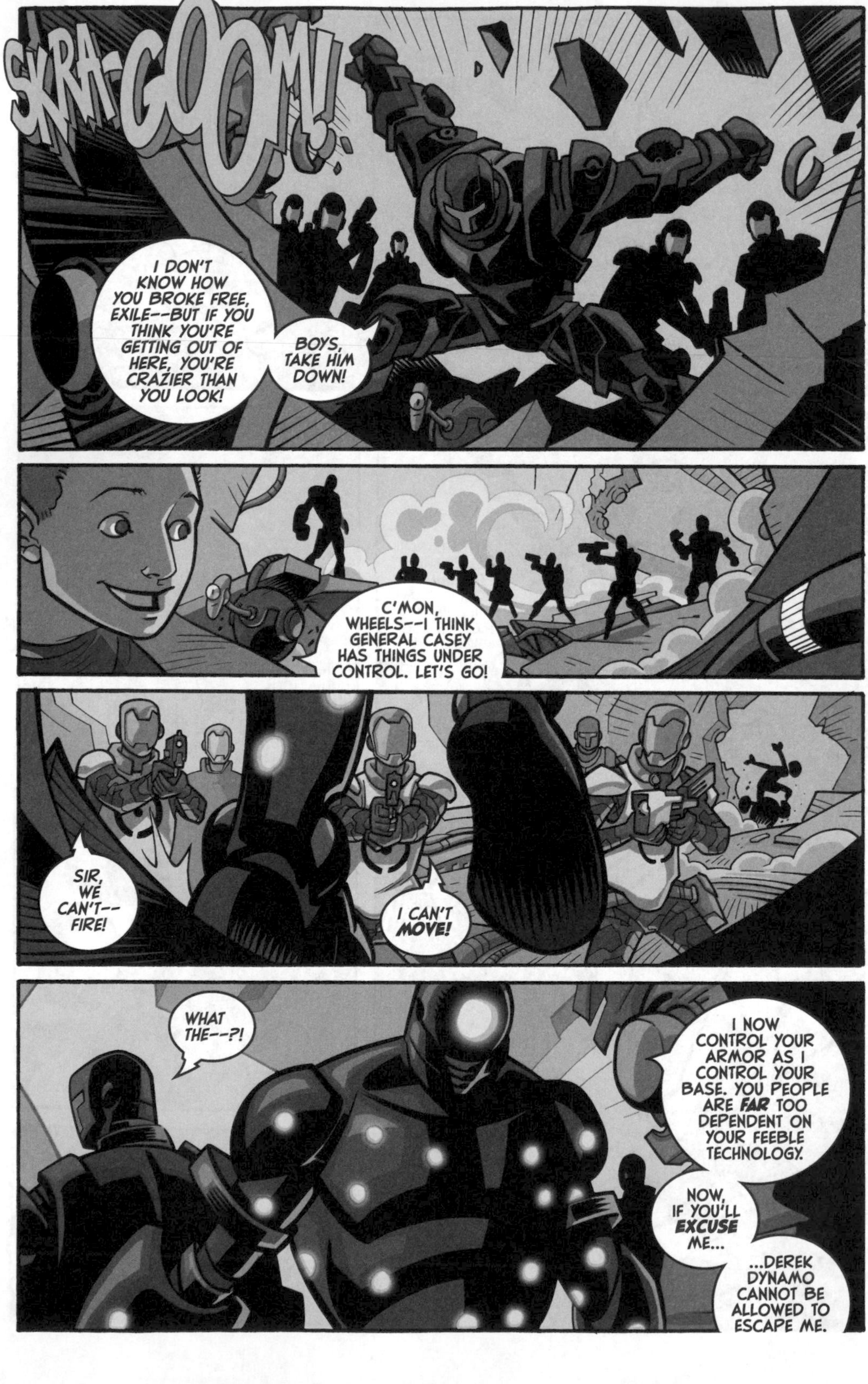
SKRA-GOOM!!
I DON'T KNOW HOW YOU BROKE FREE, EXILE--BUT IF YOU THINK YOU'RE GETTING OUT OF HERE, YOU'RE CRAZIER THAN YOU LOOK!
BOYS, TAKE HIM DOWN!
C'MON, WHEELS--I THINK GENERAL CASEY HAS THINGS UNDER CONTROL. LET'S GO!
SIR, WE CAN'T--FIRE!
I CAN'T MOVE!
WHAT THE--?!
I NOW CONTROL YOUR ARMOR AS I CONTROL YOUR BASE. YOU PEOPLE ARE FAR TOO DEPENDENT ON YOUR FEEBLE TECHNOLOGY.
NOW, IF YOU'LL EXCUSE ME...
...DEREK DYNAMO CANNOT BE ALLOWED TO ESCAPE ME.

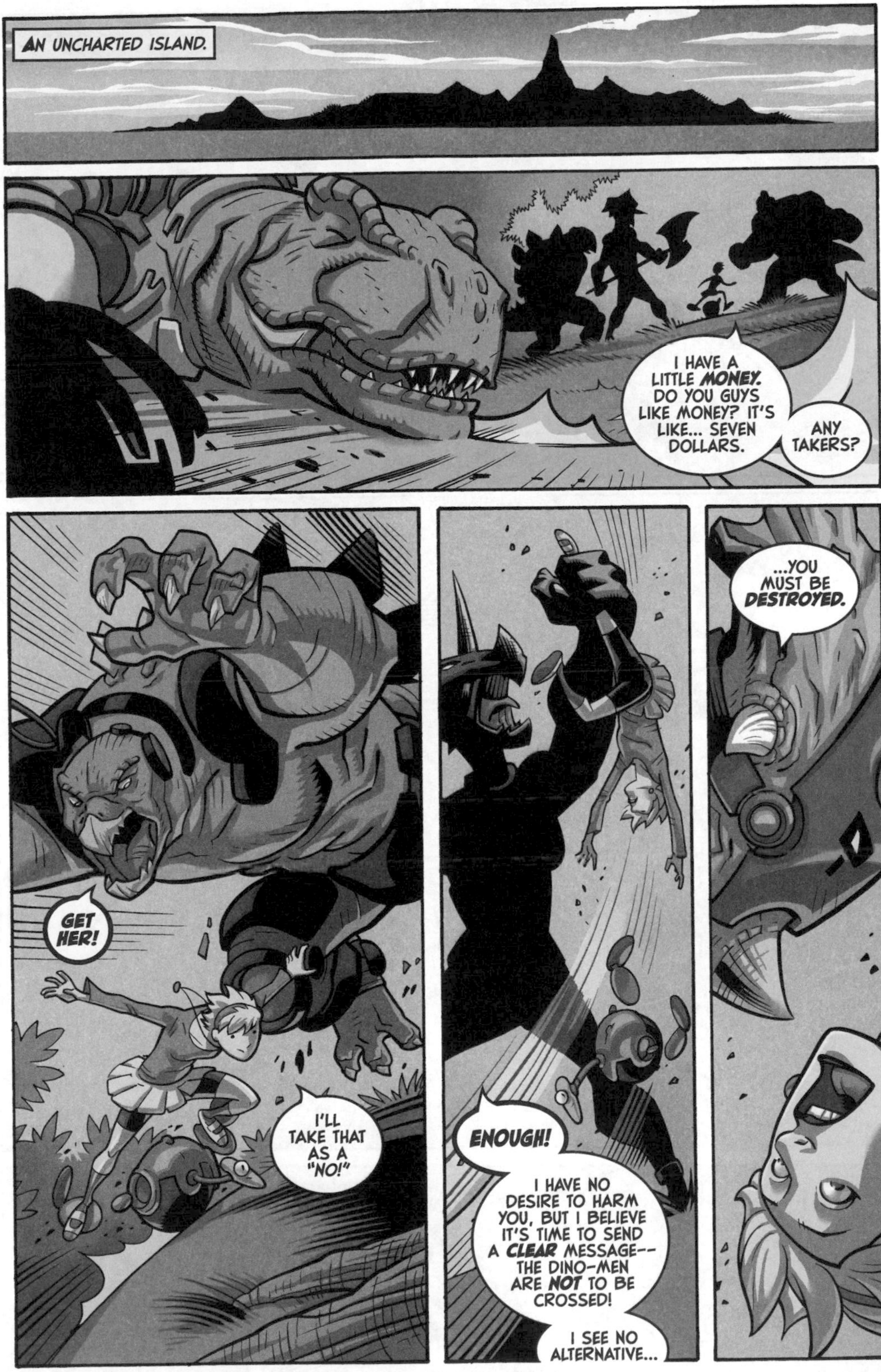

AN UNCHARTED ISLAND.
I HAVE A LITTLE MONEY. DO YOU GUYS LIKE MONEY? IT'S LIKE... SEVEN DOLLARS.
ANY TAKERS?
GET HER!
I'LL TAKE THAT AS A "NO!"
ENOUGH!
I HAVE NO DESIRE TO HARM YOU, BUT I BELIEVE IT'S TIME TO SEND A CLEAR MESSAGE-- THE DINO-MEN ARE NOT TO BE CROSSED!
I SEE NO ALTERNATIVE...
...YOU MUST BE DESTROYED.

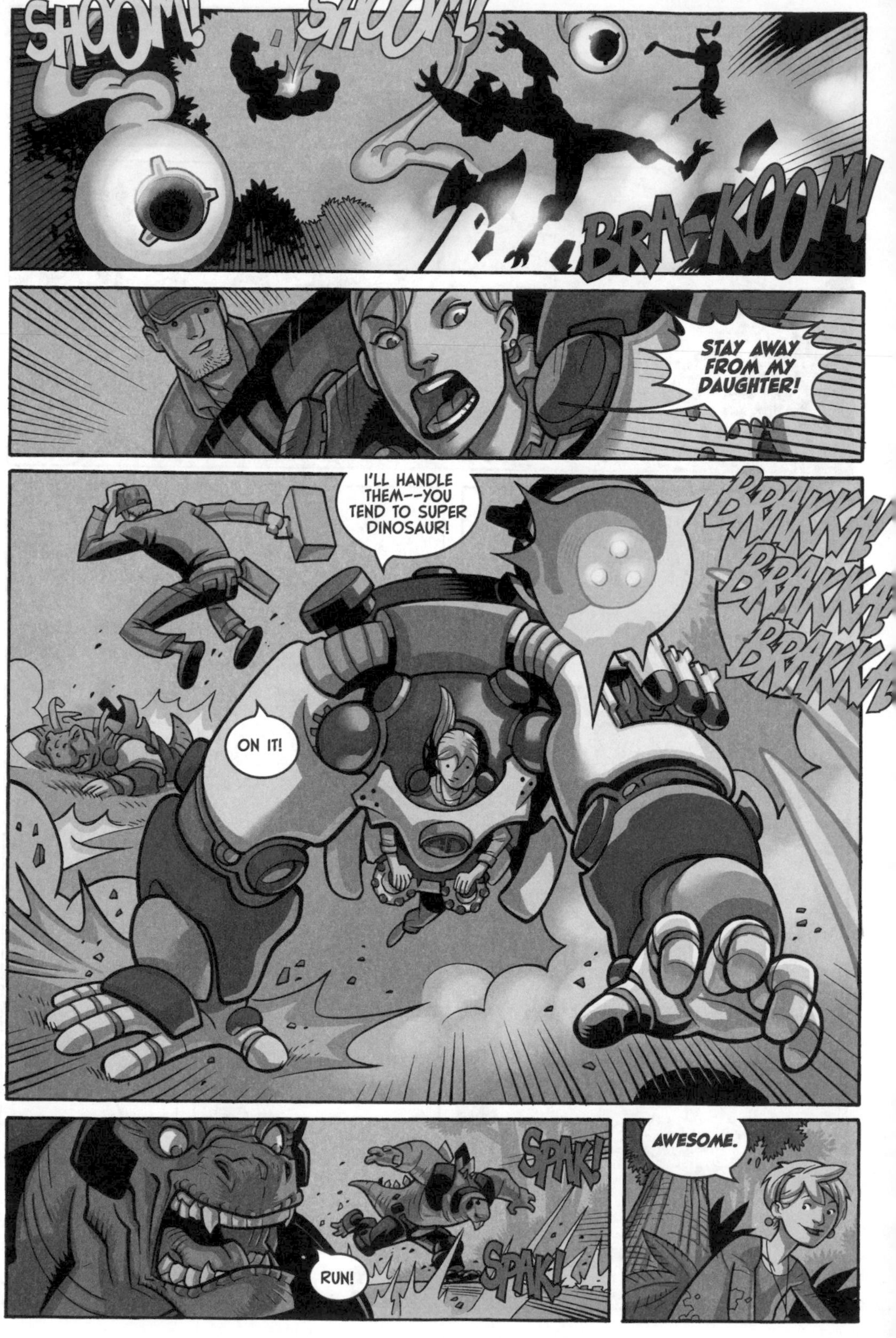
SHOOM!
SHOOM!
BRA-KOOM!
STAY AWAY FROM MY DAUGHTER!
I'LL HANDLE THEM--YOU TEND TO SUPER DINOSAUR!
BRAKKA! BRAKKA! BRAKKA!
ON IT!
SPAK!
SPAK!
RUN!
AWESOME.

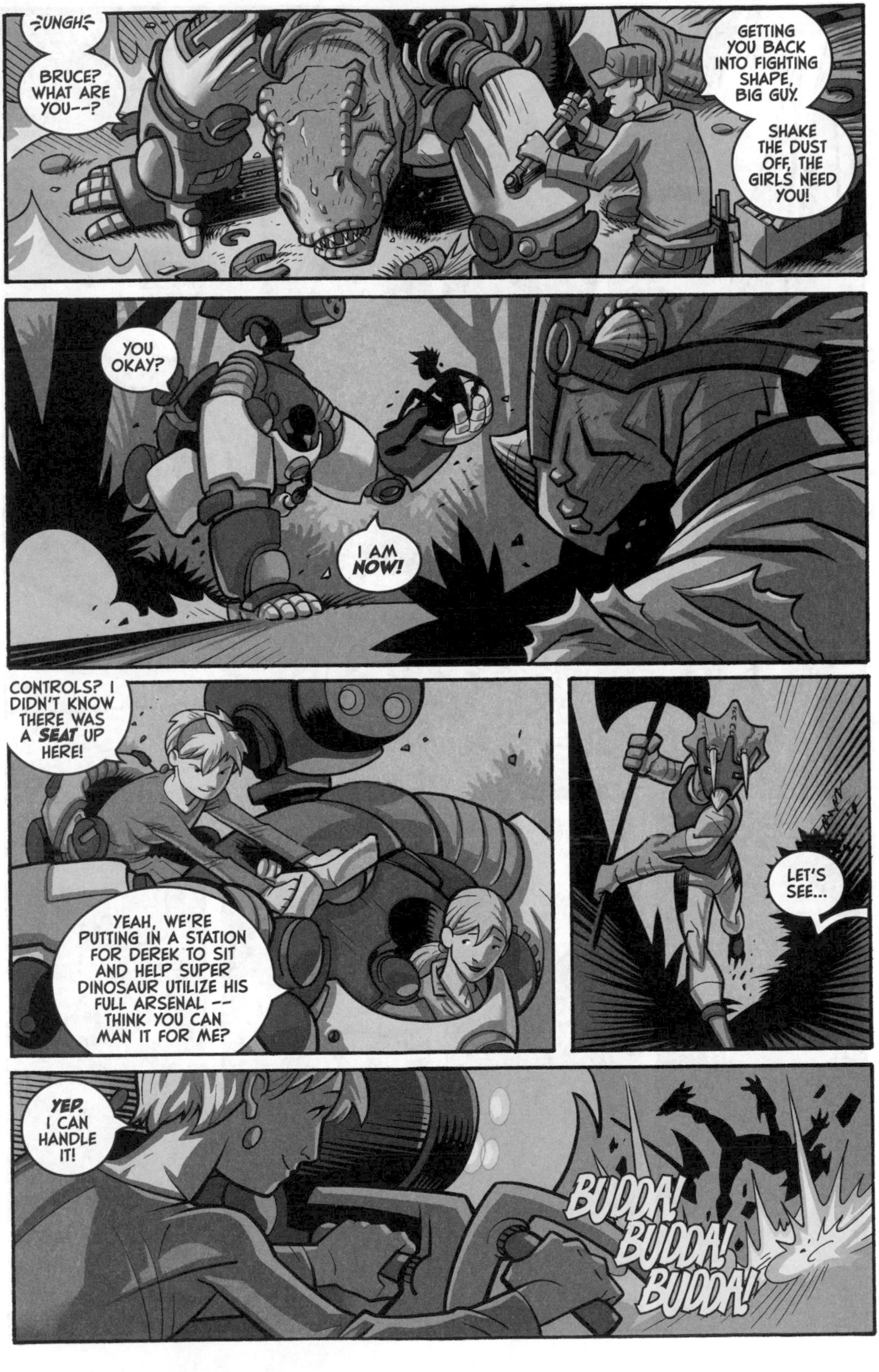
UNGH
BRUCE? WHAT ARE YOU--?
GETTING YOU BACK INTO FIGHTING SHAPE, BIG GUY.
SHAKE THE DUST OFF, THE GIRLS NEED YOU!
YOU OKAY?
I AM NOW!
CONTROLS? I DIDN'T KNOW THERE WAS A SEAT UP HERE!
YEAH, WE'RE PUTTING IN A STATION FOR DEREK TO SIT AND HELP SUPER DINOSAUR UTILIZE HIS FULL ARSENAL -- THINK YOU CAN MAN IT FOR ME?
LET'S SEE...
YEP. I CAN HANDLE IT!
BUDDA! BUDDA! BUDDA!

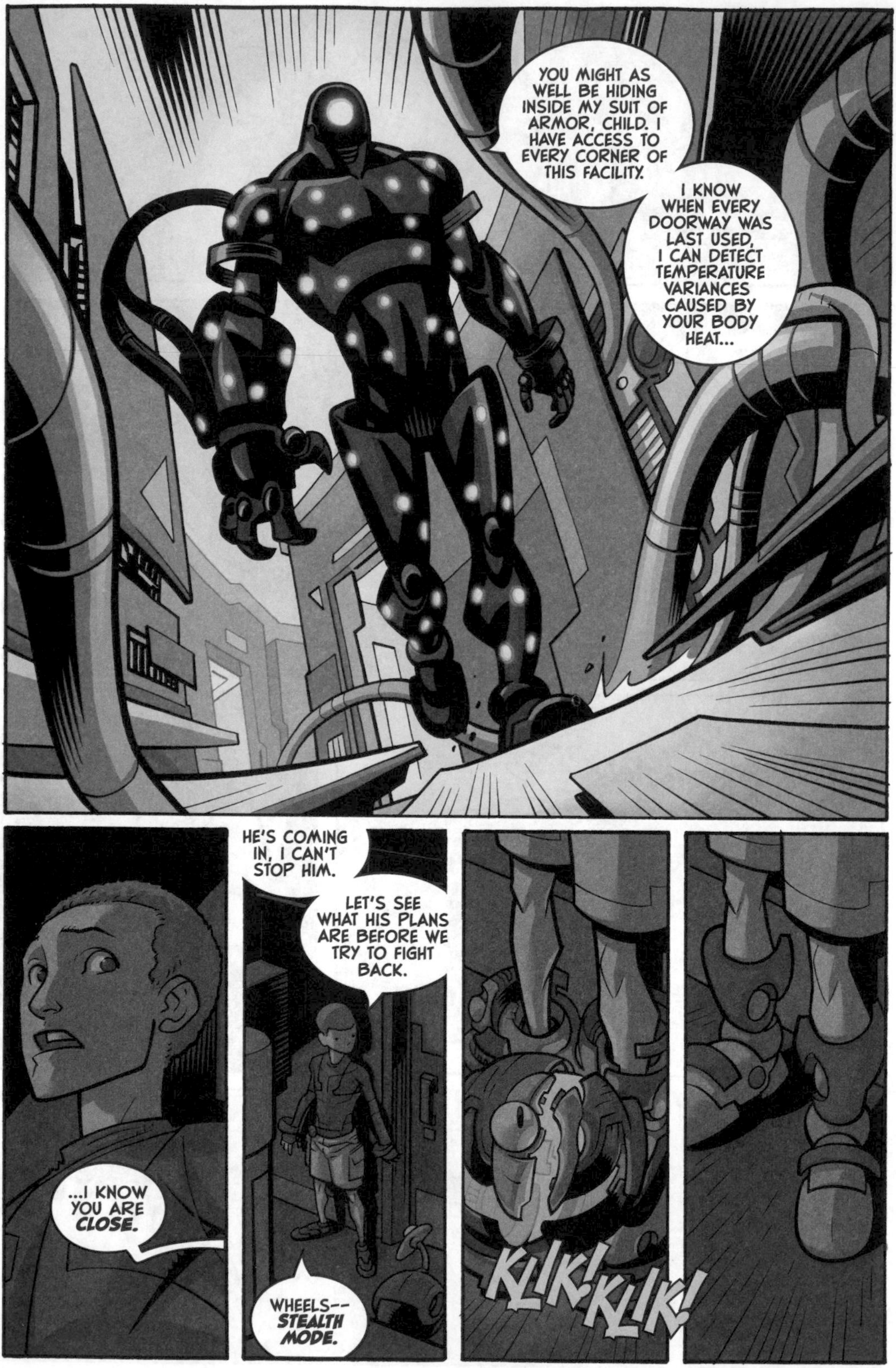
YOU MIGHT AS WELL BE HIDING INSIDE MY SUIT OF ARMOR, CHILD. I HAVE ACCESS TO EVERY CORNER OF THIS FACILITY.
I KNOW WHEN EVERY DOORWAY WAS LAST USED, I CAN DETECT TEMPERATURE VARIANCES CAUSED BY YOUR BODY HEAT...
...I KNOW YOU ARE CLOSE.
HE'S COMING IN, I CAN'T STOP HIM.
LET'S SEE WHAT HIS PLANS ARE BEFORE WE TRY TO FIGHT BACK.
WHEELS-- STEALTH MODE.
KLIK! KLIK!

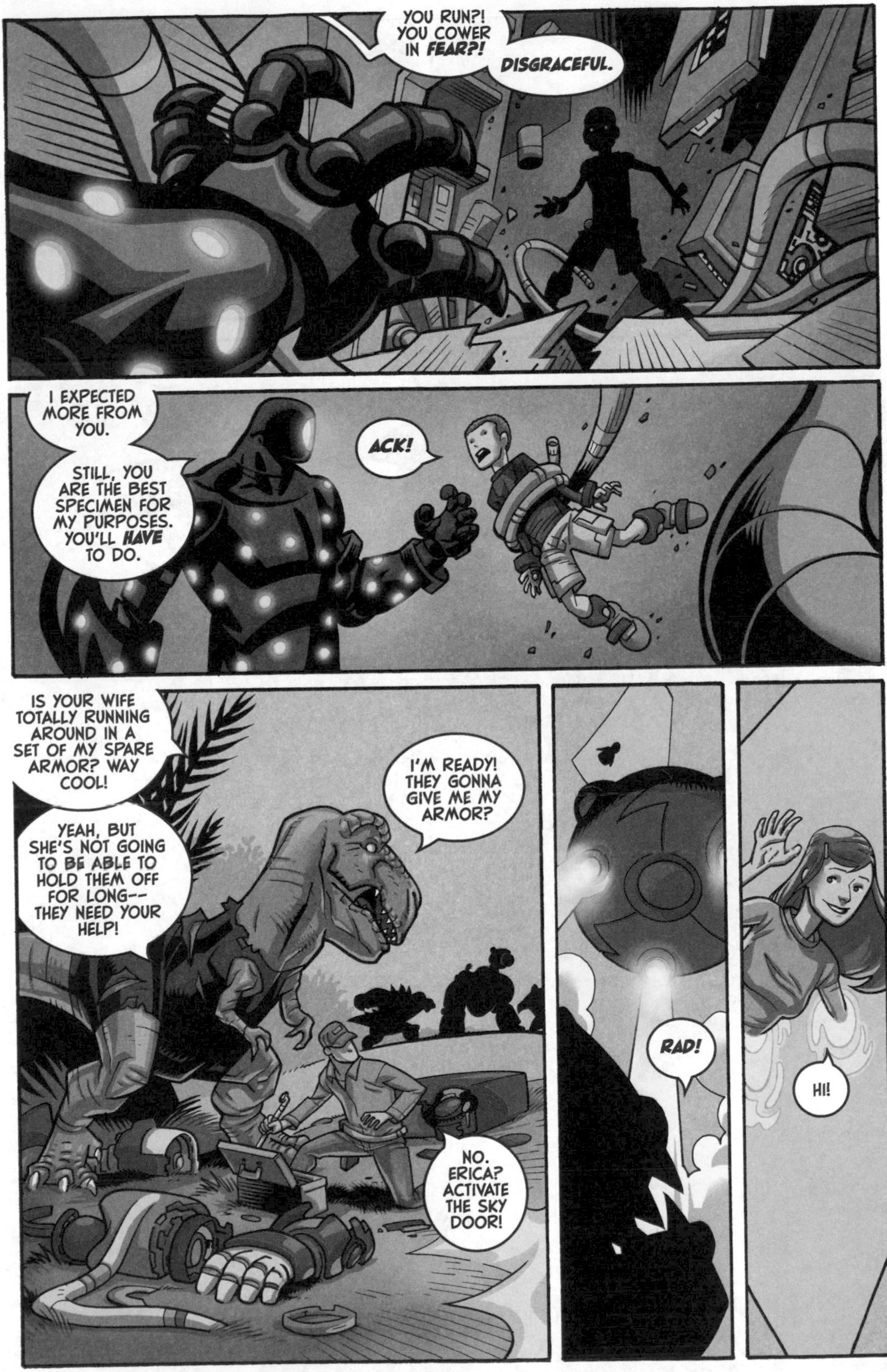
YOU RUN?! YOU COWER IN FEAR?!
DISGRACEFUL.
I EXPECTED MORE FROM YOU.
STILL, YOU ARE THE BEST SPECIMEN FOR MY PURPOSES. YOU'LL HAVE TO DO.
ACK!
IS YOUR WIFE TOTALLY RUNNING AROUND IN A SET OF MY SPARE ARMOR? WAY COOL!
YEAH, BUT SHE'S NOT GOING TO BE ABLE TO HOLD THEM OFF FOR LONG-- THEY NEED YOUR HELP!
I'M READY! THEY GONNA GIVE ME MY ARMOR?
NO. ERICA? ACTIVATE THE SKY DOOR!
RAD!
HI!

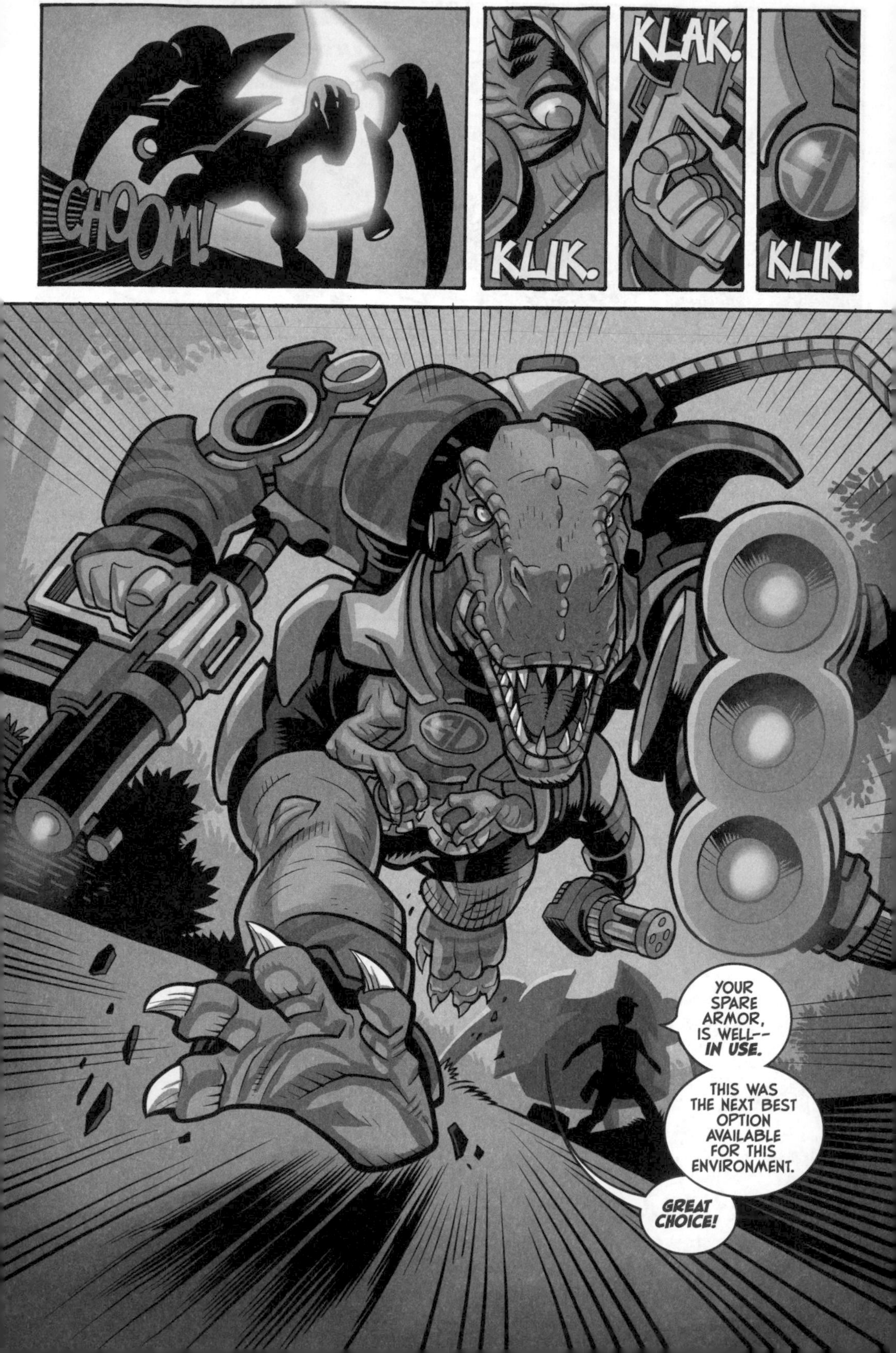
CHOOM!
KLIK.
KLAK.
KLIK.
YOUR SPARE ARMOR, IS WELL-- IN USE.
THIS WAS THE NEXT BEST OPTION AVAILABLE FOR THIS ENVIRONMENT.
GREAT CHOICE!

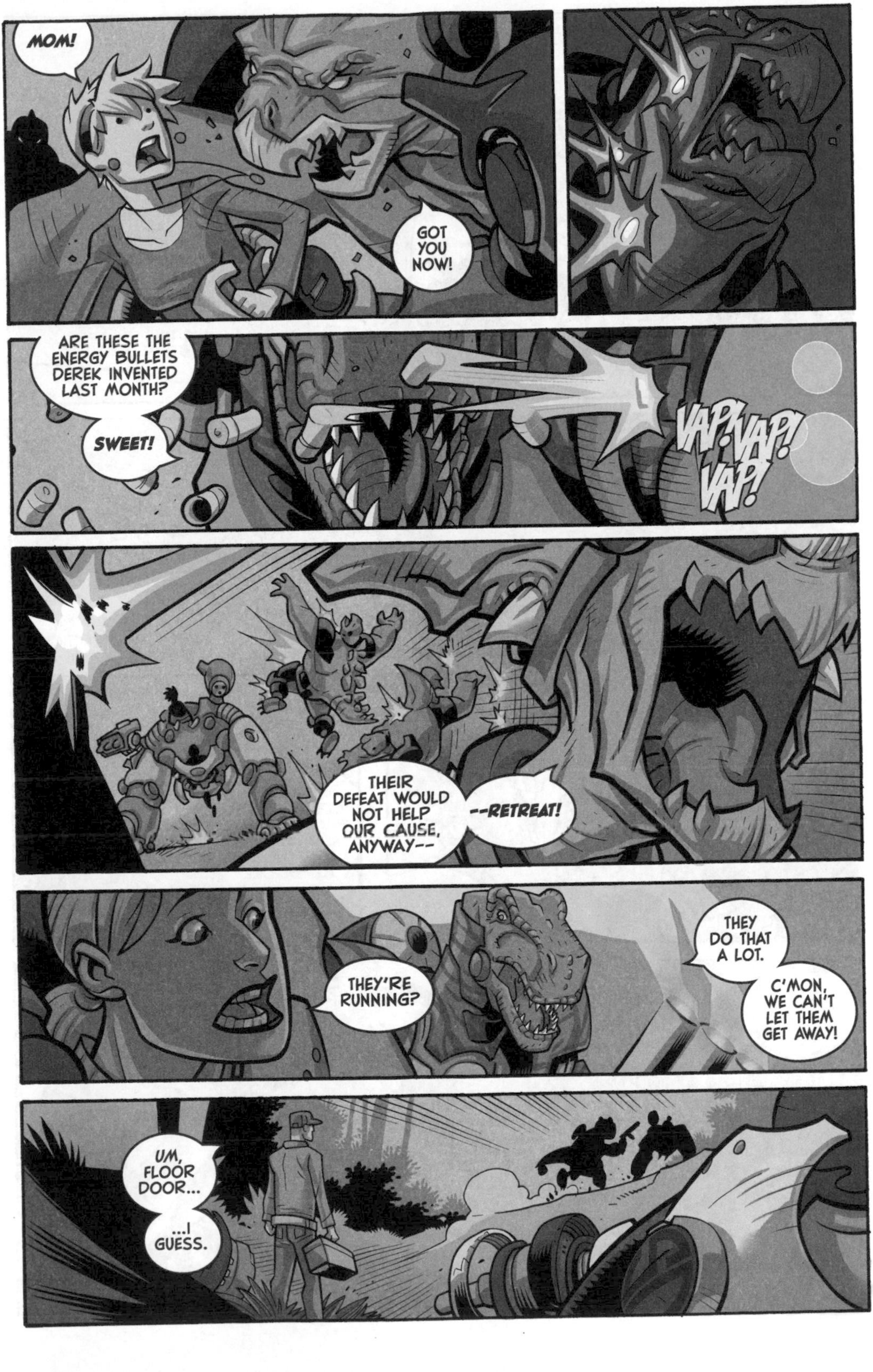
MOM!
GOT YOU NOW!
ARE THESE THE ENERGY BULLETS DEREK INVENTED LAST MONTH?
SWEET!
VAP! VAP! VAP!
THEIR DEFEAT WOULD NOT HELP OUR CAUSE, ANYWAY--
--RETREAT!
THEY'RE RUNNING?
THEY DO THAT A LOT.
C'MON, WE CAN'T LET THEM GET AWAY!
UM, FLOOR DOOR...
...I GUESS.

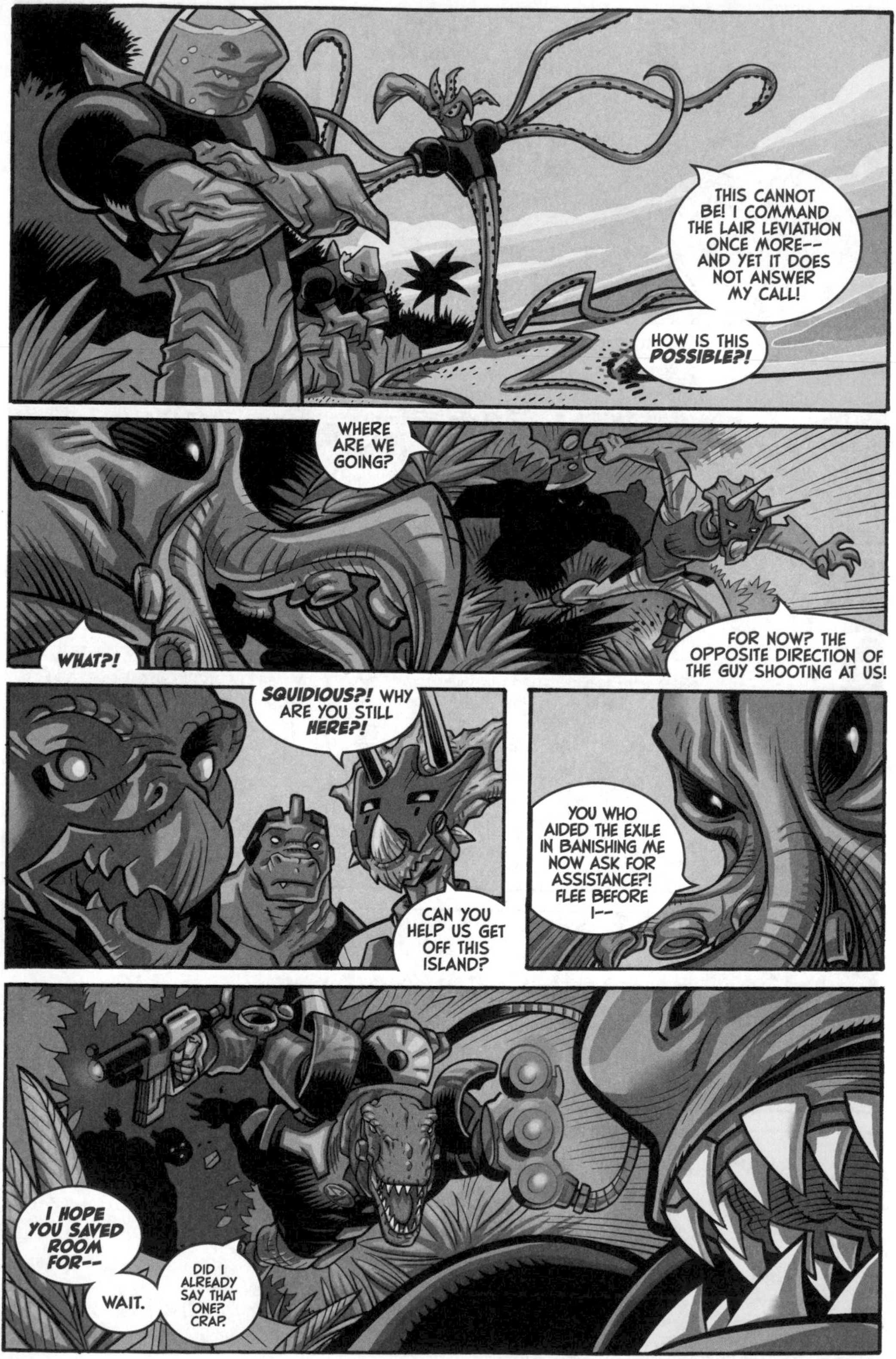
THIS CANNOT BE! I COMMAND THE LAIR LEVIATHON ONCE MORE-- AND YET IT DOES NOT ANSWER MY CALL!
HOW IS THIS POSSIBLE?!
WHERE ARE WE GOING?
WHAT?!
FOR NOW? THE OPPOSITE DIRECTION OF THE GUY SHOOTING AT US!
SQUIDIOUS?! WHY ARE YOU STILL HERE?!
CAN YOU HELP US GET OFF THIS ISLAND?
YOU WHO AIDED THE EXILE IN BANISHING ME NOW ASK FOR ASSISTANCE?! FLEE BEFORE I--
I HOPE YOU SAVED ROOM FOR--
WAIT.
DID I ALREADY SAY THAT ONE? CRAP.

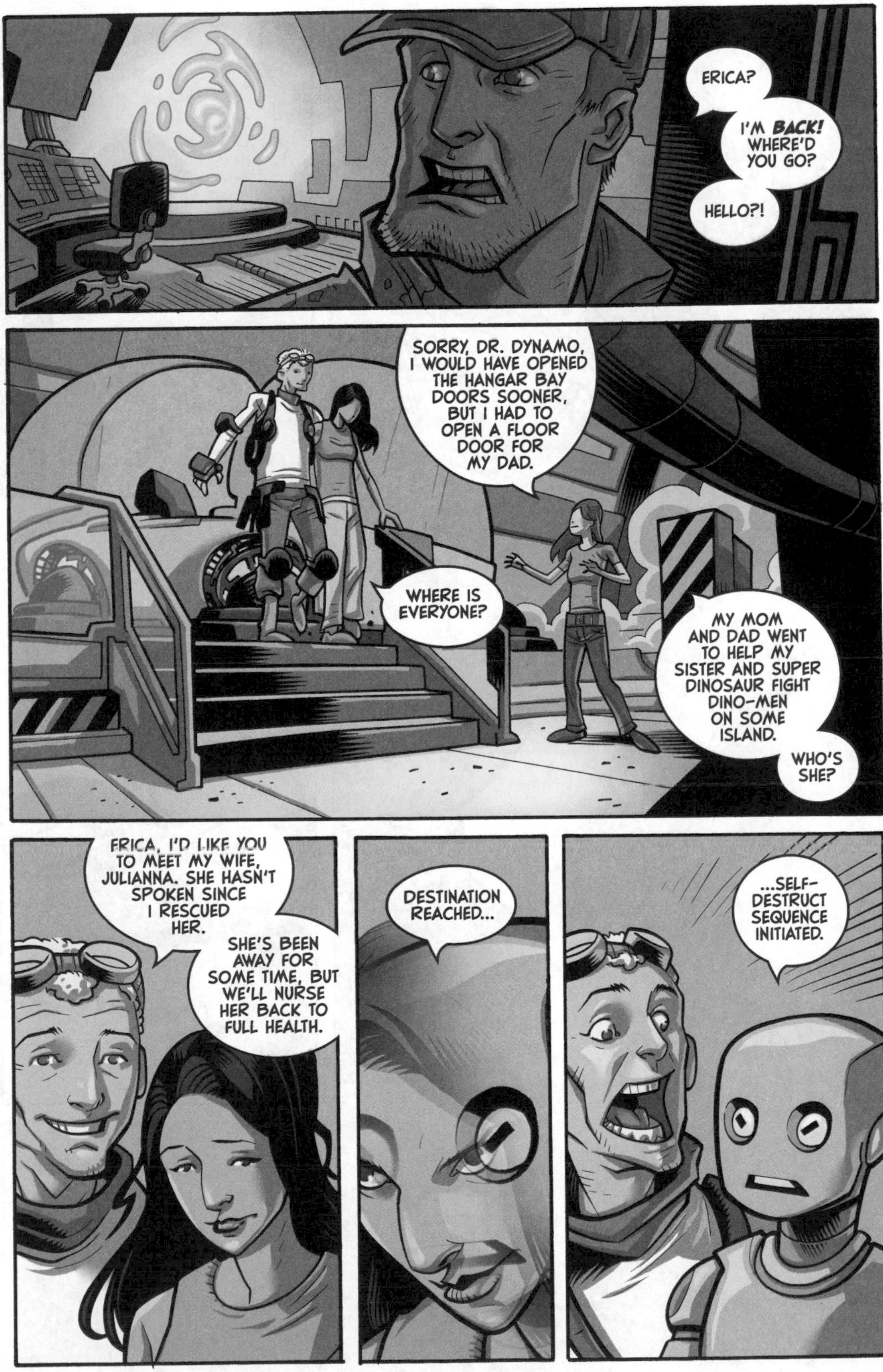
ERICA?
I'M ***BACK!*** WHERE'D YOU GO?
HELLO?!
SORRY, DR. DYNAMO, I WOULD HAVE OPENED THE HANGAR BAY DOORS SOONER, BUT I HAD TO OPEN A FLOOR DOOR FOR MY DAD.
WHERE IS EVERYONE?
MY MOM AND DAD WENT TO HELP MY SISTER AND SUPER DINOSAUR FIGHT DINO-MEN ON SOME ISLAND.
WHO'S SHE?
ERICA, I'D LIKE YOU TO MEET MY WIFE, JULIANNA. SHE HASN'T SPOKEN SINCE I RESCUED HER.
SHE'S BEEN AWAY FOR SOME TIME, BUT WE'LL NURSE HER BACK TO FULL HEALTH.
DESTINATION REACHED...
...SELF-DESTRUCT SEQUENCE INITIATED.

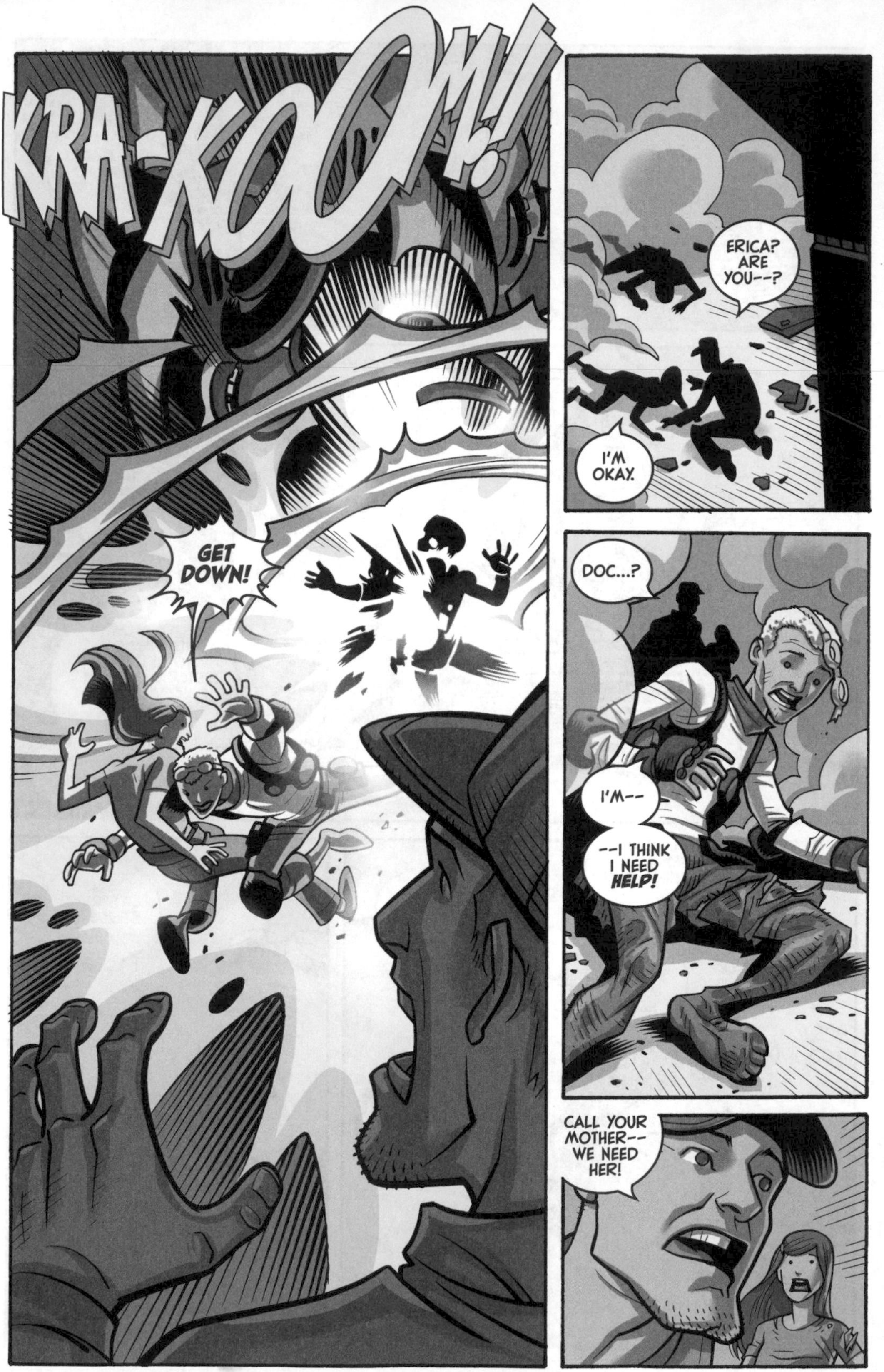
KRA-KOOM!!
GET DOWN!
ERICA? ARE YOU--?
I'M OKAY.
DOC...?
I'M--
--I THINK I NEED HELP!
CALL YOUR MOTHER--WE NEED HER!

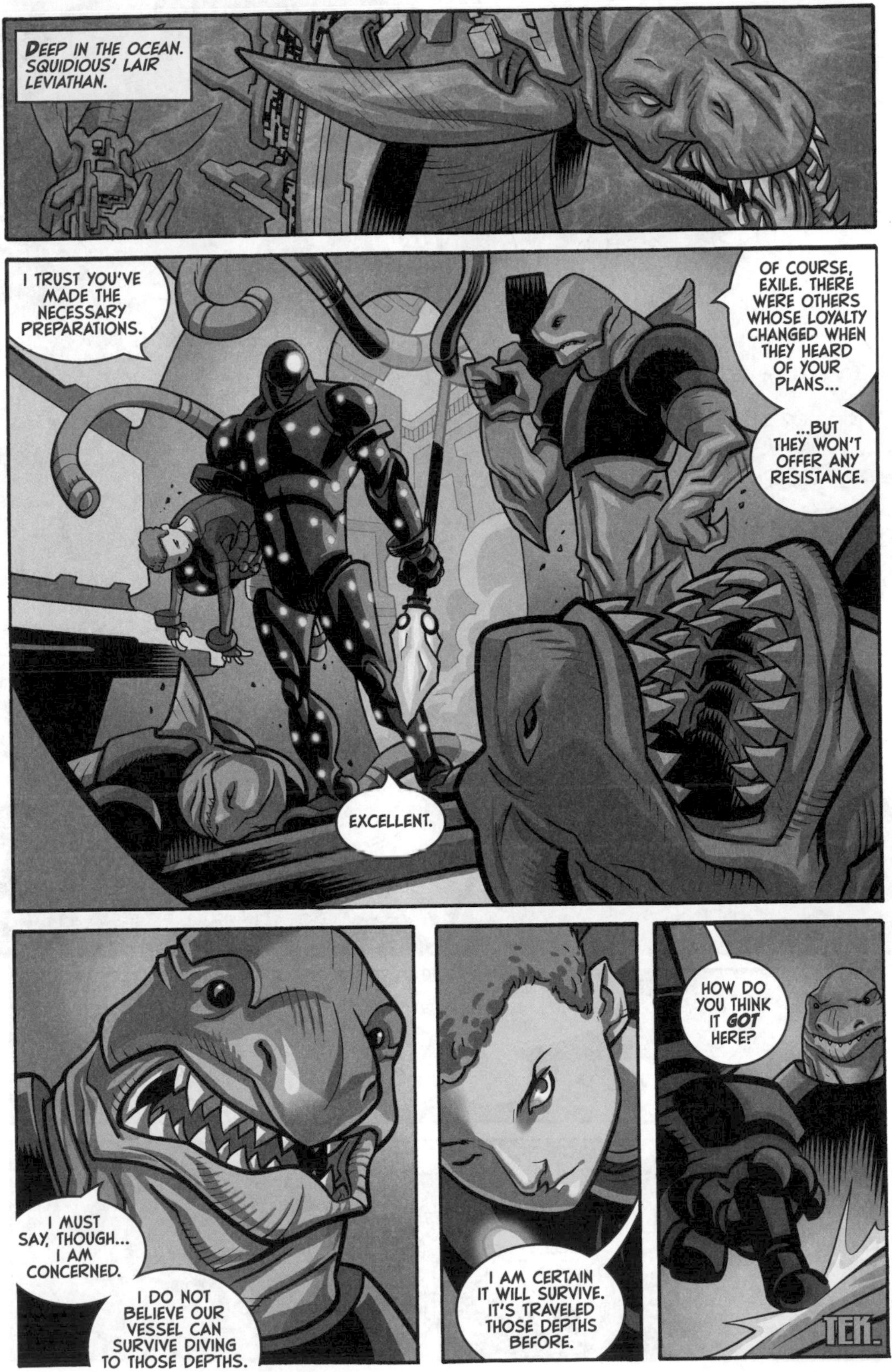
DEEP IN THE OCEAN. SQUIDIOUS' LAIR LEVIATHAN.
I TRUST YOU'VE MADE THE NECESSARY PREPARATIONS.
OF COURSE, EXILE. THERE WERE OTHERS WHOSE LOYALTY CHANGED WHEN THEY HEARD OF YOUR PLANS...
...BUT THEY WON'T OFFER ANY RESISTANCE.
EXCELLENT.
I MUST SAY, THOUGH... I AM CONCERNED.
I DO NOT BELIEVE OUR VESSEL CAN SURVIVE DIVING TO THOSE DEPTHS.
I AM CERTAIN IT WILL SURVIVE. IT'S TRAVELED THOSE DEPTHS BEFORE.
HOW DO YOU THINK IT GOT HERE?
TEK.

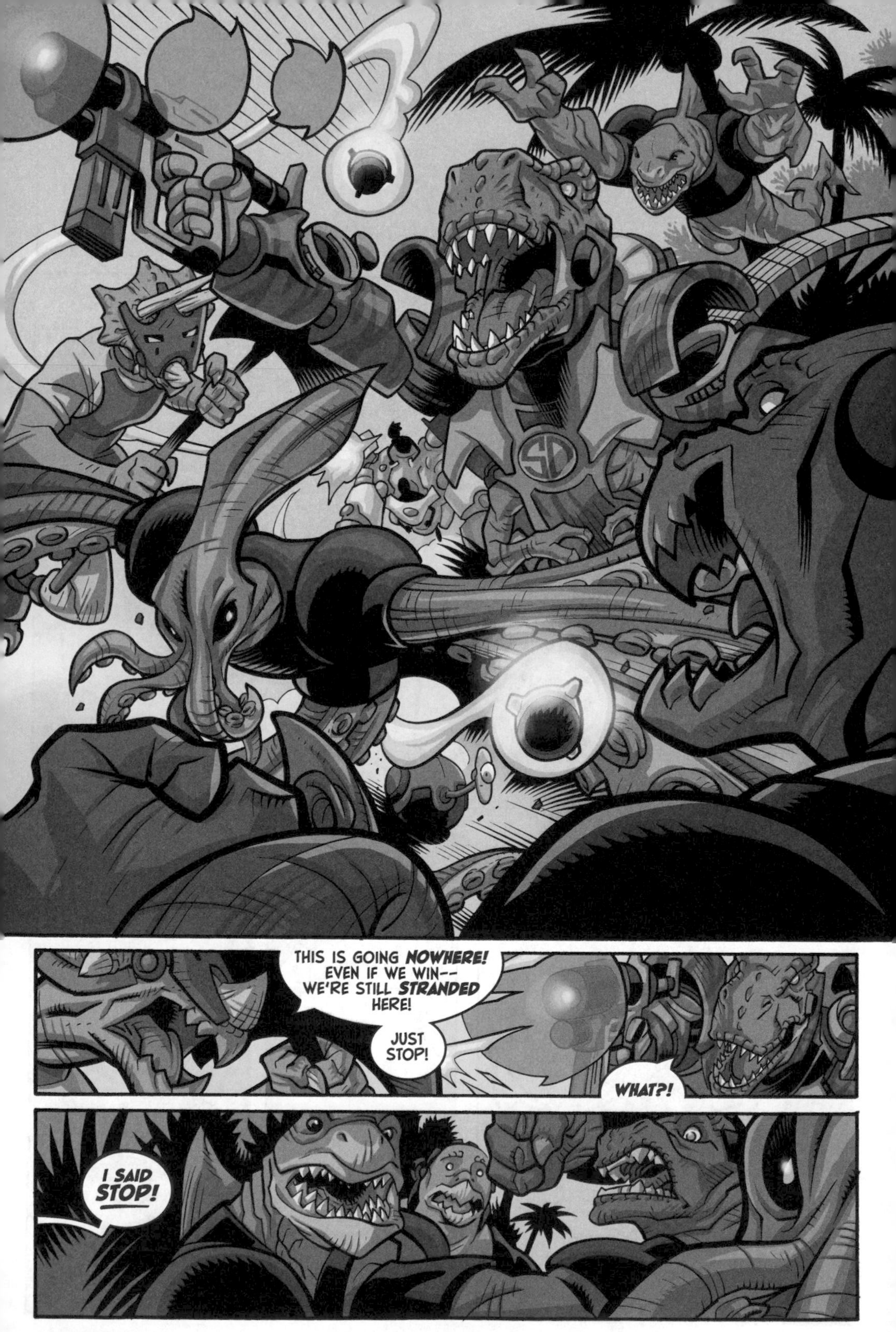
THIS IS GOING NOWHERE! EVEN IF WE WIN-- WE'RE STILL STRANDED HERE!
JUST STOP!
WHAT?!
I SAID STOP!

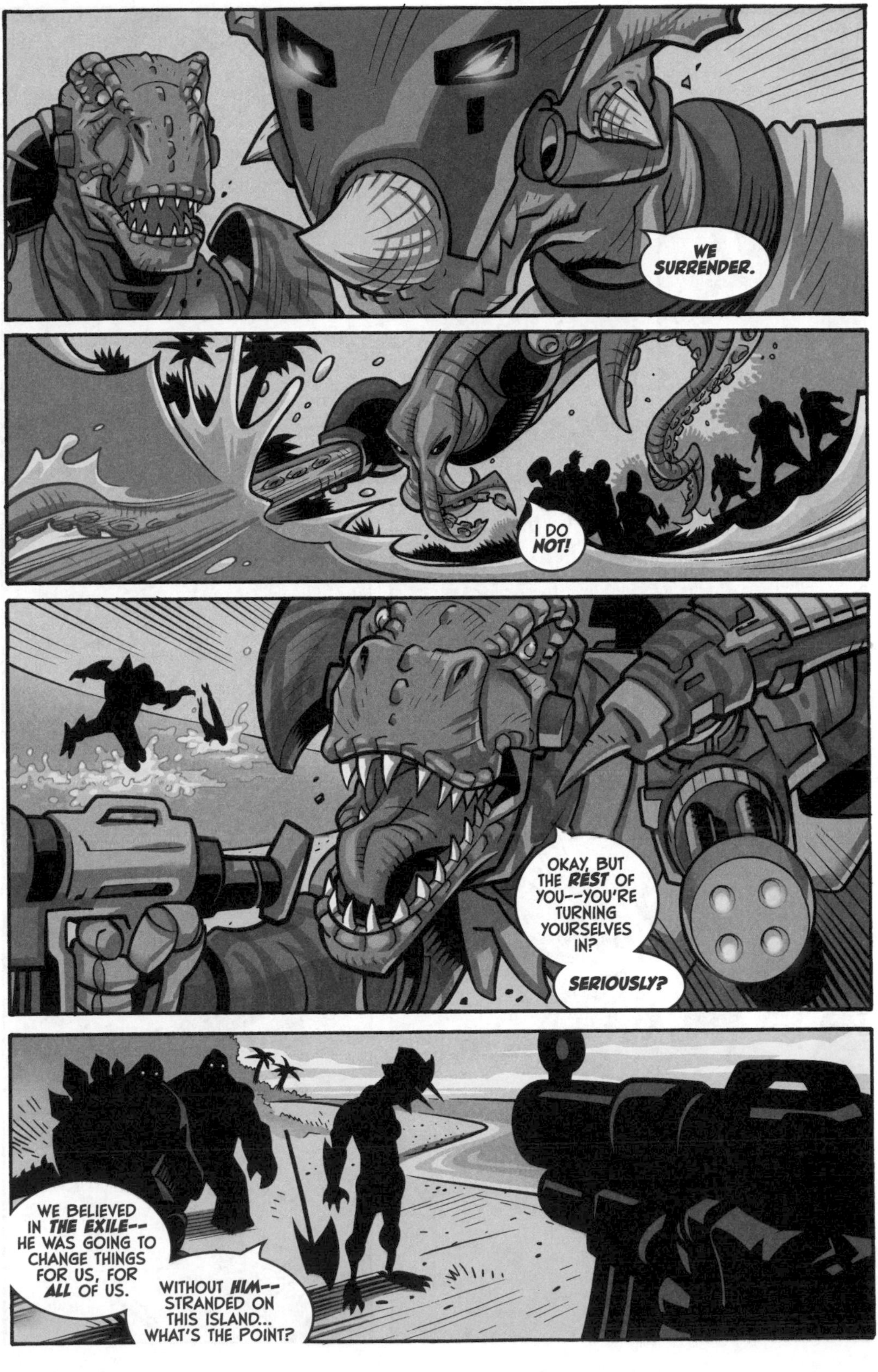
WE SURRENDER.
I DO NOT!
OKAY, BUT THE REST OF YOU--YOU'RE TURNING YOURSELVES IN?
SERIOUSLY?
WE BELIEVED IN THE EXILE-- HE WAS GOING TO CHANGE THINGS FOR US, FOR ALL OF US.
WITHOUT HIM-- STRANDED ON THIS ISLAND... WHAT'S THE POINT?

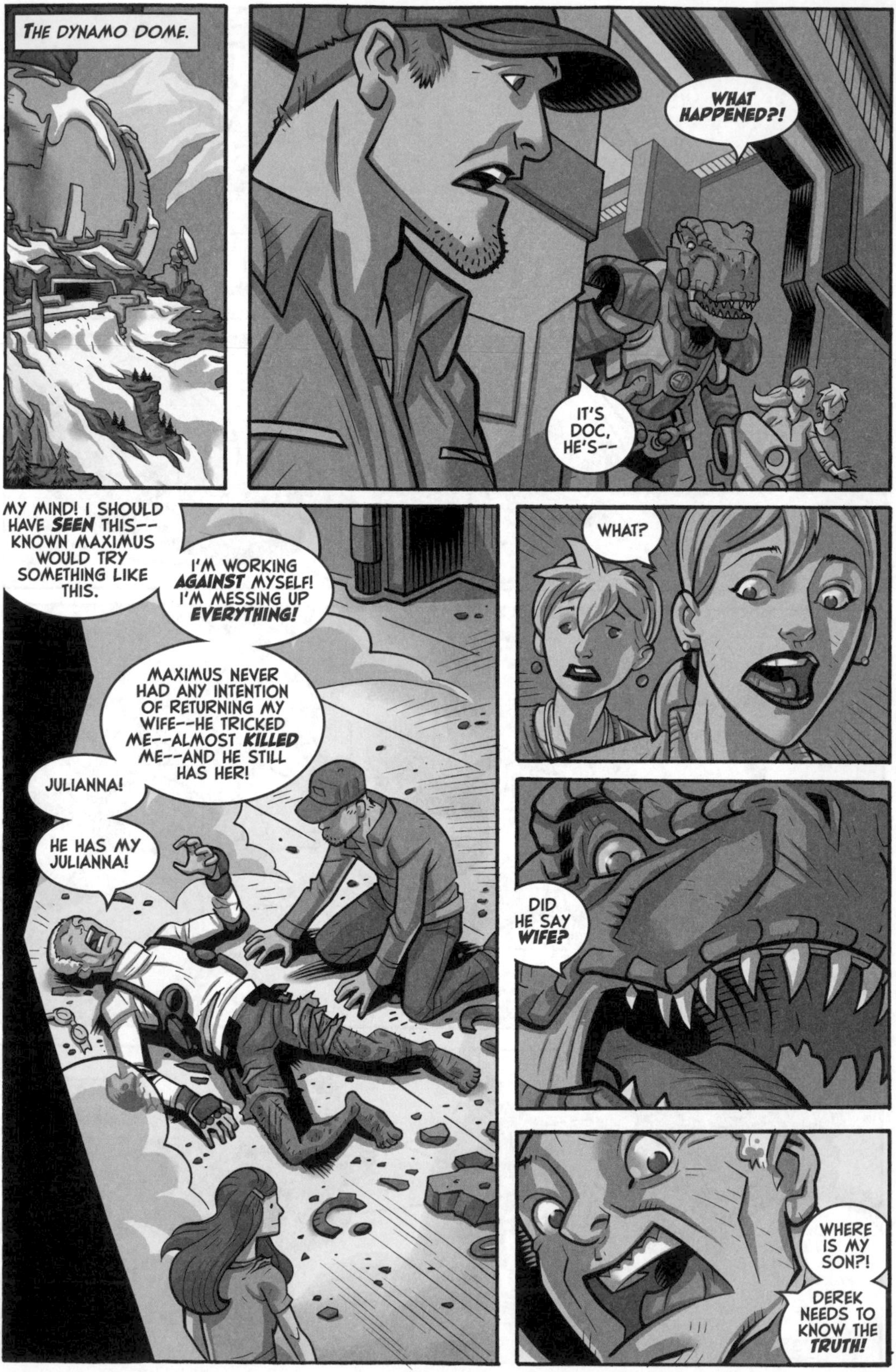
THE DYNAMO DOME.
WHAT HAPPENED?!
IT'S DOC, HE'S--
MY MIND! I SHOULD HAVE SEEN THIS-- KNOWN MAXIMUS WOULD TRY SOMETHING LIKE THIS.
I'M WORKING AGAINST MYSELF! I'M MESSING UP EVERYTHING!
MAXIMUS NEVER HAD ANY INTENTION OF RETURNING MY WIFE--HE TRICKED ME--ALMOST KILLED ME--AND HE STILL HAS HER!
JULIANNA!
HE HAS MY JULIANNA!
WHAT?
DID HE SAY WIFE?
WHERE IS MY SON?!
DEREK NEEDS TO KNOW THE TRUTH!

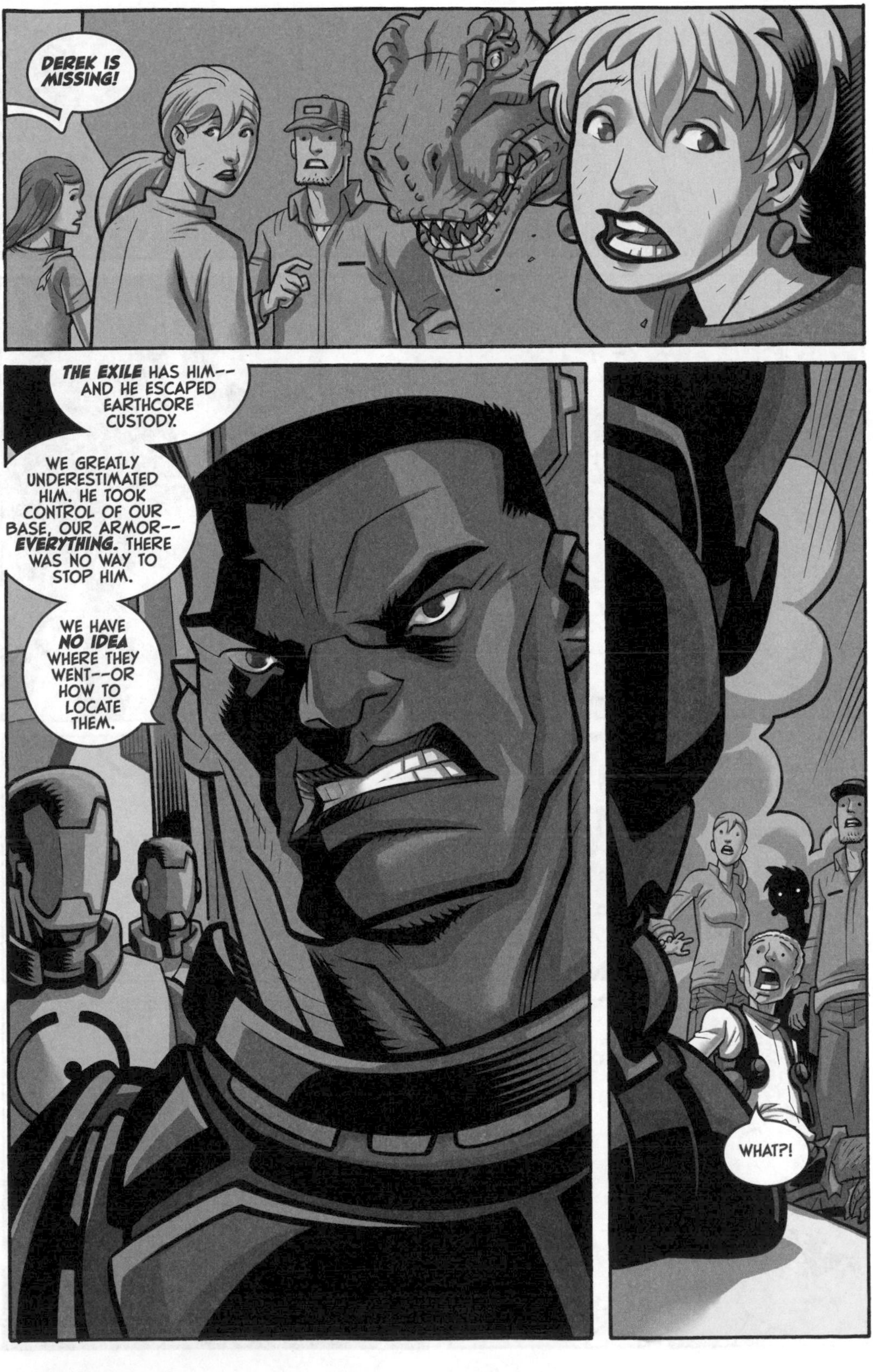
DEREK IS MISSING!
THE EXILE HAS HIM--AND HE ESCAPED EARTHCORE CUSTODY.
WE GREATLY UNDERESTIMATED HIM. HE TOOK CONTROL OF OUR BASE, OUR ARMOR--EVERYTHING. THERE WAS NO WAY TO STOP HIM.
WE HAVE NO IDEA WHERE THEY WENT--OR HOW TO LOCATE THEM.
WHAT?!

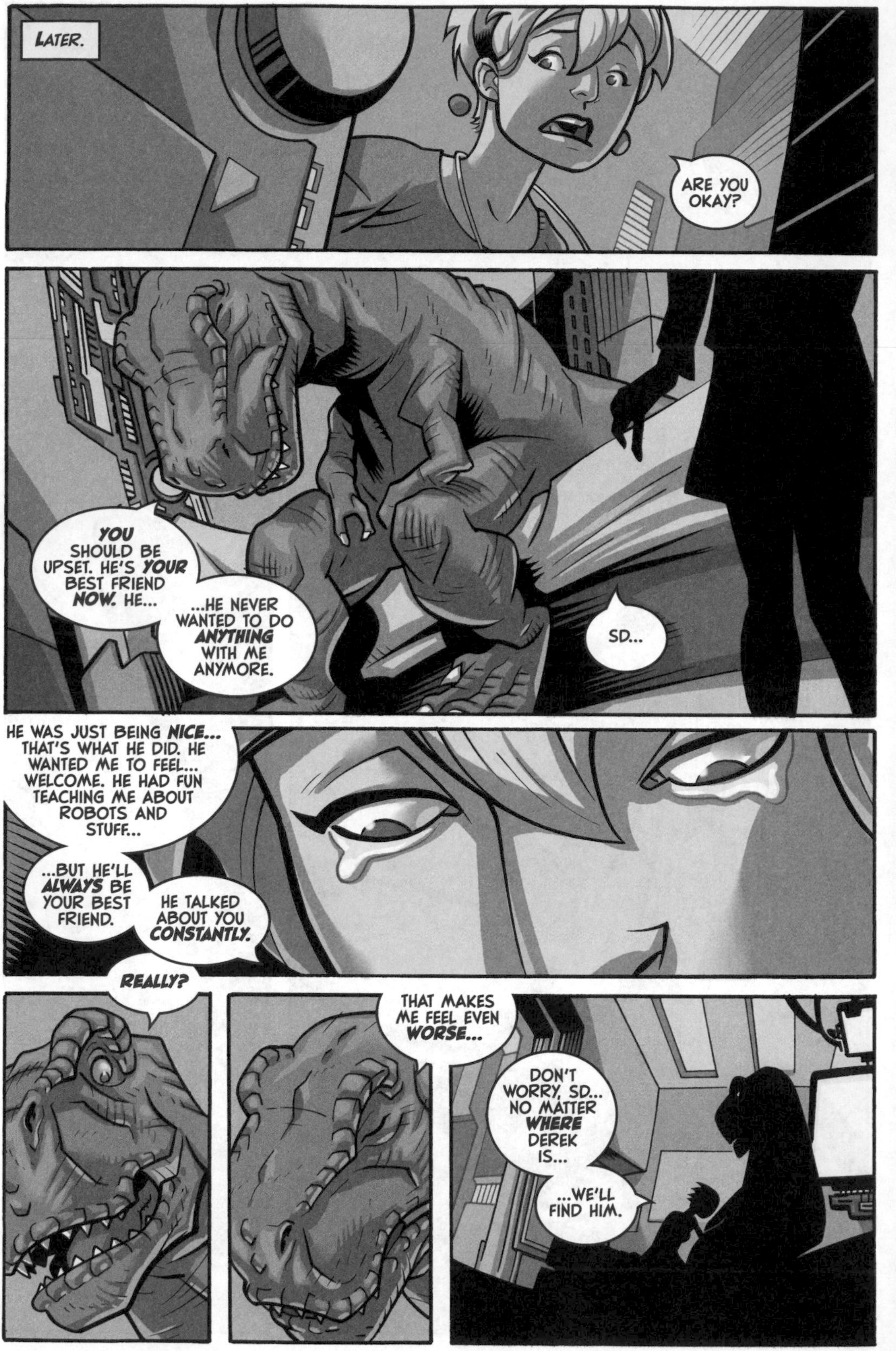
LATER.
ARE YOU OKAY?
YOU SHOULD BE UPSET. HE'S YOUR BEST FRIEND NOW. HE...
...HE NEVER WANTED TO DO ANYTHING WITH ME ANYMORE.
SD...
HE WAS JUST BEING NICE... THAT'S WHAT HE DID. HE WANTED ME TO FEEL... WELCOME. HE HAD FUN TEACHING ME ABOUT ROBOTS AND STUFF...
...BUT HE'LL ALWAYS BE YOUR BEST FRIEND.
HE TALKED ABOUT YOU CONSTANTLY.
REALLY?
THAT MAKES ME FEEL EVEN WORSE...
DON'T WORRY, SD... NO MATTER WHERE DEREK IS...
...WE'LL FIND HIM.

I **KNEW** YOU WERE PRETENDING. YOU'VE BEEN IN FAR TOO MANY BATTLES TO SIMPLY BLACK OUT FROM STRESS.

TELL ME, DO YOU EVEN KNOW WHERE WE **ARE**?

IF YOU HAD MANAGED TO ESCAPE... WHERE WOULD YOU HAVE **GONE**?

I READ THE PRESSURE READINGS. YOU MADE THIS CREATURE DIVE DEEPER THAN ANY OF SQUIDIOUS' PEOPLE WANTED TO GO--

--AND THEN YOU TURNED IT AROUND AND WENT BACK UP TO THE SURFACE.

DID I? OR IS THAT JUST WHAT IT **FELT** LIKE.

THE THING IS... THERE IS NO **INNER** OCEAN AND **OUTER** OCEAN... THERE IS ONLY **ONE** OCEAN.

COME.

I'LL **SHOW** YOU.

PSSSH.

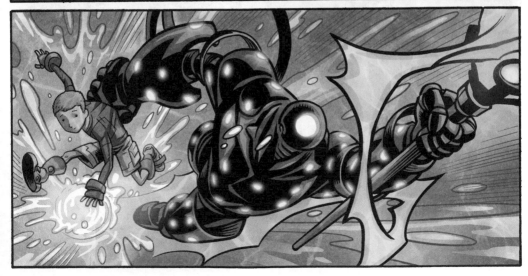

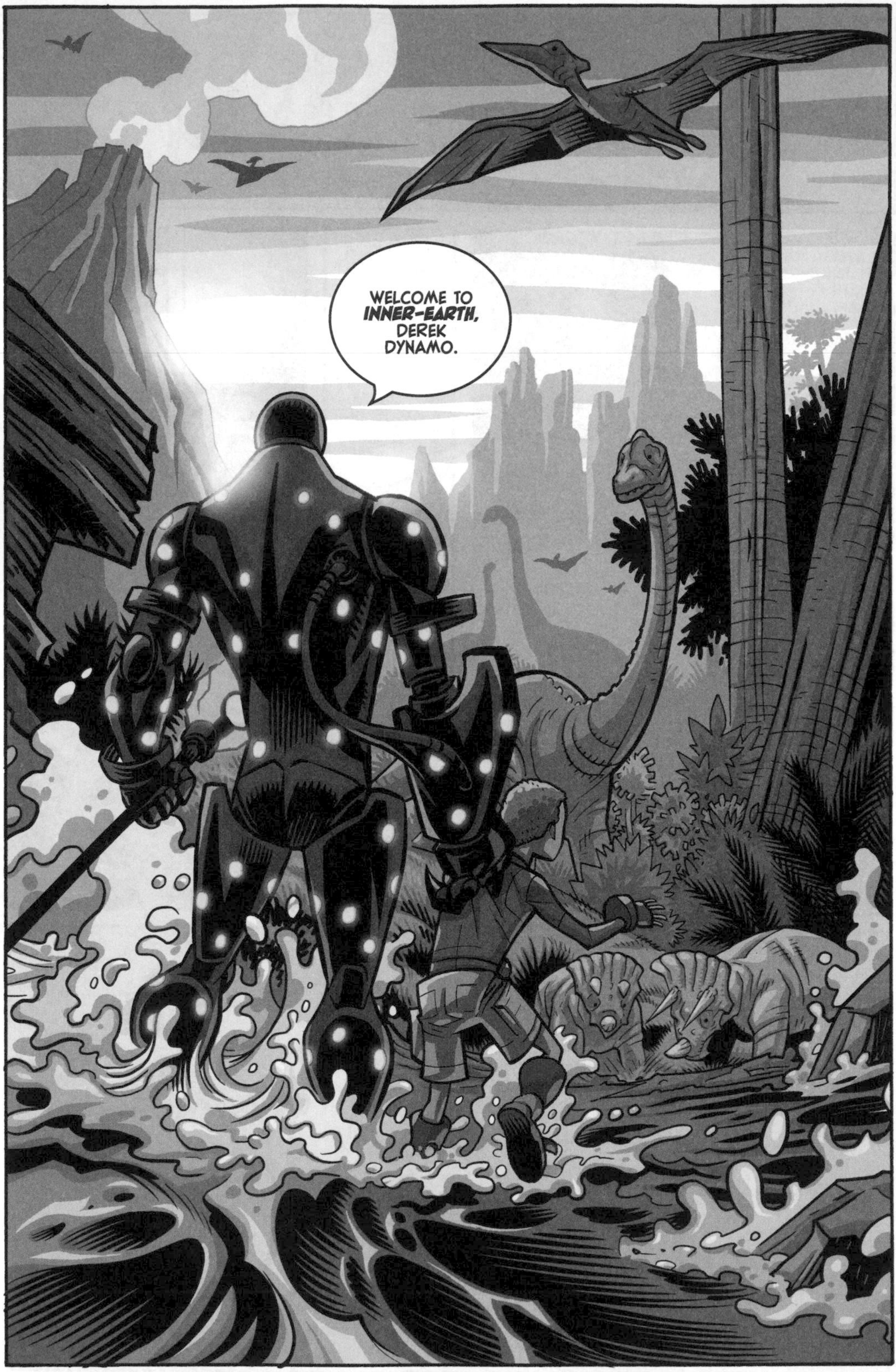
WELCOME TO INNER-EARTH, DEREK DYNAMO.

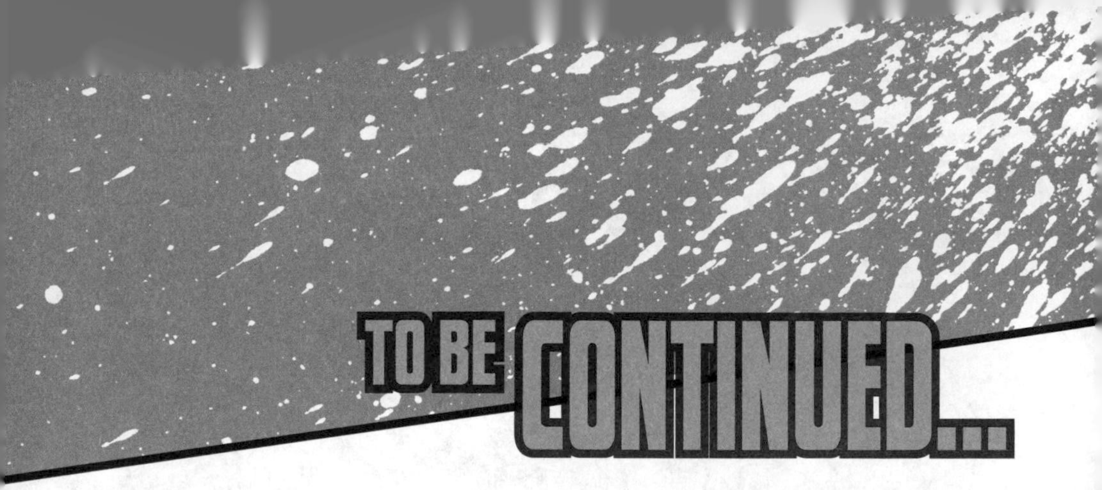
TO BE CONTINUED...

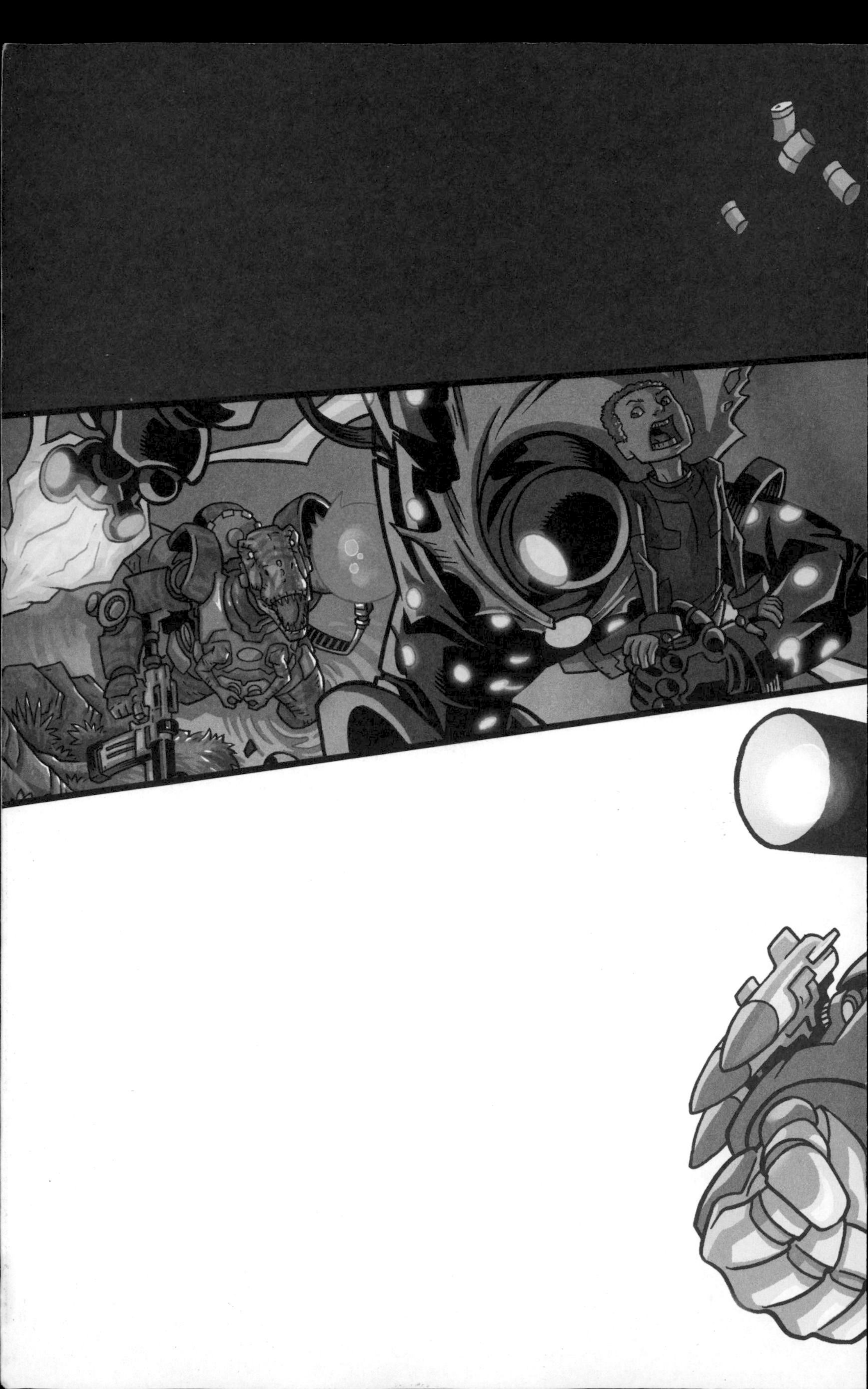